WAITING FOR OLIVIA

"Damn it!" Corinne hissed, out of breath.

Inside her car once again, she set the plastic container of acid on the passenger floor. Tugging off her gloves, she tossed them on the passenger seat. Then she took off the safety goggles.

Sitting at the wheel, she waited to see if the police showed up. She didn't think Olivia or her father had spotted her, but she needed to make sure. She was so mad at herself for not dousing her at the front door when she'd had the chance. She'd had such a clear shot, too. But she'd lost her nerve. The second opportunity had been blown when the father had come to the back door.

Corinne glanced at her watch and decided to give it another ten minutes. If a police car didn't come down Alder Lane in that time, she'd give it another try.

She was determined to get Olivia tonight—one way or another. . . .

UNSPEAKABLE

KEVIN O'BRIEN

PINNACLE BOOKS
Kensington Publishing Corp.
www.kensingtonbooks.com

PINNACLE BOOKS are published by

Kensington Publishing Corp.
119 West 40th Street
New York, NY 10018

All Kensington titles, imprints, and distributed lines are available at special quantity discounts for bulk purchases for sales promotions, premiums, fund-raising, educational, or institutional use. Special book excerpts or customized printings can also be created to fit specific needs. For details, write or phone the office of the Kensington special sales manager: Kensington Publishing Corp., 119 West 40th Street, New York, NY 10018, attn: Special Sales Department; phone 1-800-221-2647.

ISBN-13: 978-0-7860-3158-0
ISBN-10: 0-7860-3158-1

First printing: June 2013

10 9 8 7 6 5 4 3 2 1

Printed in the United States of America

First electronic edition: June 2013

ISBN-13: 978-0-7860-3159-7
ISBN-10: 0-7860-3159-X

This book is for Cathy, Gene, David, Steve, Tyler,
Kate, Beth, Matt, Megan, Kerry, Brendan,
Bill, Annie, Tim, Beven, Margaret, and Bernie . . .
With love from Uncle Kevin.
You guys are the coolest!

ACKNOWLEDGMENTS

I couldn't have written this book (or any of them!) without the help, patience, and guidance of my wonderful editor and friend John Scognamiglio. Thank you, John. I'm grateful to everyone at Kensington Books. What a fantastic group of people! Thanks to all of you—with a special shout-out to my generous friend Doug Mendini.

Many thanks to my dear agents, Meg Ruley and Christina Hogrebe, and the gang at Jane Rotrosen Agency. You guys are the best!

A huge thank-you to my Writers Group for their help, encouragement, and friendship. John Flick, Cate Goethals, Soyon Im, David Massengill, and Garth Stein—I love you guys.

Another big thank-you goes to my Seattle 7 Writers pals, especially my fellow core members: Garth (again), Jennie Shortridge, Kit Bakke, Erica Bauermeister, Dave Boling, Carol Cassella, Randy Sue Coburn, Laurie Frankel, Stephanie Kallos, and Tara Austen Weaver. Check us out at www.seattle7writers.org.

My thanks also to the terrific people at Levy Home Entertainment.

I'd also like to thank the following friends who encouraged and inspired me—and pushed my books to their friends: Nancy Abbe, Dan Annear and Chuck Rank, Pam Binder and the gang at PNWA, Marlys Bourm, Amanda Brooks, Terry and Judine Brooks, Kyle Bryan and Dan Monda, George Camper and Shane White, Barbara and John Cegielski, Barbara and Jim Church, Penny Clark Ianniciello, Anna Cottle and Mary Alice Kier, Tommy Dreiling, Paul Dwoskin and the crew at Broadway Video (Tony, Sheila, Chad, and Dan), Tom Goodwin, Dennis and Debbie Gottlieb, Cathy Johnson, Elizabeth Kinsella, David Korabik, Erik Larson, Cara Lockwood, Stafford Lombard, Roberta Miner, Jim Munchel, Meghan O'Neill, my pals at Open Road Media (especially Jane Friedman, Jeff Sharp, Luke Parker Bowles, and Danny Monico), Midge Ortiz, Eva Marie Saint, John Saul, and Mike Sack, the gang at Seattle Mystery Bookshop, John Simmons, Roseann Stella, Dan, Doug and Ann Stutesman, George and Sheila Stydahar, Marc Von Borstel, and Michael Wells.

Finally, thanks to my wonderful family.

CHAPTER ONE

"*I'm sorry! Please, don't do this . . . please. . . .*"

Olivia Barker locked her office door and backed away until she bumped into her desk. She couldn't stop shaking. She just wanted him to go—so she could breathe right again.

The young man in the waiting room pounded on the other side of her door. "For God's sake, don't turn me away!" he cried. The doorknob rattled as he tugged at it.

Olivia's office was designed to have a calming effect on her clients. The color scheme was a soothing sea foam and beige. Along with her modern oak desk, there was a sofa from Dania. But during the sessions, Olivia and her clients usually sat facing each other in the two comfy, pale green chairs. The lighting remained dim, and a little waterfall trickled down a rock sculpture in one corner. It was supposed to be a tranquil, relaxing environment. But for the last fifteen minutes, Olivia had felt as if the office walls were closing in on her.

Behind her was a window—with a view of dusk looming over Lake Washington. She'd watched the room grow darker and darker while the young man had talked to her in a voice that made her skin crawl. When he'd finally emerged from his trance, she'd promptly switched on a light. She'd practically shoved him out of her office, and then shut the door on him.

He was still on the other side of it. His relentless knocking got louder and louder.

"Go away!" she called, her voice quivering. "I mean it!"

"You're the only one who can help me!" He rattled the doorknob again. "Please, I'm sorry about what happened! You can't turn me away. You're the only one. . . ."

Olivia shot a look over her shoulder at the window. Would anyone outside hear her screaming for help? She turned toward the door again. "You need to leave!" she announced over all the pounding. "There are other businesses on this floor, and you're disturbing them."

Her office was on the top floor of a three-story building in Seattle's Madison Valley neighborhood. Specialty shops and trendy restaurants had sprouted up in the past few years. A pricey antique store was on the ground level of Olivia's building. Down the hall from her were offices for a chiropractor, a masseur, and two lawyers.

But what she'd just said about disturbing the other businesses had been a lie. Everyone on her floor—except for the masseur—had closed up at five. And the masseur was on vacation. No one else was there. No one else could hear the young man beating on her office door. No one could help her if he broke down that door and attacked her.

She never should have agreed to see him in the first place.

He'd told her on the phone yesterday that he'd spotted her ad online:

HEAL YOURSELF THROUGH HYPNOSIS!
Let Olivia Be Your Guide to a Better You!
Lose Weight, Quit Smoking, Conquer Fears and Phobias,
Increase Self-Esteem, Break Bad Habits
& Build a Happy Tomorrow!

Olivia thought the ad was simply awful. But some so-called marketing analyst had come up with the cheesy copy. He'd also wanted her to include her photo, saying that with her pretty face and shoulder-length auburn hair, she might attract even more clients. Olivia was worried she might attract the wrong type of client. So the ad ran without a photo. But the cheesy copy must have worked, because business was pretty good. At the same time, Olivia felt like a big phony.

What was the phrase? *Those who can't do, teach.* That was her. She was trying to lose weight and quit smoking—all without much success. She'd recently looked up one of those "your ideal weight" charts online—probably sponsored by some fat-burning pill or weight-loss program. She didn't scroll down far enough to find out the name of the company determining just how fat or skinny she was. All she saw on her computer screen was that for her age, thirty-four, and her height, five-feet, five-inches, at a hundred and twenty-eight pounds, she was nine pounds over her "ideal weight" for a white woman. She had no idea what her race had to do with it. There was nothing on the form asking if she had any children or if she was

single or widowed or divorced. That was more important than race, wasn't it?

There were no children, and the divorce wasn't final
yet. She told herself that half a pack of Virginia Slims a
day and nine excess pounds weren't so terrible under
her current circumstances.

She did her best to help her clients conquer what she
couldn't. She'd been eking out a living at it for a month
now—sort of. It wasn't quite a *living*, but she was making some money. Olivia used a combination of hypnosis and therapy in her work. But she didn't call herself
a *therapist*—no, not anymore.

Just three months ago, she'd been a counselor/thera-
pist at the Portland Wellness Cooperative, working
with some genuinely troubled patients. She'd thought
she was doing some good. That had been before everything went to hell, and suddenly, there was nothing left
for her in Portland anymore. She'd moved—*retreated*
had been more like it—to Seattle. Olivia had made up
her mind back then that she didn't want to deal with
people whose problems were any more serious than a
bad habit or a curable addiction.

She had a success rate of about 75 percent with her
clients—or so the marketing analyst had recently told
her. Many of those clients came back because they felt
better after their sessions with her—or maybe because
she'd become their new addiction. The majority of
them were women. She'd taken on a few alcoholics, but
most of the serious problem drinkers she steered toward AA, promising to waive her fee if they joined.

The young man had said he needed her help to quit
drinking. He didn't want to go to AA. "I drink to fall
asleep most of the time," he'd told her over the phone
yesterday. "It started out as kind of an insomnia cure,
and I've been drinking pretty heavily for almost two

years now. I'm a student and it's really starting to affect my grades. I want to quit, but I can't seem to. Anyway, I'm hoping you can help me. Maybe we can discuss it when I see you tomorrow. If it doesn't work out, it doesn't work out. No harm done, y'know?"

He'd said his name was Russ Leander. But according to Olivia's caller ID, the call had come from *Stampler, C.*

She should have known right then something was wrong.

She'd assumed the young man on the other end of the line had been in college, and he'd borrowed his roommate's cell phone.

But thirty-five minutes ago, she'd opened her office door to find this kid in her waiting room—and clearly he wasn't yet college age. Sitting on the sofa in the small anteroom, he looked about fifteen years old. He was reading a magazine from the stack of periodicals on her end table. Gangly and pale, he had a mop of uncombed black hair and hauntingly beautiful blue eyes. His face seemed to be in transition from gawky adolescence to handsome young adulthood. He wore jeans, a faded red hooded sweatshirt, and black Converse All Star high-tops. Something about him was familiar. When he glanced up at her and set aside the *People* magazine, he appeared so vulnerable—and nervous. He quickly got to his feet.

Clutching the doorknob, Olivia stared at him. "Russ?"

He shoved his hands in his pockets, and nodded. "Yeah, hi, are you Olivia?"

"I thought you'd be older," she said. "Listen, I'm sorry, but I don't take on clients under the age of eighteen, not unless they're accompanied by an adult guardian. How old are you exactly?"

"Well, I'm eighteen," he answered. "I—I just look young."

"You don't happen to have your driver's license with you, do you?"

He glanced down at the carpet and said nothing.

She started to feel sorry for him. "Are you even old enough to drive?" she asked quietly.

"Of course I am. In fact, I drove here, okay? I'm sixteen, I swear." His face turned red, and he avoided her gaze. "I'm sorry I lied. I just really need your help. The truth is I—I actually don't have a drinking problem. I only said that so you'd agree to see me. . . ."

Folding her arms, Olivia leaned against the doorway frame.

"I'm telling you this now, because—well, I have a good feeling about you," he said. "I know it sounds weird, because we've just met. But I can kind of tell about some people, and you seem like a nice person. Maybe you can help me. . . ."

"Help you with what?" she asked, frowning.

"Well, I—I got hypnotized recently, and something really strange happened while I was under. I can't explain it, because I don't remember. But this—this *occurrence* was so bizarre. I'm scared something might be wrong with me. I need you to hypnotize me again, so I can find out why this *thing* happened."

Olivia's eyes narrowed. "Who hypnotized you?"

"A friend," he answered, swallowing hard. "I was at her house with another friend last weekend, just goofing off, and she said she knew how to hypnotize people."

"And you don't remember this *thing* that happened while you were under? Were you guys drinking or messing around with drugs at the time?"

He shook his head. "No, I swear."

"Well, Russ, contrary to those hypnotist routines in nightclub acts, it's very rare that a subject can't remember what's occurred while under hypnosis."

"I think my case must be very rare, too," he replied.

"So—what exactly happened? If you can't remember, certainly your friends must have told you what went on."

"I—I'd rather not say." He reached into his back pocket for his wallet. "Look, I have money. I just need you to put me under, and ask me some general questions about who I am—"

"I'm sorry, Russ." She shook her head. "You need to find yourself another hypnotist."

"I've tried other hypnotists!" he said, waving a handful of twenties under her face. "I've been to a bunch of different hypnotists in the last couple of days. None of them can even get me into a trance. Please, you're my last hope."

"What about your friend? Why don't you go back to her?"

He let out a defeated sigh. "I can't. I just can't."

Olivia studied him. He didn't look like the violent type at all. Still, she wondered if he'd attacked this girl who had originally hypnotized him. Was that why he couldn't go back to her? Whatever he'd done while under hypnosis, he must have done to that girl.

"Please, ma'am," he said, still holding out his money. "I came all the way over on the ferry from Poulsbo and drove here just to see you. Don't turn me away. All I'm asking for is a few minutes of your time. If you can't get me into a trance, I'll go away. You can keep the money. . . ."

"I can't believe you just *ma'am*ed me," Olivia said with a roll of her eyes. She opened the door wider. "Put the wad of cash away, for God's sake. I'm not taking money from a sixteen-year-old."

"Thank you," he said, heading into her office. He tucked the bills back inside his wallet. "Really, thank you. Like I said, I had a good feeling about you the moment I saw you. Practically all the other hypnotists I've been to—they were rip-off artists. They just wanted my money, I could tell." He glanced around the office. "Plus I really like your place here. This is very nice, very professional, too."

Shutting her office door, Olivia stared at him and wondered again why he seemed so familiar—his looks, the sound of his voice, everything. He came across as such a sweet kid, and she felt sorry for him. But she couldn't get past the notion that this could turn around and bite her on the ass. It still wasn't too late to kick him out.

"Where do you want me?" he asked, looking at the sofa—and then at the chairs facing each other. He nodded at the one where her patients usually sat. "Is it okay if I sit here? I think the light's good here. Would you mind recording me on my cell phone?"

Olivia hesitated. "I'd rather not. I use my hands a lot when I'm putting a subject under."

He set the phone on the edge of her desk. "Well, is it okay if I put it here?" he asked. "It won't be in your way. It's really important I get this recorded. I need to see what's happening to me when I'm under. I've set it up. It's in record mode now. You don't have to do anything. . . ."

"Fine," she muttered. She watched him check the phone to see if he had the chair in focus. His hands were a bit shaky.

Olivia usually spoke with her clients for at least a half hour and got to know them a little before putting them under. But this young man wasn't opening up to her, and he wanted to be hypnotized right away.

"Thank you for letting me do this," he said, heading back to the chair and sitting down. "I really appreciate it." He shifted restlessly in the chair. "God, all of a sudden, I'm really nervous. . . ."

"Well, just relax," Olivia said. She pulled an ottoman in front of him and sat down. She patted his arm. "Think about a place where you feel safe, Russ. Visualize it—a place where you're happy and safe and away from it all. Think of yourself in this protected place. . . ."

"This is how my friend got me into a trance," he said. "None of the other hypnotists used this method."

She kept patting his arm. "It works even better if you stay quiet and just go with it, Russ."

"Yeah, of course, I'm sorry." He shrugged uneasily. "But I guess I should tell you my name isn't really Russ. It's Collin. I'm sorry. No more lies. That—that's the last one. . . ."

Frowning, Olivia drew her hand back. He seemed so ashamed that she couldn't chastise him. She sighed, and patted his arm again. "Okay, *Collin*, let's get you back in this safe, peaceful place. It's a place you've been before. . . ."

He closed his eyes and nodded. "I'm there," he said with a dreamy smile. "It's this little shack in the woods by Shilshole Bay—on some property my grandfather owns. I used to run away and hide there. I'd bring my sleeping bag, food, and some cans of Sterno. Even when it was cold out, I'd still be warm. . . ."

"That's right," Olivia said. "You're comfortable there. You want to sleep. But I'd like you to open your eyes, and look at my hand. Focus on it." She held her hand out, palm forward, and slowly moved it toward his face and back again. "Keep focusing, Collin. You're safe and snug, and now your eyelids are getting heavy. . . ."

As she talked to him in her soothing tone, Olivia watched him relax. He slumped a little in the chair, and his young face appeared even more innocent and sweet as he floated deeper into a trance. He closed his eyes again.

"You're in that safe, warm, cozy place," Olivia continued. "Your friend brought you here last time, and something happened. Can you tell me what happened, Collin?"

He didn't respond. He seemed so deep in sleep, she almost expected him to start snoring.

"Collin, you can hear my voice, can't you?"

Again, no response.

In the silence, Olivia heard a door close down the hall. It was probably the chiropractor, leaving for the day. She was alone here with this boy. The room was getting dark. She glanced back at the window, and saw the streetlights were on. She turned toward Collin again.

His eyes were open. Something had happened. His face seemed to change—and not just his expression. He suddenly looked older, and his icy stare cut right through her. "Who the fuck are you?" he asked. The hard-edged voice wasn't his.

Though she wanted to shrink back, Olivia resisted any sudden movement. Slowly, she moved from the ottoman to the other chair that was facing him. "I'm Olivia," she said, a bit short of breath. She kept her tone quiet and even. "You came to me for help, remember?"

His eyes shifted from side to side. "So where's the fat girl and the Mexican guy with the transistor radio?"

Olivia didn't understand the question at first, and she squinted at him. "Are you talking about your friends from the last time you were hypnotized?"

A creepy little smile tugged at one corner of his mouth. "Those losers aren't *my* friends." Then something behind her seemed to catch his eye. "Hey, you've got a transistor radio, too . . ."

Olivia glanced over her shoulder at his cell phone on her desk. Why was he calling it a *transistor radio*? Who under the age of forty even remembered transistor radios?

When she turned toward him again, he was standing up.

She nervously shifted in her chair. "Collin, please, sit down," she said, trying to keep her voice calm. "Collin . . ."

He brushed past her and reached for the cell phone. "Stupid bitch," he muttered. "I'm not Collin. I'm *Wade*." He frowned at the cell phone as he inspected it from every angle. "What the hell is this thing? I thought it was a radio. The Mexican guy kept waving it around at me the other night."

Half-twisted around in the chair, Olivia warily watched him. Just three minutes before, a sweet, polite, nervous kid had programmed that phone to record this session. And now, the same kid had morphed into this cocky creep standing behind her. And he acted as if he'd never even seen a cell phone before. He looked different and sounded different. He called himself Wade. If she didn't know better, Olivia would have sworn this was indeed someone different—maybe even someone dangerous.

"Please, *Wade*, sit down," she heard herself say. "C'mon, put that back and have a seat across from me—so we can talk. I'd like to get to know you better."

Setting the phone on the desk, he smirked at her. "Well, hey, I could really dig that." As he ambled past her, he put a hand on her shoulder—then let it slide down until he touched the top of her breast.

Olivia felt her skin crawl and she recoiled. "That was inappropriate," she said evenly. "If you try anything like that again, we're done here. Do you understand?"

"Hey, I barely copped a feel. . . ."

"I'm serious," Olivia said, glaring at him.

He plopped down in the chair, and started biting his fingernail. "Listen, lady," he grumbled. "I'll give you a break for now. But keep in mind, the last time someone talked to me like that, I slit the bitch's throat. I kid you not."

"Are you—are you telling me that you killed someone?" Olivia asked.

"I'm telling you to watch your mouth, honey," he growled. "You're goddamn lucky I happen to like the way you look." He leaned back and slung his leg over the chair's armrest. "I like the setup here, too. This is real cozy with just you and me talking. Believe you me, I was getting pretty tired of talking with that whiney fat chick and José Jiménez, Junior."

Baffled, Olivia shook her head. "Why does that name sound familiar?"

"My name José Jiménez," he said with a grin and a put-on Spanish accent.

Olivia remembered it was part of comedian Bill Dana's routine from the early sixties. She'd seen old clips of him on TV—and in her soon-to-be-ex-husband's favorite movie, *The Right Stuff.* It was strange to hear this teenager quote from a comedy routine that was over fifty years old.

Either he deserved an Oscar for his acting, or he had

a second personality—radically different from his own. But in her four years as a therapist, Olivia had never encountered a patient with multiple personality disorder. Nor did she know any other therapists who had stumbled upon a genuine case.

Olivia stared at the young man slumped back in the chair across from her. She wondered if he'd been telling the truth about slitting a woman's throat.

"You're older," he said, licking his lips. "But you're a lot better looking than the fat chick."

"I really wish you wouldn't refer to her that way," Olivia said. "Why don't you call her by her name instead?"

"I don't know her name—or the Mexican guy's name." He shrugged. "I told you, they're Collin's friends, not mine."

"So—you don't like Collin's friends. What's your opinion of Collin?"

"Oh, Collin, he's pretty fucked up."

"How well do you know him?"

"I've been here with him for a long, long time—years in fact. I've just been waiting for the right time to come out." With a smug smile, he cocked his head to one side. "This is working out exactly as I wanted. I'm scaring the shit out of him. But I've barely gotten started. I'm really gonna mess with his mind—and then I'll kill him."

Olivia frowned. "How will you do that without killing yourself?"

He chuckled and slowly shook his head. "You don't get it, lady," he said. "You don't get it at all."

"Would you like to explain it to me, Wade?"

"No, not really."

"I had a feeling you'd say that." She cleared her throat. "I'd like to talk with Collin now. . . ." This was her prompt to bring him out of his hypnotic state. She waited to see the change in his manner as Collin emerged from the trance. But there was nothing, no transformation. "Collin?"

He chuckled again. "Shit, and here I thought we were getting along so well. Why do you want to talk to him? What? Do I make you nervous? Are you scared of me?"

"Not at all," she lied. "I just want to check in with Collin for a minute or two. Collin? Collin, I'm talking to you now. You hear my voice. . . ."

"Collin? Collin?" he chanted mockingly. *"Come save me from your nasty friend!"*

Olivia felt a pang in her gut. Suddenly, she couldn't breathe right. She felt as if she were stepping on the brakes of a speeding car, only to have nothing happen. She realized she had no control over her subject.

She didn't want to think about the last time this had happened.

She just wanted that sweet, polite young man to reemerge. "I'm addressing Collin now," she said, her voice a bit shaky. "Collin, when I snap my fingers, you will wake up. . . ."

"Wake up, Collin!" he said, snickering. *"Rise and shine!"*

Olivia snapped her fingers.

With the smirk still on his face, he slowly stood up.

"You need to sit down." She snapped her fingers again. "Collin, wake up. . . ."

He wandered toward the door. "I don't think he's coming back, lady." He grabbed a sturdy hardback chair and tilted it against the door, wedging the top of it beneath the doorknob.

Panic swept through her. "What are you doing?"

"I'm just making sure no one interrupts us." He

gave the chair a shake as if to make sure it was firmly in place.

Olivia got to her feet. "I'm talking to Collin now," she said, her heart racing. She glanced over at her desk—then at a letter opener by the blotter. "When I—when I snap my fingers, you'll wake up. . . ."

His back was to her. He was still standing over the chair. Olivia snapped her fingers, and then watched him put his hand up against the door. "Collin?" she said, backing up. She edged closer to her desk.

He had his hand to the door and his head down. It took Olivia a moment to realize he was bracing himself through a dizzy spell. "Collin?"

He turned to gaze at her. That innocent look had returned to his blue eyes. "What happened?" he asked.

Olivia didn't answer him. She couldn't stop shaking.

He glanced down at the chair he'd just wedged against the door, and he suddenly seemed so confused. He still had his hand on the door. "What's going on? Did Wade come back?"

Staring at him, Olivia kept thinking this was a setup or a scam of some kind. His multiple-personality act was a good one, but she didn't believe it. For all she knew, this *Russ-Collin-Wade* kid really had slit some poor woman's throat and now he wanted to lay the groundwork for an insanity plea—should he get arrested. Maybe he knew what had happened to her in Portland four months ago, and he'd figured she would be an easy mark.

"I told you before," she said. "Except in extremely rare occasions, hypnotized subjects always remember what happens to them while they're under. They *don't* change personalities and they can't be made to do anything they wouldn't do while fully conscious. I don't know what you're selling, but I'm not buying any."

Tears came to his eyes. "Jesus, he came back, didn't he? I'm sorry if he scared you—"

"I'd like you to leave now," she said, cutting him off. She circled around to her desk drawer and fished out a piece of paper with a preprinted list on it. Then she grabbed his cell phone. Heading across the room, she gave him back his phone and presented the sheet of paper to him as if it were an official summons. Her hand was trembling. "I can't help you," she said steadily. "This is a list of qualified therapists and psychologists in the area. I suggest you contact one of them."

His mouth open, he shook his head at her. He looked so scared and lost.

Olivia felt her skin crawl as she brushed past him and extricated the chair from under the doorknob. She couldn't look at him.

"Please, if Wade came back, I need to know why he's doing this to me," she heard him say. "You're the only hypnotist who even got me in a trance. No one else—"

"I don't care!" she yelled, pushing the chair aside. "Get someone else to help you! I want you out of here. . . ." She flung open the door.

He just stood there and gazed at her. Tears ran down his face.

"Go!" she screamed. "Get out!"

He still wouldn't move. So Olivia angrily shoved him out the door.

"Wait, no!" he cried.

Shutting the door and locking it, she'd thought she would feel better. But she didn't. That had been ten minutes ago, and he was still out there.

The pounding had ceased, but she could hear him playing back their session on his cell phone—the session he claimed not to remember. The sound of that voice again—Wade's voice—made her shudder.

"Would you go away?" she yelled to him. "I can't help you. Go to someone on that list I gave you. . . ."

She heard the cell phone recording stop. "You don't understand, it's got to be you!" He jiggled the doorknob again. "I'm sorry for what happened in there. But that wasn't me. Please! I'm scared. I think he—he might have come out while I was asleep or something. I think he might have killed some people. . . ."

Olivia felt sick to her stomach. She'd been afraid of something like this. She anxiously glanced at her desk phone. "I'm calling the police!" she warned. "I mean it—"

"No, don't!" he cried. "I'm sorry. I'll go now. I'm sorry. . . ."

Olivia grabbed the receiver, but then hesitated when she heard his footsteps retreating down the corridor. She wasn't certain about calling the police. What could she tell them? She didn't even know the boy's real name. He'd claimed to be from Poulsbo, on the Kitsap Peninsula, but he'd told her a bunch of lies. The part about possibly killing someone, was that a lie, too?

Strange how as soon as she'd threatened to call the police, he'd immediately apologized and withdrawn. Had he really gone? She couldn't hear anything out in the hallway. Yet she still didn't want to unlock her office door.

Olivia moved over to the window. Raindrops started slashing at the glass. She had a view of the sidewalk—two stories below, in front of the building's entrance. Biting her lip, she spotted him wandering away from the building. His shoulders were drooping, and he kept wiping his eyes. A woman passing him on the sidewalk stared. Olivia realized he was crying again.

All at once she felt horrible for throwing him out of her office. Maybe it wasn't an act after all. Maybe the poor kid was genuinely in trouble.

She noticed someone on the other side of the street who seemed to be watching him, too. When Collin or Russ or whatever he called himself stopped to blow his nose, the man across the street stopped, too—behind a phone pole. Olivia wished she could see his face. "What the hell?" she murmured to herself.

Collin took out his cell phone and started walking again. The man on the other side of the street from him began to move, too—in the same direction. Collin stayed close to the storefronts, their awnings shielding him from the rain. Olivia looked for the man across the street, but she didn't spot him. Was he hiding again? Her breath fogged the window as she leaned close to the glass and searched for the man. There was still no sign of him. Meanwhile, Collin turned down a side street.

Olivia heard a little click behind her, and swiveled around. The light on the base of her cordless phone was blinking. She'd shut off the ringer for their session, so all calls went directly to voice mail. She checked the caller ID:

**STAMPLER, C
206-555-5028
THUR 10-04 5:43 PM**

"Good God, kid, leave me alone," she muttered, nervously running a hand through her auburn hair. She waited until the light went off. Then she picked up her phone and pressed four digits. *"You have one message,"* the automated voice told her. *"Press one to play messages. . . ."*

Olivia almost deleted it, but decided to listen to what the kid had to say. Maybe she'd end up playing it for the police. She pressed one: *"Hello, I—I'm really sorry to bother you again."* He sounded a bit throaty from crying. *"I know I must have scared you in your office. But that wasn't me. If you're scared, please, think for a minute about how scared I must be. I don't understand why this is happening to me. You—you deserve to know the truth. My name's Collin, like I told you—but I'm Collin Cox. I don't know if you've heard of me. I'm an actor. But—well, what happened in your office, it was no act. It happened before when my friend hypnotized me, and I'm worried it might have happened again while I was sleeping.. Please, call me back at this number, okay? You're the only one who can help me. I really don't know what else I can—"*

The machine cut him off, and then there was a beep.

Olivia set the phone back in its cradle. She listened to the rain tapping at her window.

Of course she knew who Collin Cox was. That was why he seemed so familiar. He was the little boy from that thriller *The Night Whisperer* several years ago. Everyone knew the scene in which he was sleeping and suddenly sat up in bed to announce, *"The killings are about to start."* He hadn't made many movies since then. But he'd been in the news four months ago. While she'd been going through her own nightmare in Portland, Collin Cox, the former child star, had been making headlines for his part in a grisly double homicide.

"You're the only one who can help me," he'd said.

Her office seemed so still all of a sudden—with just the gentle rain outside and her rock-sculpture waterfall trickling. The door was still locked, and the boy was gone. Yet Olivia felt the walls closing in on her again.

CHAPTER TWO

Three months before: Seattle—Friday, July 13, 1:15 a.m.

On the night of the murders, Collin couldn't sleep. His mother and her boyfriend, Chance, were having a party downstairs with a bunch of Chance's sleazeball friends. Even with the tower fan on high speed beside his bed, it didn't create enough white noise to drown out the racket down there. They were really getting rowdy. *What a bunch of a-holes*, he thought, pulling the sheet over his head. Though he was hot and sweaty, Collin figured the sheet might muffle the racket a bit.

But he could still hear them. He thought about reading some more. He'd recently watched *The Diary of Anne Frank* on TCM. Shelley Winters had won an Oscar for it. So now he was reading the book. But he just couldn't concentrate tonight.

He thought about getting up and sleeping in the storage area off the closet. It might not be as noisy in there. But a part of him was stubborn. It wasn't so much the noise keeping Collin awake and annoyed. It was the presence of Chance's creepy friends in the house.

He and his mother lived in a dilapidated two-story white stucco in South Seattle. It was a rental. A check for the landlord came every month from his grandparents, who lived in Poulsbo. Collin and his mother had moved up from L.A. last year at his grandfather's request. "Old Andy wants to keep an eye on us—or on *me* rather," Collin's mother had explained with a roll of her eyes. "So Seattle, here we come. Otherwise, your grandfather won't be sending us any money, and then we're totally screwed."

His mom had already gone through all of his earnings from the film and TV appearances. With the Screen Actors Guild safeguards for child performers, Collin was never sure how she'd managed to get her hands on his movie money. He suspected she'd been sleeping with his lawyer or his accountant—or both. Anyway, the money was history.

So was his career—pretty much. Collin was a has-been at age sixteen.

Back when he was eight and supporting them both as a child model, he'd beaten out scores of other boys auditioning for a horror film about the occult, *The Night Whisperer.* It was Collin's first film. His agent had said there might be some idle time on the set. But no one had counted on all the delays and mishaps. The house where they shot several scenes caught on fire and burned to the ground. One of the technicians was electrocuted in a freak accident, landing him in the hospital for nearly a week. A stuntman lost a leg filming a car crash scene. Collin hadn't known him. Nor had he known the director's brother, who drowned in a boating accident during the third week of production. But Collin had been devastated when Marianne Bremer, the seventy-four-year-old actress playing his grandmother, died of a heart attack midway through filming. Ironically, her character was supposed to perish from a heart attack in a particularly scary scene. Collin had come to like the nice lady. Her replacement had been a crusty, chain-smoking old hag who had warned him up front, *"I hate kids, so don't try any cute stuff in our scenes together."* She was some big-name actress from Broadway or old Hollywood. Everyone else on the set had seemed to think she was incredibly funny and cool, but Collin had never warmed up to her. For his reaction to her death in the movie, he had to think of Marianne—and that made the tears come.

With everything that had gone wrong while filming, rumors had spread about a curse connected to *The Night Whisperer*. People said it was because the movie dealt with the occult. But Collin couldn't help thinking something inside him had brought on this curse. These terrible things were happening because he was bad.

The anxieties he'd experienced at the time must have contributed to his performance. *Entertainment Weekly* had said: *Collin Cox, the incredibly cute kid at the center of these creepy goings-on, delivers a remarkable performance in his film debut. He's unaffected and endearing in every scene.* Collin had had to look up what *unaffected* meant.

The Night Whisperer had become an instant classic. His line, *"The killings are about to start,"* whispered when he sat up in bed after a nightmare, was almost as famous as the movie itself.

Despite winning the People's Choice Award for Most Promising Newcomer, Collin's career had fizzled after three more films. It was disheartening, because his directors and most of his costars had seemed to like him.

But then there was his mother. It was embarrassing to hear what people said about her. Apparently, she'd made all sorts of demands from the studio during the production of each of his films. Those demands had included: her pick of rental cars—always the most costly models, one of which she totaled; an expense account for her own personal wardrobe; and lodgings at the plushest Hollywood hotels. The studio managed to hush it up when they were kicked out of the Chateau Marmont after the police busted up a party in their bungalow. "When the cops showed up, that was about four thousand dollars' worth of coke down the toilet," Collin had heard his mom tell a friend later. "I'm sure it didn't do the Chateau Marmont's plumbing any good."

Collin couldn't entirely blame his mother for his foundering career. He blamed himself, too. He hadn't realized how much his looks had changed in the three years after *The Night Whisperer*. But one afternoon at a newsstand, he'd seen a current, unflattering candid photo of himself on the cover of *The National Examiner*. He was at a film premiere, sporting a bad haircut and sprinklings of acne. Inset was a publicity photo of him from *The Night Whisperer*, a picture his mother had once described as "absolutely adorable." The headline above the two photos read: *What Happens When Child Stars Are No Longer Cute?* The caption below said:

GROWING PAINS: Collin Cox is one of those sweet-faced kids from movies and TV who hasn't aged well. From cute chicks to ugly ducks . . . Check out our gallery of FORMER CHILD STARS—NOT A PRETTY PICTURE! PAGE 3!"

Of course, Collin had picked up the tabloid at the newsstand and turned to page three to find himself in the company of other child actors—some from two or three decades back—who had become overweight or bald or drug-addicted or just plain homely, like him. The captions were cruel. Not only that but all sorts of nasty items and blog posts about his declining looks had popped up on the Internet.

"You're just going through an awkward phase," his mother had told him. "The preteen years suck. I promise, by the time you're sixteen, you'll be beating the girls off with a stick."

It wasn't what a twelve-year-old needed to hear. Four more years of everyone thinking he was ugly? The movie deals dried up. He guest-starred on some TV shows, but those stints did little to advance his career. It was as if he'd become this great big disappointment to everybody—including his mom—simply because he'd gotten older.

Or maybe it was *The Night Whisperer* curse?

By the time they were ready to leave for Seattle, the only work Collin could find in Los Angeles was at supermarket openings and horror film conventions. At each one, after being introduced, he was required to say, *"The killings are about to start!"* It usually got a laugh and some applause. But he always felt like a jerk at those things.

Starting as the new kid at his Seattle high school, Collin figured he wouldn't have too much trouble making friends because, after all, he used to be sort of famous.

To his utter humiliation, the kids in his new school regarded him as a freak—and a failure. Even the theater arts gang snubbed him. He wasn't sure why, maybe out of jealousy or spite. Or maybe because he'd had a chance they all would have killed for—and he'd blown it.

He spent a lot of his free time riding on different Seattle bus routes, exploring the city. At home, he holed up in his bedroom, drawing. He revived a cartoon he'd created back when he'd been a little boy, *Dastardly Dave & the Shilshole Kid*. Dave and the Kid were good-guy cowboy outlaws—just like Butch Cassidy and the Sundance Kid, from his mother's favorite movie. In his new, PG-rated version, Dave and the Kid were wronged by characters patterned after Collin's unkind classmates. These villains always met a gruesome end. It was usually a somewhat comical, justified demise, too—like something out of *Willy Wonka*.

Once in a while, Collin would run away to a little shack by Shilshole Bay, which he'd discovered during a visit to Seattle years ago. He and his mom had been walking along some beach property his grandfather owned. In the woods, he'd found the shed, which he'd cleaned out and turned into a fort over the weekend. When he'd returned to Seattle earlier this year, he'd been amazed to see the place still standing. He'd cleaned it out again and bought a lock for the door. Whenever it got too awful at home, he'd take the bus to Shilshole and camp out in the little shack. He felt safe there—away from his mother's creepy friends.

His mom had started seeing Chance about four months ago, and he'd moved in with them shortly after that. She'd made Collin swear not to tell his grandparents about their new lodger. Chance had long, dirty gray hair and a neck tattoo. Plus he always smelled like stale cigarettes. Collin did his best to avoid him, which was easy, because Chance slept all day and went out most nights. But his seedy friends would drop by the house at all hours. It didn't take long for Collin to figure out Chance was a drug dealer. He was also a damn thief. A week after Chance moved in, Collin's People's

Choice Award disappeared from the bookshelf in his bedroom. Collin confronted his mom, who swore Chance would never steal from them. *Yeah, right.* If it wasn't Chance, it was one of his scuzzy, drug-addict friends who had made off with the lead crystal prize. Collin figured his award must have ended up in some pawnshop or on eBay.

Chance was always inviting over his buddies to party—as if the place were his. Those were the nights Collin felt safer in a sleeping bag in a shack in the middle of the woods.

He wished he were there now—instead of tossing and turning and trying to ignore the noise downstairs. They all roared with laughter about something. Collin pulled the sheet down from over his head to squint at the digital clock on his nightstand: 1:36 AM.

Downstairs, his mother shushed the others and whispered something.

"Oh, who gives a shit?" he heard Chance reply. "He doesn't have school in the morning. It's summer. The smart-ass ex-movie-star can sleep late tomorrow. . . ."

Collin listened to them laugh about something else. Then there was the sound of footsteps on the stairs, and after a few moments, his bedroom door yawned open. Collin sat up and frowned at the silhouette in the doorway.

"I thought that last round of laughter might have woken you," his mother said. "Chance said the funniest thing about—"

"I've been trying to fall asleep for the last hour," Collin interrupted. "But I can't, because of all the stupid noise downstairs. When are they leaving?"

She shrugged. "I wish they'd leave, too. But I can't exactly kick them out."

"Yes, you can, it's your house. How many people are down there anyway?"

"Just Chance and me and four of our friends," she replied.

"They're *his* friends, not yours," Collin said. "And they're scumbags, let's face it."

With a sigh, she strolled into the room. He could see she had a bottle of pills in her hand. From the hallway light, he also saw the lines on her face. Blond and petite, she used to be so pretty. Now she looked kind of beat up and wore way too much makeup. She had on a black T-shirt and jeans. She kept touching her nose and her lips, a sure sign that she'd just recently snorted some cocaine. The pills rattled in the bottle as she sat down on his bed.

"What happened to you?" she asked. "You used to be so sweet. My sweet little boy, that's what you were. What happened?"

Sitting up in bed, Collin said nothing. His eyes avoided hers. When he was mad at her, he always had a hard time looking at her.

"Listen, I'm sorry about the party," she finally said. "It was a crazy, last-minute thing. If I'd known we were having company, I would have sent you to stay with Grandpa and Dee for the weekend. . . ."

Collin remained silent. Lately, he'd thought about asking if he could go live with his grandparents—full-time. Maybe then he'd have a normal life.

A woman downstairs let out a screech of laughter, and the others joined in.

"Christ, it sure is loud down there," his mom admitted. She opened the bottle of pills and shook one out. "No wonder you're so pissy tonight. You just need a little help falling asleep. I'll try to hustle them out of here soon. Meanwhile, have one of these. . . ."

He knew the pill was Ambien. She used to give him half a pill whenever he was too keyed up the night before a morning call on the movie set. He'd been ten years old at the time. She'd give him a whole pill when leaving him alone for the night. He'd once overheard her telling a friend on the phone, "Hey, I need to have a life, too. And where can you get a sitter? It's either knock him out with a pill or tie him down in his bed until I return home. And I'd just as soon not tie him down, thank you very much. Besides, why do you care all of the sudden?"

A few years back, Collin had read stories about some of the pill's side effects—like sleepwalking, people preparing and eating food while asleep, sleep-*driving*, and even having sex while asleep. After that, Collin had refused to take any more Ambien.

Tonight he didn't want to argue with her. He reached for the glass of water on his nightstand, plucked the pill from her hand and swallowed it. A lot of those side-effects stories were pretty far-fetched anyway.

"You can sleep in tomorrow," his mother said, twisting the cap back on the bottle. She reached over and messed his already messy hair. "Tell you what, Collie, tomorrow afternoon, we can finally go check out the Experience Music Project—just you and me. What do you say?"

Collin wanted to say he was too old to hang out with his mother all afternoon. Why not just wear a T-shirt that said, I'M A PATHETIC LOSER? Besides, she and Chance would probably sleep until three in the afternoon tomorrow. There was no way in hell they'd get to the EMP in time to see anything. Though he knew it would never happen, Collin worked up a smile and nodded, "Sounds good, Mom."

She leaned over and kissed him on the forehead.

"Sleep tight." Then she got to her feet and retreated toward the hallway. The last thing Collin saw before she closed the door was her silhouette, and she was rubbing her nose again.

Then the room was swallowed up in darkness.

Collin told himself it was nice she'd checked in on him. The gesture reminded him that she genuinely cared about him—in her own screwed-up way. As much as he imagined a better life with his grandparents on the Kitsap Peninsula, he couldn't leave her. Who else would take care of her, clean up after her, and protect her from herself?

Collin's father had tried to take care of her long ago. They'd met at a ski resort, where he'd been an instructor. They'd gotten married two days later. When Collin was four months old, his dad had left in the middle of the night—in his jeep and with all of his ski equipment.

Collin had been three years old when his father came back—to ask for an annulment so he could remarry. His mom didn't believe Collin when he claimed to have a vague memory of his father from that day—handsome and tan with wavy brown hair. He'd worn a blue jean jacket. Collin remembered his dad picking him up and holding him over his head. He remembered the jeep, parked in front of their town house.

Aaron Cox and his fiancée had died three months later when that same jeep spun out of control and hit a truck on Highway 145 outside Telluride, Colorado. Collin's mother hadn't gone to the funeral. She'd been in her first stint in a drug rehab facility at the time, and little Collin had been staying with his grandparents at their beachfront home in Poulsbo.

He wished he were there now. He had his own bedroom—with a TV and a connecting bathroom. From his window, he looked out at Liberty Bay. It was always so quiet there.

He now longed for that same quiet—just waves lapping against the shore outside. But Chance and his lowlife friends were laughing and carrying on downstairs. Even with the Ambien in his system, Collin still couldn't fall asleep. He tore off his bedsheets and sat up.

The drug must have worked from the ground up, because his legs felt wobbly as he climbed out of bed. Collin had on his South Park T-shirt and plaid boxer shorts. He grabbed his pillow, which smelled of Clearasil, and hugged it to his chest. Lumbering into the closet, he pulled the string for the overhead light and shut the door behind him. Already, the noise downstairs became muffled. He staggered past the row of clothes on hangers. They concealed a narrow door— about four feet tall. Opening it, he reached inside and switched on the light. He lost his footing for a second. Empty hangers rattled and clinked as he stumbled back into them. He braced himself against the wall, and then pulled the string to turn off the closet light.

Collin ducked into the storage space, which was surprisingly cool on this muggy summer night. He'd fixed it up with a cheap bathroom rug, a bookcase full of books, his sleeping bag, and a battery-operated lantern. He kept the area clean. It had a small window, which he opened a crack. He tossed his pillow on top of the sleeping bag. Then he switched on the lantern and weaved back toward the tiny door to close it and turn off the light.

This secret room reminded him of that little shack by Shilshole Bay. When he needed to be alone and couldn't get away from home, this crawlspace was the next best thing. Except for some muted laughter, he couldn't hear them anymore. And he couldn't keep his eyes open.

Collin crawled inside the sleeping bag and tucked the pillow under his head. He felt a cool, gentle breeze coming through the open window.

The next thing he knew, he and his mother were scurrying around under the shadow of the Space Needle, looking for an entrance into the Experience Music Project. Every door they tried was locked. He kept thinking they didn't have much time before the place closed. He was so angry at her, because she'd told Chance where they were going. Collin desperately wanted to get inside the building before Chance caught up with them. At last, he found a door that opened, and he tried to pull his mother inside.

"God, no, wait!" she screamed.

He heard Chance cursing.

Suddenly, he was awake. He knew he wasn't at the Experience Music Project. He'd sweated inside the warm sleeping bag. He remembered the weird thing about Ambien was that it gave him vivid, realistic dreams. But he could have sworn that had actually been the sound of his mother's voice just a moment ago. And the spew of loud obscenities from Chance seemed to come from beneath the attic's floorboards.

Collin kept still and listened. He heard some indistinct conversation. It sounded like other people talking. He wondered what time it was. Hadn't the party broken up yet?

He started drifting off again. He thought of Dastardly Dave and the Shilshole Kid—except they weren't cartoon cowboys. They were real, and he was the Shilshole Kid. He and Dastardly Dave were on foot, being chased through the woods by an evil sheriff and his posse. He kept thinking that once he and Dave made it to that little shack, they'd be safe. No one would find them there.

He heard a loud snap—like someone had broken off a tree branch.

"Oh, sweet Jesus, my baby!" his mother screamed. *"Don't hurt him! Collin, get out of here! Oh, no . . ."*

He couldn't tell where his mother's voice had come from. Maybe she was waiting for them in the shed. He did what his mom told him to, and ran even faster. He gasped for air, and felt his lungs burning. Through the tree branches, he spotted the little shack up ahead. But he'd lost track of Dave.

Somewhere nearby, he heard a muted whimpering. It sounded like an animal was trapped and wounded here in the woods. All Collin could think was this ailing creature would give away his position. The wheezing sound went on and on.

"Shut up!" Collin finally yelled.

Or had he? He told himself again that it was just the pill he'd taken. None of this was real. He was dreaming.

"Son of a bitch!" someone grunted. It was a stranger's voice. *"Can you believe it? The fucker's still alive. He's still breathing. Finish him off. . . ."*

The Shilshole Kid reached the cabin at last. He burst inside and shut the door behind him. He'd wait for Dave's special knock. But as he turned around, he realized he wasn't in the shack in the woods. He was in a dark attic, and about ten people were huddled together, hiding in there. He didn't recognize any of them, except the somewhat frumpy-looking blonde in one corner of the room. It was Shelley Winters. "Shhhh, Collie," she whispered. "You have to be quiet. The Nazis are outside. We can't let them find us. Stay still, baby. . . ."

"Of course," he whispered.

There was the rumble of footsteps up the stairs. It sounded like at least two people.

"No witnesses!" someone said. *"Where's the kid? She's got a kid. . . ."*

Collin heard a door creak open. *"Shit, somebody was in here,"* one of them said. *"The fan's still on."*

His heart was racing. Collin didn't dare move a muscle—or breathe. He heard another door yawn open. Gazing over toward the little trapdoor, he couldn't see it at first—and then an outline of light from the other side suddenly appeared at the hinges. Hangers rattled.

All at once a loud shot went off. Collin flinched.

"Christ, what the hell is he doing down there?"

There was a scuttle of footsteps, and the hangers clanked again.

It sounded like the Nazis were leaving. Collin could hear them going down the stairs. They were arguing about something, but he couldn't make out what they said. Were they talking in German? He stared at the line of the light around that little door. He was still too afraid to make a move. The voices started to fade.

"We have to remain quiet," Mr. Frank whispered. "No one move a muscle."

Collin didn't know how long he lay there motionless. It didn't sound like anyone had left yet. There was still a lot of movement in the house—voices whispering, doors opening and shutting. He glanced over at Anne Frank, who sat quietly and stroked a cat in her lap. The young, dark-haired girl gave him a sweet, reassuring smile.

At last, he thought he heard some car doors slamming. Then tires screeched.

"Just lie still," Mr. Frank whispered. "It might not be over yet."

Huddled in the sleeping bag, Collin tried not to move. He wondered if those men were really gone.

"You just need a little help falling asleep," he heard his mother say. "I'll try to hustle them out of here soon."

He wanted to thank her. But he was too tired to even talk. It was blessedly quiet now, and he slept.

When he opened his eyes again, it was morning.

Collin sat up in the sleeping bag. The early morning light through the small window made his cozy getaway look like the ugly attic space it was. He always tried to keep it clean, but this morning, he could see the splintery, wooden floorboards, and all the dust and cobwebs. He made out—just barely—the faint outline of light around the narrow little door to his closet.

He remembered almost stumbling last night when he'd reached for the closet's pull-string light. But he'd turned it off. Why was the light on now?

The house seemed too quiet. He thought about Chance's party last night. It had sounded as if it had gotten pretty crazy. A fight had broken out or something. Collin figured his mom and Mr. Personality were asleep right now. They probably wouldn't be waking up for hours yet.

He had no idea what time it was. Crawling out of his sleeping bag, he grabbed his pillow and staggered toward the small door. He still wasn't sure why the closet light was on. He opened the door and ducked through it. Collin pulled the string and turned off the closet light. Then he moved on to his bedroom, where the tower fan was blowing cool air toward his bed. He remembered that voice in his Nazi dream: *"Shit, somebody was in here. The fan's still on."*

He set the pillow on his bed and squinted at the clock on the nightstand: 8:02 AM. He stepped into a pair of jeans. Gazing down at the beige rug on his bedroom floor, he noticed some faint, crimson marks that hadn't been there before. They looked like partial shoe prints—in faded, dried blood.

With uncertainty, Collin continued into the hallway. He remembered his weird, vivid, Ambien-fueled nightmare from last night. All that fighting, screaming, the chaos and the gunshot, it was just a dream.

But why was there blood on his bedroom rug?

He never went into his mother's room, certainly not when he knew Chance was in there with her. But he turned down the hall and saw the door was slightly ajar. Collin remembered his mother's screaming and wondered if Chance had beaten her up last night. Chance hadn't knocked her around yet, but Collin had always figured he was capable of it.

The bedroom door creaked as he pushed it open farther. The bed was unmade and empty. Some dresser drawers had been left open. The closet door was open, too, and the light was on. Boxes and suitcases had been yanked down from the shelf and clothes dumped on the floor. Someone had been searching for something—maybe drugs.

Collin noticed the same faded crimson smudges on his mother's pale blue carpet. He told himself it could be reddish mud or just about anything. Most of Chance's friends were slobs—as well as potential thieves. They could have tracked in something from outside.

Collin turned and headed back down the hallway. Stopping by the bathroom, he glanced beyond the half-open door. "My God," he muttered.

The linen closet door was open, too—and so was the mirrored medicine cabinet above the sink.

He started toward the stairs. "Mom?" he called with

a tremor in his voice. "Mom, are you home? It looks like we got robbed. . . ."

At the top of the stairs, he hesitated. Maybe the intruders were still inside the house. He stood there for a moment, feeling sick to his stomach. He backed up, and then retreated into his room. Propping open his window was a solid piece of wood—almost the length of a baseball bat. Collin grabbed it and headed toward the hallway again. Behind him, the window squeaked as it slid down toward the sill.

"Mom?" he called once more. With the piece of wood clenched in his fist, he started down the stairs. His legs felt wobbly again—as if the Ambien was still in his system. He nervously clung to the banister with his other hand.

"Mom? Mom, are you—" He didn't finish. The words caught in his throat.

Halfway down the stairs, Collin saw the chaotic pattern of dark red footprints on the front hall's hardwood floor. He could see the living room from here, too. The shades were drawn, and the lights were still on. He saw the bodies—both of them, hog-tied with their hands behind their backs. Beneath them, the blood soaking the tan shag rug almost looked brown. His mother was lying on her side, turned away from him. Strands of her blond hair were clumped together with blood. Collin couldn't see her face.

Chance was lying beside her. When Collin had seen him last night, he'd been wearing a yellow T-shirt. Now, it was crimson, with countless slashes and tears from knife wounds. Chance must have been cursing at them right up until someone had put that gag in his mouth. Collin knew he hadn't died easily. He'd heard the killers talking about it. He'd also heard one solitary gunshot. That must have been what had obliterated most of Chance's face. From his nose to his gray-brown hairline, it was just a bloody pulp.

Collin felt his legs give out and he sank down until he was sitting on one of the steps. Numbly, he stared down at the horrible scene in the living room. His mother looked so pitiful lying there. He couldn't see her face, but he knew someone must have shoved a gag in her mouth, too. He remembered her screaming: *"Oh, sweet Jesus, my baby! Don't hurt him! Collin, get out of here! Oh, no . . ."*

Those were the last words he'd heard from her.

Collin stared at that sad, lifeless thing sprawled on the living floor. He couldn't believe it was his mom.

And he couldn't believe that at the end, she'd actually been thinking about him.

CHAPTER THREE

It was her second day of not smoking, and Olivia Bischoff was going a little crazy.

Usually after lunch, before heading back to work, she'd duck into the alley behind the old medical building and sneak a cigarette. It was a filthy place to feed her filthy habit. But she wished she were there right now, puffing away on a Virginia Slim.

Instead, she was in a pretty garden courtyard that was part of the Portland Wellness Cooperative's small campus. On sunny days like this, the half-dozen café tables in the courtyard were premium lunch spots. Olivia's supervisor, Dr. Winifred Frost, had snagged them a table. On it now were the remnants of their lunches: two salad containers, two Diet Coke cans, and Olivia's Yoplait, which she was still finishing.

"Do you not want to talk about it?" Winnie asked. Dr. Frost had become *Winnie* to her about a year ago—after Olivia had finished her six-month training period as a therapist-counselor. Olivia now had her own patients and her own office—just down the hall from Winnie. At forty-seven, Winnie was like the big sister

Olivia never had. When she first met her, Olivia thought Winnie looked sort of like an ostrich—tall and skinny, with large brown eyes, a wide smile, and a slightly weak chin. Her brassy, brown hair was always a bit mussed—like a bird's crown. Yet Olivia no longer noticed the avian similarities in her friend. She thought Winnie was exotic-looking and pretty. She was divorced—with two handsome brainy sons, one in college and another in high school.

"Do I not want to talk about what?" Olivia asked, over her last spoonful of Yoplait.

"About how much you're dying for a cigarette," Winnie said.

Olivia rolled her eyes. "Go ahead, talk. It's all I think about. I may gnaw away at this spoon until there's nothing left—I'm so orally fixated."

"Try chewing on cinnamon sticks or cloves." Winnie crumpled up her napkin and stuffed it inside the plastic container with her salad. "For the record, I think what you're doing is fantastic. I mean, you've been a slave to the habit for—how long?"

"Seventeen years," Olivia admitted. "I started senior year in high school, Marlboros."

It had been her boyfriend's brand. He'd been good-looking and grungy, always arguing with the English teacher about the real meaning of different literary classics. He'd liked to converse with homeless people, and hang out in cemeteries. Smoking had given Olivia something to do while she tagged along for these sometimes monotonous yet deep, intellectual endeavors. He'd dropped her for a college freshman over spring break. The relationship had left her with a serious smoking habit—and a weakness for edgy, brooding guys. Of the two susceptibilities, cigarettes were far more comforting and dependable. Smoking had gotten her through all those long study sessions in college—and later on, when she was earning her master's in social work at the University of Washington. So at least cigarettes were good for something—unlike most of the good-for-nothing guys she dated.

But that was all in the past.

Now she had a great husband—and a compelling reason to kick her pack-a-day habit. They were trying to have a baby. She hadn't planned on telling Winnie any of this until she was actually pregnant. It wasn't something she was eager to share with her supervisor after eighteen months on the job. But Winnie was also her friend, and she needed to confide in someone.

"Good for you for quitting," Winnie said. She toasted her with her Diet Coke can, and then took a swig. "Awful as it is, I know you enjoy your cigarettes. I hope he appreciates the sacrifice you're making."

"*He*? What makes you so certain the baby—when I get pregnant—will be a boy?"

"I was talking about Clay," Winnie replied, one eyebrow arched. "What's that handsome husband of yours giving up? What sacrifice is Clay making?"

Olivia let out a stunned little laugh. "Hey, he isn't too thrilled with this sex-on-a-schedule routine, but he's there for me each time."

"God love him. What a trouper."

Olivia frowned. "You just don't like Clay. It's that simple."

He wasn't like all those intense, self-involved, troubled types she'd been attracted to in high school and beyond. Clay Bischoff was different. With receding blond hair, beautiful blue eyes, and a confident smile, he won everyone over. Though he had been a bit of a party boy when she'd met him, he'd also held a high-powered job at a PR firm. Plus he'd really been there for Olivia when her mom had been dying of pancreatic cancer. She still remembered one of the last lucid things her mom had told her: *"That Clay is a nice young man. You should stick with him for a while."*

Her mother hadn't told her to marry him, but that was what Olivia had done. She'd even managed to cut back on cigarettes for him—and never smoked in their Queen Anne apartment. She'd always stepped outside for a smoke.

Then Clay had accepted a job offer in Portland, where he'd grown up. They socialized a lot with his old school chums. Olivia wasn't exactly crazy about them—or their wives. Smoking became her excuse to step outside during some of the more intolerable *"Hey, remember when . . ."* social gatherings. By the time Clay and some of his friends had formed a softball team, Olivia was exceeding a pack a day.

That had been almost a year ago, when she'd decided they should have a baby. Clay had been all for it. She'd made three other attempts to quit smoking since then, and each time, when she'd gotten her period, the disappointment had been so overwhelming she'd broken down and started smoking again. She'd probably leaned on Winnie and complained about Clay a bit too much during those setbacks. Her friend had a skewed opinion of him.

"I'm just saying," Winnie sighed, while gathering up her salad container and Diet Coke. "You're going through withdrawal right now, and some months down the line, you may have to take maternity leave from here. Clay isn't making any sacrifices for this. He hasn't even said anything about giving up his Little League—"

"It's not a Little League," Olivia muttered. "It's a men's softball team, and they play for charity."

"Charity begins at home," Winnie replied, getting to her feet, "which is where your husband and most of his friends should be. Instead they're ignoring their wives and families to go swing at a baseball and relive their old high school glory days. I mean, really, three nights of practice a week—and a game every Saturday? That's N-U-T-Z, nuts."

Olivia got up from her café chair. "You know, every time I'm unhappy and I confide in you, it comes back to bite me in the ass." She quickly gathered up what remained of her lunch and took it to the trash can.

Winnie followed her. "Oh, don't pay too much attention to me, honey. You're talking to a golf-widow divorcee, who discovered her husband was two-timing her with a twenty-eight-year-old paralegal. I'm bitter and jaded." They threw out their trash, and then Winnie gave her a nudge as they headed into the old medical building together. "For what it's worth, I'm not sure about how great a dad Clay will be, but I know you'll be a wonderful mom."

Olivia worked up a smile. "You really think so?"

"At least, you'll be a better mother than the one Collin Cox had."

Olivia laughed and pressed the button for the elevator. "Well, that's high praise. Thanks for the vote of confidence."

It was all over the newspapers, tabloids, and TV that Collin Cox's recently slain, drug-addicted mother was a potential candidate for World's Worst Stage Mother Ever.

In the elevator on their way up to the sixth floor, Winnie asked if she wanted to go out for a drink after work. Olivia figured she'd conquer one vice at a time for her yet-to-be-conceived baby. For now, she could drink. Besides, Clay had softball practice tonight. Olivia said yes.

She had a half hour before her next patient, but found her message light blinking when she got back to her office. It was Sheila at the admissions desk. One of Olivia's regulars, Layne Tipton, was waiting for her: *"He knows he doesn't have an appointment, but it's quite urgent, he says. Anyway, I thought you might be able to squeeze him in before your one-thirty. . . ."*

The admissions people practically never let patients in without an appointment. But twenty-year-old Layne Tipton was so damn handsome almost everybody made exceptions for him. He was just the kind of guy who would have broken her heart in college.

Olivia found the brooding, dark-haired, dark-eyed young man nervously pacing around the waiting area. He wore a black T-shirt that showed off his muscular arms—one almost completely covered with tattoos and the other untouched. His jeans were torn in several places and he had a jacket tied around his waist. Despite his ragtag attire, he still looked like a fashion model. Olivia noticed the other people in the area looking at him. Most of them probably had no idea someone so gorgeous could have so many problems.

"Hi, Layne," she said, coming up behind him.

He swiveled around and gaped at her with his beautiful sad brown eyes. "I really need to see you," he whispered. "Something happened. . . ."

"It's okay," she said. "I've got some time for you." She patted him on the shoulder, and led the way down the narrow corridor to her office. The halls of the old medical building had been cheaply updated years ago with fluorescent lighting overhead and gray carpeting.

As she neared her office door, Olivia glanced back at Layne, plodding behind her.

"I got fired yesterday," he whispered. "Another customer at the garden store complained to my stupid boss, and he fired me. Then this morning, my mom found out—and oh, God . . ."

As soon as he stepped inside her office, he made a beeline for his usual spot at one end of the tan sofa. He plopped down on the couch, buried his face in his hands, and cried.

Layne had grown up with an abusive, manipulative mother. He'd attempted suicide twice—once by slashing his wrist, and again with pills. He'd admitted to Olivia that before starting to see her, he'd even bought a gun to use on himself. For a while, he'd lived on the streets and hustled. He'd been arrested for all sorts of infractions—from shoplifting to assault to public indecency. The last charge had stuck, and put him on the list of registered sex offenders in Oregon. He'd been caught with his pants down in some bushes in a public park, satisfying an older gentleman for fifty dollars.

In his hustling days, Layne had been "gay for pay." He said he wasn't interested in sex with men beyond the monetary rewards. But Olivia was pretty certain he found a warped sense of importance and acceptance in those sexual encounters. Apparently, Layne's mother knew about some of his minor brushes with the law, but he'd managed to keep her in the dark about his hustling days. He'd recently moved back in with her after a stretch at a halfway house.

With a notepad and pen in hand, Olivia sat across from him in the easy chair. While he sobbed, the fan hummed in one corner of the room. The two big windows behind her desk were open to their six-inch maximum, allowing some air to circulate through the stuffy office. The windows had a view of the alley where Olivia usually took her cigarette break.

"All right." She handed Layne a Kleenex. "Let's talk about what happened at work."

He blew his nose, wiped his eyes, and told her about his run-in with a "bitch customer" at the garden store, where he'd been employed for two months. Olivia felt sorry for the customer. Layne didn't seem to grasp when he was being rude or incredibly tactless with people.

"I'll be honest with you, Layne," she finally said. "From everything you've told me, I'm not sure this woman did anything to deserve your hostile treatment. Are you sure you weren't mad about something else—and maybe decided to take it out on this woman who was just buying some azaleas?"

He squirmed in the corner of the sofa. "I should have known you'd side with her."

"Well, it's obvious you went to work yesterday in a bad mood. And it's also obvious your getting fired isn't what's really upsetting you right now. Otherwise, you'd have called me or come in here yesterday, when it happened—"

"Of course, I'm upset about it!" he argued. "That fucker boss of mine, he's such a prick! I'd like to slit his throat. Believe me, if I ever see him again—"

"Layne, you don't mean that. Didn't he give you a break by hiring you?"

"The bastard told my mother that I had a record!" he screamed.

"All right," she said calmly. "Okay. Let's talk about it. What happened exactly?"

Layne started crying again. "I didn't want her to

know I got shit-canned—so I—I left the house like I was going to work this morning. I hung out at the library and the park. . . ."

"Were you looking for company?" she asked, without judgment in her tone.

"No!" he said, shaking his head over and over. "I just didn't want her to know I'd gotten fired. But she called the garden store, and my boss started giving her all sorts of shit. He went on and on about how much I've screwed up—and how he'd done me this big favor letting me work in his crappy store when I had a *criminal record*. That fucker! I could kill him. . . ."

Olivia had a feeling Layne's boss wasn't the one who had gotten hostile over the phone, not from what she knew about Layne's mom. Mrs. Tipton was a piece of work.

"Your mother already knows you have a record of sorts," Olivia said.

"Yeah, but the asshole told her to look it up online!" Layne started sobbing again. "She had no idea about the public indecency charge. Now she knows I'm on the registered sex offender list. . . ."

"You spoke with her?" Olivia asked.

Tears streamed down his face. "She doesn't want to see me ever again. She threw all my shit out of the house. *Don't come home*, she said. . . ."

"Okay, Layne," she said, patting his knee. "We're going to work this out. Everything seems awful now, but believe me, it's not the end of the world. . . ."

He seemed inconsolable. He wouldn't stop weeping. Olivia handed him the box of Kleenex. She remembered hypnosis helped him work out his issues with his mother. While hypnotized, he'd managed to remember and calmly describe for her some of the horrible things his mother had done to him in the past. As a child,

when he'd wet his bed, she'd make him stand in the
bathtub with the urine-soaked sheet over his head all
night. One evening when he'd been nine years old,
she'd caught him in his room, naked and staring at
himself in the mirror. She dragged him naked outside
and tied him to a tree in their backyard. "I'm sure it
was only for an hour or so," Layne had explained. "But
it seemed like half the night, because it was—like, November, and I was freezing my bare ass off. Plus I
was afraid to scream for help, because I didn't want
anyone to see me naked. I was so sick the following
week. . . ." It was while under hypnosis that Layne had
lifted the back of his shirt and shown her the faint scars
where his mother had whipped him with a belt years
ago.

"Okay, Layne, I want you to take some deep
breaths," she said. "You always feel better after I've
hypnotized you. We can work some of these things out.
Does that sound good?"

He wiped his eyes and nodded.

"You know the routine," she said. "Think of a place
where you're safe and happy."

"I don't have a place like that," he sighed.

"I know, but don't you remember? You made one up
in your head. I want you to go there now. Everything's
so peaceful. You don't have to close your eyes to see
it. . . ." She held her hand out—the palm toward him.
Layne numbly stared at it. Taking her time, Olivia
moved her hand toward his face and back again.
"You're tired, and all you want to do is sleep. . . ."

She watched him relax and slump back on the sofa.
She continued to coax him into a trance with her soothing voice and the careful movement of her hand—until
he closed his eyes. He let out a tiny sigh.

"You're in a deep sleep, Layne, and a very safe

place," she told him. "When I snap my fingers and call your name, you'll wake up. But first I want to talk with you about some things. And you'll feel good getting them off your chest. Can you hear me, Layne?"

"Yes, Mama," he whispered.

Olivia balked. For a moment, she didn't think she'd heard him right. "Layne, this is Olivia. We're talking together in a quiet, safe place. . . ."

"I'm sorry!" he cried. "Please, don't hate me. . . ."

"Layne, this is Olivia," she said loudly—over his sobbing. "Can you hear my voice?"

He coiled up in the corner of the sofa. He was shaking. "Mama, please, I didn't mean for it to happen. . . ." He kept apologizing, and yet the tone of his voice grew angrier and angrier. Opening his eyes, he glared at her and started to uncoil. It looked as if he might spring off the sofa at any minute. "You can't do this to me, goddamn it!" he screamed. "It's your fault I'm this way! You're the one who should be sorry. . . ."

"Layne, I want you to wake up—"

"What do you expect from me? I was just your fucking whipping boy. That's all I was, and still am. Well, go ahead and take your failures out on me. . . ."

Olivia wondered if Winnie could hear him down the hall. At this point, she would have welcomed some help from another therapist. She didn't know how to deal with him.

"Layne, wake up!" She snapped her fingers. "Can you hear me, Layne?"

It wasn't doing any good.

"The only way I'd ever make you happy was if I were dead!" he ranted, saliva flying from his mouth. "Well, I tried that! Fuck you. Why don't *you* die?"

Olivia slowly got to her feet. "Layne, wake up!"

He curled up in the corner of the sofa again and wept inconsolably.

Olivia felt so helpless. She backed toward the office door and opened it. She glanced down the hall at the closed door to Winnie's office. She knew most subjects under hypnosis normally emerged from a trance on their own after a few moments if their guide couldn't reach them. But what was happening now with Layne wasn't normal.

"Everything's all right, Layne," she said. "You're safe here. . . ."

Backing out of the office, she turned and hurried down the hall. She pounded on Winnie's door, and then flung it open.

Her supervisor was in the middle of a session with a middle-aged woman. Lying on the sofa, the patient let out a startled cry and quickly sat up. From a chair beside the couch, Winnie got to her feet. "What is this? Olivia, you know better than to barge in—"

"I'm sorry, Winn," she cut her off. "The sink in the bathroom is backing up."

That was their code for an emergency situation with a patient. Olivia had only used it twice before, and neither case had seemed quite this serious. She remembered Layne's suicide attempts. Then all at once, she thought about the large windows in her office—and the six-story drop to the cobblestone alley below. All he had to do was smash one of those windows.

Winnie told her patient that she'd be right back and hurried out to the hallway. She shut the door. "Who is it?" she whispered.

"Layne Tipton," Olivia answered, heading down the hall with her. "I hypnotized him to make him calm down, but he just got worse. I can't get him to snap out of it. . . ."

"You shouldn't have left him alone."

"I didn't know what else to do. . . ."

Winnie grabbed her arm just as she was about to rush into the office. "We don't want to do anything too sudden or startling," Winnie whispered. She stepped in front of Olivia in the doorway, and then stopped dead.

Layne stood with his back to the window. He fumbled for something inside the jacket he'd had tied around his waist earlier.

"Layne, I'm Olivia's friend," Winnie calmly said. "We want to help you. I know that—"

"I'll show you!" he screamed. He pulled a gun from the jacket and aimed it at them.

It happened so fast, Olivia barely had time to gasp before two loud shots rang out.

"Oh!" was all Winnie said, and then she collapsed. Her body hit the floor with a thud—right at Olivia's feet.

Paralyzed, she stood and stared at Layne as he fired the gun again.

Olivia felt the stinging, searing blow to her shoulder. She staggered back into the hallway. She braced herself against the wall to keep from falling. Horrified, Olivia gazed down at the pool of blood beneath the crumpled form of her friend. When she looked up again, her eyes met Layne's.

For a moment, he seemed to realize what he'd done. His mouth dropped open and he shook his head at her. It was as if he'd finally come out of his trance.

Helpless, she watched him turn the gun on himself—just under his chin.

"No, wait!" she screamed.

He fired, and the blast of the final shot reverberated in the room. Layne's blood and brains splattered against the window behind him. Then his body flopped down on the floor.

Olivia stared down at him. But her vision began to blur. She could hear someone running up the corridor. She didn't know who it was, but they were calling out to her. She couldn't answer. Her body was shutting down and her legs gave out from under her.

Everything started to get dark.

But she was thinking about her friend, Winnie—and about Layne.

At last, poor Layne had found a peaceful, quiet place.

Olivia woke up and squinted at the window in her hospital room. The afternoon sun shone through the open blinds. The TV bracketed to the wall was on mute, and tuned to a baseball game. Any one of three people could have turned it on: her husband, her dad, or her college-age brother. The latter two had come down from Seattle, and were staying at a Best Western.

Blindly reaching for the button at her side, she elevated the head of the bed until she was almost sitting up. The IV tube in her arm flopped around a bit as she reached for her water glass and took a sip. The nightstand also had a stack of magazines: *People, Us Weekly, InStyle*, and several others. If she never saw another photo of a Kardashian again, it would be too soon.

She rubbed her eyes and focused on the visitor's chair. She recognized Clay's baseball cap, sitting on the cushion. Clay must have stepped out for a minute.

A foil *Get Well Soon* helium balloon was tied to the arm of that chair. It was from Clay's niece, Gail, who had stayed with them for two weeks last summer. Cool air from the vent by the window made the balloon dance.

Olivia gazed at the menagerie of plants, flowers, and cards on the dresser. On the cover of one card was a cartoon of a guy with a broken leg; a rectal thermometer joke was on another; and a photo of a sexy, shirtless intern was on yet another. The shooting incident that had put her here in the hospital had occurred just three days ago. She appreciated the cards, but wasn't quite ready to laugh yet. Several of those cards and flower arrangements were from Clay's baseball buddies and their spouses. It was nice of them to think of her, and she felt guilty for not having tried harder to make friends with them.

She felt guilty about a lot of things right now.

The pain in her left arm was a constant reminder of what had happened. The shooting incident at the Portland Wellness Cooperative had made the front page of *The Oregonian.* The ongoing postmortem analysis of Collin Cox's murdered mother and her lover had gotten bumped to page two. Reporters had been hounding Clay and her coworkers. Clay had the hospital operator screen all the calls to her room.

Her official condition was stable. They'd removed the bullet from her shoulder, but she'd developed an infection. This morning was the first time her temperature had finally dropped below a hundred and one. The doctor thought she might go home the day after tomorrow—and he recommended bed rest after that. He advised against her attending Winnie's funeral on Tuesday. Clay had promised to attend for her.

"You're awake," he said, strutting into the room with a Starbucks Frappuccino bottle. He looked sporty in his khaki shorts and red polo shirt. He had a healthy tan and his dark blond hair was sun-kissed flaxen. "Can I get you anything?"

"No, thanks," she said, working up a smile. "How long have you been here?"

"About forty-five minutes." He turned to look up at the TV. "Who's winning?"

"I have no idea." She didn't even know who was playing.

He swiped his cap off the chair and sat down. "Feeling a little better?"

She just nodded.

"Well, the home phone was ringing off the hook today," he said, taking a swig of his Frappuccino. "Liz Noll called this morning from Seattle. She and Tom send their love. Also your friend, Nancy—um, Nancy What's-her-name from your old job with Group Health . . ."

"Nancy Abbe," Olivia said.

He nodded. "I gave her your number here. Also Margaret and Bev left messages."

Olivia nodded again. "That's sweet." Margaret and Bev were work friends—and for just a second, Olivia wondered why Winnie hadn't called, too.

Then she remembered, and her shoulder started to hurt again.

"You sure I can't get you anything?" Clay asked.

"No, thanks, honey." She looked toward the window and sighed. "I—I keep thinking *'what if?'* I mean, if I'd stayed with Layne, maybe I could have stopped him somehow."

"And maybe he would have shot you dead—and then shot a lot more people on your floor before killing himself. We've been through this before, sweetheart. No one blames you. You want to blame anyone? Blame him—or maybe blame the douche bag who sold a gun to a crazy person." He set down his Frappuccino. "I mean, hell, didn't the guy have a record?"

Before she could answer, the telephone on her nightstand rang.

"Stay put. I'll grab it," Clay said, getting to his feet. He snatched up the receiver. "Hello? *Who*?" He covered the mouthpiece and looked at her with one eyebrow raised. "You want to talk to a Debi Donahue?"

Debi was another coworker. It had been Debi's voice Olivia had heard in the corridor just as she'd blacked out.

"Of course, I'll talk to her," Olivia said, reaching out with her good hand. "You know who Debi is, silly. She was the first one on the scene. It was in all the news stories, honey. . . ."

Clay shrugged apologetically. "Hi, yeah," he said into the phone. "You can put her through." He handed Olivia the receiver.

Olivia sat up a little. "Hello, Debi?" she said into the phone.

There was silence. She wondered if the operator had lost the connection.

"Deb?"

"Is this Olivia Barker Bischoff?" asked the woman on the other end of the line. It wasn't Debi's voice.

"Yes. Who is this?"

"You evil bitch," the woman whispered.

"What?" It suddenly occurred to Olivia that anyone could have gotten Debi's name out of the newspaper. "Who is this?"

"Layne was fine until you started in on him with all your analyzing and headshrinking. You caused it. You're going to pay for what you did to my son. . . ."

"What's going on?" Clay asked. "Honey, are you okay? Who is it?"

Olivia listened to the line go dead.

Clay grabbed the phone from her. "Hello? Who's there? Goddamn it, who is this?"

Olivia turned her head away from him and started to cry.

She didn't think the pain in her shoulder would ever go away.

CHAPTER FOUR

"Honey, are you going out?"

Collin hesitated by the door leading out to the garage. He glanced back at his grandmother at the breakfast table in their gourmet kitchen. At sixty-seven, she still had a buxom figure and a pale, creamy complexion—though, close-up, her face looked slightly careworn. Her wavy blond hair was cut short. She always smelled like lavender, which was also her favorite color. At the moment, she wore a lavender blouse and khakis. She was on the phone with a friend, and held her hand over the mouthpiece. Her engagement ring—given to her by Collin's grandfather twenty-three years ago—had a big diamond that sparkled in the light.

Dee wasn't his actual grandmother. Collin's real grandmother had died after a long bout with cancer back when his mom was just a kid. His grandfather married Dee eight years later. Collin's mom never really warmed up to Dee. She used to say Dee looked like a floozy ex-stripper. Collin thought that was pretty harsh, especially since his mom wasn't exactly a saint or anything. Dee had always been sweet to him. Besides, she was the only grandmother he had.

She'd been fretting and fussing over him for the last ten days. Now she was looking at him with concern. "Where are you headed?" she asked.

Collin shrugged. "I thought I'd ride my bike to town and grab a late breakfast."

Dee frowned, and then put the phone to her ear. "Hold on just another second, Mary Lou. Sorry." She covered the mouthpiece again. "I'm sorry, sweetie. If your grandfather was here to give the okay, that's one thing. But I really don't think you should go out alone just yet."

He cracked a tiny smile. "Well, it's not like I'll be alone, Dee. You can be sure they'll give me a police escort."

Ever since the murders, an unmarked police car had been parked on Skog-Strand Lane by the front gate of his grandparents' beachfront home. Four Seattle police detectives worked in shifts, watching the house—and watching him.

"Why go out for breakfast when I can make you perfectly delicious pancakes?" Dee asked. "Plus the fridge is crammed. Those cold cuts from the deli are in there." Dee was always telling him what was in the refrigerator. "And we have those toaster waffles you like. . . ."

He shrugged. "Thanks anyway, Dee. I just want to go out."

That much was true. But he planned to go to Hot Shots Java, where the pretty blond barista, Melissa, worked. She was a year or two older than him. On his last visit to his grandparents, when he'd stopped by the coffee shop, Melissa had complimented him on his shirt and given him a free iced latte. She'd had the sweetest smile. He'd gotten kind of tongue-tied around her. Collin hoped she still worked there. But he didn't want to tell his grandmother that. She might think something was wrong with him for having some girl on his mind so soon after his mother's death. The truth was, he'd been thinking about Melissa for the past few days.

"I really need the exercise," he explained. "I'm feeling kind of cooped up here lately."

With a sigh, she talked into the phone again. "Sorry, Mary Lou, can I call you back in a couple of minutes?"

Slump-shouldered, Collin turned and wandered toward the breakfast table while his grandmother made another call. His grandparents' kitchen was like something in one of those Home & Garden TV shows: hardwood floors, stainless-steel appliances, and all the new gadgets. Behind Dee was a sliding glass door to a patio—with stone stairs that led down to the beach. The late morning sun reflected across the rippled water of Liberty Bay. At least a dozen boats were out there. Collin could see he was missing a gorgeous day. He'd dressed for it, too—in cargo shorts, a blue polo shirt, and his black Converse All Stars.

"Hi, hon," his grandmother said into the phone. "Sorry to interrupt your game. You weren't late teeing off, were you? Good. Say, listen, Collin wants to ride his bike into town, and I have to admit, I'm a little nervous in the service about it. . . ."

His mouth twisted over to one side, Collin watched her on the phone. *Nervous in the service* was one of his grandparents' expressions that he never quite understood. After staying with them for a while, he heard himself using the same bizarre phrases and words they used—like *cockamamie, all catawampus,* and *for crying out loud.*

"Uh-huh. Well, if you're copacetic with it, so am I," Dee was saying. "I just wanted to check with you first. Uh-huh. Okay, here he is." She held the cordless phone out to Collin. "Your grandfather wants to bend your ear for a sec."

Bend your ear, that was another one. And what did *copacetic* mean? Sounded like a laxative. Collin took the phone from her. "Hi, Grandpa," he said.

"Hi, kiddo," his grandfather replied on the other end. "It's fine if you want to go out. My guess is you'll have the cops on your tail wherever you go anyway. . . ."

"That's what I was trying to tell Dee." He threw his grandmother an exasperated look.

"Well, they're a pain in the neck, but those detectives are there for a good reason," his grandfather reminded him. "Anyway, bring your cell phone with you. Be careful. And call us if you think you'll be gone for more than two hours. Okay, kiddo?"

"Okay," he answered. "Thanks, Grandpa."

Minutes later, Collin was in the three-car garage, donning his bike helmet. His grandmother had shoved a twenty-dollar bill in his hand, "just in case." He'd kissed her good-bye, twice assured her that he'd be careful. He hit the automatic garage door opener, and with a hum, the big door started to ascend. Collin wheeled his bike out to the driveway, and stopped to gaze at his grandparents' beautiful, sprawling cobblestone home. Through the arched window above the big double doors in front, he could see the elaborate, Chihuly-inspired glass chandelier. He'd stayed with his grandparents dozens of times, but never really noticed how impressive the place was. Now that he'd be living here permanently, he was in awe of their home.

Behind him, there was a click, and the garage door began its descent. His grandparents were already clearing a spot for a third car—for him. They just hadn't bought it yet.

He couldn't help thinking that he'd gotten just what he'd wanted. He was living with his grandparents now, and they were spoiling him—as they always had. Since he'd moved in, they'd bought him a new desktop computer for his bedroom, and a new iPhone. He felt horrible even thinking it, but this was a far cry from living in a dumpy rental where his award got stolen and he'd have been lucky to find milk in the refrigerator.

Collin hopped on his bike and peddled down the driveway, which wound through the tall trees and manicured shrubs. The gate opened automatically, and he spotted the silver Dodge Charger parked near the end of the driveway. Someone was in the car, behind the wheel. It looked like Al, the stocky one.

Collin slowed down and glanced over his shoulder as the gate shut behind him. There was a code box and a speaker on this side of the entry. From the inside intercom by the kitchen door, Collin could listen in on the cops' conversations. He'd hear when they were talking in the car with the windows rolled down—or if one of the guys stepped out of the Charger to make a personal phone call. His grandmother caught him listening once, and chided him: "Eavesdroppers never hear anything nice about themselves!" That was true. Still, some of the things he overheard were pretty interesting.

The one cop he liked was a good-looking guy with a mop of wavy brown hair. He usually used his own car, a black Honda Civic. He was about thirty years old, and the youngest among them. His name was Ian, and from the cell phone calls he made some nights, it sounded like he had a girlfriend in Seattle, Janice, who was giving him grief for accepting this surveillance assignment. Collin had heard Ian talking to her about him: *"Considering his mother and what he's been through, you'd think he'd be really screwed up, but he seems like a nice, normal kid. I feel really bad for him. . . ."* After that, Collin thought about bringing a Coke out to Ian while he was on duty. But then he'd be expected to do the same thing for the rest of them. And the rest of them were jerks.

Al, sort of the ringleader of the three, had a nasal, whiny voice. To his cohorts, he always referred to Collin as "the little faggot movie star." Collin's grandfather was "the old fart," and Dee was "Old Biddy Big Tits." Al was one to talk—with his man-boobs jiggling in those tight Izod knockoff shirts he always wore. Collin heard Al tell one of his buddies: *"If you ask me, I think we've got the murderer right here. I say the kid offed that worthless mother of his and the guy she shacked up with."* It was hard for Collin to ignore that comment.

Al—along with the other two cops—loathed Ian. When not bad-mouthing Ian behind his back, all they did was nap in the car. From the intercom, Collin could hear them snoring.

His grandfather didn't like any of them, and unjustifiably lumped Ian in with the others. "Seattle's Finest," he'd grumble from time to time. "They must have scraped the bottom of the barrel to come up with the guys for this detail." At the same time, he always grudgingly acknowledged that the cops were there to protect them.

The police still hadn't figured out who had murdered Collin's mother and Chance. They believed the double homicide was drug-related. All the open closets indicated the killers were looking for drugs. Chance was a dealer. It was a logical conclusion. Another, less popular theory was that it had been a Manson murder type of situation. Collin had a feeling he was a suspect in the killings—and the detectives outside were watching him as much as they were protecting him. He'd already told the police everything he'd heard in his "dream." The "no witnesses" remark he'd overheard had the police worried about his safety.

Two days after the murders, still in shock, Collin had spent several hours listening to recordings of suspects the police had rounded up. The anonymous voices recited what Collin had heard that night:

"The fucker's still alive. He's still breathing. Finish him off. . . ."

"Where's the kid? She's got a kid. No witnesses. . . ."

Collin didn't recognize any of the voices. But hearing those words again and again only made him relive the nightmare, and he'd imagine what had been going on while he lay there in his sleeping bag one flight up. According to *The Seattle Times*, his mother had been stabbed eleven times, including two deep knife wounds in her neck. Chance had been stabbed seventeen times, mostly in the stomach and chest. The one bullet in his face had finally killed him.

It dawned on Collin that while all this was happening, he hadn't done anything. At no time had he ever sat up in his sleeping bag and realized, "The killings are about to start."

He frowned at Al, on his iPhone, sitting alone in the Dodge with the window down. He seemed to glance back at him from behind his sunglasses. His forehead was all shiny with sweat, and he looked annoyed.

Collin pedaled past him on his bike. Then he heard the Dodge's engine start up. Skog-Strand Lane was a dead end weaving through the woods, with only three other houses—all secluded beachfront mansions like his grandparents' place. Collin could see the bay through the trees. The warm sun and fresh air felt good against his face. He wished he was alone. He didn't like hearing the car hovering behind him. He pedaled faster and turned onto one of the main drags, Viking Way.

So far, the four detectives hadn't protected him from anyone dangerous—just a few reporters. The double murder of Collin Cox's mother and her lover had been the lead story on *Entertainment Tonight* for three nights in a row. It had made the front pages of national newspapers. The tabloids had a field day going on about the *Night Whisperer* curse and how the murders had happened on Friday the thirteenth. Collin saw his mom exposed as a screwed-up, drug-addicted, negligent stage mother. Maybe her problems had been an open secret in the movie industry, but now everyone knew. Collin was stupid enough to read the articles online—along with the reader comments. He couldn't believe how many awful people were out there in cyberspace, posting their opinions and making judgments about someone they'd never met. The consensus among them was that his mother had deserved exactly what she'd gotten.

He'd been photographed and filmed ad nauseam, mostly outside the police station in South Seattle. It had been almost as crazy as some of the movie premieres he'd attended. The photographers had also swarmed in on him again four days ago outside Lake View Cemetery on Capitol Hill for his mother's burial. The funeral had been delayed, because her autopsy had taken nearly a week to complete. When Collin saw the recent photos of himself online, the captions often referred to him as *handsome former child star Collin Cox.* Praise, at last. His mother had said he'd outgrow his "awkward phase" by age sixteen. Or maybe people just felt sorry for him. It didn't matter, and didn't make up for the horrible things they said about his mom.

Collin received a barrage of emails from talent agents—including two who had previously abandoned him. But the movie deals they proposed were cheapie exploitation stuff. The TV offers were all reality shows. Someone even talked about possibly getting him on *Dancing With the Stars,* and asked how long a mourning period he'd need before he could step into a ballroom-dancing getup and compete on the show.

Last week, his Facebook fan page, which he hadn't updated in over a year, jumped from around 8,400 to 177,489 fans—at last count.

He might have enjoyed all the press and the attention a few years ago, but not now.

His grandfather had used his still-formidable clout to keep Collin's current whereabouts out of the newspapers. For twenty-five years, nearly a third of the people in town had been employed at his grandfather's mill, Stampler Wire and Cable. He'd used his influence with the local press, who downplayed the fact that the late Piper Cox was onetime industrial tycoon Andrew Stampler's daughter.

A few determined reporters had tracked Collin to his grandparents' house in Poulsbo. But Ian and the other detectives kept them off the property.

That didn't mean he had to like Ian's coworkers. He figured Al was going to be on his ass all the way to town. And, as was typical of him, Al was a jerk about it, too. Every once in a while, the car would fade back and give Ian some space—but never for long. He'd hear Al gun it and come up right behind him. Gravel crunched under the Dodge's tires as it loomed closer. Collin really wanted to flip him the bird.

Instead, he turned onto one of the foot trails threading through Nelson Park, an eleven-acre piece of land overlooking the bay. As he got closer to the park's picnic grounds, he smelled food barbecuing. He heard kids laughing and screaming. There wasn't much to the park, except the water views, an old barn, and a quaint waterfront museum/souvenir shop. Yet scores of tourists milled around, checking the place out. Collin steered his bike onto the grass to avoid all the people on the trail, and then he headed into town.

Front Street, the hub of the Scandinavian village, was Tourist Central today. He pedaled past Muriel Williams Park—with its gazebo, dockside restaurants, and the tall, solemn-looking Viking statue on a pedestal. It was a mob scene. He wove around all the tourists until he finally reached Hot Shots Java.

During his last visit, when Melissa had flirted with him, he'd felt like an adult in the funky, hip café— among the other arty coffeehouse types on their notebook computers, reading their books or writing in journals. He remembered the soft jazz music and the rich coffee smell.

After locking up his bike and helmet on the post outside, Collin checked out his reflection in the window, and then stepped into the café. His former *sanctum sanctorum* was now crowded and noisy—with a couple of babies crying, a gaggle of teenage girls talking and laughing loudly, and some guy practically screaming into his cell phone.

His heart sank even lower when he didn't see Melissa behind the counter. He stepped to the back of the long line, and hoped she might be in the kitchen or something. The longer he waited in the line, the more depressed he got.

The last time he was here, he'd dreaded catching the ferry home the next day. On several occasions, his mom had forgotten to pick him up when he'd returned to Seattle Sunday night—or she'd kept him waiting outside the ferry terminal for almost an hour. He remembered returning from the last visit, certain she wouldn't be there. But she'd been waiting by the car, smiling and waving at him. That was the funny thing about his mom. Just when he thought she was a total screwup who didn't care, she would surprise him.

The line moved forward a bit, but Collin hesitated. His throat started to close up and he felt tears stinging his eyes. A gasp came out, and he tried to pretend he was coughing. He'd had a few crying jags since his mother's death, but always in private. Even at the funeral, he'd managed to remain dry-eyed. Now he couldn't stop the tears. He had to get out of there.

His head down, he threaded around the crowded café tables and hurried to the alcove for the bathroom. But they had only one restroom, and it was locked. Wiping his tears, Collin ducked out the screen door beside it. The exit could have been for employees only. But at this point, he didn't care. He just had to get away from all those people.

The screen door slammed shut behind him. He stepped down and found himself in a narrow, dead-end alley. It was like an old driveway—with patches of grass and weeds sprouting up through the crushed gravel. A big air conditioner unit hummed along the brick wall of another store at one end of the alley. On the other end, a tall chain-link fence was closed—with a chain lock wrapped around the post. Collin ducked behind several empty milk crates and a garbage bin. It smelled like rotten fruit and sour milk. But at least he was alone.

He buried his face in his hands and sobbed. Nothing about it was a *good cry*. He felt miserable and achy. His throat hurt and his nose dripped with snot. He kept thinking even though she'd disappointed him so often, she was still his mother. She'd been home to him. He couldn't believe he'd never see her again. And he couldn't stop crying.

But then he heard the screen door yawn and slam shut. Collin swiveled around and gaped at the tall, thin, forty-something dark-haired man. The guy held out a fistful of napkins for him. He must have grabbed them off the stack at the café's cream-and-sugar station. "Here, Collin," the man said.

Collin didn't budge from where he stood. He quickly wiped his eyes with his hands. He didn't recognize the man. He glanced over at the locked chain-link fence at the one end of the alley. The only way out of there was to go back inside through the coffeehouse. And the stranger was blocking the door.

"I'm sorry," Collin said in a voice raspy from crying. "Do I know you?"

"Not yet," the man said. "I recognized you when you came into the café. I figured maybe you could use a friend right now—or at least a tissue." He let out a little laugh. "Don't worry. I'm not a stalker or anything like that." He waved the napkins at him. "Here . . ."

From his experience with certain fans, Collin remembered the ones who said, "Don't worry, I'm not a stalker," right up front were usually the most trouble. He couldn't put his finger on it, but something about the guy was a little off. With his blue eyes, dark hair, and square jaw, he should have been handsome, but he wasn't. The features just didn't mesh together right. He had a slightly nerdish quality that was more creepy than endearing.

Collin dug into the pockets of his cargo shorts, hoping to find his own Kleenex. But he didn't have any. He gave the man a wary glance and took the napkins from him. "Thank you," he muttered. He blew his nose. "I don't want to be rude, but I kind of want to be alone."

"I haven't seen you cry like that since your grand-mother died in *The Night Whisperer*," he said. "You should have gotten an Academy Award for that—or at least, a nomination."

Collin wiped his nose again. "Thanks, nice of you to say. I'm sorry, but I don't feel very social right now. . . ."

But the man still didn't get the hint. "I've seen all your movies, your TV appearances, too," he said. "A lot of them are on YouTube. I didn't care for the episode of *Brothers & Sisters*, but it wasn't your fault. I'm sure it's something your manager or agent made you do."

"Sorry you feel that way," Collin said, frowning. He started to brush past him on his way to the screen door. "Excuse me. . . ."

The stranger touched his arm, and Collin recoiled. The man backed off a step. "Hey, I'm your friend, Collin," he said with a hand over his heart. "I just hate to see you looking so sad. I've read all about your mother. It shows how compassionate you are that you'd still cry for her. But really, she isn't worth your tears. . . ."

Shaking his head, Collin glared at him.

"Rick, I think he's talked to you all he wants to."

The stranger spun around.

Collin glanced over at the one detective he liked. Ian stood on the stoop, holding the screen door open. He wore a blue oxford shirt with the sleeves rolled up, khaki shorts, and sandals. From behind his sunglasses he seemed to be staring at the other man.

"Who are you?" the stranger asked, indignant. "How do you know my name?"

"I recognized you when you came into the café," Ian said in an ironic tone. "But don't worry, Rick. I'm not a stalker or anything like that." He took off his sunglasses and smiled at Collin. "Can I offer you a lift home?"

Wiping his eyes, Collin nodded. He brushed past the man and followed Ian back inside the café, letting the screen door slam shut behind him. He tossed the used napkins in a trash can by the sugar-and-cream station.

"I hear you managed to ditch Al," Ian said over his shoulder as he started toward the front of the coffeehouse. "Congratulations, I wish I could ditch him myself. I wasn't supposed to go on duty for another half hour, but Al called and put me on search-and-rescue duty. Lucky for me, I saw you locking up your bike outside."

"Lucky for me, too," Collin said. "Who was that guy back there?"

Ian stopped near the end of the customer line. "Were you going to order something?"

With a sigh, Collin glanced toward the counter one more time for Melissa. But she wasn't there. He shook his head. "I kind of lost my appetite."

Ian moved to the door and held it open for Collin, but a young couple hurriedly walked in before him—without a glance at Ian. "You're welcome a lot, dip-shits," Ian growled at them. They ignored him.

Collin actually found himself chuckling. "Thanks," he said, heading outside.

"I'm sorry, but sometimes I hate people," Ian grumbled, stepping out after him. "After having Al scream at me on the phone to find you—like it was my fault you were MIA—I'm not in the best of moods right now. Then again, look who I'm complaining to. I should count my blessings. Listen, I snagged a parking spot about two blocks away. I'll give you a lift home. We can put your bike in my trunk. Sound good?"

Collin nodded. "Yeah, thanks." Crouched down beside his Schwinn, he worked the combination lock and unfastened the chain. Then he grabbed his helmet.

Ian put his sunglasses back on, and they started down the crowded sidewalk together. "So who's that Rick guy anyway?" Collin asked. He glanced over his shoulder to see if the man had followed them. There was no sign of him. "Is it a big secret? Is he dangerous?"

"No, he's just kind of a pest," Ian finally answered. "His name's Rick Jessup, and when he said he wasn't a stalker, I don't know who he was trying to kid—you or himself. Twice, we've chased him off the beach in back of your grandparents' house. We've caught him hanging around Skog-Strand Lane several times, too. I've personally sent him on his way a few of those times. I should be insulted he didn't recognize me."

"Does he live around here?"

"He lives in Seattle—with his wife and two kids, poor things. Three nights ago, officers caught him creeping around your rental house—the crime scene. He said he was looking for his cat. We checked with Rick's neighbor, and the Jessups don't own a cat."

"So is he—like a suspect?" Collin asked.

"The same neighbor was up with a toothache the night of the murders. He was pretty sure all the Jessups were home. Rick's Chevy Camaro was in the driveway all night. Speaking of cars, here's mine." He nodded at the black Honda Civic parked in front of the bookstore.

Ian helped him load the bike in the Civic's trunk. He got behind the wheel while Collin slid onto the passenger seat and lowered his window. "Thanks for finding me when you did," Collin said as they pulled into the congested traffic on Front Street. "I'm glad it was you who found me, and not that big turd, Al."

Ian let out a laugh, but then stifled it. "Listen, can you do me a favor?" he asked, watching the road ahead. "Forget what I said about wanting to ditch him. That was really unprofessional of me. Like I mentioned earlier, I'm just in a lousy mood today."

"Is it because of your girlfriend?" Collin asked. "What's her name? Janice?"

Ian gaped at him for a second. "How do you know about Janice?"

Collin figured since Ian had been pretty straightforward with him, he ought to reciprocate. So he explained about the intercom by the gate to his grandparents' driveway. "I'm sorry," Collin said. "I didn't mean to spy on you guys. I was just kind of bored—and it was something to do. I hope you're not too pissed off at me or anything."

With his hands on the steering wheel, Ian sighed. "I'm not pissed off, just kind of embarrassed. Anyway, for the record, Janice and I had a talk last night, and she thinks we should 'take a break.' So—yes, you're right. That accounts for much of my lousy mood today."

"I'm sorry," Collin mumbled.

"It's not your problem," Ian said. "Have you overheard anything else that was private or humiliating for me?"

"Well, when you were alone in the car three nights ago, you must have been listening to your iPod, because I heard you singing along with 'We Built This City on Rock and Roll.' "

"Jesus, that really is humiliating."

"You were kind of off-key, too."

"When you work surveillance nights, you resort to a lot of tricks to keep yourself awake."

"The other guys, I hear them snoring all the time."

Ian took his eyes off the road for a moment to throw him a crooked smile. "Well, I guess you've got the goods on all of us."

"You're the only one who's nice. The rest of them are jerks. They . . ." Collin hesitated. "They say creepy stuff about you behind your back."

"I already know that," Ian said, turning onto Viking Way. "I was downsized out of the public relations department and given a crash course in detective work—three months' training. It was either that or I'd get laid off. Anyway, this is my first assignment. These good old boys don't believe someone could do what they do with just three months of training. The truth is they aren't exactly the cream of the crop. All of them have poor fitness records."

"Is that why they got sent here to Poulsbo?" Collin asked. "I mean, no offense, but really, are you guys here to do anything besides chase away Rick Jessup and the occasional paparazzi?"

"I probably shouldn't answer that," Ian said, frowning. "I've already shot off my mouth too much. I don't know why. Maybe it's because you're the first person I've really talked to over here—besides Al and company. Plus ever since *The Night Whisperer*, you've always reminded me of my kid brother. Anyway, I'll tell you this much, Collin. . . ." He glanced at him. "We think the danger is real. Our presence here is serving a purpose. Until they catch your mother's killers, you shouldn't go off on your own."

Collin squirmed in the passenger seat, and looked out the window. "I overheard Al telling one of the other guys he thinks I killed my mother—and her boy-friend."

"Al's an idiot."

Collin kept staring out the window. The wind whipped through his black hair. "Maybe I did kill them—only I don't remember, because of the Ambien I took. I've heard all sorts of stories about people doing strange things while they're taking these sleep drugs." He turned to look at Ian. "I'm the only one who survived. The cops must think that's weird. Tell me the truth, you guys are watching me to make sure I don't try to run away or kill somebody else."

Ian shook his head. "If that was the case, we'd be pretty reckless with your grandparents' lives, letting them spend night after night with a murder suspect. You shouldn't pay attention to anything Al says. He's a board-certified moron."

Collin turned toward the window again. Ian hadn't really answered his question. Collin had read online that in the rental house, all the bloody footprints on the rugs and floors had been indistinguishable partials. Investigators weren't sure how many killers there were. His vague account of an intruder talking to a cohort—and then a shot from downstairs—seemed to indicate at least three suspects were involved. But did the police believe him?

The cops probably had their theories about how he'd murdered his mom and Chance, how he'd gotten the gun, and where he'd hidden it—along with the knife. Collin imagined they had some explanation for how he alone could have tied up the two of them.

Collin had heard only one stranger's voice that night. He'd also heard his mother and Chance.

She used to call Chance "baby" sometimes.

Collin still wondered if he'd killed them in his sleep.

Had his mother been begging him to spare her boyfriend? He remembered her screaming: *"Oh, sweet Jesus, my baby! Don't hurt him! Collin, get out of here! Oh, no . . ."*

He continued to stare out the window, and for the rest of the car ride, he didn't utter a word.

Chapter Five

The skinny-dippers weren't out there tonight.

It was sheer luck he'd spotted them from his bedroom window four nights ago. Collin had heard the girl's high-pitched laughter—an alert that someone had snuck onto his grandparents' private beach. Sometimes, watching whoever showed up on that strip of shore was more entertaining than TV or the Internet. After all, it was happening in his own backyard. That was why the binoculars from his grandfather's study had found a new home on his bedroom windowsill. They weren't exactly high-powered state-of-the-art, but they were better than nothing. Since he'd been living in a perpetual state of boredom and horniness lately, he was always hoping for some skinny-dipping trespassers.

On Monday night, he got his wish. As soon as he heard that girl giggling, Collin switched off his bedroom light and reached for the binoculars. From what he could see, she was brunette, pretty, and college age, with a rocking body beneath her T-shirt and shorts. The guy looked like a dopey jock, and he was already taking off his clothes when Collin got the binoculars out. She squealed as he plunged naked into the water. He called to her and cajoled her into joining him.

"Thank you, God," Collin whispered, watching her shuck the T-shirt over her head. Then the bra came off—and the shorts, and finally the panties.

He felt like such a pervert, spying on them, but the vision of that brunette frolicking naked in the moonlight took his breath away. The two of them were in shallow water some of the time, and Collin couldn't believe the guy didn't have a woody. Meanwhile, he was ready to pass out. They were splashing each other when a boat pulled up close to the sandbar. A light glowed in the small craft's cabin. The girl seemed to notice. The couple scurried to the shore and put on their clothes. Collin couldn't tell if it was a police boat or what. But the damn thing sure put a crimp in his night.

For the last three evenings, he'd kept checking for the skinny-dippers again. They hadn't returned. But the boat had.

It was out there again tonight.

Collin sat at his desk, playing *Castle Attack* on his computer. The rest of the house was quiet. His grandparents were asleep—way down at the other end of the hall, in their own little wing practically.

During his previous visits, he'd thought of this as *his* bedroom. Framed prints of sailboats adorned the walls. The curtains and bedspreads were a blue and white print with anchors, life preservers, flags, and crossed paddles. The desk lamp had a base that was a replica of a ship's helm. "It's a wonder our guests don't get seasick sleeping in there," his grandfather joked.

Now that Collin had actually moved in, the quarters did indeed feel like a guest room—or a hotel room.

Dee even stocked the attached bathroom with travel-size soap, shampoo, toothpaste, and all the rest. No one was supposed to stay there permanently.

Collin's stuff from the rental house clashed with Dee's maritime motif. His collection of bobblehead baseball figures looked out of place, lined up along the windowsill. He still hadn't hung up the illuminated Coca-Cola clock he'd had since he was eleven. It was plugged in and set against the wall with stacks of his books, games, and DVDs. His grandfather had offered to help hang his framed poster of *The Night Whisperer*—along with several plaques, film awards, and citations. There were also pictures of him with some big-name celebrities—photo ops from different events he'd attended. His grandfather couldn't understand why he didn't want to decorate the bedroom with his awards and memorabilia. But Collin hadn't had them on display since he and his mother had left Los Angeles. He didn't see any point in reminding himself of who he used to be.

Staring out the window, he wondered if the boat out there on the bay belonged to some persistent paparazzo or reporter. Most of them had already lost interest—even though his mother's murder remained unsolved. The only people still paying attention to him were the police. Was it a police boat?

Collin turned off the computer monitor in the middle of *Castle Attack* and switched off the helm lamp on his desk. He grabbed the binoculars, and focused in on the small craft. He guessed it was about as close to the beach as it could get. A light was on in the front—along with one dim cabin light. If it was a police boat, it wasn't marked like one.

He wondered if the person on the boat had come back with hopes of seeing the skinny-dippers, too. He could see someone standing on the deck. The lone shadowy figure looked like a man, and he seemed to be holding something in front of his face. Collin couldn't tell what it was—maybe a camera. Or maybe the guy had a pair of binoculars of his own. He didn't seem to be scoping out the beach. In fact, he seemed to be looking directly into Collin's window.

"What the hell?" he murmured. He stood in the dark for a few minutes—until he saw the man retreat inside the boat's cabin. Then the vessel's lights went off. Collin kept a lookout, but he didn't see the man again. After a few minutes, a cloud must have moved in front of the moon, because everything got darker. He could hardly see the boat anymore.

Blindly groping around on the floor, Collin found his sandals and slipped them on. He couldn't help wondering if someone was watching and waiting for him to go to bed. Were they making sure everyone in the house had gone to sleep before coming over to kill them?

Setting the binoculars on his desk, Collin told himself he was being paranoid. He headed down the back stairs to the kitchen, where he pulled a Coke from the refrigerator. Slipping out the front door, he started up the driveway. The night air felt balmy. On both sides of him, outdoor lights illuminated the bushes and the big trees. It was quiet, and the sound of gravel crunching under his sandals seemed oddly exaggerated. Even with his cop friend on duty at the end of the long driveway, Collin still felt a bit nervous taking this lonely walk at night.

Whenever Ian worked the late shift, Collin brought food out to him—usually some snack and a Coke. Often he'd grab a Coke for himself, too, and they'd lean against the car, munching chips and "shooting the breeze" (another one of his grandparents' sayings). Usually, they talked about baseball or the movies, keeping the conversation quiet, so as not to wake his grandparents.

Old Andy had heard them talking one night last week, and told Collin, "I don't think it's such a good idea for you to pal around with that cop, kiddo. You ought to be making friends your own age. It's best you leave him alone to do his job."

His grandfather didn't seem to understand that Ian was his only friend right now. In fact, the young cop was the closest thing to a friend Collin had had in a long time. While making movies, Collin had gotten close to costars and crewmembers of all ages. They'd been like family to him. It always broke his heart when the filming ended, because those ties were severed and everyone moved on. It was never the same. Collin knew his cop friend would be moving on eventually. But right now Ian was like the big brother he never had. Collin didn't want to lose that. So when he promised his grandfather that he'd leave the young detective alone to do his work, it was a total lie.

He wondered why, after three weeks, the police were still parked outside his grandparents' house. Was his life really still in danger? Or was it because they suspected he'd killed his mother and her boyfriend? He kept coming back to that question. Ian scoffed at it. Did he really think he'd murdered two people in his sleep? How had he tied them up by himself? Where did he get the gun? Where were the shoes he'd used to create the bloody footprints? He couldn't have done it by himself—and certainly not while asleep. He was being ridiculous. The double homicide had all the earmarks of a drug-related hit, and until they found the killers, the police would be protecting their only witness.

Collin had decided to believe him. But it meant the police had every reason to think someone wanted him dead.

Maybe it wasn't so crazy to imagine some killer on that boat watching the house. Had the guy really been waiting for the last bedroom light to go off? With everyone asleep, it would be easier to break in undetected and then start the killing.

No witnesses, he'd heard the man say on that awful night.

Near the gate at the end of the driveway, Collin stopped dead. From where he stood, he could see the front of Ian's Honda Civic. He pictured himself going up to it, only to find Ian at the wheel with his eyes wide open and his throat slit.

Wouldn't the cop guarding the house be the first to go?

He pressed the button for the gate, and with a hum, it slowly swung open. Collin took a few more steps to the end of the driveway, all the while staring at the car. There was no one in the front seat, and the passenger window appeared to be cracked. Or was it a reflection on the dark glass? He couldn't tell.

Somewhere behind him, a twig snapped.

"Collin?"

He swiveled around and accidentally dropped the can of Coke.

Ian gaped back at him. He stood a few yards in front of the car—near the side of the road. He wore a gray T-shirt and jeans, and held a gun. Collin hadn't seen him with a gun in his hand before.

"God, you scared the crap out of me!" Collin whispered. "What's going on?"

Ian tucked the gun in the back waist of his jeans. "I

thought I heard something," he said. "I was checking it out. I'm a little jumpy tonight. They put us on alert."

"What do you mean? What kind of alert?"

He picked up the can of Coke from the pavement. "Was this for me?"

Collin nodded.

Ian tapped the top of the Coke can several times. "Every once in a while, they try to scare us with something—some tidbit—so we don't get too comfortable in the job. Today happens to be one of those times." He held the Coke away from him as he opened it. A bit of spray came out. Then he raised the can at Collin. "Thanks," he said, taking a swig.

"So what happened?" Collin asked.

Ian warily glanced toward the house. "We need to talk." He nodded at the car. "Hop in—and don't slam the door. You might wake up your grandparents."

Collin climbed into the passenger side of the Civic and carefully closed the door. He noticed the window wasn't cracked at all. It was just the shadows of tree branches. Ian ducked behind the wheel and stashed the gun under his seat. With the key, he turned on the car's electric system for a moment to raise the windows. Then he turned it off again.

"This alert you're on," Collin said. "Did they put an extra guy on a boat to watch the house from the beach side?"

Frowning, Ian shook his head. "No. Why?"

"There was a guy out on this small boat, pretty close to the shore. It looked like he was scoping the place out."

"When did you see this?"

"About ten minutes ago. But the boat sailed away shortly after I switched off the light in my bedroom. I have a weird feeling this guy is watching my room in particular. The boat was there last night, too."

"Was it there at the same time last night?"

Collin nodded. "Yeah, I didn't give it much thought. But then I saw it again tonight. . . ."

Sitting back, Ian drummed his fingers along the side of the steering wheel. "I don't think it's connected to this other matter. Maybe it's one of those damn paparazzi. Still, I'll make sure someone follows it up."

"What's this 'other matter'?" Collin asked. "Is it the reason you're on alert?"

Ian said nothing and sipped his Coke.

"C'mon, I won't blab that you told me. We're friends."

"That's just the thing, Collin," he sighed. "We aren't friends. I'm here to protect you and your grandparents. You shouldn't be coming out here and talking to me until one or two in the morning. You don't do that with any of the other detectives—"

"That's because they're jerks."

"Well, you lied to me," Ian frowned. "You said your grandfather was fine with these midnight bull sessions. Last night, he pulled your little trick with the intercom and heard us talking. This morning, your grandfather got on the phone with my boss in Seattle. Then my boss got on the horn with me, and he gave me an earful—"

"Ian, I'm sorry. . . ."

"Making matters worse," he continued, gazing past the windshield, "the other detectives on this watch know about it now, and I'm getting all sorts of flak for fraternizing with a surveillance subject. I won't even go into all the crap they're insinuating. Anyway, you're a great kid. But I think from now on, you ought to leave me alone to do my job."

Collin stared at him. "So—I'm a 'surveillance subject.' You just admitted it. You guys aren't here to protect me. You're here to *watch* me—to make sure I don't kill anybody else."

"Oh, for God's sake," Ian growled. He turned toward him. "You are not a suspect, Collin. How many times do I have to tell you? We're about ninety-nine percent sure the killings were drug-related. Okay?"

Collin didn't say anything.

"You wanted to know about the alert?" Ian asked. "Fine, I'll tell you. I'm already up to my neck in trouble anyway, what the hell. The main suspect in the murders is this scumbag drug dealer named Leon Badger. He has a regular posse working with him. We think they killed Chance over some stupid drug-turf issue. That's what we're getting from our sources. We've been trying to locate Badger and his gang for the last three weeks, but they've been one step ahead of us all the way. Obviously they know the heat's on, and they've been in hiding. Only this morning, a couple of Badger's guys were spotted in the Seattle ferry terminal—minutes before the Bainbridge Island ferry loaded up. Unfortunately, we lost the guys at the terminal. We're not sure if they boarded or not. So that was the alert, Collin."

Wide-eyed, Collin stared at him. "Do you—do you think one of them could have been the guy I saw on the boat?"

Ian seemed to mull it over for a moment. "It's doubtful. The last ferry left Bainbridge a few minutes ago. If they were here last night at this time, and again tonight, they wouldn't be traveling by ferry. No, I'm not sure who you saw, but I'll try to find out. Maybe it's our old friend Rick—though I haven't seen him in a while." He sat back in the driver's seat again and heaved a long sigh. "Anyway, as usual, I've told you way too much. You probably won't sleep a wink tonight, because of me and my big mouth. It's probably for the best we pull the plug on our midnight bull sessions. Okay? In fact, you should head back inside now—before your grandfather wakes up and realizes . . ."

Ian didn't finish. His eyes shifted to the rearview mirror.

A light swept across the car, illuminating the interior for a moment.

Collin turned and squinted out the rear window.

A car had turned into Skog-Strand Lane. Collin couldn't see the make or model, just the headlights piercing through the darkness. "Is that one of your guys?" he asked.

Ian shook his head. "They would have let me know backup was coming."

Collin watched the vehicle slow down. He still couldn't see what kind of car it was. There weren't any streetlights on the tree-lined private road.

Eyeing the rearview mirror, Ian slowly reached under the driver's seat. "Listen, do me a favor. Crawl back to the seat behind you, where my jacket is. Crouch down on the floor and cover yourself with the jacket."

"Are you serious?" Collin whispered. His heart was racing.

"Just do what I'm asking you!" he hissed.

Collin managed to squeeze through the space between the two front seats. Twisting himself around, he plopped onto the backseat. The car's headlights illuminated the inside of Ian's Civic for another fleeting moment.

The lights suddenly went out. But Collin could still hear its motor humming—and the faint sound of gravel crunching under tires. Then it stopped. Peeking out the rear window, Collin could see the vehicle was a black SUV. "Maybe he's lost—or he stopped to take a pee," he murmured.

"Get on the floor and cover yourself up."

Collin put the coat over the back of his head, but continued to peer out the rear window.

"The tires are riding low," Ian murmured—apparently to himself. "There are at least two or three people in that SUV."

Collin didn't say anything. But he remembered the newspapers reporting that two or three people might have carried out the murders of his mother and Chance. He studied the SUV, sitting there motionless. It was too far away to read the license plate. "Do you think they see us?" he asked.

"Well, I don't want them seeing you. So for the third and final time, Collin, stay down until I tell you the coast is clear."

Collin followed his instructions, crouching on the floor with the jacket over him. He hated the darkness—and the silence. He wanted to ask Ian what was happening, but decided it was best to shut up and just count to himself. He heard him shifting around in the driver's seat.

"Hello, Bainbridge Island Police," Collin heard him say. "This is Detective Haggerty with the SPD, guarding the Stampler house at 27 Skog-Strand Lane. I have a suspicious vehicle that has come up the street here and stopped, an SUV, black in color. I'm too far away to see the plates. Please stand by, officer may need assistance. . . ."

Collin listened to the front door click open. The car's interior light went on. He dared to peek out from under the jacket. Past the door opening, he could see

Ian only from the neck down. He had one hand behind his back, ready to grab his gun. He murmured something into the phone.

In the distance, the SUV's engine started up. Collin listened to the gravel under its tires again. He peeked over the edge of the backseat in time to see the SUV turning around—with its headlights off. Only as it neared the end of Skog-Strand Lane did the vehicle switch on its lights. Ian was saying something into the phone about a false alarm, and then he thanked them for their help.

Collin shrugged off the jacket. "So—that's it?" he asked. "You aren't going to put out an APB on the car or anything?"

"I don't think it's necessary." Ian opened the back door for him. "For all we know, it could have been a couple parking there so they could neck or something. I probably scared them a hell of a lot more than they scared us."

Collin wasn't so sure about that. He was still shaking as he climbed out of the backseat.

Ian patted him on the shoulder. "I think we've had enough excitement for one night," he said. "You better get inside before your granddad wakes up and sees you out here."

Collin hesitated. "Are you sure you'll be okay all alone?"

He nodded. "I'll be fine. Give the light above the front door a blink so I know you made it inside okay."

"All right," he said with uncertainty. Then he turned and started toward the gate. His hand shook as he punched in the code to open the gate. It swung open.

"Collin?" Ian whispered.

He turned around.

His cop friend smiled. "Just so you know, I've enjoyed our bull sessions."

Collin nodded. "Me, too," he said. Then he turned and hurried up the driveway.

Quietly opening the front door to his grandparents' house, he listened for a moment. It didn't sound like anyone was awake upstairs. He closed the door, locked it, and then flicked the outside light switch on and off.

He hoped Ian would be okay out there tonight.

Collin crept up the back stairs to his room and closed the door. But he didn't turn on the light. His eyes had already adjusted to the darkness. He looked out the window at the bay.

There was no sign of the boat. But like his cop friend outside, he was still on alert, still waiting for something bad to happen again.

CHAPTER SIX

Tukwila, Washington—Saturday, August 4, 8:20 p.m.

With his eyes closed, he tilted his head back and let the warm water from the showerhead spray him in the face. Standing behind him in the tub, Noreen soaped his tattooed back and buttocks. Noreen was crazy for his butt.

Leon Badger found an after-sex shower with her more endurable than the postcoital cuddling Noreen sometimes demanded. Like they were supposed to lay there and *spoon* for thirty minutes while his two burnout buddies in the next room watched *Futurama*. The small, two-bedroom ranch house belonged to a friend of Noreen's who was in Mexico. For the last few days, the four of them had been practically living on top of each other. They couldn't stay in one place too long. The cops had been looking for them for almost a month, ever since the Friday the thirteenth murders. Making matters worse, Leon had just made a lucrative but risky cocaine deal three days before in Vancouver, B.C.

Apparently, he'd treaded on the turf of a crazy Canadian drug lord named Big Sam, who had emigrated from Taiwan. Leon had heard some scary stories about Big Sam—beheadings, torture, and all sorts of medieval shit. So tomorrow, he and his cohorts, Cody and Les, were loading up the SUV and driving to Arizona. They'd lay low there for a while.

Noreen—whose soapy, magic hands were now rubbing his taut stomach—had no idea they were leaving her behind. His buddies weren't shedding any tears about it either. Cody, who was so good with a knife, swore he'd come close to carving up Noreen several times. Cody was always asking Leon what he saw in her.

Noreen was skinny and pale, with short jet-black, maroon-streaked hair and an interesting array of piercings and tattoos. She was crazy in the sack, and practically wore him out. Leon figured he'd miss the sex, but she was getting too clingy.

With her petite breasts pressed against his back, she began to fondle him. But then through the clear shower curtain he saw the bathroom door open. "What the fuck—"

Noreen let out a shriek. "Get out of here!"

"Hey, relax, man!"

Leon yanked open the curtain just enough to glare at Les. "What the hell do you think you're doing?"

His bald, goateed friend waved some of the shower steam away. "Hey, don't bite my head off, man. I couldn't find your wallet. We got to pay the pizza guy when he shows up. . . ."

"In the pocket of my jeans," Leon barked, pulling the shower curtain shut. The hooks squeaked against the curtain rod. "Look over by the bed, on the floor somewhere. If I find more than forty bucks missing, I'll nail your ass to the wall. And close the bathroom door—the bedroom door, too."

"Yeah, yeah," his friend grumbled. Leon heard the bathroom door shut.

The interruption had sort of killed the mood. So Noreen gave Leon a shampoo, and he reciprocated.

A few minutes later, while they toweled off, Noreen announced that she was "positively starving." She donned her yellow kimono and opened the bathroom door. A waft of cool air hit Leon. He wrapped the towel around his waist, and then wiped a clear streak through the fogged medicine chest mirror. Slicking his damp, tangled, long black hair back from his face, he gazed at his pale reflection. He told himself he'd work on his tan in Arizona.

He started after Noreen into their mess of a bedroom. She was a lousy housekeeper. The whole place was a sty. He watched her working a towel on her hair as she stepped over piles of dirty clothes on the floor. "God, I really am famished," she said. "They better leave some food for us. . . ."

Leon could hear the TV blaring in the living room. It got louder as Noreen opened the door. "Hey, save us some pizza," she announced, her head down as she continued to towel-dry her hair. "I ordered the pepperoni, so don't—"

She didn't finish.

There was a muffled sound, like someone hitting a hollow pipe.

Leon saw his girlfriend step back from the doorway. Stunned, she gazed down at the blood seeping from a hole in her yellow kimono—just above her right breast. She turned toward him with a bewildered expression. She coughed and blood spilled over her lower lip.

He started toward her, but there was another muffled pop. He realized it was a shot from a silencer. This time, it hit Noreen in the temple. Leon felt the warm blood spray him in the face. Wincing, he shut his eyes.

When he opened them again, he saw Noreen flop down on the floor—amid their dirty clothes. In the bedroom doorway stood the two hit men. They wore lightweight, nylon running suits. One was in blue, the other in black. Their faces were a blur. But the one in black had a gun with a silencer. The one in blue carried a samurai sword. Behind them, Leon glimpsed his friends, Les and Cody, lying dead on the living room floor. The walls were splashed with blood. Two pizza boxes were stacked by the front door.

"Where's the money and your stash, Badger?" the gunman asked, shouting over the TV.

Leon Badger fell to his knees. He stared up at the two men. He knew the crazy drug lord in Vancouver had sent them. Even if he told them where he'd hidden his drug supply and the latest cash haul, he'd still die.

But Leon realized if he told them, at least he might die quickly.

Poulsbo—Wednesday, August 8, 9:52 p.m.

Collin watched the two chefs on *Chopped* each try to make a dessert out of ramen noodles, marzipan, root beer, and figs. Dee was a Food Network junkie. But at the moment, she was on the other end of the family room sofa from him—with her head tipped back, eyes closed, and mouth open. She almost looked dead—if not for her ample bosom heaving up and down beneath the top of her pink jogging suit.

On the other side of him, his grandfather was dressed in a yellow Izod polo shirt, green and blue plaid golf slacks, and brown slippers. He was asleep on his lounge chair.

Collin got to his feet and wandered out the front door. It was a warm, muggy night. He couldn't help wondering what *normal* guys his age were doing on a hot summer evening like this—night baseball, the movies, imbibing an unlawful six-pack of beer in a buddy's backyard, swimming, or maybe even some coed skinny-dipping.

And here he was watching the Food Network with his dozing grandparents. Sometimes, it was hard to believe he had once been a movie star.

Swatting a mosquito on his arm, he plodded down the driveway toward the gate. He glanced at the trees and bushes on either side of the drive—so perfectly still it was almost eerie. Approaching the gate, Collin gazed at the end of the driveway and Skog-Strand Lane—where the on-duty detective's unmarked car always used to be.

As of this morning, no one was guarding the house anymore. The policemen had all gone back to Seattle. He hadn't even gotten a chance to say good-bye to Ian.

It was all over the news. On Monday night, a Tukwila woman returned from a Puerto Vallarta vacation to find her house sitter and two male companions shot to death in her home. A third man had been beheaded. He was identified as Leon Badger, thirty-six, a drug dealer sought by Seattle Police for—among other things—questioning in the Piper Cox/Chance Hall murder case. The other victims were his associates. In the house and inside Badger's SUV, the police found a few items reported missing from Piper Cox's rental home—including a pair of silver candlesticks, some costume jewelry, and a DVD of *The Night Whisperer*. They also found a match for the bloody shoe print from the Friday the thirteenth murder scene—a size-eleven boot belonging to one of Leon's men, Cody Williamson, whose weapon of choice had been a knife. The single gunshot, which had blown off part of Chance Hall's face, had come from a Glock 38. The police discovered the murder weapon in a kitchen drawer of the Tukwila house.

Despite all this evidence, Collin couldn't quite accept that his mother's murder had been solved. It just seemed too convenient. All the killers were dead. There would be no arrests, no confessions, and no trial. He wondered if it was possible whoever executed this Badger guy and his group had planted that evidence in the Tukwila house—and in the SUV.

He was curious about Badger's SUV. Could it have been the SUV he and Ian had seen on Skog-Strand Lane late Saturday night? Collin figured he'd never know for sure. Nor was he likely to find out about the strange man who had been spying on his bedroom from that boat. Ian had tried to follow it up, but couldn't get any leads. Collin hadn't seen the boat—and its creepy helmsman—since Saturday night.

He kept staring at the empty, darkened road at the end of the driveway. Since he'd moved in with his grandparents after the murders, the cops had always been there, guarding the house. He didn't like to see them go—even the a-holes like Al and his buddies. He suddenly felt so vulnerable in that big, secluded house—with just his grandparents.

He retreated up the driveway to the house. Stepping inside, Collin double-locked the front door. He kept telling himself they'd be okay tonight. They really didn't need the extra protection of someone watching the house.

He couldn't hear the TV in the family room anymore. But above him, on the second floor, there was the sound of footsteps and his grandfather clearing his throat. Collin quietly headed up the back stairs and ducked into his room. He was about to close the door when he heard someone coming up the hall. He stuck his head out the doorway.

"Hi, kiddo," his grandfather said, ambling up the corridor. "We were looking for you."

"Oh, I just went outside for a few minutes." Collin stepped aside to let his grandfather into the room. "I locked up."

His grandfather nodded. Six-foot-three and solidly built, Old Andy still cut a handsome, imposing figure. He had slightly receding silver hair and blue eyes. He looked his age—sixty-seven—but then he'd always seemed old to Collin. As long as he could remember, his mother had referred to his grandfather as "Old Andy."

His grandfather glanced around the bedroom with an appraising eye. "You know, if you'd like, I can help you slap a coat of paint on these walls, whatever color you want. Maybe you'd like to pick out some new bed-spreads and curtains. This is your room now."

"Well, thanks," Collin said, shrugging. "It's okay for now, I guess."

"This weekend, you and I are going to find a car for you. What do you say?"

Shrugging, Collin worked up a smile. "I have a bike. I really don't need a car, Grandpa."

"You'll be thinking differently when it's cold and rainy out—and you want to get together with your bud-dies or you have a date." He put his hand on Collin's shoulder and squeezed it. "Now that it's safe to go out on your own, you should travel in style. You've still got a few weeks of summer left. There's no reason you shouldn't go out and have fun, make some friends—fellas your own age. . . ."

Collin figured this was his grandfather's way of explaining why he didn't want him to be friends with Ian. He worked up a smile.

His grandfather hugged him. "Please, let us spoil you a little. We enjoy it, and God knows you deserve it, kiddo. You haven't had it so easy. So let us do this for you. Okay?"

All Collin could do was nod and hug him back. "Okay, thanks, Grandpa," he whispered.

The old man pulled away, and patted him on the shoulder. "Good," he said. His eyes were a little misty as he shuffled out of the room.

Collin closed his door, then plodded over to his desk and sat down. He clicked on the computer, and saw he had new mail.

His email address was private, but occasionally a resourceful fan's email reached him. Opening his mailbox, he looked at the new listing:

8/8/2012 – arealfriend@humblelo . . . Wishing
You Well, Collin

He clicked on READ, and the email came up:

Dear Collin,

I am so glad that your mother's killers have been put to death. I breathe a sigh of relief with you and wish you healing and happiness. I hope you are able to rest easy from now on. The whispers in the night you hear are me praying for you.

☺

Collin frowned. He was pretty sure the person who had signed with a smiley face hadn't meant to come off as creepy, but he or she had.

He got most of his fan correspondence over Facebook. He'd found the best way to deal with the weird messages and postings was to ignore them. Occasionally, he gave a quick, brief response—just to acknowledge it and move on. That was what he decided to try now with this smiley face weirdo:

Dear ☺

Thanks for your well wishes.

Sincerely, Collin Cox

He hit SEND, and just moments later, he heard a click, signifying a new email. Collin went back to his mailbox and saw the new message:

8/8/2012 – MAILER-DAEMON. . . . Returned Mail

"What the hell?" he murmured. Smiley Face's email address had been temporary or suspended.

"You've gotten creepier fan letters," Collin mumbled to himself. He went back to the email and deleted it.

He was still staring at his computer monitor when something outside his window caught his eye. It was a speck of light out on the dark water. He sat at his desk and watched it. That man on the boat was back.

Collin realized he'd been wrong earlier.

Someone was watching the house tonight after all.

CHAPTER SEVEN

Portland—Friday, August 10

"I read about what happened," said her four o'clock patient. She sat down in the love seat across from Olivia in the hardback chair. Candace Lavery was a thirty-one-year-old divorcee who sometimes cut herself. Through hypnosis, Olivia had helped Candace curb the self-mutilation, but hadn't entirely broken her of the habit. That was why the slightly dowdy brunette wore a long-sleeved tee and jeans on this hot afternoon. She had to keep the scars covered.

"I told my friends—the ones who know I'm getting help—I told them, 'That's my therapist at Portland Wellness. It was her patient who went crazy and started shooting those people.' They couldn't believe it."

In addition to her self-harming compulsion, Candace didn't have much tact. She glanced around the room and frowned. "I guess I shouldn't be surprised they gave you a different office, though I think this one's smaller—and darker. Is anyone using your old office, or is it still considered—like a *crime scene*?"

"It's vacant right now," Olivia replied, with her notebook and pen in hand. For her first day back to work in three weeks, she wore a tan skirt and a white, three-quarter-sleeve blouse. She had her own scar to conceal—on her shoulder. She wouldn't be wearing sleeveless dresses for a while. At least the bandages were off. The ache in her shoulder hadn't completely gone away yet. Every morning, she did the stretch exercises the hospital therapist had taught her.

As for emotional healing, she'd had talks with the social worker from the hospital and from a coworker from Portland Wellness. They asked her all the right, probing questions, and told her all the right things. She knew the drill. It was her business. Olivia knew she shouldn't blame herself for what had happened. And if any of it had been her fault, she had to forgive herself. Everyone told her so.

But there was one voice of dissent—a bitter, crawly, menacing voice that came to her over the phone.

There hadn't been any more calls from Mrs. Tipton while Olivia had been at the hospital. Maybe the operator had screened them. However, on her third day home in their Laurelhurst town house, Olivia's cell phone rang at eleven-thirty at night. She'd been taking bed rest as her doctor had prescribed, but was wide awake at the moment. She kept the cell on her night table, and her first thought had been about Clay, asleep beside her. He'd been working late to catch up on all the days he'd missed thanks to her. The poor guy was exhausted. She thought for sure her Van Morrison "Moondance" ringtone had woken him. She quickly grabbed her cell and answered it without checking the caller ID. Clay stirred in bed beside her.

"Hello?" she whispered, sitting up in bed, her back to Clay. Except for a faint, bluish glow from the adjoining bathroom's nightlight, the bedroom was dark.

"Did I wake you?" the woman on the other end asked.

"No," Olivia said, rubbing her forehead. "I'm sorry, who—who is this?"

"I wouldn't think you'd be able to sleep, considering what you did to my son," Mrs. Tipton hissed. "You filthy whore—taking advantage of a vulnerable, confused young man. Layne was fine until you poisoned his thinking with your sick, psychological—"

Olivia clicked off the phone. She felt sick to her stomach. She stood up and started toward the bathroom.

"What's going on, babe?" she heard Clay mumble. "You okay?"

"Fine," she managed to say. "Go back to sleep."

Olivia ducked into the bathroom and closed the door. She fell to her knees and clung to the sides of the toilet, but nothing happened. She sat down on the tiles and waited until she could breathe right again. If this nausea in the middle of the night had occurred a month before when she'd been hoping so much for a baby, she might have been optimistic about what it meant.

But this had nothing to do with new life—just lives lost.

She had no idea how Layne's mother had gotten her cell number. Maybe Layne had tracked it down at one time, and Mrs. Tipton had discovered it among his things.

Olivia didn't tell Clay about the call until morning. He was furious, and wanted to contact the police. But Olivia insisted they wait and see if Mrs. Tipton called again before taking any action. In the meantime, she would just screen all her calls. Mrs. Tipton's number was blocked; and over the next few days, Olivia had at least twenty blocked-number hang-ups on her cell—a lot more than usual. She couldn't be sure how many of those aborted calls had been from Layne's mother.

Olivia got a voice mail message after a week of screening calls: *"I suppose you think you're being so clever not answering your phone. Well, you might be able to dodge me, but you can't escape responsibility for what happened to my son. He was in your care. He depended on you, and you warped his mind. You turned him against me, you miserable bitch. I wished he'd aimed higher and shot you in the head—instead of just wounding you."* She started crying on the recording. *"It's your fault. He's dead because of you. I'm not going to let you forget. . . ."*

Clay played the message for the police, who paid a visit to Mrs. Tipton. Olivia figured the sad, demented woman had probably been through enough after losing her only child. She asked that Layne's mother merely be given a stern warning to cease and desist. One of the police detectives who had spoken to Mrs. Tipton told Clay in confidence that the woman lived in a messy, neglected two-bedroom rambler in Portland's Hollywood District. The cops thought they'd gotten through to her—and made it clear she'd face criminal charges if she continued this harassment on the phone. Apparently, Mrs. Tipton had apologized to them—with tears.

Two days later, someone hurled a rock through their living room window.

Mrs. Tipton was taken to the police precinct for questioning, and then released. She'd insisted that she didn't even know the Bischoffs' address.

Olivia figured that trip to the precinct must have instilled enough fear into Layne's mother. The number of unidentifiable hang-ups on Olivia's cell phone was suddenly cut in half.

With her arm out of a sling and Mrs. Tipton no

longer on the warpath, Olivia felt like she was just starting to get her life back. Still, she wasn't ready to return to work, not after what had happened there. Clay didn't see it that way. "Honey, I think you've stayed too long at the pity party," he'd told her the night before last. "You should go back to work—at least half-days. The longer you stay home, the harder it'll be to pick up where you left off there. You're going to lose all your regular patients. And speaking of losing patience, I've lost mine. You're here all day, moping and doing nothing else. It's not like I've expected to come home to *House Beautiful* these past couple of weeks. But lately, the place looks like a dump. And I'm tired of ordering takeout because there's never any food in the house."

At first, Olivia had been livid he could be so insensitive. But then she'd figured this had been her husband's "tough love" strategy. It had worked, too. She'd decided to show him. The very next day, she'd gone out and bought five bags of groceries—not an easy haul for someone with a sore arm. She'd given the house a Windex-Pledge-vacuuming treatment. Then she'd called Portland Wellness, and told them she was ready to come back to work.

So here she was at the end of her first day back— with her last patient. In a way, Candace's almost child-like tactlessness was a nice contrast from Olivia's colleagues' forced smiles and efforts not to stare. She knew everyone around her was uncomfortable, just waiting for her to have a breakdown or something.

Candace was right about the new surroundings, which seemed cramped and dark. She was now down on the other end of the hall from her old, empty office. They kept that door closed and locked.

Candace was the only patient she actually put under hypnosis that day—her first subject since the session with Layne. It was like getting back on the bicycle after a horrible accident. Olivia was nervous and uncertain at first, but Candace took to suggestion well. At the end of it, when Olivia snapped her fingers and Candace actually woke up, it was such a relief. The usually sullen Candace was in an upbeat mood as she walked out of the office.

So was Olivia a few minutes later. She'd made it through this long first day back. On her way to the elevator, coworkers told her it was great to see her again. A couple of people mentioned having lunch together later in the week. Walking across the lobby to the garage elevators, she had a smile on her face.

As she pressed the button for the elevator, Olivia felt someone hovering behind her. She glanced over her shoulder at a woman of about sixty with mousy, gray-brown hair. Despite the sunny, mid-eighties temperature, the woman wore a trench coat. A sheer pale green scarf dangled from one of the pockets, in which she had her hand tucked. Unsmiling, she glanced at Olivia, then quickly looked away.

Olivia moved to one side, putting some breathing room between them.

The elevator bell rang and the door whooshed open. Olivia stepped inside and turned to press the button for garage level C. The woman came in after her. Olivia noticed the green scarf on the lobby floor. She automatically stopped the elevator door from shutting. "Oh, you dropped your scarf," she said.

The woman barely looked at her as she stepped out to retrieve the scarf. Stuffing it in her pocket, she hurried onto the elevator again. Olivia let go of the door and it slid shut.

As the elevator made its descent, she frowned at the woman. Olivia didn't expect her to fall on her knees in gratitude for holding the elevator. But would a smile or a simple *thank you* have killed her?

Then again, maybe the woman didn't say anything because she didn't want Olivia to recognize her voice.

Olivia remembered Layne's mother—and her scathing message: *"He's dead because of you. I'm not going to let you forget."*

During her few trips out of the house—even just down the driveway to get the mail—Olivia had always been on the lookout for Mrs. Tipton. But she'd never laid eyes on the woman.

Was she looking at her now?

Olivia told herself she was being silly. How could Layne's mother know she'd started back to work today? Besides, Mrs. Tipton had stopped harassing her almost a week ago.

The woman's eyes met hers for a moment, but then she glanced away. Olivia stared at how her hand was inside the pocket of her trench coat. It looked like she had something else in there besides the scarf. Was she concealing a gun—the same way Layne had hidden a Smith & Wesson in his jacket?

The elevator came to a stop, and the doors opened. Olivia waited for the woman to walk out first. A cell phone's muffled ring startled her. The woman stopped just outside the elevator, almost blocking the exit. She pulled the phone out of her trench coat pocket. "What?" she barked into it. "No, I just came from the pharmacy. They'll have my pills tomorrow. I'm in the garage now. I can barely hear you. . . . I said I'm in the garage. . . ."

Olivia walked around her. She knew from her voice, the woman wasn't Layne's crazy mother. She could still hear her by the elevator, yapping into the phone. Then the sound of her irritating voice gradually faded.

Olivia approached the row where her car was parked, but an SUV blocked her view of her red Beetle. Fishing into her purse for the car keys, Olivia walked around the SUV, and then stopped dead.

The front hood of her VW was streaked with brown and black slush. Dried rust-colored bubbles coated the marred surface. She immediately glanced up to check if an overhead pipe had dripped on the hood. But there was nothing. It was no accident. It looked like someone had doused the hood of her car with acid.

Stunned, Olivia stepped back. She noticed the deflated front tires, flat against the concrete floor. For a few moments, she just stood there with her mouth open.

She could hear tires screeching on the parking level above her. And in her head, she could hear Mrs. Tipton's crawly voice.

"I'm not going to let you forget. . . ."

"I'm telling you, we never should have let that crazy bitch off with just a warning," Clay said, watching the road ahead. Olivia sat in the passenger seat with the window down. The wind whipped through her auburn hair. They were in Clay's Lexus, driving back from the Portland Wellness campus, where they'd talked with the police for the last hour.

Now Mrs. Tipton had property damage and malicious mischief added to her harassment charges. Photos were taken of Olivia's VW. The police were pretty certain that indeed some kind of acid had been poured over the car's hood. Three of the four tires had been slashed. The tow company hauled her Beetle to an auto body shop. Clay knew something about cars, and estimated Mrs. Tipton's handiwork would set them back about three thousand dollars.

"Didn't you tell me that she used to beat her kid and do all sorts of screwed-up shit to him?" Clay asked.

"Yeah," she murmured. "But for the record, I never said anything. That was patient-doctor confidential stuff."

"My lips are sealed," Clay said, turning onto their street. "But God, after all the crap she pulled on him, it burns me that she's accusing *you* of screwing up her kid. That's just so typical. No accountability. Well, she's gonna pay now. I hope they throw her sorry ass in jail. . . ."

He pulled into their driveway and parked. As Olivia retrieved the mail from the box at the end of the driveway, Clay called to her: "How about if we just order a pizza, stream a movie, and try to forget about bat-shit crazy Mrs. Tipton for the rest of the evening?"

"I'm all for that," Olivia sighed. They walked to the front door together.

The alarm went off—as it always did whenever they stepped inside the house. Clay reached for the box on the wall on the other side of the front door and punched in the code. The beeping ceased.

Olivia had a feeling something wasn't right as soon as they were inside the living room. She could smell it. Flies were buzzing around, and Olivia fanned them away.

"What the hell?" she heard Clay mutter.

Her nose told her some food in the kitchen was going bad. Maybe it was something in the garbage. As she headed for the kitchen, the smell got worse—and so did the flies.

Olivia saw it from the dining room. The refrigerator and freezer doors were open. Food had been emptied out and thrown on the linoleum floor. The cupboards had been ransacked, too. Her glassware and plates were broken. Shards littered the counter—along with the floor, which was covered with a mound of spoiled food and garbage. Flies buzzed around the pool of spilt milk and juice. Yogurt oozed out of smashed containers. Melted ice cream, spoiled meat, and lettuce mingled with cans of soda and beer. The hot summer sun had been streaming through the kitchen window all day, and now a rank odor filled the room. The congealing mess had attracted an army of ants—as well as the flies.

"What the hell is going on here?" Clay asked, coming up behind her.

Olivia turned and hurried into the bedroom. When she saw all her clothes on the bed, she cried out. Her closet and dresser drawers had been emptied out. Horrified, Olivia rummaged through the pile of torn, shredded garments. Someone had hacked away at every piece with a knife or a pair of shears. The same someone had scrawled *BITCH* in lipstick over the smashed mirror on her dresser.

Olivia didn't have to wonder who that someone was.

According to the police, Mrs. Tipton claimed she'd been with a friend in Beaverton the entire day. Her friend backed her up on it, too. Apparently, Layne's mother became quite indignant with the police, and maintained she was the one being harassed now. The police had to let her go.

It was a mystery how anyone could have broken in, entered the security code to silence the alarm, done all that damage, and then set the alarm again before leaving and locking up. It made no sense. So much of the food Olivia had just recently bought had been destroyed. Anything that had been opened or unsealed before the break-in had to be thrown out. Olivia couldn't be sure whether or not it had been tainted. Everything in their medicine chest and all her toiletries had to be tossed out as well.

Oddly, none of Clay's things had been touched. Their big-screen TV in the living room, his precious music/entertainment system, his computer, and his clothes had been spared.

Stranger still was the change in Clay's attitude after speaking with the police alone that night. He'd walked with them to the squad car, and stayed out there for fifteen minutes. Olivia had asked him what they'd discussed, and he'd said, "Nothing." But after that, he no longer ranted about crazy Mrs. Tipton.

"I'm sure the old bat got it all out of her system," he maintained. "Let's just have the insurance pay for the damage to your Beetle, and we'll get you some new clothes. The quicker we can move on from this, the better off we'll be. . . ."

Olivia was baffled. Clay didn't seem to understand how violated she felt. Their home had been invaded. She practically had to insist they change their locks and the alarm code. She mentioned that the police were shuffling their feet with this investigation, and instead of agreeing with her, Clay replied, "I'm sure they're doing all they can." He kept talking about "moving on."

The auto body shop had her VW repaired and ready for pickup the following Wednesday. Olivia hadn't slept much the night before. That morning, she sat at the breakfast table with a cup of coffee. She wore a new bathrobe she didn't like as much as her old one. Clay, in his suit and tie, sat across from her with his

Special K and juice. Following the break-in, she'd cleaned up the kitchen the best she could, but milk had seeped and dried in the cracks under the cabinets. To combat the foul odor, Olivia had set out two Renuzit "Ocean Breeze" air fresheners. So now the kitchen smelled like fabric softener—with a hint of sour milk.

"I think I figured out what's going on here," she said over her coffee cup.

"What's going on where?" Clay asked, hunched over his cereal.

She frowned at him. "Tell me the truth. When you talked with the police the other night, what did they say to you?"

"Nothing they didn't already tell you, just the same old shit they said all night long."

Olivia sighed. "So they believed Mrs. Tipton and her friend. They didn't think she had anything to do with what happened here—and what happened to my car."

Clay shrugged. "I guess."

Sitting back, she folded her arms. "There's something you're not telling me. The police aren't investigating this anymore, are they?"

Clay put down his spoon. It clanked against the cereal bowl. "No, they aren't."

"They think *I* did it, don't they? They think I destroyed about a thousand dollars' worth of food, plates, and glasses. Then I went into my bedroom and slashed up my wardrobe. And for good measure, I wrote a nasty note to myself on my dresser mirror. Is that right?"

Clay squirmed in his chair and glanced down at his cereal bowl.

"Did they have any theories as to why I would do

such a thing?" she asked. "Did they say I did it for attention? Or was I acting out on some guilt complex?"

He rubbed his forehead. "Honey, they suggested it might be someone we know—or yeah, perhaps you might have—"

"Clay, Friday morning, I left for work fifteen minutes after you did," she interrupted, raising her voice. "I was at work all day—until I called you about the car."

He said nothing.

"Do they think I did that, too?" she asked, incredulous. "Do they think I sabotaged my own car? Do *you* think so?"

He shook his head. "Sweetheart—"

"So—I'm supposed to have done that number on my car *and* our house? Is that why I practically had to demand we change our locks? I mean, why change the locks if I'm the one doing all the damage, right? Is that why you keep telling me, 'Let's just move on . . .'?"

"I think it's too early in the morning for this right now," he said wearily. "I haven't had enough coffee yet." The chair let out a squeak, sliding against the floor as he stood up. He took his cereal bowl and juice glass to the sink. "Honey, I'm on your side here. The police mentioned that since you've been through a lot lately, it was possible you could have had a meltdown and pulled this stunt. But I basically told them they were full of shit."

From her chair, she watched him rinse his dish and glass. "Right now, I just want things to be normal again." He shut off the water, and then dried his hands. "I truly believe that crazy old Tipton bitch has gotten it out of her system now. She knows she's toast if she tries anything else. If we let this keep eating away at us, then she'll win. So I'd like to forget the whole mess and get on with our lives."

Olivia didn't respond. She sat there and stared down at the kitchen table.

He leaned over and kissed her forehead. "Listen, I need to get to work. We can talk about this tonight. You sure you don't need a lift to the auto body place?"

"No, I'll take a taxi," she said quietly. She couldn't believe it. A minute after telling her the police thought she was crazy, Clay was going off to work—like it was just another morning. Olivia kept staring at the table. She listened to him getting ready to leave.

She heard the front door shut, and then she started to cry.

In the taxi on her way to Curtis Auto Body Repair, Olivia kept mulling over how Mrs. Tipton had managed to pull it off. Crazy as she was, Layne's mother must have been pretty damn cunning. How did she do it?

The house was empty for hours at a time, especially back when Olivia had been in the hospital. Mrs. Tipton could have hired someone to break in and figure out the codes—or get an extra key made. Hell, she could have had the same hoodlum-for-hire trash the place on Friday—while she was in Beaverton with her friend.

One big glitch with this scenario was that—according to Layne—his mother didn't have two dimes to rub together. So how could Mrs. Tipton afford to pay someone to carry out her dirty work? And any housebreaker-for-hire certainly would have stolen a few items for himself. Clay had a lot of expensive gadgets. But nothing was missing from the house.

Olivia could almost understand why the cops thought she'd done the job herself. A distraught woman snaps, trashing her own house and her car—it was the easiest, most logical explanation, considering the circumstances. But they were wrong. And so was Clay—for even thinking it was possible.

That hurt the most.

From the backseat of the cab, Olivia noticed the dumpy-looking storefront with an open garage door. It was up ahead and on the right. They had a blue sign above the garage with yellow lettering: CURTIS AUTO BODY REPAIR. The cabdriver pulled over in front of the place. It was a busy, commercial area—with four lanes of heavy traffic and cars zooming by. Olivia thought she might get run down as she paid the driver through his open window.

The taxi pulled away, and she started toward the garage entrance.

"Olivia? Olivia Barker-Bischoff?"

She recognized the voice—and then she heard a car's tires screeching.

Olivia turned around and saw the stout woman running towards her from across the busy street. A second car skidded to a stop and honked at her, but the woman ignored it. She had short-cropped gray hair and big tinted glasses. Wearing a peasant blouse and unflattering khakis, she carried a large straw purse. She had sort of a determined waddle as she barreled toward her. "Olivia Barker-Bischoff!" she repeated, sounding slightly crazy.

On the sidewalk in front of the auto body shop, Olivia just stared at the woman who she knew must be Layne's mother.

Mrs. Tipton was out of breath and sweating by the time she reached the sidewalk. "I thought that was you!" she said, shaking a finger at her. Olivia backed up a little.

"Listen, you," she said, catching her breath. "If the

police bother me again with another one of your wild, false accusations, I'll get a lawyer and sue you! I'm sick of your persecution and harassment—"

Olivia let out a stunned laugh. "You're sick of *my* harassment? Are you serious?"

Mrs. Tipton glared at her from behind the tinted glasses. "Outside of a couple of phone calls you certainly had coming, I haven't done a thing to you!"

"You're lying," Olivia shot back. "I know you broke into my house somehow. And I know you did that number on my car, too. What—are you following me now?"

"Why in God's name would I be following you? I don't want anything to do with you. And for your information, I don't break into people's homes or ruin their cars—"

"No, you hire someone to do it for you."

"Lies!" Mrs. Tipton declared. "Your filthy soul will rot in hell! It's bad enough you turned my son against me and poisoned his thinking with all of your modern psychological muck. He was fine before he started seeing you—"

"Layne wasn't *fine*, Mrs. Tipton," Olivia cut in. "He was deeply troubled—thanks mostly to his upbringing. Whatever you do or say to me, it won't change the fact that you were a horrible, abusive mother—"

"That's not true!"

"Layne told me some of the things you did to him when he was a child, the beatings and the cruel punishments. You should have been thrown in jail, you sick, crazy . . ."

Mrs. Tipton hauled back and took a swing at her, but Olivia recoiled. The older woman missed her. She stumbled and grabbed a streetlight pole to keep from falling. She started to cry. "You're lying!" she screamed.

"Layne wouldn't tell stories like that! He was a good boy. . . ."

Olivia could only shake her head at the woman. She'd already said way too much. She took a deep breath. "Just leave me alone, Mrs. Tipton."

With tears streaming down her face, Layne's mother started to back away. "You're a lying, evil bitch!" she screamed over the traffic noise. "I don't have to listen to this filth. . . ."

Olivia turned and headed toward the auto body shop.

"I wish I *had* broken into your house. I would have burned it to the ground!" she heard her yell. Mrs. Tipton started to scream something else, but the sound of screeching tires drowned her out.

Olivia swiveled around to see an old silver Buick LeSabre careening toward Layne's oblivious mother. The older woman was still screaming and shaking her fist at her. All at once the car plowed into her with a horrible thud. It knocked Mrs. Tipton into the air. Her big purse flew in a different direction. She toppled over the hood and smashed against the windshield, shattering the glass.

Something hit Olivia in the leg. She glanced down and saw it was the woman's shoe.

Stunned, she looked up again as the car ground to a halt. Mrs. Tipton's lifeless body just rolled over at the base of the windshield and stayed there. Blood started seeping through her clothes.

Olivia heard other tires screeching and people screaming. Someone from the shop ran out and yelled, *"What happened?"* over and over.

With a hand over her mouth, Olivia stood paralyzed in front of the auto body repair shop. She couldn't believe that just a moment ago, Mrs. Tipton had been screaming at her.

Now she stared at the dead, mangled body pressed against the LeSabre's cracked windshield. Streaks of blood covered the silver car's hood.

"I'm not going to let you forget," Mrs. Tipton had told her in that first phone call.

Now Olivia knew she never would.

"I guess I'm here because I'm in a pretty screwed-up relationship," she said, perched on the love seat in Olivia's office. "I'll bet you get that a lot."

Sitting in the chair across from her, Olivia worked up a smile. "Often enough," she said. "But each story is different."

Corinne Beal was a pretty twenty-six-year-old with big green eyes and long, straight blond hair. She worked at a cosmetics counter and had the classic features that went with the job. At the same time, she also had sort of an elongated horse face. Still, with her fashion model's body, she looked stylish in her rust sweater and black Capri pants. She was a new patient who had specifically asked for Olivia.

It had been five days since Olivia had seen Layne's mother die right in front of her. She kept replaying it in her head, and each time, she flinched when she remembered how that old Buick had slammed into Mrs. Tipton, silencing her angry tirade.

She'd missed work that Wednesday, of course, and stayed home the following day. But Clay had insisted she try for at least a half-day at work on Friday. He'd said her best therapy was helping other people, and the sooner she got back into her work routine, the better. She'd understood it was more tough love from Clay,

but he'd been right. She'd gotten through that Friday—
and the weekend—okay. She'd even bought some more
clothes. With Clay's help, she'd moved the refrigerator
and finally cleaned up the last stinky remnants of dried
milk on the floor. The smell had been a constant reminder of Mrs. Tipton.

Olivia focused on her job. Right now, that meant
Corinne Beal and her screwed-up relationship.

"Well, I'm pregnant," her new patient announced.
She let out a long sigh. "And the father—my lover—
he's married."

"Does he know you're pregnant?" Olivia asked.

Corinne nodded silently.

"Do you intend to have the baby?"

"Yes. And he wants this child as much as I do. He's
told me so."

Olivia tried not to frown. Part of her job was not to
show judgment of any kind. "What about the wife?
Does she have any idea what's going on?"

Corinne let out a sad little laugh and shrugged.
"She's clueless. Sometimes I think he's never going to
tell her, and he's just stringing me along. Yet I know in
my heart and in my head, he loves me. He just doesn't
have the guts to leave her right now."

Olivia scribbled in her notebook. "Let's backtrack
for a moment," she said. "Did you know he was married when you first started seeing him?"

She nodded. "Yeah, but he was miserable. He told
me that he hasn't been happy with her for a long time.
I'm not the type of person who would set out to break
up a happy home."

"I understand," Olivia said. Again, she was trying to
sound nonjudgmental. "Just to get an idea of everyone
involved here, do he and his wife have any children?"

"No children." Smiling proudly, Corinne rubbed her

stomach. "This is his first. I think the wife is barren or something."

"Has he told you that he plans to leave his wife?"

"Yes. I know he's working out a strategy, and that takes time. But I'm getting impatient. Plus my hormones are all out of whack. I've really had some crazy days. The morning sickness isn't so bad, but oh, the mood swings! Is that normal?"

"I think every pregnancy is different," Olivia said.

"I've done some things I'm not too proud of. But I figure, you can't really blame me when my body's going through all these changes."

"What kind of things have you done?" Olivia asked, jotting in her notebook.

"My lover's wife was in a—an accident a few weeks ago and spent a few nights in the hospital," Corinne explained. "And while she was there, I stayed in their house and slept with him in their bed. . . ."

Olivia looked up from her notes. "How did that make you feel?"

Corinne gave a flicker of a smile. "It made me feel like I belonged there instead of her."

Olivia's eyes wrestled with hers. "While you were staying in their house, and his wife was in the hospital, did you—did you have a copy of the house key made?"

Corinne nodded.

Olivia suddenly felt sick to her stomach. "And did you memorize the security code?"

Corinne nodded again.

"And I suppose you've followed his wife around," Olivia said in a shaky voice. "So—you know where she works, and—and where she parks her car. . . ."

"I even drove it a few times while you were in the hospital," Corinne said, her head cocked to one side. "Believe it or not, I'm really sorry for all the damage.

In fact, I'm kind of embarrassed it even happened. But like I say, I can't really be held accountable when my hormones are all screwed up. . . ."

She didn't look the least bit sorry.

"Does—does Clay know what you did?"

Corinne licked her lips and nodded. "The thing is, Clay doesn't love you anymore," she said. "He's in love with me. He said he's going to pay you back for all the clothes I ruined. When he gets around to it—and he will soon—Clay's going to ask you not to press charges. And he's going to ask you for a divorce."

Dumbstruck, Olivia stared at her. If she'd felt violated before when she'd discovered someone had invaded and trashed her home, it was nothing compared to this. She thought of Clay telling her the police thought she was crazy. She remembered Mrs. Tipton, screaming at her that she hadn't touched anything of hers. And once again, Olivia could see that big car barreling into Layne's mother.

She felt so sick, she started trembling. "You need to leave," she said quietly. "You need to leave right now. . . ."

Corinne got to her feet. "Listen, I didn't come here to gloat. I happen to be—"

"GET OUT!" Olivia screamed.

Gaping at her, Corinne froze.

"GODDAMN IT, GET OUT OF HERE!"

Corinne let out a scared little cry. She ran to the door, flung it open, and ran out to the hallway.

Olivia listened to her footsteps retreating down the corridor.

For a moment, she felt better—but only for a moment.

CHAPTER EIGHT

Poulsbo—Saturday, September 29, 10:43 p.m.

"Hey, how about if I hypnotize one of you guys?" Gail asked. She stood in front of the big-screen TV, which she'd finally turned off. "I know how to do it. My aunt taught me. I'll hypnotize one of you and we'll record the session. It'll be a kick. What do you say?"

"I say it sounds kind of lame," Collin sighed.

He tried to act like he wasn't interested. But in truth, he was scared of what might happen—and not about the stupid stuff Gail might make him do, like kissing her, or taking off his pants or something. He was worried he might tell the truth about who he was.

He and his friend, Fernando, sat on the mauve sectional sofa in the Pelhams' basement recreation room. An empty pizza box and some cans of soda sat on the coffee table in front of them. Gail Pelham was into performing arts, and Collin figured she'd chosen the theater posters on the basement walls: *Wicked, Phantom of the Opera*, and *Mamma Mia*. She'd just forced him and Fernando to watch *Bye Bye Birdie* on TV. It wasn't bad, and Ann-Margret was sexy. But he and Fernando could have done without Gail singing along with every musical number.

Gail Pelham and Fernando Ryan were Collin's only friends at North Kitsap High. They knew him as *Collin Stampler*, who had moved from Seattle after his mother had died in a car accident. Collin figured he'd tell them the truth eventually. He just wasn't ready for everyone in school to know yet. He didn't want people treating him like a freak. For now, he just wanted to blend in.

Tonight everyone who was *anyone* in their class had been invited to Rachel Porter's beach party. It was supposed to have a bonfire, a band—and, since Rachel's folks were out of town, a lot of beer. It was also invitation only. Collin, Gail, and Fernando weren't invited.

So Gail had insisted the three of them hang out tonight. "We'll celebrate our lack of coolness together," she'd told Collin. It was Gail's way of saying, *The hell with them.*

Despite some lingering baby fat, for which the other girls teased her, Gail was pretty with a bright, dimpled smile and curly red hair. Apparently, her hair had been "shit-brown" the year before—so said the tweets by some of the popular mean girls. Though she could be annoying at times, Collin had a little crush on Gail, maybe because she was the only girl in school paying attention to him. She'd been desperately upbeat most of the evening. Before announcing she wanted to hypnotize somebody, she'd replayed and sung along with the *Ed Sullivan* number from *Bye Bye Birdie*—twice.

"C'mon, don't be a spoilsport," she said, standing between them and the TV. "I know hypnosis, and I swear, I won't make you do anything you'll be embarrassed about later."

"Well, then what fun is that?" Fernando asked.

Half-Mexican and half-Irish, Fernando looked like he was about fourteen. He was also a dead ringer for Sal Mineo in *Rebel without a Cause*. Though born on the Kitsap Peninsula, he'd still picked up a trace of accent from his Mexican mother.

He patted Collin on the shoulder. "Oh, what the hell, we might as well let her hypnotize us—or she'll play that stupid *Ed Sullivan* number again." He reached into the pocket of his cargo pants and pulled out his iPhone. "You go first. I'll record it for posterior. . . ."

"*Posterity*," Gail said. She didn't get it when Fernando was kidding. "Okay, Collin . . ."

He shook his head. "I'm not a good subject. Someone once tried to hypnotize me for one of those after-dinner shows, and it didn't work at all." He was lying. He just didn't want to be hypnotized. He couldn't afford to let down his guard. What if he opened up about his mother's murder—and started bawling?

"C'mon," Gail pleaded. "Let me at least give it a try. . . ."

"He's afraid you'll make him show us his wiener," Fernando said.

Gail clicked her tongue against her teeth. "My aunt told me that you can't make a subject do anything under hypnosis they wouldn't normally do while conscious. So there's nothing to be afraid of. C'mon, Collin, don't be a party pooper."

He grabbed the iPhone from Fernando. "Okay, but *you* go first, and I'll record it."

"Fine," Fernando declared, sitting back and folding his arms. "I'm ready. Bring it!"

Collin was hoping Fernando would resist, and then they could drop the whole thing. But now they were going through with it. He felt a nervous twinge in the pit of his stomach.

Gail made him move over to the ottoman, so he'd
have a better angle for recording the session. She took
his spot on the sectional and leaned in close to Fernando. Collin thought she might go fetch a charm or a
pocket watch on a chain—something to dangle in front
of Fernando's eyes. But Gail just used her hand, slowly
moving it toward his face and then back again, over
and over. "Okay, Fernando, I want you to focus on me.
Now, think about a place where you like to relax and be
at peace. . . ."

With the iPhone, Collin started to record the session. He was surprised at how cooperative Fernando
was as a subject. He didn't resist or make any sarcastic
comments. He took it all in.

That was because—unlike him, obviously—Fernando wasn't afraid.

A lot of things scared Collin lately. Ever since the
detectives had stopped guarding his grandparents'
house, he'd had a tough time falling asleep at night. He
couldn't help feeling something awful would happen.
The house was so big. Someone could break in, and
he'd never hear them. Plus there were so many places
for an intruder to hide. It was so isolated there, too. No
one else lived close enough to hear if he screamed for
help. Collin didn't tell anyone, but he slept with one of
his grandfather's old golf clubs under his bed. As much
as he'd loathed most of them, he missed having the police guards outside.

About a week after they'd left, Collin had received
an email from Ian Haggerty:

Hey, Collin,

**I'm back in Seattle working on a new assignment
with that same wonderful bunch of guys you got
to know & love. Lucky me, right? I hope you're**

doing okay & taking some comfort knowing your
mom's killers have been found.

I feel bad that I didn't really get a chance to say
good-bye. Thanks so much for smuggling food &
Cokes to me all those nights. Believe me, I really
appreciated it. Thanks also for your terrific
company & your friendship. It was great getting
to know you, Collin.

Take Care,
Your Friend, Ian

Collin had emailed him back:

Hi, Ian,

Thanks for your email. Sorry you've got to work
with the same bunch of a-holes. I don't miss
them at all. But I miss you. I hope you're doing all
right too. Thanks for guarding the house and
everything. If you ever come back to Kitsap, I
hope you come by and say hello.

Your Friend, Collin

Collin hadn't expected him to respond or visit the
Peninsula again, and he didn't.

Though the police were gone, someone else was still
watching the house from time to time. That man on the
boat kept coming back to that same spot just beyond
the sandbar off the beach behind his grandparents'
house. Collin never saw the boat in the daytime, only
late in the evening. He told his grandfather about it,
and Old Andy didn't seem too concerned: "Oh, during
the summers, they'll have a patrol boat out there occasionally. They watch the beaches at night. That's probably what you're seeing."

Collin wasn't so sure about that. If he'd truly believed his grandfather, then on those nights when he was so lonely and scared, he might have taken some comfort seeing the boat out there. Instead, it just made him more edgy, and he'd pull down his bedroom shade.

He was tense all the time lately.

And right now, he didn't feel like opening himself up to hypnotic suggestion—not even in front of his only two friends.

But Fernando had no such qualms. With the iPhone in his hand, Collin watched him. His friend sat with his eyes closed, answering Gail's questions. Yes, he could hear her. Yes, he was comfortable. Yes, he knew where he was. He was in his safe place.

"That's very good," Gail said. "Now, I'd like you to open your eyes so you don't trip or anything. I want you to get up and pretend you're Ann-Margret in the movie we just watched. I want you to sing the *Bye Bye Birdie* song."

With a slightly dazed expression, he opened his eyes. "Ann-Margret," he murmured. Then he slowly got to his feet.

Collin kept the iPhone trained on Fernando as he shuffled toward the TV.

Fernando turned toward them with that same blank look. "Are . . . you . . ." He hesitated. "Are you . . . sure you wouldn't rather see my wiener?"

Gail shrieked, and Collin burst out laughing.

"You totally had me fooled!" Collin admitted, switching off the iPhone camera.

"You guys are such suckers." Fernando smirked.

"I hate you!" Gail said, grinning at him. "I'm not even talking to you!" She turned to Collin. "Okay, it's your turn, and I want you to take it seriously."

Collin shook his head. "There's no way I can top that."

"Oh, better let her try her voodoo on you, or she'll sulk all night." Fernando reached for his iPhone. "Here, gimme. I'll record it. You get in the hot seat. . . ."

Collin told himself to just pretend, the way Fernando had. With a sigh, he moved back over to the sectional. Gail said Fernando had killed the "receptive mood," and so now the three of them had to take a few minutes to calm down again. "Laugh if you need to get it out of your system," she said. "And then we're going to be quiet, and concentrate on our breathing. . . ."

"Oh, yeah, thanks for reminding me," Fernando replied. "I almost forgot to breathe."

She shushed him. They were silent for a minute. She told Collin to focus on her hand as she slowly moved it toward his face, then back again. "Think of a place where you feel safe and everything is peaceful. No one can bother you there. . . ."

Collin thought of the little shed in the woods by Shilshole Bay. If he was actually going along with this nonsense, he would imagine himself there. He listened to Gail's supposedly soothing voice and figured he'd string her along for a while. But he wasn't going to do any musical numbers from *Bye Bye Birdie*.

"Are you in your safe place?" she asked.

He closed his eyes and nodded. He remembered when he was a kid, playing in that shack in the woods. For a while, when he was five or six, he had an imaginary friend named Dave. He'd pretend he and Dave were cowboy-outlaws, and the shed was their hideout. *Dastardly Dave & the Shilshole Kid*. That little shack was where it had started—before he'd turned the idea into his own comic strip adventure series.

His mother had been worried about him for a while. "You know that Dave isn't real, don't you?" she'd asked.

"Yeah, I made him up," he'd told her, matter-of-factly.

Eventually she'd gone along with it. *"Why don't you and Dave go outside and play while I visit with my friend?"* she'd tell him. Or: *"I need to go out for a while. Dave will keep you company. Go to bed when the little hand is on the nine. . . ."*

Whenever he was afraid, he used to tell himself that Dave was there—and Dave wasn't a scaredy cat. *Brave Dave* wasn't afraid of the dark, and he wasn't afraid to walk down that side of the street where the neighbor's dog barked at him. He knew Dave was make-believe, but it still helped to have him around sometimes.

"Collin?" It was Gail's voice.

He heard someone snap their fingers. "Okay, c'mon now, Collin, cut it out. . . ."

Opening his eyes, he gaped at her and blinked. "What?"

"Bullshit artist!" Fernando declared, chuckling.

"Very funny," said Gail, shaking her head. "I have to admit, that was kind of creepy. I almost believed you."

Collin glanced at both of them. "What are you talking about? Aren't you going to hypnotize me?"

"Oh, give me a break," Fernando moaned. "It was a pretty good act. You almost had me, too. But when you started talking about seeing Elvis, that's when you pushed it too far."

"And where did you get that voice?" Gail asked, her eyes narrowed at him. "That didn't sound like you at all."

Baffled, Collin shook his head. "You guys, I swear to God, I don't know what you're talking about. I didn't go into a trance, did I? I couldn't have. I closed my eyes for—like, three seconds. . . ."

"Yeah, about ten minutes ago," Fernando said. "Listen to him. Give it up." He started working his thumb over the pad of his iPhone. "Tell you what, I'll email your performance to you. Personally, I thought mine was better."

Collin stood up. He rubbed his forehead. "I don't understand. Did something really happen? How could it?"

"Collin, we know you're faking." Gail sighed impatiently. "Only in rare cases do hypnotized subjects not remember what happened while they were under. So quit pretending—"

"You guys, I'm not pretending!" He reached for Fernando's iPhone. "Let's see that."

Fernando shoved the phone in his pocket. "Please, don't make me sit through that act again. It was funny the first time. But let's not run it into the ground. I'd rather watch that *Ed Sullivan* number again. I sent you the video. You can look at yourself later." He stood up and stretched. "In fact, you can look at yourself sooner than later, dude. I'm tired. I think we should wrap it up here. . . ."

Collin still couldn't fathom how he'd lost ten minutes like that. It was scary—and maddening the way Gail and Fernando acted as if it were all a joke. He kept insisting to his friends that he hadn't faked anything.

Before heading to the car with Fernando, he turned to Gail one last time on the Pelhams' front porch. "Listen, I'm totally serious," he whispered. "I don't know what went on down there. Can't you tell me?"

Frowning, she crossed her arms in front of her. "I think you need to stop," she said quietly. "I mean, enough is enough. It's not funny anymore, Collin. It wasn't even funny when you were acting like that. In fact, it was kind of disturbing."

Collin wanted to tell her that it was no joke, that he

was scared and confused. He opened his mouth to speak, but then he decided to shut up. He turned away and started for the car.

As he drove Fernando home, all Collin could think about were those lost ten minutes. But he didn't mention anything to his friend—and he didn't ask about the video. *Enough is enough*, Gail had said. Obviously, Fernando felt the same way. The two of them were quiet—until Collin turned down Fernando's block.

"Just so you know," Fernando said, at last. "You drive like an old fart."

Collin wasn't taking any chances with his shiny red Ford Taurus. Though last year's model, it was new from the dealer. "Thanks a lot," he said, pulling into the Ryans' driveway. "You can walk home next time. Listen, seriously, I just have one question for you."

Fernando opened the car door. "What's that?"

"Can you hear the drums?"

Fernando rolled his eyes. "Oh, up yours, like that's the first time I've heard that." He gave Collin's shoulder a punch. "By the way, that was a pretty good act you put on back there in Gail's basement."

Collin worked up a smile. "Thanks. See you later."

His smile waned as he watched his friend head inside the house. Collin backed out of the driveway and drove to the stop sign at the end of the block. There wasn't any traffic tonight. Shifting to park, Collin let the car idle while he pulled his phone out of his jacket pocket. He had to see the video now. He couldn't wait until he got back to his grandparents' house. He tried to power on the phone, but realized the battery was too low. "Damn it," he muttered.

Heading for his grandparents' house, Collin became

even more anxious about the video. What had gone on during those missing minutes? His foot got heavier and heavier on the accelerator as he sped down Viking Way. He hoped Fernando's email came through okay. He'd go nuts if he didn't get to see it tonight.

His grandparents had left some lights on downstairs for him. Collin came in from the garage, locked up, and checked the front door, too. The digital clock on the kitchen stove read 12:20 AM. He crept up the back stairs to his room, and then quietly closed the door behind him. Clicking on the computer, he saw Fernando's email at the top of the mail listing:

9/29 – cooldudefernando@g . . . You're SO full of S-H-I-T

The icon showed an attachment. Collin clicked on it. Aside from the subject head, Fernando hadn't written any text. Collin ignored all the standard warnings, and downloaded it. A few moments passed before the window appeared with a frozen image—showing him on the sectional sofa in Gail's basement. His eyes were closed. The picture was a bit fuzzy. From the lighting in the room, everything looked slightly murky with an orange/brown tint.

Collin clicked on the arrow to play the video. He waited another near-unendurable half-minute for it to start playing. He watched himself sitting there with his eyes still shut. He heard Gail, off-camera, murmuring something to him. Collin tuned up the volume, and listened to her ask, "Are you in your safe place?"

He nodded in response. Collin remembered that much. He glanced at the counter at the bottom of the picture, and saw the number of minutes and seconds left for the video: 6:57.

"You're very sleepy . . . so tired," Gail was saying. "You're in your safe place, and all you want to do is drift off to sleep. But you need to listen to me and stay awake just a little longer. I'm going to count down from five, and then you can go to sleep, all right?"

Collin watched himself nod again. He'd seen her go through this procedure with Fernando, but didn't remember her doing this with him. His eyes were still closed. Gail started counting backward from five. By the time she reached *one*, his head gradually tipped back and his mouth dropped open.

The image wobbled a bit. He guessed Fernando hadn't been able to keep the iPhone steady. On-screen, Gail quietly asked if he could hear her voice. Did he understand what she was telling him? Was he comfortable?

He lifted his head slightly, and then nodded in response to every query.

"Do you know where you are?" she asked.

He nodded again. "The safe place, the hideout . . . Shilshole Bay . . ."

Bewildered, Collin leaned closer to the computer monitor. The voice that came out of him wasn't his own.

The image went out of focus for a second. "What the hell?" Fernando said.

Gail shushed him. Collin watched the shot come into focus again. His eyes were open now, and he stared off camera at Gail, whose shoulder was at the very edge of the frame.

"Okay, Collin," Gail said. "You're somewhere near Shilshole Bay, and you're safe. You're listening to my voice right now—"

"I'm not Collin," he said. "I'm Wade. . . ."

With a hand over his mouth, Collin stared at the

screen. He didn't remember any of this. None of it made sense.

Gail leaned in close to him. "What's your last name, *Wade*?"

"Grinnell, Wade Grinnell," Collin heard himself say in that strange voice.

Grabbing a pen from his desktop, he scribbled the name, *Wade Grinnell,* on the Post-it pad. He put a question mark after it.

On screen, he scowled at Gail and then at Fernando behind the camera phone. "Who the hell are you? Is this another goddamn police interview? You guys don't look like cops. . . ."

"The police have interviewed you?" Gail asked.

He smirked at her. "Yeah, don't you know? I'm a dangerous character. . . ."

"What are the police accusing you of, *Wade*?" Gail put a sarcastic emphasis on the name.

"Well, they say I've been an awfully bad boy to some girls like you—and their mommies, daddies, and little brothers. That's all I'm going to tell you, baby." He turned to squint at the camera. "What do you have there, José? A transistor radio?"

"Collin!" Gail said, scandalized.

He was shocked at how racist he sounded. But Fernando just chuckled, and the camera shook. Bewildered, Collin stared at the video, and kept shaking his head. It was like watching someone else entirely. *Wade* pointed to something in front of him—off camera. "What the hell is that, a TV?"

"Oh, give me a break," Fernando muttered.

"Of course it's a TV," Gail said.

"Is this your place?"

"Yes," she replied impatiently. "Yes, *Wade*, I live here with my parents and my younger brother."

"Shit, you must be loaded. Are they here now?"

"Yes, everyone's upstairs, asleep."

"So where does your old lady keep her purse?"

"You're not serious," Gail muttered. The camera panned over to her, shaking her head. "You know, that really isn't funny."

"Hey, cool it, bitch," he grumbled. He turned toward the camera again—and Fernando. "Who are you listening to on that thing? Chubby Checker? Elvis? Y'know, I saw Elvis while he was shooting that movie at the fair a few weeks back. Talk about nuts, it was a goddamn mob scene with all those screaming, fainting chicks. . . ."

"You saw Elvis," Gail repeated skeptically.

"You mean he hadn't left the building yet?" Fernando cracked. The camera wobbled. "God, you are so full of shit!"

His fist clenched, he shot a lethal, threatening look toward the camera. His eyes were so cold. "What the fuck did you just say to me, asshole?"

"That's enough, Collin!" Gail said.

For a moment, it looked like he'd lunge at the camera—and Fernando.

"Collin?" It was Gail's voice again.

He watched himself on the screen, and a chill raced through him.

His eyes rolled back, and his mouth fell open.

Gail snapped her fingers. "Okay, c'mon now, Collin. Cut it out. . . ."

He suddenly focused on her. "What?" he asked, in his normal voice.

"Bullshit artist!" Fernando said, off camera.

The video abruptly stopped and returned to the first, grainy image of him with his eyes closed—from seven minutes before.

Collin sat there in a stupor. He couldn't understand

why he'd acted like that. It was so bizarre to hear a stranger's voice coming out of his mouth. The things he'd said about Elvis Presley, Chubby Checker, and transistor radios made absolutely no sense. Collin wondered if watching that old movie had triggered those sixties references. At least now he knew why Gail had found the whole session pretty disturbing. *"I'm a dangerous character,"* he'd said with a smile, but it looked like he'd meant it. He'd seemed proud of it.

It wasn't him in that video. It was somebody else.

Collin glanced down at the name he'd scribbled on the Post-it:

Wade Grinnell?

Seattle—Sunday, September 30, 1:32 a.m.

"Oh, the hell with it," Olivia muttered.

She threw back the sheets to her four-poster bed and switched on the nightstand lamp. She'd thought *Saturday Night Live* might help take her mind off things, but it was a rerun. She'd watched part of it anyway, and then gone to bed depressed—only to toss and turn for an hour.

Olivia put on a robe over her faded University of Washington nightshirt, and then wandered over to her purse, which hung on the back of the desk chair. She dug out her cigarettes and took an ashtray from the desk. Opening the window all the way, she sank down in the stuffed easy chair beside it. The chair had a pink, green, and white flowery pattern that matched her bedspread.

Olivia's father had kept her room the same as when

she'd moved out—back in 2000. Above the double bed, there was a framed movie poster from *Titanic*, which she'd adored at age nineteen. After college, even though she'd outgrown the movie, she'd left the poster up there. She'd decided not to change anything in her room—so she couldn't get too comfortable living at home with her father.

How in the world could she have known she'd be moving back here at age thirty-four?

With the ashtray in her lap, she lit up her cigarette, took a long drag, and exhaled toward the window. She used to put away nearly a pack a day in this room, and thought nothing of it. But for this return stay, she'd resolved not to smoke in her father's house—even though he'd claimed he didn't mind at all. She usually stuck to these self-imposed restrictions and stepped outside to smoke. But tonight she was making an exception.

Olivia surveyed the room again. In addition to Kate and Leo "flying" at the front of the doomed luxury liner, she had a framed print of some ballet dancers by Degas. There were also about twenty box-framed photos of her with her high school and college friends at various functions—all pre-1999. She'd been a bridesmaid to several of the girls in those pictures. But she'd fallen out of touch with most of them. Some still sent Christmas cards—or hit her up for a present with the occasional birth announcement. A few still lived in Seattle, and were single—like her. She probably should have reached out to reconnect with them, but she just didn't have it in her right now. She hadn't even told any of them that she was getting a divorce. What had happened to her was so utterly humiliating, she didn't want anyone to know the details. It certainly would have

made a juicy, ongoing story for the Internet: SHOOTING
SPREE SURVIVOR TORMENTED BY HUSBAND'S PREGNANT
GIRLFRIEND. A brief article about it had made it to *The
Oregonian*. That was as far as it went, because she'd
agreed not to press charges against Corinne Beal. Clay
had paid her for all the damage. Olivia had taken
everything that was hers and moved back in with her
dad in Seattle. That had been eight weeks ago.

But it wasn't until tonight that she'd actually changed
her Facebook status to *single*.

Facebook—that was what had plunged her into this
dark, dismal mood tonight. She'd made the mistake of
checking Facebook—and clicking on a photo from a
ten-year anniversary party for Barb and Jim Church.
They'd been friends of Clay's in Portland, nice people,
too. She didn't want to un-friend them just because she
and Clay had split up.

Olivia had known by clicking on that Facebook
photo for more pictures from the party she'd been setting herself up to get hurt. The party had been yesterday. Of course, Clay had attended, and of course,
Corinne had gone with him. Olivia just hadn't counted
on them both looking so tan, healthy, and happy—goddamn them. Every photo of Clay had Corinne beaming
at his side. They appeared to be having a great time.
Though Olivia had found one shot of the two of them
with Barb Church in the background, and Barb seemed
to be giving Corinne the evil eye. Olivia had liked that
shot. It had been the only picture of her husband and
Corinne that didn't make her feel like someone was
stabbing her in the heart.

Olivia had been tempted to "like" every photo from
the party—except the ones with Clay and Corinne. But
that had seemed silly, so she hadn't "liked" any of

them. She had, however, commented on Barb's post: *Happy Anniversary to a Cute-some Twosome!*

And then she'd changed her status to *single*.

Olivia stubbed out her cigarette, fanned at the air, and got up. She switched on her laptop computer. She wanted to see if anyone had commented on her new status change on Facebook. Not yet, but then she'd posted it only four hours ago. And with eighty-six friends, she figured there might be a wait.

However, she did have a new email—from her sixteen-year-old niece. She was on Clay's side, his sister's daughter. This was the second email she'd sent since the breakup. The subject head was: What's New, Buenos Aires?

Dear Aunt Olivia,

You were on my mind tonight, and I just thought I'd check in with you. I have a crush on this very cute new guy at school. Blue eyes to die for! He and another friend came over tonight for pizza and a movie. I'm still not sure how he feels about me. No kiss good night or admission of his undying love or anything. In fact, he was acting pretty weird tonight. Maybe he's a vampire or something! Tune in tomorrow! ☺

Uncle Clay came over with his girlfriend two weekends ago. Let's just say I'm not a fan. My mom would kill me for telling you this, but I've heard her say the same thing. I think Uncle Clay is a huge dope.

Anyway, thanks so much for emailing me back last time. I hope you're getting settled and liking your new job. I also hope we can stay friends. Maybe we can go out on a double-date

sometime . . . you and some hot new guy & me
and my kind of weird, cute semi-almost-boyfriend!
OK, now I'm the one who sounds weird. I just
think it would be cool if you met him. Anyway, I
should get to bed. Take care, Aunt O!

XXXX – Gail

PS: I lost 2 lbs. last week!

PPS: I tried out for girls' choir last week. Here's
hoping I get in!

Slouched in her desk chair and staring at the screen,
Olivia actually found herself smiling a bit. She clicked
on the REPLY icon:

Dear Gail,

Well, if you're looking for the 2 lbs. you lost last
week, I found them! They're currently clinging to
me, thanks to 2 guys I know named Ben and
Jerry. Seriously, congratulations, Gail. And FYI,
you've got a very cute figure. So I hope you're not
starving yourself.

That's fantastic that you auditioned for girls' choir.
They'd be fools not to take you. You're so
talented. I'll keep my fingers crossed. Let me
know what happens!

It was so sweet of you to email. Thanks for thinking of me. I'm really happy that we're keeping in
touch, Gail.

The new business is keeping me very busy. I happen to agree with you about your uncle. That's all
I'll say about that! Actually, I'm doing great and
have no complaints.

Please say hi to your parents and Chris for me.
Keep me posted about this blue-eyed boyfriend of

yours! And yes, maybe I'll get to meet him sometime.

Meanwhile, take care of yourself, cutie!

XXXXXX – AO

She quickly sent the email—so she wouldn't spend
the next thirty minutes reworking the paragraph that
mentioned Clay.

Olivia shut down the computer and then plodded
back to her four-poster bed. Shrugging off her robe,
she glanced at the *Titanic* poster above her headboard.
She wasn't going to change a thing in this room, because she was determined to move out on her own—
and soon.

She thought about her email to her niece. *Actually,
I'm doing great and have no complaints,* she'd written.

Crawling to bed, Olivia reached for the lamp on the
nightstand. "Yeah, I'm doing great," she muttered to
herself. "I'm king of the world."

She switched off the light and hoped for sleep.

Poulsbo—Sunday, 1:50 a.m.

Collin restlessly paced around his bedroom.

He'd watched the video a second time, and still
couldn't figure out what was happening to him. He
stopped pacing, and glanced again at the Post-it on his
desk:

Wade Grinnell?

He'd never heard of the guy. Could it be a real person?

He sat down. Hunched over the computer keyboard,
he went onto Google and typed "Wade Grinnell." He

hit ENTER, and studied the search results that popped up. The first few listings were references to Grinnell College in Grinnell, Iowa. But something at the bottom of the first results page caught his eye:

SEATTLE WORLD'S FAIR – 40 YEARS LATER

www.seattletimes.com/features/4/21/2002.html

Century 21 Exposition Timeline: Thursday 10/11/62 – 17-year-old **Wade Grinnell**, a suspect in the El Mar Hotel murders (see 7/9/62) is killed by a speeding train while running from police . . .

Biting his lip, Collin leaned in closer to the screen and clicked on the story, from a *Seattle Times* article in 2002. It was a timeline of events in Seattle during the World's Fair, which was called the Century 21 Exposition, starting with the opening day on April 21, 1962. He scrolled down the list of mini-milestones— toward the date in October when this Wade Grinnell character had been run over by a train. But a photo of a young Elvis Presley made Collin stop. He read the caption below it:

Wednesday 9/5/62 – Even the first day of school can't keep mobs of teenage girls away as Elvis Presley, 27, arrives in Seattle to shoot *It Happened at the World's Fair.* His first scene is filmed on the Monorail, and features in a small role 19-year-old Miss Seattle Linda Humble, who is also a Space Needle elevator operator.

Collin scratched his head. He hadn't heard of this Elvis film about the Seattle World's Fair. Yet under hypnosis, what was it he'd said? *"Y'know, I saw Elvis while he was shooting that movie at the fair a few weeks back. Talk about nuts. . . ."*

Had the real Wade Grinnell actually seen Elvis? That would have been five or six weeks before Wade had been struck by a train and killed. Collin wondered how he suddenly knew stuff from fifty years ago that had happened to someone else—someone dead.

He anxiously tapped the arrow key and inched further down the timeline until he saw the date of Wade Grinnell's death:

Thursday 10/11/62 – Seventeen-year-old Wade Grinnell, a suspect in the El Mar Hotel murders (see 7/9/62), is killed by a speeding train while running from police in Interbay Rail Yard. A family of four, visiting the fair from Medford, Oregon, had been bound, gagged, and stabbed to death in their connecting hotel rooms. Police believe Grinnell may have also been responsible for a fire at another hotel, in which five people in town for the fair were killed *(see 8/8/62)*.

He remembered telling Gail while in the trance: *"They say I've been an awfully bad boy to girls like you—and their mommies, daddies and little brothers."*

A family of four, it said. Kids were murdered. Who was this guy?

Staring at the monitor, Collin couldn't help thinking about his mom and Chance. While he'd slept, his mother and Chance had been bound, gagged, and stabbed to death.

He told himself that he couldn't have killed his mother and Chance. Ian had already given him a long explanation of why that was totally implausible. He hadn't murdered anyone in his sleep. But he couldn't help wondering if this Wade person had come out that night.

On the keyboard, he arrowed back up to July 9, the date of the El Mar Hotel murders:

Monday, 7/9/62 – A family of four is brutally slain at the El Mar Hotel in Capitol Hill. In town for the World's Fair, Ronald Freitag, 31, and Betty Parsons Freitag, 28, of Medford, Oregon, were tied up, gagged and stabbed to death on their bed in the El Mar. Their children, Ron, Jr., 7, and Kim, 5, were similarly executed in the connecting room. While robbery is believed to have been the motive, Freitag had less than one hundred dollars on him; the rest was in travelers' checks. His wallet and his wife's purse were ransacked. Even little Kim's rubber coin purse was emptied. *(See 10/11/62 for related story.)*

Collin couldn't believe it. The son of a bitch had gone through the little girl's coin purse. Before or after he'd stabbed her and her family to death? Collin felt sick to his stomach. Now he realized why Wade had been interested in where Gail's mother kept her purse.

How could this be happening?

Had Gail given him some kind of pre-hypnotic suggestion that wasn't on the video? Had she read up on this murder case and manipulated him somehow? No, he'd seen the whole session on video—from the time he'd drifted off until he'd awoken—and she hadn't coached him at all. This Wade guy had emerged on his own.

Collin knew the *related story* on October 11 was the paragraph about Wade's death. It had mentioned that Wade might have been responsible for a hotel fire in August—with even more victims. With a shaky hand, Collin hit the arrow-down key until he found the story:

Wednesday, 8/8/62 - Five people perish after
a fire swept through two connecting rooms in
the Hotel Aurora Vista on Aurora Boulevard.
Brandon and Irene Pollack of Wenatchee,
Washington, came to Seattle for the fair with
their three children and Pollack's younger
sister, Loretta, 17. Investigators believe the
fire may have started late Tuesday night from a
smoldering cigarette, but the possibility of arson
hasn't been ruled out. Irene Pollack, 33, survived
the inferno, but is hospitalized with extensive
third-degree burns.

There was no reference to Wade Grinnell—or his
death. They didn't cite any follow-up or related stories.

Collin caught his reflection in the darkened glass of
his bedroom window. Was he looking at an image of
Wade Grinnell now? Were he and Wade Grinnell like
twins?

He shifted in his chair and arrowed back to the
Google home page. He clicked on the *Image* option,
and squinted at the display of small photographs that
came up on the monitor. He was searching for a guy
about seventeen years old, who might look as if he'd
just stepped out of the sixties movie from earlier
tonight.

No one fit that description on page one.

He found only two photos of young men. Clicking
on them, he discovered they were just Facebook photos
of students from Grinnell College. A few of the images
might have been from the fifties or sixties, but they
were of women, kids, and older guys. It was the same
way for the next five pages.

He clicked out of Google and brought up the video
for a third time. Cringing, he watched it again. In a

strange, awful way, everything he'd said while in a
trance now made sense. He'd become this Wade Grinnell person. "This can't be happening," he murmured
to himself.

How many times had Wade Grinnell taken over
while he was unconscious? This was the first time he'd
been captured on video. But there could have been
other episodes. If Wade had come out before while he'd
been asleep, his mother would have noticed. Then
again, maybe she hadn't known about Wade until the
last night of her life.

"Stop thinking that," he whispered, squeezing his
eyes shut. Tears rolled down his cheeks. He took a few
deep breaths.

It came down to one person who might be able to
help him figure out what was going on here. That person had been dead for fifty years, Wade Grinnell. And
the only way to reach him was to go into a hypnotic
trance again.

Collin wiped his eyes, then got up from his desk and
ducked into the bathroom. He slurped some water
from the sink faucet. Returning to his desk, he sat
down again and composed an email to both Gail and
Fernando:

Hi, You Guys,

I know you think I was joking tonight when you
hypnotized me. But I wasn't. I can't explain what
happened.

Can the three of us get together again tomorrow?

Collin hesitated. He looked at the clock in the bottom corner of his computer monitor: 2:37 AM. It was
already *tomorrow*. He backed up and changed it:

Can the three of us get together again today (Sunday)? I need you to hypnotize me again, Gail. And I need you to record it for me, Fernando. I'm really depending on you guys. I'm serious.

Please forgive me for acting so creepy while I was under. I didn't know what I was saying or doing until I saw the video. Sorry about the José crack, Fernando.

Please don't tell anyone else about this. I'm counting on you guys to keep it secret. Thanks.

See you later, I hope.

Collin.

CHAPTER NINE

Poulsbo—Sunday, September 30, 4:50 p.m.

"I'm going on record here," Fernando announced, his arm stretched out as he filmed himself with his iPhone in the front seat. "My friend, Collin Stampler, is totally full of shit. Here he is, about to give another performance. Take it away, Collin."

Collin wasn't sure whether or not the rain tapping on the car's roof would screw up the video's sound quality. He and Gail were in the backseat of the Taurus. His car was the only one in the lot at Nelson Park on this rainy, gray afternoon. The three of them had families at home and Sunday dinner commitments. So Collin had picked up Gail and Fernando and then driven here. He didn't want any distractions while Gail tried to hypnotize him again.

Playing back his sarcastic introduction, Fernando said the lighting was "good enough." All the windows were cracked open to keep the phone's lens from fogging up.

Collin was nervous, and his hands were sweating. He'd barely slept last night. Part of him had been afraid to fall asleep—for fear that *Wade Grinnell* would emerge again.

Gail had a tired, *let's get this over with* look on her face. "Are you ready?" she sighed.

He pulled a piece of notebook paper from his back pocket, and handed it to her. "I wrote these questions I want you to ask—in case this Wade guy comes back."

Rolling her eyes, Gail took the piece of paper from him. Unfolding it, she glanced at the list of questions for a few moments, and frowned. "Collin, this isn't funny at all."

"It's not meant to be," he murmured. "Please, go along with me on this. I really need your help." He turned to Fernando. "Both of you."

Gail let out an exasperated sigh. "All right, fine." She held her hand in front of his face and gradually moved it back and forth. "I want you to focus on my hand, Collin. Take long, deep breaths and think of a place where you feel very safe. . . ."

His eyes felt heavy, and he closed them. Collin listened to the rain on the car roof, and her voice. A tiny part of him was scared Wade would emerge and never let him come back. Or maybe Wade would do something horrible to Fernando and Gail.

I've been a bad boy to girls like you. . . .

He listened to her counting backward from five. But he didn't hear her get past two.

"Shit, man, that's really screwed up," Fernando said. He switched off his iPhone.

In the backseat of the car, Collin gazed at Gail. "What just happened? You've got to believe—"

Before he could finish, she slapped him across the face.

Startled, Collin recoiled. He gazed at her and blinked. The slap stung.

"I don't want you back here with me," she said, scooting toward the window. "Just drive me home. We're not going to talk about this. I don't want to hear another word from you."

Collin quickly climbed out and then got in behind the wheel. His left ear was still ringing from her slap. He started up the engine. He wanted to say he was sorry for whatever he'd done, but figured he should just shut the hell up. He pulled out of the parking lot.

The *whoosh-whoosh* of the Taurus's windshield wipers somehow seemed louder than normal—probably because it was so quiet in the car. Collin's stomach was in knots as he watched the road ahead. The pavement felt a little slick from the rain.

"Listen," he finally said. "You guys need to understand, that wasn't me. Okay? You think I'm joking or trying to punk you, but I'm not. This is serious. I'm really scared. . . ."

"Collin, I wouldn't push it if I were you," Fernando warned. He was manipulating the keypad of his iPhone. "Now, I've sent you the video. If you're smart, you won't post it anywhere, because it makes you look like a real asshole."

Collin glanced in the rearview mirror at Gail. She turned her head away and sniffled. He was pretty sure she was crying back there.

When they finally pulled into her driveway, Gail loudly cleared her throat. "I used to think you were a real nice guy, Collin," she said. "If you seriously don't know what happened back there, then you need professional help, because you're sick. And if this is your idea of a joke, I *still* think you're sick. Either way, I don't want to see you anymore."

He turned around. "Gail, please, I'm sorry—"

But she'd already opened the car door and ducked outside. She slammed the door shut, and then ran in the rain to her front porch.

"Jesus, Fernando," he murmured, gripping the steering wheel. "What happened? Did I attack her or something? I really don't remember, I swear."

"Are you on the level?" his friend asked.

"Yes, goddamn it! I've been trying to tell you guys that since last night. I'm worried I might have a split personality or something. There's even more to it than I can tell you. This Wade guy, he . . ." Collin hesitated. How could he explain it without sounding totally crazy?

He took a deep breath and watched Gail step inside the house.

"Are we going to get moving?" Fernando asked nervously. "I don't want to be sitting here when her dad comes out of the house ready to pound the shit out of you. He's liable to take a couple of swings at me for not doing anything."

Collin felt the knots in his stomach tighten. He backed out of the driveway. "Okay, we're moving. Would you please tell me what happened?"

Fernando sighed. "Well, the way you touched her and talked to her was really—I don't know, *slimy*. If you really don't remember, you'll see it on the video. I should have stopped you, but I didn't realize how much you were scaring her."

Collin braked at the stop sign at the end of her block. "Poor Gail, I had no idea. . . ."

"Hey, I think I'm gonna get out here," Fernando said. "I feel like walking."

Collin turned to him. "Are you crazy? Your house isn't for another two miles, and it's pouring out."

"I don't care. I'll hitch a ride if I get tired." He opened the car door.

"Was I really that awful, Fernando?" Collin asked.

His friend said nothing for a moment. The sound of rain filled the silence.

"The thing of it is," Fernando finally replied, not looking at him, "I thought I knew you. But it just occurred to me, I only met you—like, two weeks ago. After seeing you in that trance, it's like I don't know you at all. Anyway, I kind of want to be alone and walk for a while. Don't take it personally or anything. I—I'll see you in school tomorrow. Okay?"

Before Collin could respond, Fernando climbed out of the car. He closed the door and started walking along the shoulder of the road. The rain pelted him, and he turned up the collar of his jacket. Collin wanted to get out and run after him. But he stayed in the car.

It hurt that his only two friends didn't want anything to do with him.

He left the car idling—and the wipers on. Switching on the hazard lights, he took his iPhone out of his pocket, and retrieved the email from Fernando. While it downloaded, he watched his friend ambling along the side of the road, getting smaller and smaller in the distance.

Fernando had been right about the sound and light quality of the video. The rain on the car roof practically drowned out Gail, who talked in a whisper. The picture was murky, and he was almost in silhouette with the light coming through the rear window behind him. Collin adjusted the volume—while, in the video, Gail put him into a trance.

"You're in your safe place now, Collin," she said.

"And you're very comfortable. I'm going to ask you some questions. Are you ready?"

There was silence for few moments. The image shook a bit.

"Collin, you made a list of questions I'm supposed to—"

"I'm Wade," he said—in that same strange voice from the evening before.

"Hello, *Wade*," Gail said coolly. "We talked last night, remember?"

"Sure. I see you have your boyfriend with you again. *Sí, señor?*"

Fernando didn't say anything, and neither did Gail.

"Shit, listen to that rain," he said, stretching his arm across the top of the backseat. "Too bad it can't be just you and me in here, honey."

"Yeah, it's really a shame," Gail muttered. She glanced at Collin's list of questions. "Last night, you mentioned the police interviewed you about something. Did it have to do with the murders at the El Mar Hotel?"

"Well, now, doll, where did you hear about that?"

"A friend told me," Gail replied, improvising.

"Maybe your friend should keep his fucking mouth shut," he growled.

"I think he's just watching out for you, covering your back, y'know?" Collin had to hand it to her for keeping her cool. Gail nervously cleared her throat. "He—he also thought maybe the police were trying to connect you to the—the fire at the Hotel Aurora Vista."

"Yeah, well, a couple of hotels got torched, and a bunch of people got fried," he said. "Snap, crackle, pop. But they haven't been able to pin any of those jobs on me. And you can tell your smart-ass friend—whoever he is—that the El Mar wasn't the only new hotel where some tourists got chopped up."

"Chopped up?" Gail repeated.

"Yeah, stabbed. Which one is the El Mar? They have so many of those new, crummy hotels to cash in on the World's Fair crowd. Is the El Mar where the mommy and daddy and their two little kiddies got chopped up in connecting rooms?"

"There were children? You mean a whole family was stabbed to death in this hotel?"

"Yeah, they checked out early." He chuckled, and touched her arm. "It was in the papers. But they buried it on page two or three. After all, if it made the front pages, it might hurt business at the fair."

"And the police think you had something to do with these murders?"

"Like I say, they can't pin anything on me."

"When did this happen?" Gail asked. She was going off script.

"A couple of months ago," he replied.

Collin realized this Wade guy still thought it was 1962.

"I don't remember hearing about any multiple murders or fires in a Seattle hotel recently," Gail said. She turned toward Fernando in the front seat and looked at the camera. "Do you know what he's talking about?"

"No," he heard Fernando grunt. "I don't get any of this. . . ."

Gail seemed rattled. The sheet of paper with the questions shook in her hand. She glanced down at it. "Have the police talked to any of your friends—or your family?"

"They were bugging my sister, Sheri, but she didn't tell them anything."

"Do you know . . ." Gail trailed off and said nothing

for a few moments. She shifted in the seat. "Would you please take your hand off my knee?"

"Where do I put it? Here?" He stroked her shoulder, and then touched her face with the back of his hand. "Are you a virgin?"

She recoiled. "You're not funny! Cut it out!"

"You're sitting here with me in the backseat of a car—and in the rain, no less." He stroked her curly red hair, and then kissed her neck.

"Stop it!" Gail cried.

He pulled back. "Who are you trying to kid?" he hissed, his hand squeezing her face so her lips puckered. "If you aren't asking for a good banging, I don't know what. Let your pipsqueak boyfriend watch if it gets him off. I don't care. Don't be such a fucking tease. You goddamn virgins are all the same. . . ."

"Hey!" Fernando barked. "What are you doing?"

Gail knocked his hand away. "Okay, that's enough! Stop it! Collin?" She snapped her fingers.

Collin watched his head tip back for a moment. Then he seemed to come to and stared at Gail. "What happened?" he asked—in his normal voice.

"Don't give me that," Gail growled at him. She crumpled up the piece of paper and threw it at him. "You know what you were doing. . . ."

"Shit, man, that's really screwed up," Fernando said, off camera.

Then the video stopped.

Just a moment later was when she'd slapped him.

Dear Gail,

I'm so sorry for the way I acted when you hypnotized me. I watched the video Fernando shot, and it was scary to hear myself saying those things in that weird voice and acting that way. Believe me, I wasn't conscious during that. Nothing like this has ever happened to me before. I think you're right when you said I probably need some professional help. I don't know why this is happening.

You were very brave to ask all those questions I wrote down and to deal with me when I was acting so screwed up. I understand why you'd never want to see me again. But I hope you'll give me another chance. Let me know if there's any way I can make it up to you. Corny as it sounds, it was really nice of you to be my friend when I was the new kid in the school, and everyone else was ignoring me. Thank you for that, and please forgive me.

Your Friend (still, I hope),
Collin

Sitting in front of his computer monitor at his desk, Collin read over the email. He winced at how pathetic he sounded, but clicked the SEND icon anyway. He'd just sent a similar email apology to Fernando. He felt horrible about what had happened. At the same time, a part of him was kind of ticked off at both of them for being so thickheaded. Why did they refuse to believe him? Couldn't they see the awful person who came out while he was under hypnosis wasn't him? Then again, Fernando had been right. They hadn't known him for long. In fact, they still thought he was someone named Collin Stampler. They had no idea who he really was.

Neither did he anymore.

The house still smelled of his grandmother's pot roast. They'd eaten dinner about an hour ago. At the table, his grandfather had asked if anything was wrong.

"You act like you have the sword of Damocles hanging over your head," he'd remarked.

Collin hadn't been sure what that was—besides another one of his grandparents' bizarre expressions. He'd just lied and said he was fine. After helping his grandmother clear the table, he'd mentioned he had homework and retreated up to his room.

On the desk in front of him, he smoothed out the crumpled piece of notebook paper with the questions Gail was supposed to have asked Wade. He looked at the last two questions—questions Gail hadn't gotten around to asking, because he'd scared her off:

Do you know Chance Hall and his girlfriend, Piper?
Why are you doing this to Collin? Who is he to you?

Those had been the two most important questions he'd written down, and they'd gone unanswered. Still, he'd found out a lot from the session in the car—most significantly, that there were other murders and deadly fires at Seattle hotels during the World's Fair. And Wade Grinnell may have been responsible for those as well. He'd never denied culpability; he'd merely said, *"They can't pin anything on me."*

Collin wondered why the other hotel fires and slayings weren't mentioned in the Century 21 Exposition timeline article. Had the stories been buried?

On the computer, he pulled up Google and tried a search for "Seattle World's Fair Murders." Nearly all the results on the first five pages had to do with H. H. Holmes, who confessed to twenty-seven murders, but may have slain at least a hundred more during the 1893

Chicago World's Fair. A bestselling book on Holmes, *Devil in the White City*, kept popping up, too. There was nothing about any murders during the 1962 Seattle World's Fair.

Collin tried another Google search—for "Sheri Grinnell." But it didn't lead to anything substantial. He gave up after scanning five pages of search results. He figured she was either married with a different name or long dead.

Frustrated, he went back to the Century 21 Exposition timeline article and reread the paragraph on the Hotel Aurora Vista fire. He stared at the last sentence:

Irene Pollack, 33, survived the inferno, but is
hospitalized with extensive third-degree burns.

Collin figured she'd be eighty-three years old if she was still alive. The family had come from Wenatchee, about two and a half hours east of Seattle. It was a long shot, but he tried a Google search for "Irene Pollack, Wenatchee."

He saw something on the second page of the search results:

LEAVENWORTH LIBRARY ANNOUNCES KIDS' CORNER READINGS

www.wenatcheeworld.com/features/02/16/11/library-readings.html

Bestselling Children's Author **Irene Pollack**-Martin will be reading from her Lucky Ladybug series. . . . **Pollack**-Martin is a frequent visitor to the Children's Center at **Wenatchee** Valley Hospital. . . .

Biting his lip, Collin clicked on the link and watched the full story come up. He knew Leavenworth was close to Wenatchee, but still had a feeling he was wasting his time. He read the article. Back in the seventies,

Irene Pollack-Martin had written a series of picture books about the perilous adventures of a "plucky, lucky ladybug named Bernadette."

"Shit," Collin muttered. He forced himself to read on. He kept hoping to find something about this kids' author losing her husband and three children in a hotel fire. Instead, the article went on about how her books had been out of print for twenty-five years, but she still went around reading them to kids at a hospital in Wenatchee and now at the Leavenworth Public Library Kids' Corner. Then in the last paragraph, he finally found something:

> Twice-widowed, Pollack-Martin, 82, started her readings on Sunday afternoons at the Riverview Manor Retirement Center in Leavenworth. According to the Center's program manager, Katie Reynolds: "With so many people visiting on Sundays, we have up to two dozen kids in the lounge for Irene's readings. The children just love it." Pollack-Martin has been a resident at the Center since 2009.

Collin scribbled on his Post-it pad: *Riverview Manor Retirement Center, Leavenworth*. The article was from last year, so her age matched the Irene Pollack who had survived the Hotel Aurora Vista fire.

He looked up the phone number for the Center, and then called them on his cell phone. Someone answered after two rings: "Riverview Manor. How can I help you?"

"Hi," Collin said. He suddenly realized he hadn't figured out what to say. "Um, do you have a—an Irene Pollack-Martin staying there?"

"I can connect you," the operator said. "I also have a direct line for Irene in case we get cut off. Do you have a pencil and paper handy?"

"Um, yes," Collin said, grabbing his pen again. "But first. I—I want to make sure I have the right Irene Pollack-Martin. Was she—in a fire at one time? I'm looking for the *Irene Pollack* who lost her husband and children in a fire back in 1962."

There was a silent beat at the other end. "I'm sorry," the operator finally said. "We don't give out personal information about our residents. Ms. Pollack-Martin's phone number for future reference is 509-555-0416. If you'll hold on, I'll connect you."

With a shaky hand, Collin scribbled it down. "Thank you," he said.

While the phone rang on the other end, he glanced at the clock in the corner of his computer monitor: 9:13. He realized he'd probably wake her up—if she was anything like his grandparents. They'd both nodded off in front of the TV downstairs about an hour ago.

"Hello?" she answered on the third ring.

"Hi, Mrs. Pollack?"

"Yes, I'm Mrs. Pollack-Martin. Who's calling?"

"Hi, um, you don't know me," he said. "My name's Collin Stampler, and I'm sorry to call so late. I—I'm doing a paper on you for my English class. We're supposed to write about an author, and I chose you. My mom used to read your books to me when I was a kid."

"Well, that's very flattering," she said. "What did you say your name was?"

"Collin—Collin Stampler."

"Do you live here in Leavenworth, Collin?"

"No, I'm in Poulsbo. But I—well, I'm coming to Leavenworth tomorrow," he heard himself say. "Would it be possible to meet you? I was hoping I could ask you a few questions—and get some quotes."

"I don't see why not," she answered. "Are you in high school?"

"Yes, North Kitsap High. A bunch of us are coming over on a field trip, and I asked for time off to talk with you. Um, would around noon be okay?"

"That's fine. Where would you like to meet?"

He glanced at the Post-it pad. "I can meet you at Riverview Manor, if you'd like."

"Well, that's easy enough for me," she said. "When you get here, just tell the front desk to ring me, and I'll come meet you in the lobby. How does that sound?"

"That's terrific, thank you. Um . . ." He couldn't hang up yet. He had to find out if this was the right Irene Pollack. "I was wondering if you have any children—that I could talk to. I figured it would be good to get a quote from the—the child of a children's author."

Silence.

"Hello?" Collin asked.

"No, I don't have any children. But you could talk with some of my neighbors here and get some quotes about me from them if you'd like. So—tomorrow at noon?"

"Yes . . . yes, thank you."

"You're welcome, Collin. Good night." She hung up.

He clicked off his cell phone.

He'd planned to square things with Gail and Fernando at school. But that wasn't going to happen now. He'd be driving to Leavenworth instead.

Collin slouched back in his desk chair. *Good night*, the lady had said.

He knew he probably wouldn't sleep a wink.

CHAPTER TEN

Poulsbo—Monday, October 1, 7:50 a.m.

Fernando usually walked the two miles to school, unless the weather was crummy or he was feeling lazy. Then he'd hitchhike. This morning he felt lazy.

He'd been walking along the shoulder of the road with his thumb out for the last ten minutes. There was a lull in traffic. So he pulled his phone out of his backpack and texted a message to Collin. He wanted to assure him that he wasn't pissed off at him or anything:

> **Ey, Collin, I got yr emsg lst nyt. U wr sure acting weird yday. Bt I thk Gail wz heaps mor freaked ot bout it thN I wz. I'm really not >☹@U or NE fin. So let's mEt n d caf n talk @ lnch 2day. Sound QL?**

Fernando was trying to think of something funny to say before signing off, but then he heard a car approaching. He turned and stuck out his thumb again. There were no other cars on the road except for the black Saturn approaching him. Fernando could have sworn that same car had passed him five minutes ago.

Then again, it was probably just a different black Saturn.

He kept his thumb out and watched the car slow down as it cruised by. It was hard to see how many people were in the vehicle, because the morning sun glared off the windshield and windows. The car passed him. But then he heard gravel crunching under the tires, and Fernando realized the Saturn had pulled over. Turning around, he shoved the phone in his jacket pocket and ran toward the car. He noticed two men sitting in the front seat. The one on the passenger side reached back and opened the car door for him.

Fernando took off his backpack and tossed it on the seat. He saw the man in the passenger seat, and his face lit up with a smile. "Well, hey, I was just heading for school. Thanks for stopping. . . ."

He ducked into the back and shut the car door.

The Saturn pulled onto the road again, and then it started to pick up speed.

Fernando never got to finish his text to Collin.

Leavenworth, Washington—Monday, 11:52 a.m.

"Hi, I'm here to see Irene Pollack-Martin. She's expecting me."

Collin had a pen in his pocket and a notebook in his hand. He wore a lightweight red jacket—and a skinny, dark tie, which he'd hidden in his pants pocket while leaving the house this morning. If his grandmother had seen him wearing a tie to school, she'd have thought something was weird. But Collin had figured a tie was a nice touch for this interview with Mrs. Pollack-Martin.

The stocky, fifty-something brassy-haired receptionist wore a burgundy blazer over her white blouse. Sporting something that looked like a Bluetooth headset, she sat on a tall stool behind the counter, with a computer keyboard and monitor in front of her. Over to one side of her was a tall glass vase full of long-stem flowers.

Riverview Manor looked more like a three-star hotel than a rest home. It was a few blocks uphill from the main drag of Leavenworth, a charming Bavarian village nestled just east of the Cascades. All the stores and hotels had gingerbread architecture and signs with old-fashioned lettering. It was like a town in the Alps. Collin had almost expected the people to be wearing yodeler hats and lederhosen. But all he saw were a lot of normally dressed tourists.

The retirement center looked a like big, sprawling four-story Swiss chalet. Flowerboxes adorned all the first-floor windows. The stone-tiled lobby had big comfortable chairs and a working fireplace along one wall. There were also wheelchair access signs and handrails everywhere—a reminder that this was a retirement home. He'd noticed a lounge off the lobby, with a big-screen TV, card tables, and an entire wall of shelves crammed with books. Collin figured that was where Irene Pollack-Martin had her readings. Right now, there were four old women playing cards at one of the tables and an elderly man shuffling around with a walker. Everyone else must have been at lunch.

After nearly four hours of driving, Collin needed to pee. He hadn't noticed a restroom sign in the retirement center's lobby. Collin squirmed a bit and drummed his fingers on the front desk while the stout receptionist typed something on her keyboard.

"You said Mrs. Martin is expecting you?" she asked.

"Yes, um, my name's Collin Stampler."

She hummed for a few moments, and then said into her mouthpiece: "Hello, Mrs. Martin. It's Greta at the front desk. You have a handsome young gentleman here to see you. His name's Collin Stampler. . . . Um-hmm . . . I certainly will. See you soon, then." She looked up at him and smiled. "She'll be down in a jiff, honey."

"Thanks," Collin said. "Do you have a restroom?"

The woman directed him to the facilities down the hall. When he stepped into the men's room—with handrails all around and a tall, ugly, beige plastic seat extension on the toilet in the stall—he was once again reminded that this was a rest home. He tucked his notebook under his arm and used the urinal on the other side of the stall.

Washing his hands in front of the mirror, Collin noticed he looked tired and pasty. His hair was a mess from driving with the window open. He smoothed it back with his damp hands. Then he slurped some water from the faucet, wiped his mouth, and ducked out of the restroom.

As he headed up the corridor toward the lobby again, Collin heard a woman talking. He recognized Irene Pollack-Martin's voice from their brief conversation on the phone last night. ". . . called out of the blue and asked if he could interview me for an English assignment. How about that?"

Collin saw her from the back. She stood near the vase of flowers, and sort of held on to the desk. She didn't have a walker or a cane, so he guessed she welcomed having something to hold on to while standing there. She was thin and had neatly styled gray hair. The pale green dress she wore made Collin wonder if she'd gotten *gussied up* (another one of his grandparents' expressions) for him.

"Well, speak of the devil," the receptionist said. "Here he comes now."

Irene Pollack-Martin turned toward him. She had a smile fixed on her careworn face. She looked like one of those old actresses who had aged gracefully. At least, she didn't look eighty-three.

But as soon as her eyes connected with his, the smile disappeared.

Irene Pollack-Martin's hand came up over her mouth and she shrank back. Her other hand swept over the counter, knocking over the glass vase full of flowers. It hit the floor with a loud crash and an explosion of glass. The tall-stemmed flowers landed in a heap on the stone tiles. All at once, the graceful, spry older woman looked frail and elderly. Staring at him, she shook her head.

"Mrs. Martin?" the desk clerk asked with concern. "Mrs. Martin, are you all right?"

"Oh, my God," she whispered. Mrs. Pollack-Martin looked as if she were about to faint. "I can't believe it. . . ."

Dumbfounded, Collin gazed back at her. He was paralyzed.

He knew right then. She'd seen him before.

She'd seen Wade.

Silverdale, Washington—Monday, 12:07 p.m.

Fernando ran as fast as he could. He followed the thin, crude trail that snaked through the woods, hoping it might lead to a road or someone's cabin. Then he'd have a chance of getting some help. Scratches from the brush and cold, clammy sweat covered his near-naked body. All he had on were his white briefs. His lungs burned, and his bare feet were bloody and sore. How soon before they became numb to the pain? Right now, he could still feel every twig and rock underfoot.

He pressed on, fueled by terror and a dizzy sense of the sudden freedom. When they'd finally pulled off the dirt road and parked at a clearing in the woods, he'd thought for certain they were going to kill him. They'd led him behind a rotted-out shack with torn screens, old garbage on the floor, and cobwebs everywhere. Then they'd made him take off his clothes.

He'd gotten down to his undershorts when they heard bushes rustling nearby. Startled, the driver of the black Saturn swiveled around and fired his gun. He hit a deer, which had come into the clearing. The deer stumbled down on its hind legs. It seemed to shake uncontrollably. The driver fired at the wounded creature again and again until it collapsed on the ground.

By then, Fernando had already bolted off in the other direction. That had been at least an hour ago—maybe two. He wasn't really sure anymore. He'd spent so much of that time hiding in gullies or ditches. He kept hearing the car in the distance. Every once in a while, the motor would stop, and then he'd hear the car door open. They'd talk back and forth, but the words were always indistinguishable. He still hadn't shaken them. Fernando kept hoping to run into some hikers or nature nuts, anyone who might help him.

Stopping for a moment, he ducked behind a tree and tried to catch his breath. He listened to the bushes rustling and twigs snapping—not very far away. One of them was closing in on him. Fernando crouched down near the cold ground. His salty sweat seeped into the cuts and scratches all over his body. It felt like his skin was on fire. He couldn't stop shaking. He thought of that wounded deer.

"Hey, Fernando, c'mon," called the driver of the

black Saturn. "I know you can hear me. It was all a gag. Collin put us up to it. C'mon, dude, we weren't really going to hurt you. We were just supposed to scare you. We'll give you your clothes and your phone back. Fernando?"

He didn't believe him for a minute. The guy's voice seemed to be fading. Fernando slowly straightened up and crept off in the other direction. After a while, he couldn't hear him at all, and he broke into a sprint. He thought he saw a paved road through the trees ahead.

For a second, he glanced back to make sure no one was behind him. All at once, the ground disappeared beneath his feet—and he was falling. He toppled into a gully, and cried out in pain as he landed on his arm. He heard something snap. For a few moments, he lay there in shock, unable to move. He'd gotten the wind knocked out of him.

"Fernando, did you hurt yourself?" the driver called. "I think I know where you are, but give me a yell so I can help you!"

He heard the footsteps through the brush coming closer—and then the man's raspy breathing.

With his one good arm, Fernando tried to push himself up, but he couldn't. His feet had become numb. They couldn't support him anymore. He collapsed on the ground again and let out a defeated cry. Helpless, he lay there in the rocky ditch.

The sun was in Fernando's eyes when he gazed up.

The driver of the black Saturn had found him. The man stood at the top of the ditch—a dark silhouette against the noon sun. Fernando couldn't see his face. But he saw the policeman's nightstick in his hand. "Why are you doing this?" Fernando whimpered.

Coming toward him, the man shook his head. He slowly raised the nightstick. "Stupid little shit," he grumbled. "You shouldn't have been hitchhiking in the first place. . . ."

Fernando squeezed his eyes shut. He heard the nightstick whipping through the air—right next to his ear—and then a crack.

He didn't hear anything after that.

Leavenworth—Monday, 12:20 p.m.

"I'm okay now," Mrs. Pollack-Martin said. She was sitting in one of the cushioned easy chairs in the lobby. A nurse in purple scrubs hovered over her, taking her blood pressure, while Greta, the receptionist, fanned her with a copy of *People* magazine. "I'm so sorry about the flowers," Mrs. Pollack-Martin went on. "I don't know what happened. . . ."

Collin sat on an ottoman in front of her. Every time she met his gaze, she looked away. The nurse had pushed up Mrs. Pollack-Martin's sleeve to strap on the Velcro cuff, and Collin could see the pink burn scars on her thin, pale arm.

"Really, everyone, I'm fine," she insisted. "Thank you, Sheila. And Greta, I'm sorry again about the flowers. I'll pay for the vase. . . ."

"Oh, don't sweat the small stuff," the receptionist said, retreating toward her desk. "It was no antique. Five-ninety-nine at Target."

The Velcro made a loud ripping noise as the nurse took off the blood pressure cuff. She patted Mrs. Pollack-Martin on the shoulder. "You're all right," she said. "Just sit there for a few minutes, catch your breath, and let this young man look after you." She stashed the blood-pressure-gauging device in a doctor's bag and headed down the corridor.

His notebook in his lap, Collin was suddenly alone with her.

Mrs. Pollack-Martin self-consciously rolled down her sleeve. "I must apologize," she sighed, still not quite looking at him. With a shaky hand, she reached for the water glass on the table beside her and took a sip. "I'm not making a very good first impression, am I? It was just kind of a shock when I first saw you, because you remind me of someone from years ago— fifty years ago, in fact."

"And I look like this guy?" Collin asked.

Her eyes finally met his, and she worked up a pale smile. "Yes. He was just about your age, too."

"Do you remember his name?"

"No, I never got his name. I only saw him a couple of times—briefly."

"Something tells me this guy who looked like me wasn't very nice."

Mrs. Pollack-Martin glanced away again, and she nervously rubbed her arm.

"What did he do?" Collin pressed.

She shrugged. "I'm not certain he did anything, really. He just showed up at a very bad time." She smiled at him again. "Anyway, you didn't come here to talk about that. You wanted to ask me some questions about my books."

"Do I really look like this guy?" Collin pressed.

She nodded. "There's an uncanny resemblance, yes. But I can see the differences now. He was handsome, like you, but he also looked sort of cold and—I don't know—unfeeling. You don't seem like that at all." She shrugged and took another gulp of water. "Maybe it's how I picture him in hindsight, but even when he smiled, he seemed cruel. I suppose that sounds silly."

Collin shook his head. "It doesn't sound silly at all."

He'd seen the way Wade had smiled in those videos, and she'd just described it to a T. Collin cleared his throat. "You said he showed up at a bad time. What happened?"

"I thought you wanted to talk about my books. Wasn't that your assignment?"

"Well, I'm writing about you, too," he answered carefully. "I mean, if this was a significant event in your life, I'd like to include it in—in my paper."

"All right, then. If you really want to know . . ." She glanced over her shoulder.

Collin followed her gaze, and saw a custodian had just finished cleaning up the water, the scattered flowers, and the glass from the broken vase. Beyond him were the elevators.

Mrs. Pollack-Martin got to her feet. "Well, if I'm going to tell you this story, I'll need a glass of wine. And there's a cold ginger ale with your name on it in my refrigerator. C'mon . . ."

In the elevator, on her way up to her apartment on the fourth floor, she still seemed a bit wobbly and held on to the handrail. "You know, it's funny about getting old," she said. "I can't remember what I was doing the day before yesterday, but I can tell you everything about that day fifty years ago."

The elevator stopped and the doors opened. Collin held out his hand to help her, but she just patted his arm. "I'm all right, thanks," she said, starting down the corridor, which had handrails along the beige walls. She stopped in front of apartment 405 and took her keys out of her pocket. She put the key in the door. "Oops, looks like I forgot to lock it again," she muttered, opening the door for him.

From the living room window, Collin saw a small golf course, the river, and the mountains beyond that.

The place was nicely furnished, modest and clean, but she had the heat cranked up kind of high. A silver tabby emerged from the kitchen. The cat rubbed against his leg and meowed.

"That's Smike," she explained. "Do you know *Nicholas Nickleby*?"

Collin shook his head. "Not very well." He and the cat followed her into the kitchen.

"I named him after a character in the book." Mrs. Pollack-Martin fished a can of ginger ale and a bottle of white wine from her refrigerator. "My Smike is an illegal immigrant. I smuggled him in here four years ago when he was a kitten. We're not supposed to have pets. So in case anyone asks, you've never seen him." Getting out the glasses, she nodded at the small breakfast table—beside a window with another view of the mountains. "Have a seat. It'll be easier if you want to take notes. Besides, you can see all my book covers."

There were ten of them on the wall, all framed—her lucky ladybug series: *Ladybug's Day at the Park*, *Ladybug's European Vacation*, *Ladybug's Day Off*, and so on. Collin sat down at the table, where she had the newspaper folded over to the crossword puzzle, almost finished.

Mrs. Pollack-Martin moved the paper aside and set down his ginger ale and a glass of ice. "You might have noticed, I don't have any family pictures around," she said. "Go into any other apartment in this building, and you'll find photos on display of children and grandchildren." She glanced at her book cover collection. "I guess these are a poor substitute. I keep my family pictures in a photo album. Having them on display wouldn't really give me any comfort. You see, I lost my first husband and my three children in a hotel fire in 1962. My sister-in-law was with us. She died, too."

Mrs. Pollack-Martin turned away. Collin thought she was going to retrieve her glass of wine. Instead, she kept walking—around the corner and into the living room. Collin waited. He was about to call out to her when she returned with a photo album. She had her thumb at a certain page and opened it to show a black-and-white photo of a family posed in front of a Christmas tree. It was like something out of an early episode of *Mad Men*. She was strikingly beautiful with her big dark hair and her cocktail dress. The husband looked like one of the Mercury astronauts with his blond crew cut. He wore a suit and thin tie. The three kids, also dressed in their Sunday churchgoing finest, ranged from slightly dorky to damn cute.

Ice clinked as she sipped from her wineglass. She pointed to the photo. "That's me—way back when—and my husband, Brandon," she said. "And those are our children, Brian, Felicia, and Audrey. This was taken at Christmas 1961, eight months before the fire."

She set down her glass and pulled the photo album to her side of the table. "There's a picture of my sister-in-law, Loretta, in here. She was a very pretty girl—right around your age. Ah, yes, here she is. . . ."

Mrs. Pollack-Martin slid the album back in front of him and pointed to a studio portrait of a cute, young brunette with dark, exotic eyes. She was looking off to one side, and wore a white, round-collar blouse that looked like part of a school uniform. The photo was signed in slightly faded blue ink: *To Brandon & Irene – SMOCK, SMOCK, SMOCK! XXX – Loretta.*

Collin had no idea what *Smock, Smock, Smock* meant, but assumed it was a private joke or something.

"When we invited Loretta to come with us for the World's Fair in Seattle, she was so excited," Mrs. Pollack-Martin said. "I was thrilled to have some help with the kids. My husband and I planned to take off one night, and Loretta said she'd babysit. He'd heard about this 'Gay Nineties' nightclub at the fair. It was supposed to be the big hot spot." She smiled and sipped her wine. "This was the other kind of *gay* and the other *nineties*." Her smile waned. "I remember after the fire, feeling so horrible for my husband's mother. She was a widow. Brandon and Loretta were her only children. Both of us lost everyone in that fire. I kept thinking, if we hadn't invited Loretta to come with us, then my mother-in-law would have at least had one of her children to comfort her. At the same time, if we hadn't invited Loretta, I doubt the fire would have happened. Things might have been very different." She nodded to the collection of book covers. "I'd probably have photos of my grandchildren up there on that wall."

Collin sipped his ginger ale. He wondered if he should be taking notes—at least to keep up the pretense that he was there to interview her for an English assignment.

"Has your family been in the Seattle area for long, Collin? Do any of them remember the World's Fair in 1962?"

He shrugged. "I think my grandfather was away at military school at the time."

"Well, it was about the biggest thing to happen for *everyone*," she said. "We lived in Wenatchee. We made our reservations at the hotel months ahead of time. The Hotel Aurora Vista had a pool, which would be perfect for the kids, since the trip was in August. I remember all of us piling into the station wagon for the drive to Seattle. This song, 'Johnny Angel,' was a big hit at the time, and Loretta had a crush on a boy in her class named Johnny Something. The song must have played on the radio five times during the trip. We all sang along with it and teased her. Everyone was laughing, even Loretta. We were all so keyed up."

She glanced down at the photo album for a moment. "We took so many pictures that first day at the fair," she said. "I think we must have shot two rolls of film. Of course, none of it survived. It all went up in smoke. But the strange thing is I still have those pictures so clearly in my mind—even though they never got developed. I remember the crowds and the smells, and the hot sun on my face that day. We saw the 'Car of the Future,' and took in the Bell Telephone exhibit. We couldn't get over the new touchtone phones they were introducing—and all the other innovations. Oh, and the food—from all over the world! No one had ever heard of Belgian waffles before this. The kids stuffed their faces at the Food Circus. There were so many exhibits and international shops. Everything seemed so futuristic with the Space Needle and the Monorail. At one point, my husband and Brian went to the space exhibit while Loretta and I took the girls to the little amusement park attached to the fair. That's where I first saw the young man. He seemed to be following us. Loretta thought he was handsome. He was just about her age, and I think she might have been encouraging him a little, too. But there was something about him I didn't like. I couldn't put my finger on it at the time. Anyway, I took my older girl, Felicia, on the Ferris wheel. And looking down, I noticed Loretta talking with the young man." She looked across the table at Collin. "His hair was exactly like yours. . . ."

He realized it was still slicked back from when he splashed water on his face down in the lobby restroom.

"I remember when we finished with the Ferris wheel ride, I went to look for Loretta and Audrey, and they'd disappeared. It took ten minutes before we found each other. I asked Loretta what she and that boy were talking about. Apparently, they had talked about Marilyn Monroe, who had just committed suicide. It had happened the day before we'd left for Seattle—so sad. Anyway, I asked Loretta if she knew this young man's name or where he was from. Loretta claimed she didn't know. But she let it slip that he'd asked where she was staying in town. I remember saying to her, 'You didn't tell him, did you?' I mean, he was a complete stranger. Loretta gave me an odd look, and said, 'Of course not.' But somehow I knew she was lying."

As Mrs. Pollack-Martin spoke, Collin could almost see the amusement park and all the rides in the shadow of the Space Needle. He could hear people screaming and laughing over the canned carnival music. He'd never been to that amusement park, and wasn't even sure if it was still there. But somehow she'd made him *recollect* it.

"That night, after dinner, we were exhausted," Mrs. Pollack-Martin continued. "I'd put Audrey to bed in the connecting room. Felicia was going to share the twin bed with her, while Loretta had the other bed. The hotel had gotten a cot for Brian. With them all crammed into that one small room, we weren't sure how it was going to work out. But everyone was so pooped and so happy to have air-conditioning, I don't think they cared where they slept. The kids were in their pajamas, watching TV in my husband's and my room. Loretta had gone to sit out by the hotel pool, and said she'd be back in time to watch *Hawaiian Eye* at nine o'clock. She wasn't even gone an hour, but I have a feeling she might have met that young man from the amusement park. Of course, I'll never know. She came back a little after nine, and the kids moved into the connecting room with her. I checked in on them around nine-thirty. Both my girls were asleep. Brian was sitting at the foot of Loretta's bed, watching TV. Loretta was on top of it in her nightgown, painting her toenails. I blew them both a kiss and ducked back into our room—my husband's and mine. That was the last time I saw them alive."

The cat jumped into her lap, and Mrs. Pollack-Martin absently stroked its silver coat. Collin felt a bit self-conscious, because she kept looking right at him. Tears filled her eyes.

"A little before ten, I thought I heard someone whispering right outside our window. I put my ear to the connecting door, and heard the TV still going. I figured it was nothing. The Hotel Aurora Vista was long and L-shaped, with two floors. Every room had an outside entrance with a window beside it. We had a second-floor corner unit, near the stairs outside. So—it wasn't so alarming to hear voices or doors closing. People passed by our window to get to their rooms. Still, I told the police about it later. I don't think they cared. They were fixated on the fact that when I left our room, my husband was lighting up a Newport. We'd decided to have a nightcap, and I'd volunteered to go fetch the ice. I left the door open a crack. I remember I had on Capri pants, sandals, and a sleeveless top. When I stepped out of our room with the ice bucket, I smelled gasoline. I thought someone's car had a leak or something. Our room looked down on the parking lot, but we had a Space Needle view, too. The rooms in back of us were poolside. The ice and vending machines were there—on the opposite corner of the hotel. I lingered a couple of minutes by the pool. It was such a beautiful night.

"On my way back to our room, I spotted the young man from the fair. He was heading out of the parking lot—on foot. He looked over his shoulder back at the hotel. I don't know if he noticed me or not. But he ducked behind some bushes. A few moments later, I heard tires screeching. I thought he must have come there looking for Loretta. That was when I smelled the smoke. Then, at the bottom of the stairs, I heard a crackling noise . . . and my children . . ."

Mrs. Pollack-Martin winced, and her voice became shaky. "My kids, they were screaming. I raced up the stairs, and saw in the windows of both rooms that the curtains were on fire. Everything else was just black from all the smoke trapped in there. I dropped the ice bucket and reached for the door to my kids' room. The knob singed my hand, but I tried to open it anyway. I pushed and pulled—and nothing. Then I tried my husband's and my room. It was the same thing. I remember calling to my children to get down on the floor. They were coughing and—and screaming for me. . . ."

Mrs. Pollack-Martin started to cry. "I banged on the window, and finally grabbed the ice bucket. It was one of those heavy, clunky insulated things. I used it to smash the glass. It just made the fire worse, and the flames shot out. It was like an explosion. I could barely see anything, but I reached into where the fire and black smoke billowed out. I could smell my flesh burning. At the same time, I felt one of my children's hands grab mine. But it was only for a few seconds, and then they let go. I'll never know if it was Brian or Felicia. . . ."

She took a napkin from the holder on the tabletop, then wiped her eyes. "Some other hotel guests had come out of their rooms. One of them had called the fire department. With all the smoke, I couldn't see any-one—and I could hardly breathe. All I wanted to do was climb in there and get to my kids. I didn't even re-alize my blouse had caught on fire until someone knocked me down and covered me with a blanket. Most of my hair burnt off, too."

She sighed and shook her head. "If that person hadn't rescued me, maybe I could have pulled one of my children out of the fire. But I doubt it."

"I'm so sorry," Collin whispered.

"I spent nearly four months in the hospital," Mrs. Pollack-Martin continued, more controlled now. "The investigators said it appeared as if my husband might have hit his head on a table in the room. They think he stumbled, knocked himself out, and the cigarette he was smoking started the fire."

She dabbed her eyes, and frowned. "Brandon had a couple of drinks that night, but he wasn't stumbling, staggering drunk. And I'm sorry, but I wasn't gone very long. A stray cigarette couldn't have started a fire of that magnitude. Both rooms were swallowed up in flames in a matter of minutes. The fires must have started near the doors, otherwise the doorknobs on the outside wouldn't have gotten scorching-hot so quickly. I told the investigators that from my hospital bed. And I told them about the young man from the fair.

"You know, talking to the police was so strange, because I couldn't see their faces. They all had to wear surgical masks in my room. Burn patients are very susceptible to germs. One little drop of saliva can botch up the entire healing process, maybe even kill you. So everything around me had to be sterilized, and everyone had to wear hospital gowns and surgical masks. I was so lonely and isolated. I didn't see anyone's face for months—except on TV."

She let out a long sigh, and Smike jumped off her lap. "Anyway, the newspapers called it an *accident* and turned the whole thing into a cautionary tale for the tourists. *Don't smoke in your hotel bed.* The burns on my arms and torso were horribly painful, but what hurt even more was having everyone think my sweet husband had gotten drunk, fallen, and started that fire."

"Didn't they try to track down the guy from the fair?" Collin asked.

Mrs. Pollack-Martin took another swallow of wine, draining the glass. "They took me seriously enough to show me some mug shots of juvenile delinquents— based on my description of the young man. But I didn't see him in any of the photos. I heard they had a suspect, this young man who might have killed another family at a hotel, but he was hit by a train. That was happening when I was having skin graft operations, so I was pretty out of it at the time."

"Did you ever see a photo of the guy who was hit by a train?" Collin asked.

She shrugged. "He could have been in one of those mug shots the police showed me, I don't know. That entire period is like a fog to me now. I was in so much agony, physically and mentally. Plus I was loopy from pain medications. By the time I got out of the hospital, I'd become numb to everything. You'd think a good mother wouldn't give up, that she'd dedicate herself to finding the killer of her family. But I was weak—and so uncertain. I mean, I'll never know if that young man really had anything to do with the fire. Did he let himself into our room—after I'd left the door open? Did he hit my husband over the head, and then set fire to the kids' and our room? Why in the world would he have done that? Because my sister-in-law had flirted with him? It doesn't make sense. I realized I'd drive myself crazy if I didn't put it all behind me and move on.

"So—I went back to Wenatchee, taught school, got married again, and I wrote some children's books— based on stories I used to tell Brian, Felicia, and Audrey." She seemed to work up a smile. "I guess that's what you really came here to discuss. I'm sorry to go on and on about the fire. Except for my second husband, Jim, I haven't talked about it with anyone else. I don't know why I picked you to unload on. I'm sorry, Collin."

He shook his head. "No, it's okay. I'm glad you told me." He squirmed in the kitchen chair. "About this young man, you never saw him again? The police didn't give you any more leads or anything?"

She reached over and patted his arm. He could see the scars on her hand now.

"No, nothing," she answered. "I stopped thinking about him. I even managed to forget what he looked like . . ."

Collin looked up, and her eyes locked with his.

". . . until I saw you," she said.

CHAPTER ELEVEN

Bainbridge Island ferry—Monday, 6:20 p.m.

From the railing along the ferry's top deck, Collin stared at the terminal lights in the distance. A chilly wind off the choppy gray water whipped through him, and he turned up the collar of his red fall jacket. The setting sun left streaks of orange, gold, and scarlet on the darkening horizon.

A twenty-something couple with their arms around each other came and stood beside him. Collin heard the girl tell her boyfriend: "Wow, it looks like the sky is on fire."

He thought of Mrs. Pollack's family, and remembered the scars on her arm and her hand. He remembered how she'd looked into his eyes as she'd told him about the fatal hotel fire. Walking him to her door, she'd apologized again. She'd wondered aloud why she had unburdened herself on him, a complete stranger.

Collin thought about it, and realized he wasn't a stranger. She'd first seen him fifty years ago. So maybe Mrs. Pollack needed to look in the face of the young man who had taken her family away from her—and tell him just what he'd destroyed.

Collin moved away from the nuzzling couple so he could be alone.

Why was this happening to him? He couldn't help wondering if he'd been Wade Grinnell in a former life. Did he really look like the guy—or had Mrs. Pollack-Martin just seen something inside him?

It didn't make sense. As far-fetched as it seemed, he thought about reincarnation. But if he'd been Wade Grinnell in a previous life, wouldn't he have recognized the family he'd killed? Four hours ago, he'd looked at their photos and felt nothing but pity. He certainly should have had some kind of flashback or recall studying Loretta's photo. But she didn't look familiar at all.

From the Seattle ferry terminal earlier, he'd called his grandparents. He'd told his grandmother that he was busy with a class project at the school library and he would be home around six-thirtyish. She'd seemed to believe him.

Collin shivered. It was cold out on the top deck. He thought about telling his grandparents what was going on—or at least some of it. But they'd been through enough with his mother's murder three months ago. They really didn't need to hear he was going crazy.

He heard a bell sound, and then a recorded voice came over the loudspeaker: *"Your attention, please. We're now arriving at our destination. Please take a few moments to make sure you have all your personal belongings before disembarking the vessel. Drivers and passengers, please return to your vehicles at this time. Walk-on passengers, disembark using the overhead walkway. . . ."*

The twenty-something couple at the deck railing turned and strolled away, their arms still around each other. Collin took one last look at the ferry terminal

and all the lights—looming straight ahead. Then he
ducked into the main cabin, where he got a welcome
blast of warm air. Shuddering gratefully, he headed for
the stairwell to the parking deck.

He found the Taurus and noticed a folded piece of
paper on the windshield, tucked under the wiper. Mystified, Collin grabbed the slip of paper and unfolded it.
The note was written in block letters:

*SHOULDN'T YOU HAVE BEEN
IN SCHOOL TODAY?*

Collin glanced around, wondering if somebody was
sitting inside one of the cars, watching him right now.
He thought about that solitary boat out on the bay for
so many nights in the last several weeks.

Suddenly, his cell phone rang. It startled him. He
grabbed the phone out of his jacket pocket. He thought
it must be the person who had left him the note. Obviously, they were still around here on the ferry someplace.

But Gail's name and number came up on the caller
ID screen. After how he'd behaved toward her yesterday in the car, Collin was glad she still wanted to talk
with him. He shoved the note inside his pants pocket,
and then clicked on his phone.

"Hey, Gail," he said.

"Was it you?" she asked, a bit shrill.

"What?" He put a finger in his other ear. On either
side of him, drivers and passengers were climbing into
their cars. All the talking and door-slamming seemed
to echo in the parking deck area. Collin looked around
one more time for anyone who might be spying on
him.

"Was it you?" she repeated.

He unlocked his car and climbed inside, behind the wheel. "Was it me—what?"

"You've been acting so weird, and you weren't in school today," she said edgily. "The other night you were asking where my mother keeps her purse. I just want to give you a chance to be honest with me before I say something to my parents or the police."

"What? Is this about yesterday in the car when you hypnotized me?"

"No, I'm talking about *today*, Collin. Someone broke into our house. They stole a bunch of stuff. . . ."

"My God," he murmured. "Is everyone okay?"

"Yes, we'll live. But my bedroom got the worst of it." Her voice cracked. "They tore the place apart, and stole my laptop. They even went through my journal. Was it you?"

"God, no, it wasn't me, Gail. I swear."

"Why weren't you at school today? Where were you?"

"I drove to Central Washington," he said. "I've been gone all day. I'm on the ferry right now. It's just pulling into the dock. In fact, I need to hang up soon. The lane I'm parked in is about to start moving. . . ." Up ahead, he could see the ferry crew directing the traffic off the boat. The drivers in front of him in line were gunning their engines.

"I'm not sure I believe you," she said.

"Can't you hear the other cars?" he asked—over all the rumbling.

"What were you doing over in Central Washington?"

"Following a lead I had about that—that slimy guy I turned into when you hypnotized me. It wasn't an act, Gail."

"Well, if you really have a split personality and you

can't remember some of the shit you say and do, how can you be so sure you didn't break into our house?"

"Like I told you, I've been off the island since eight o'clock this morning." He switched the phone to his other ear, put the key in the ignition, and started up the car. "Listen, I've got to hang up. Can I swing by? I'd really like to talk with you. I'll explain everything."

"Fine, yeah," she said. "I'd like to look you in the eye when you tell me again you had nothing to do with our house getting broken into."

"All right, then I'll see you in a few minutes," Collin said. "Okay?"

There was no response.

"Gail?" He realized she'd hung up.

The car in front of him started moving. Rattled, Collin clicked off the phone, and tossed it on the passenger seat cushion. Then he followed the other cars off the boat.

"Hey, guess what?" said Chris Pelham, swinging open the front door. Gail's ten-year-old brother had a big, excited smile on his freckled face. He didn't wait for Collin to answer. "We were robbed! The police were here and everything, Collin. You just missed them. . . ."

Standing on the Pelhams' front porch, he nodded soberly. "Yeah, I know. Gail told me. I'm really sorry to hear it."

"They didn't steal anything from my room," Chris said. "All my Xbox games are still here, and—"

"Christopher, don't leave Collin standing outside in the cold," Mrs. Pelham said, coming up behind her son. She was heavyset with near-shoulder-length beige hair and a pleasant, dimpled smile. She wore a loose, un-tucked navy blouse over a pair of jeans. Collin liked Gail's mother, who possessed a sort of laid-back, down-to-earth poise. But tonight she seemed haggard and tense. "Invite him in, honey," she said, patting Chris on the shoulder. "And run upstairs and tell your sister Collin's waiting for her."

"HEY, GAIL!" the boy yelled, turning away and bolting toward the stairs. "Hey, Gail, Collin's here! Gail?"

Mrs. Pelham managed a weak smile. "Hi, Collin, come on in. We're all a little—*discombobulated* right now. Mr. Pelham's on the phone with the insurance company, and Gail's upstairs, cleaning up the mess in there. We're still trying to figure out what's missing. . . ."

Collin stepped into their front hall and glanced toward the dining room on his right. The breakfront cabinet doors were open, and some of the drawers were still sticking out. To his left, their hall closet door was open, too, and the light was on. Collin remembered finding all the closet doors open with the lights on in the rental house the morning after his mother's murder.

"When did it happen?" he asked.

"Sometime today while I was at work," she sighed. "I came back with Chris after picking him up from band practice, and the place was turned upside down. Anyway, now all of us have to change our Social Security numbers—and any account numbers they might have seen. There's a whole concern about identity theft. Oh, Collin, this has been so horrible, awful . . . ," she trailed off, and put a hand to her forehead. "I'm just glad you're here. Gail could really use a friend right now. . . ."

Collin looked up and saw Gail slowly descending

the stairs. Her red hair was in a ponytail. She wore jeans and a black, long-sleeved T-shirt. She was glaring at him.

"Hi," Collin said.

She just nodded. Then she brushed past her mother and took a jacket out of the open closet. She put it on.

"Where are you off to?" Mrs. Pelham asked her.

"I'm just going outside to talk with Collin."

"Don't be silly," her mother said. "If you want privacy, you can talk downstairs. Collin, would you like something to drink? Water? A soda?"

"He's not staying long, Mom," Gail said coolly. Then she opened the front door for him.

Collin turned to her mother. "Thanks anyway, Mrs. Pelham."

He followed Gail outside. She closed the door behind him. She stopped on their front porch, folded her arms, and glowered at him.

Collin pulled some receipts out of his pocket. "Okay, first of all, here," he said, handing her one receipt after another. "My ferry ticket stubs . . . eight-fifteen this morning and just about an hour ago in Seattle, dated today. There's a gas station receipt from a Chevron on Highway 2 in Monroe at ten o'clock this morning. And here's a receipt from Starbucks at one-fifty this afternoon. Look at the location, Leavenworth, Washington, and the date, today, October first." He watched Gail examine the scraps of paper. "I was off the island all day. I couldn't have come back here and robbed your house."

With a sigh, Gail stuffed the receipts back into his hand. "Okay, so maybe you didn't," she murmured. "But why did they pick on me? They took some silver from the dining room, and some jewelry from my mom's dresser. But I got the worst of it, Collin. They stole my laptop and iPod station, and, like I said, they even looked in my diary—for God's sake—at least, I think they did. I found it opened up on my bedroom floor. Why would a burglar want to read my diary? And there was stuff on my computer I didn't want anyone else to see. Why me?" She started to tear up, and quickly wiped her eyes. "You know what else they stole? My Pluto snow globe. I've had it since I was a little girl. What good is that to some burglar? Why would they take that? It's not worth much."

She glanced toward the front yard. "You know, I can't help feeling like they're still around here, watching this house, watching me." She turned to him. "Do you think it was someone from school? I mean, some of those girls really hate me. Do you think they could have talked one of their dumbass boyfriends into doing this?"

Collin shrugged helplessly. "Maybe, only—well, I hate to admit it, but you might be right to think I had something to do with this."

She squinted at him. "Now what are you telling me?"

"Seeing how they left your house—with the drawers and the closet doors open, it reminded me of when it happened to me and my mother in the last place I lived in—in Seattle."

"You got robbed, too?" she asked.

"That was just part of it," he said, moving over to the porch railing. He gazed out at their front lawn. The trees were half-bare, and a light wind scattered a few leaves across their lawn. "Listen, Gail, I haven't been completely honest with you and Fernando—or anyone else at school. My mother didn't die in a car accident.

Someone broke into our rental house in July. They stole some stuff, and they killed my mother and her boyfriend."

"Are you serious?" he heard Gail murmur.

Collin nodded. "I was asleep upstairs the whole time." He looked through the front window into the Pelhams' empty living room. He didn't want anyone inside the house to hear him. "My mom's boyfriend was this scuzzy drug dealer. The police were pretty sure the killings were drug-related. Supposedly, the guys who did it are dead now themselves. . . ."

"Wait a minute," she said. "I know about this. I saw it on TV. That didn't happen to you. That happened to Collin Cox. . . ."

He half-smiled at her. "The Stamplers are my grand-parents. It's my mom's maiden name. I decided to en-roll as Collin Stampler so people at school wouldn't treat me like a freak."

A hand over her mouth, Gail gaped at him. "My God, you're *Collin Cox*. All this time . . . I can't believe I didn't recognize you. . . ."

"I'm sorry I didn't tell you. I was kind of working up to it."

"This is incredible. *Collin Cox*. I've been hanging out with Collin Cox. . . ."

"Nice to meet you," he said glumly. He stuck out his hand.

Gail laughed. She shook it enthusiastically, and didn't let go.

"Listen, I wouldn't be so excited about it," he warned. "I'm pretty screwed up right now. I don't know what's happening with this Wade Grinnell guy who took over when you hypnotized me. That second time you hypnotized me, he was talking pretty casually about people getting stabbed. . . ."

Gail let go of his hand and stepped back.

"This Wade, he . . ." Collin hesitated. He didn't want to tell her that Wade Grinnell was a suspected serial killer who had been dead for fifty years. He still couldn't quite believe it himself. He sighed. "Well, you saw for yourself what a slime-bucket he was. And I can't remember anything I said or did while I was under. So— I can't really be sure if he didn't emerge that night my mom was murdered."

"But it was all over the Internet," Gail said. "The guys who murdered your mother were killed. You just said so earlier, case closed. Besides, I don't know much about forensics and all that jazz. But if you— well, if you'd stabbed your mother and shot her boyfriend, don't you think the police would have picked up some kind of evidence of that?"

Collin couldn't look at her. "Maybe Wade Grinnell didn't kill them. But who's to say he didn't come out that night and see the killers? He might have even helped."

"Jesus, you're scaring me," she whispered.

"It scares me, too." He took her hand in his. "Listen, Gail, there's a way of finding out for sure. You could hypnotize me again."

She shook her head. "No, I—"

"Please? I need to know if this Wade person had anything to do with their murders. . . ."

"I'm sorry, Collin." She let go of his hand. "I don't want to go through that again. You need to find someone else to hypnotize you. In fact, you should talk to a therapist about this. A lot of them do hypnosis, too, like my aunt. She's in Seattle now. You should go see her."

Collin frowned. He'd hoped once he told Gail the truth about who he really was, she'd want to help him.

Wouldn't a big performing arts fan make some concessions for a former child star? But she was afraid, and he didn't blame her. He was scared of Wade, too.

"Listen, I'm sorry about your mother, Collin." She stroked his arm. "And I'm sorry you're having these—*episodes*. In fact, I kind of feel responsible. I'm the one who talked you into getting hypnotized in the first place. But—well, what does any of this have to do with our house getting robbed?"

"You said you think someone's watching you. I know exactly what you mean. I feel the same way." He reached into his pocket and took out the folded-up note. "In fact, take a look at this. Someone on the ferry left this on the windshield of my car today."

Gail studied it. "Are you sure it's not just a stalker? After all, you're famous. . . ." She handed the note back to him. "And I still don't understand what this has to do with our house getting broken into."

"I have a feeling my mom's killers aren't really dead," he admitted. "If Wade Grinnell emerged that night, he could have seen or done something I don't remember. These killers—if they're still around—they might think I know a lot more than I do. That's why I think someone's keeping tabs on me. If I'm right, then they must have seen us hanging out together, Gail. They probably figured I've told you something."

"My God," she whispered. "So that's why they tore my room apart—and took my computer and looked at my diary. . . ."

"My guess is they're checking our emails to each other. Did you write anything in your diary about me?"

"Well, yes, but that was before I knew you were *Collin Cox*." She started rubbing her arms as if she had a chill. "So you're saying the people who broke into our house may have killed your mother and her boyfriend?"

"It's possible," he said. "I don't know for sure. . . ."

"Then we need to tell the police."

Collin sighed. "The police think my mother's killers are dead. And when you tell them what I just told you, they're going to think I'm bat-shit crazy. Hell, maybe I am. But if you could hypnotize me again, Wade might tell us something. He could confirm a lot of this."

"You talk about him like he's somebody else," she said.

"He is," Collin replied.

She shook her head. "No, I'm sorry. I can't hypnotize you—at least, not tonight. I've had enough excitement for one day. I still say we should call the police." She warily eyed the bushes on either side of their porch. "How do you know these people aren't somewhere out there, looking at us right now?"

"Gail, if they've seen your diary and everything on your computer, they'll know you didn't have a clue about who I am—or about my mother's murder. They probably won't be back. I doubt whoever's responsible for this robbery would come back to the crime scene so soon." He took hold of her hand again. "Listen, before we call the cops—and they laugh us into oblivion— could you at least *think* about putting me under again?"

Her eyes searched his for a moment. "Okay," she finally sighed. "I'll sleep on it—if I can sleep at all tonight. Maybe by morning, the cops will find whoever pulled this break-in." She let out a stunned little laugh and shook her head at him. "I still can't believe I'm standing here talking to *Collin Cox*."

"Could you do me a favor and keep it secret for a while?"

"Can I tell my folks, at least?"

"I guess. Just ask them to keep it under wraps, okay?"

"Sure. You know, I was just thinking once I go back inside, I need to get on the Internet and Google you. But—well, wouldn't you know? Some asshole stole my computer."

Collin managed to laugh. "Would you like me to pick you up in the morning? I can drive you to school."

Gail seemed to blush a little. "Well, sure. That sounds nice. Is around a quarter to eight okay with you?"

"I'll be here." Collin wanted to kiss her. But he just squeezed her hand. "Thanks, Gail. Thanks for not laughing at me."

She nodded and smiled. "You're welcome, Collin Cox."

The man sat alone in the black Saturn, parked two houses down and across the street from the Pelhams'. From the driver's seat, he watched Collin Cox climb inside his Taurus and back out of the driveway.

The man held a snow globe with a Disney figure inside. He wasn't sure if it was Pluto or Goofy. Whatever, he'd taken a shine to it. He kept turning it upside down and letting the snow collect. Then he'd turn it right side up again, and watch the little blizzard swirling inside the globe.

There was nothing in the girl's journal and nothing in her laptop hard drive. She probably didn't have a clue what was going on.

Still, she was a loose end.

She stood on the front porch for another minute after Collin Cox's car had pulled away down the block.

He turned the globe upside down again. While the snow accumulated in the glass ball, he watched Gail Pelham step inside the house. She looked like a nice kid—from a nice family.

Too bad it just wasn't going to be their night.

Dee switched on the outside lights. "Lord, Andy, why you couldn't have done this over the weekend—or at least in the daytime—is beyond me."

She'd made his grandfather put on his fall jacket, and said the chicken casserole dinner could keep for another fifteen minutes. "Now, don't try to carry a lazy man's load!" she called to Collin and his grandfather as they headed out to the back patio.

"Lazy man's load" was another one of his grandparents' expressions, but Collin had this one figured out. It meant they shouldn't carry too much at one time to avoid taking more trips. Collin and his grandfather were going to move the patio furniture into the garage for the winter.

They started with the round wrought-iron table that had a glass top. They carried it together, maneuvering up a well-lit stone pathway to the garage's side door. "Listen, kiddo," his grandfather said, panting a bit. "I didn't want to say anything in front of your grandmother. But where did you go today?"

Collin was careful to keep the table balanced. "Pardon?"

"I spoke to my friend Art Honeycutt. He mentioned he saw you on the eight-fifteen ferry to Seattle this morning. He said you were alone. I didn't know the schools were on holiday, Collin. . . ." He teetered a bit as they approached the garage. "Hold it. Let's put this down for a second. Careful of the walkway lights. . . ."

They set the table on the sloped path. "Anyway," his grandfather continued. "I called the school and talked to a very nice lady in the principal's office. I asked if they had you marked as absent today, and she said yes. So where'd you go off to?"

Collin shrugged. "I'm sorry, I just—well, I wanted to check out the old neighborhood. I was feeling kind of sentimental. I didn't do anything except drive around for a while."

His grandfather frowned at him across the tilted table. He looked so disappointed.

"I'm sorry, Grandpa," he said. "It was a spur-of-the-moment thing. I know it was really dumb to skip school like that. But once I got on the ferry, there was no turning back."

"You told your grandmother you were at the school library."

"I know," Collin muttered. "I'm sorry I lied. It—it won't happen again."

"Well, I guess what your grandmother doesn't know won't hurt her. I straightened it out with the school and told them you were running an errand for me. C'mon . . ." His grandfather hoisted up his half of the table, and they lugged it into the garage. "Here's fine," he announced. They set the table in the corner, a few feet away from Collin's Taurus.

Collin hoped that was the end of the discussion. But as they started back on the stone trail to the patio, his grandfather stopped and put a hand on his shoulder. "I've noticed you've been acting kind of strange since yesterday morning—withdrawn," he said. "You haven't been yourself. Your grandmother and I are concerned about you."

The irony of that comment "You haven't been yourself" wasn't lost on Collin. He sighed. "Like I said,

I've been feeling sentimental—and blue. I didn't mean to worry you guys."

"You know, I didn't do such a bang-up job with your mother. I should have seen some of the signs when she first started pulling away from us. I was too busy running a company to see that my daughter was skipping school, disappearing for hours at a time, and then lying to your grandmother and me." He shook his head. "I just can't let that happen all over again, not with you. It would kill me."

"It won't," Collin murmured.

"You know, you can tell me anything, and I'll try to understand. That said, can I ask you a question? I promise I won't be upset—as long as you answer me truthfully."

Collin felt a little pang in his gut. With reluctance, he nodded. "Go ahead."

The old man's eyes narrowed at him. "Did you sneak a friend into the house late last night after your grandmother and I went to bed?"

Collin blinked. "What?"

"I got up to go to the bathroom around a quarter to four this morning, and thought I heard someone talking. It didn't sound like you, so I went down the hallway and stood outside your door. I heard this fellow mumbling something. I couldn't make out what he was saying. But it wasn't you, I could tell that much."

Collin stared at him. "I—I don't know what you heard. I must have fallen asleep with the TV on low or something."

His grandfather didn't say anything. He just frowned.

"Grandpa, I didn't sneak anyone into the house last night, I swear. I mean, you guys have been cool about Fernando spending the night here. If I wanted a friend to sleep over, I'd have asked you. Besides, I don't have any other friends." He sighed. "Anyway, I was alone—and asleep. You must have heard the TV."

Old Andy shrugged, and seemed to work up a smile. "You're right. It was probably the TV I heard. I'm hungry. Let's go eat. We can put the rest of this stuff away later."

As he headed up the stone path to the patio with his grandfather, Collin was quiet. He'd been wondering earlier if Wade Grinnell ever came out while he was asleep.

Now he had his answer.

His grandmother's chicken noodle casserole had been delicious, but Collin figured he needed a blowtorch to clean the dried, burnt crust off the casserole dish. He was washing the dishes after dinner—to give Dee a break. He was used to it after so many years of cleaning up after his mother. He decided to let the casserole dish soak, and turned off the water. Drying his hands, he pulled the note out of his pocket again:

*SHOULDN'T YOU HAVE BEEN
IN SCHOOL TODAY?*

The house phone rang. His grandmother must have picked it up in the study. After a few moments, she called to him: "Collin, honey, telephone!"

Shoving the note back in his pocket, he grabbed the cordless off the kitchen counter. "Thanks, Dee," he said into the phone. Then he heard a click as she hung up the other extension. "Hello?"

"Collin, this is Marisa Ryan. Do you—do you have any idea where Fernando is?"

"Oh, hi, Mrs. Ryan," he said. The question had

thrown him for a loop. "Um, no. Isn't he answering his cell?"

"No, and I've tried him several times."

"Well, I missed school today. I haven't talked with him since we got together yesterday afternoon. Did you try calling Gail Pelham?"

"Yes, I just talked with her. Gail and Fernando have history class together, and she said he wasn't there today. He left for school at seven-forty-five this morning, and apparently never got there. You missed school, too. Gail said something about you going for a drive to Central Washington. Please, I'm getting really worried here. If you boys played hooky together, and you're covering for Fernando—"

"I'm not, Mrs. Ryan. I'm telling you the truth. I haven't heard from him all day."

There was silence on the other end of the line.

He wondered if Mrs. Ryan knew how much Fernando traveled by thumb. Collin had always considered it a pretty risky way to get around. He didn't want to scare Mrs. Ryan or betray Fernando's confidence by saying anything. "Have you talked with the police yet?" he asked.

"Not yet," she said, her voice quivering.

"Sometimes he likes to go to the Kitsap Mall in Silverdale. Maybe we should call there and have him paged."

"I'll try that. Thanks. Listen, I've talked to Fernando about the hitchhiking. Do you know if he's still doing it?"

Collin hesitated. "I—I think so, once in a while."

She let out a frail sigh on the other end. "All right, if I can't get him at the mall, I'm calling the police—and the hospitals, too."

"Would you like me to come over?" he asked.

"No, it's okay. But will you get in touch with me if you hear from him?"

"Of course," Collin said. "And—please, call me as soon as you find out anything. And really, let me know if there's anything I can do."

"You can say a prayer that Fernando's all right."

"I'm sure he's okay, Mrs. Ryan."

As Collin hung up the phone, he felt a little sick and short of breath.

The last thing he'd said to Fernando's mother had been a lie. He didn't think his friend was okay.

In fact, he had a terrible feeling it was already too late for prayers.

CHAPTER TWELVE

"Don't go near it!" someone screamed.

Behind him, several ferry passengers stood near the bottom of the stairwell. Collin stared at the only car in the cavernous parking area. The old sixties-style station wagon was on fire. Flames shot up from the vehicle and licked the ceiling. Smoke swelled up into a black cloud that hovered over the entire space. The gasoline smell was overpowering.

All the while, the ferry churned forward on choppy waters. Beyond the smoldering haze, Collin could see they were approaching the Seattle dock. He saw the skyline, the Space Needle, and the big Ferris wheel on the pier. He heard faint carnival-type music.

Collin moved closer to the fiery station wagon. He felt the heat on his face. He heard children screaming past the crackling flames. Their distressed shrieks were heartbreaking. Through all the smoke, he saw something move inside the car. A little hand vainly banged against the window.

Collin reached for the door handle, and a trail of flames shot up his arm.

He suddenly sat up in bed.

His heart was racing. In the darkness, he blindly fumbled for the nightstand lamp until he found the switch and turned it on. He rubbed his eyes, and then felt his chest. His T-shirt was soaked through with perspiration. He glanced at the clock on his nightstand. The last time he'd looked at it had been almost four hours ago: 2:50 AM. He couldn't believe he'd actually fallen asleep. He'd been so worried about Fernando—along with everything else.

He threw off the sheets and staggered out of bed. Pulling the sweat-soaked T-shirt over his head, he dug another from his dresser and put it on.

It was too early to call the Ryans about Fernando.

Shuffling into the bathroom, Collin opened the hamper to toss in his soiled T-shirt. But he caught a strong waft of gasoline, and hesitated. He reached into the hamper and dug out the jeans he'd been wearing yesterday. It didn't make sense. He'd thrown the jeans over the back of his desk chair before going to bed. He'd planned to wear them again today.

Now they were in his hamper, and they smelled of gasoline.

"What's going on?" he muttered under his breath. Dumping the T-shirt and jeans in the bin, he hurried to his desk, where his red jacket was still draped over the chair. He sniffed it and smelled traces of gasoline. His shoes should have been by the desk chair, too. Bewildered, he checked his closet and saw his Converse All Stars on the floor. They were muddy. When had that happened? The shoes had been clean when he'd kicked them off earlier tonight.

Collin switched on the desk lamp and studied the carpet in his bedroom.

It was spotless, no footprints.

Then something occurred to him. Within the last hour or two while he'd slept, Wade Grinnell must have gone out. And he'd come back, stinking of gasoline and smoke. He must have taken off the muddy shoes before stepping back inside the house.

This time, Wade had left no footprints.

"You didn't by any chance go out looking for Fernando in the wee, small hours last night, did you?" his grandfather asked over his coffee cup, which had *World's Greatest Golfer* on it.

Collin sat across from him at the breakfast table with the Frosted Flakes box by his cereal bowl and orange juice. He didn't have much of an appetite this morning. Twice he'd tried to phone the Ryans' house for an update on Fernando. Both times, it had gone to voice mail, and he'd left messages. No one had called him back yet.

Collin guessed his grandfather had delayed his usual morning golf in respect for the Fernando crisis. Still, old Andy had dressed to tee off—in a green cardigan and plaid slacks.

Collin's grandmother, in her ivory-colored jacquard robe and slippers, leaned back against the kitchen counter. She never sat at the table. She always consumed her two pieces of toast with marmalade and three cups of black coffee while on her feet. And she was always tuned in to the *Today Show*. The volume was turned down on the flat-screen TV on the wall in their breakfast nook. Collin could barely hear Matt Lauer talking.

With ten minutes to go before he had to leave for school, Collin was still hoping for a call back from the Ryans—or maybe even Fernando himself. He was also wracking his brain to figure out where Wade had accumulated the mud on his Converse All Stars.

Collin had left the shoes in his closet and put on a pair of Skechers. He'd torn out a lift-and-sniff ad for Polo by Ralph Lauren from one of his grandmother's *Vanity Fair* magazines. Then he'd rubbed the cologne sample on his jacket to camouflage the gasoline smell. For some reason, he'd felt compelled to cover up whatever might have happened last night.

And now his grandfather was asking if he'd gone out in the "wee, small hours."

With a spoonful of cereal halfway to his mouth, Collin stared at him on the other side of the breakfast table. "Um, no," he said. "I just stayed put."

"Well, something woke me up," his grandfather said. "I thought I heard the garage door open and close, and the car running. It was around three-thirty this morning. I was a little concerned—especially after what you told us about your girlfriend's house getting broken into."

He put his spoon down. "Actually, Gail's not my girlfriend, Grandpa."

"I didn't see anything unusual outside," his grandfather went on. "But then I checked in on you, and you weren't in your bed. So—I came down here, and there was no sign of you. I figured you must have gotten up in the middle of the night and gone looking for your friend. So I fixed myself a scotch and waited up for you in front of the TV. . . ."

"Warm milk would have been better for you," Collin's grandmother interjected with a piece of toast in her hand. "You shouldn't drink so late at night."

His grandfather shot her a look, and then turned to Collin again. "Anyway, I fell asleep in my chair, and woke up a little before five. I was about to call your cell, but decided to check your room, and there you were in bed, sawing logs. It made me think I must be going crazy."

"That's what comes from drinking too much late at night," Dee said.

Collin shrugged. "Maybe I was in the bathroom when you checked on me the first time."

His grandfather nodded. "Probably," he grunted.

"Collin, honey," Dee said. "If you're picking up Gail this morning, you better skedaddle, or you'll both be late for school."

Five minutes later, Collin was scooting behind the wheel of his Taurus. He noticed a slight gasoline smell in there, too. Or maybe he'd just been expecting it.

The smell seemed to disappear after he'd driven with the windows open for a few blocks. In fact, all he could smell now was the Polo sample he'd rubbed on his jacket. It was like he'd taken a bath in the stuff.

He might have been able to cover up the stink on his clothes, but he couldn't do anything to change what his grandfather had seen and heard last night. Collin wished he knew what had happened while he'd slept. Was his grandfather right? Had his mysterious trip in the *wee small hours* had something to do with Fernando?

Collin turned onto Gail's street, and immediately hit the brake. His stomach clenched tight when he saw what was happening down the block. "Oh, no," he murmured.

In front of the Pelhams' house were an army of police cars and fire trucks with their lights swirling and flashing red. There were two ambulances as well. TV news vans were parked farther down the block, across the street. About fifty people stood in the middle of the road.

Collin inched farther down the street, then pulled over and parked. He stepped out of the car. His legs were a bit wobbly as he made his way toward the Pelhams' house. It was blustery out, and the wind carried the acrid smell of damp, burnt wood. He heard firemen and cops yelling at each other over the noisy crowd.

Wind gusts must have knocked over a few of the orange cones placed on the road. Yellow DO NOT CROSS police tape cordoned off the Pelhams' front yard. The police had used the bushes and trees at the yard's edge as posts for their flimsy, fluttering barricade.

He couldn't see the house yet. But he already knew. One look at the squad cars and fire trucks, and he knew. He should have known when he'd first smelled gasoline on his clothes this morning. Mrs. Pollack had smelled gasoline outside their hotel room that night fifty years ago.

Several of the bystanders were in their bathrobes. There were people with news cameras among the throng, too—and a reporter off to one side, talking into a handheld microphone. A teenage girl held her iPhone up over her head, photographing or recording what was going on at the house. Collin didn't see Gail, or Chris, or Mr. or Mrs. Pelham among the crowd. His heart sank. "No, please, God, no," he whispered.

Moving closer, he saw the Pelhams' front porch. Until just a few moments ago, he'd expected to find Gail waiting there for him.

Instead, he saw cops and firemen lingering by the bashed-in front door. The porch looked filthy. Water dripped from the roof. The pretty gray-shingled house was still standing, but nearly all the windows in front were broken. The white trim around each one was charred, and black smoke stains covered the surrounding shingles.

Ripples of water skirted over the front walkway, and the lawn looked saturated. Collin noticed the puddles of mud and soot, along with the skeletons of burnt bushes outside the basement windows. He thought about his soiled sneakers and wondered if Wade had crawled inside one of those windows.

"Well, the husband smoked, I can tell you that much," he overheard an older woman in a terrycloth robe tell her friend.

Collin turned to her. "Excuse me. Do you know if the family got out? Are they okay?"

Clutching the bathrobe lapels in front of her neck, she frowned at him and shook her head. "All four are dead. They've loaded three bodies into the ambulances so far. They haven't brought out the last one yet. Oh, such a tragedy. Did you know them?"

He started to tear up. "I'm a friend of Gail's," he heard himself say. "When—when did it happen? Do you know?"

"Around four this morning," she answered. "I'm the one who called the fire department. I woke up and heard the screaming across the street. Then I looked out and saw the light flickering in all the windows, and I knew something was wrong." She clicked her tongue and sighed. "If only I'd woken up just a few minutes earlier, maybe the firemen could have gotten to them in time. What with the wind this morning, we're lucky the fire didn't spread down the block." She turned toward the house, and nudged Collin. "Oh, look . . ."

Collin glanced at the Pelhams' house again and saw paramedics and firemen emerge from the front door carrying a stretcher. A gray plastic tarp covered the body. One of the firemen held the sheet down to keep it from blowing away. They carefully took the body down the porch stairs and up the walkway to the waiting ambulance. Suddenly, a gust of wind peeled back one end of the covering. A collective gasp sounded from the crowd.

All her hair had burned off, and her face was swollen, blistered, and red. But Collin still recognized Gail. Her eyes were closed and her mouth was stuck open in a horrified grimace.

The fireman quickly covered her up again—before the rest of her ravaged body was exposed.

Collin quickly turned away. He thought he was going to be sick.

He retreated toward his car. It was all he could do to keep from running away. He didn't want to draw attention to himself. He wiped the tears from his eyes and pulled out the keys. Approaching the car, he glanced in the side mirror. No one seemed to be following him. He opened the door and climbed behind the wheel. His hand shook as he started the ignition. Then he slowly pulled down the block.

At the end of the street, Collin turned and drove for five blocks. He took another turn—onto a side street. "I couldn't have done that," he whispered. "Please, God, I couldn't have. . . ."

Pulling in front of a deserted lot, Collin parked the car. No one was around. No one could see him. He switched off the ignition, and for the next few minutes he just sat in the front seat and sobbed.

"I'm trying to make some sense out of all this," his grandfather said. He took off his reading glasses and rubbed his eyes. Suddenly he looked frail. He was sitting in front of the computer monitor in Collin's bedroom.

Collin guessed this was all too much for him—too

much of a shock about the Pelhams, and too confusing about how the fire might have happened.

Collin had driven back home at around nine-thirty. Dee had already taken off for a hair appointment. He'd told his grandfather about the fire. Despite the presence of TV news vans at the Pelhams', there hadn't been anything on television about the fire yet. But Dee had phoned around ten o'clock, and apparently, it was all they were talking about at the beauty parlor.

"I'm so sorry, honey," she'd told Collin over the phone. "What an awful shock for you, so horrible. I'm going to wrap things up here and hurry home."

"You don't have to. There's really nothing for you to do. Seriously, take your time. I'm just going to lie down for a while. . . ."

After hanging up with his grandmother, Collin had decided to tell his grandfather the truth. He'd taken him up to his room and sat him down in front of his computer. He'd played for him the two videos Fernando had filmed—with Wade Grinnell emerging during the hypnosis sessions. On Google, he'd shown his grandfather the Century 21 Exposition timeline—with the paragraphs about the El Mar murders, the fire at the Hotel Aurora Vista, and the death of Wade Grinnell. He'd told him about going to Leavenworth yesterday, and described how Irene Pollack-Martin had seemed to *recognize* him from fifty years ago.

All the while, his grandfather had sat there with his mouth slightly open and the computer screen reflected on his glasses.

Collin had admitted that he didn't believe the police had found his mother's actual killers. He'd suggested the real murderers were still at large, watching him closely. He'd hoped his grandfather would understand how these killers—or at least, one of them—might have been behind yesterday's break-in at the Pelhams' house, as well as Fernando's disappearance.

Collin's back ached from hovering behind his grandfather at the computer for the last forty minutes.

Old Andy slipped his glasses in his shirt pocket and sighed. "Well, first off, I think you're wrong about your mother's killers. I think it was this lowlife drug gang who got shot themselves. And I say good riddance to bad rubbish. The police already went over all the evidence with us, Collin." He shrugged. "And I don't know what any of that has to do with this Wade character who's been dead for half a century. Are you saying you think you're reincarnated from this dead hooligan—like a Shirley MacLaine kind of thing? If that's the case, then I'm sorry, but it sounds pretty crazy."

Collin sat down on his bed. "I'm not sure what it is," he said wearily. "I wish I knew. I'd never heard of the guy until Saturday night. But that lady in Leavenworth recognized me from 1962. And you saw how I acted in those videos."

"Your friends could have egged you on earlier," his grandfather said. "And—and you told me, you'd just been watching a movie from around that same year. You know, Collin, even when you were a little boy, you took to any kind of suggestion. I'd tell you to be a tiger, and you'd growl and roar and claw at the air. It's what made you such a good actor. I think your friends were playing a joke on you. I'll bet Gail—God rest her soul—I'll bet she read about this World's Fair killer somewhere—and she made some sort of hypnotic suggestion to you, only you didn't get to see it in the video. They could have stopped filming during that part or edited it out or whatever. Have you thought about that? What is it you kids say, 'You just got dunked'?"

"*Punked*," Collin corrected him. "I already considered that, Grandpa. Gail and Fernando thought I was pulling a joke on them. And they weren't happy with me about it. In fact, Gail was really pissed off at me for the way I acted in the car Sunday while I was hypnotized. I don't remember any of it—except for what I saw in the video. . . ."

His grandfather looked so confused and lost. Collin knew exactly how he felt. He sighed. "Not being able to remember is one of the scariest things about this. Last night, I think Wade took over while I was sleeping. I think he snuck out and started the fire at the Pelhams'."

His grandfather squinted at him. "So you're saying you drove over there and set fire to the house—and all the while, you were *asleep*?"

"I'm saying I think *Wade* did it. You saw how it was in the videos. This other personality just sort of took over. All I remember from last night is waking up from a bad dream, and I was all sweaty. My clothes weren't where I left them. There was mud on my shoes—and my pants and jacket smelled like gasoline. Then today at breakfast, you told me about hearing the car engine at three-thirty in the morning, and I wasn't in bed. The lady I talked to outside the Pelhams' said the fire started around four."

"Why in the world would you want to kill the Pelhams?" his grandfather asked, frowning. "Gail was your friend—"

"That's the point, Grandpa. It's not me, it's *Wade*. I don't know why he'd kill them. I don't know why he murdered all those people back in 1962 either, but I'm pretty sure he did."

His grandfather stared at him. "So," he said finally.

"Where are these shoes with the mud on them—and the pants that smell like gasoline?"

"The shoes are in my closet, and the jeans are in the bathroom hamper."

His grandfather stood up and headed to the closet. He opened the door and picked up the muddied Converse All Stars. "Are these them? They don't look so bad."

"They didn't look that way when I took them off last night before going to bed."

His grandfather took the shoes in the bathroom, and then opened the hamper. Collin followed him in there. His grandfather fished the jeans out of the bin. "I can barely smell the gasoline," he muttered. Before Collin could say anything, his grandfather tossed the jeans and sneakers into the tub. Then he turned on the shower.

"Grandpa, what are you doing?"

He reached for the shampoo bottle and squeezed some over the shoes and jeans. "I don't believe for one minute that you'd ever intentionally hurt somebody," he said resolutely. "I know you better than you know yourself. And no one could even *make* you hurt another living soul. But if you're crazy enough to think you might have burned down that house—with your friend and her family in it—than there's probably someone out there crazy enough to agree with you. Why give them any ammunition to go after you when you're perfectly innocent?"

Collin glanced down at the jeans and the shoes— and the trail of mud that snaked toward the tub drain. "Grandpa, you can't . . ." he murmured. Yet a part of him was secretly relieved.

Leaving the shower on, his grandfather headed back to the bedroom. He stopped in front of Collin's desk and pointed at the computer screen. "I want you to erase or delete or whatever it is you do to get rid of those videos showing you acting so strange."

Collin shook his head. "Grandpa, I need those."

"You need them like you need a hole in your head," he argued. "Those videos aren't helping you one bit. They're just filling your mind with crazy notions. The last thing you need is for someone else to see these. . . ." He sat down at the desk, his bony hands poised over the keyboard. "Where's the delete function on this thing?"

"I'll do it!" Collin rushed to his side. He didn't want his grandfather screwing up his computer. Hovering beside him, he brought up the video files and sent them into the recycle bin.

"This recycle thingy," his grandfather said, "people can still go in there and pull stuff out, can't they? You need to get rid of it for good, Collin. Someone might look at that thing and—just like you—they'd come up with all sorts of nutty theories about you and that fire you had nothing to do with."

With a sigh, Collin reluctantly moved the cursor, pushed the delete button, and emptied out the recycle bin.

"What's this doohickey?" his grandfather asked, pointing to the webcam attachment. "Is that like a video camera?"

Collin nodded. "I don't really use it for anything."

"I want you to aim it at the bed and switch it on before you go to sleep tonight," he said. "Record it. That way, if you get up and start walking in your sleep tonight, you'll know. . . ."

Collin wished he'd thought of that last night.

"If we find out you're sleepwalking," his grandfather continued, "then we can talk to a doctor about it—

a doctor, not a *hypnotist*. You don't need any more of that nonsense. And listen, do us both a favor, and don't tell your grandmother about any of this. In fact, don't talk about it with anyone. It's just going to get you into trouble. You haven't done anything. Right now, you've got troubles enough, kiddo. Don't make things any worse. Let's just forget about all of this hocus-pocus reincarnation stuff, and move on. Are we in agreement here?"

For a moment, Collin didn't say anything. He listened to the shower running. He thought about his screwed-up mom, and wondered if his grandfather had employed this same brand of blatant denial in his dealings with her. A lot of good it had done for her.

They could wash the gas and dirt off his clothes, and he could delete those videos. But Collin still remembered the horrified expression on Irene Pollack's face when she'd first seen him yesterday. He couldn't let this go. He figured if Fernando ever showed up, he'd get his friend to send him the videos again. He probably still had them in his phone.

Collin looked his grandfather in the eye. "All right, Grandpa. I'll drop the whole thing." He could tell the old man believed him, too.

He was still a very good actor.

Silverdale—Tuesday, 9:20 p.m.

"I'm serious, you're pissing me off," Maya told her boyfriend.

But Liam didn't pay any attention to her. He wasn't paying much attention to his driving either, because he was texting at the wheel. The two North Kitsap High seniors were driving along Silverdale Way, on their way home from a movie at the Kitsap Mall.

One of the things Maya really didn't like about Liam—and it was almost a deal-breaker—was his habit of texting while driving. She'd seen one too many grisly public service announcements on YouTube about the dangerous pastime. It was especially unnerving when her boyfriend texted while driving at night. He kept drifting over the double yellow lines.

"I'm counting to ten, Liam," she announced. "If you don't put the phone away by the time I'm finished, I'm ripping it out of your hand and throwing it out of the window."

"Jesus, who died and made you the texting narc?" He worked his thumb over the small keypad. "I can multitask. I'm texting Matt about tomorrow. . . ."

"You know how much I hate this. Like you can't wait ten minutes until we're parked . . ."

"I'm almost done. Give me a break."

"One, two, three . . ." Maya flicked the switch to lower the passenger window. Her long brown hair started blowing in the breeze. "You're weaving, for God's sake, and there's a car in the other lane coming at us. . . ."

Liam looked up long enough to get back onto his side of the road and watch the car whoosh by. Then he glanced down at his iPhone again.

Maya went back to counting. The closer she got to ten, the more Liam started laughing. His texting thumb worked even faster now, and his eyes were riveted to his iPhone. Maya was certain they were going to have an accident.

". . . eight, nine, and ten!" she announced. "That's it! Enough!" Maya reached over and snatched the phone from him. The car swerved. She was so angry that she hurled the iPhone out the window without hesitation.

"WHAT THE FUCK?" Liam bellowed. Veering over to the side of the road, he hit the brake. Gravel rattled against the underside of the car, and the tires screeched.

Maya braced a hand on the dash as they skidded. The car finally came to a diagonal halt—with the front of it sticking in the roadway.

After a few more choice expletives, Liam straightened the car on the shoulder of the road and stepped outside. He slammed his door shut and then stomped down a ditch into some bushes bordering a dark, wooded area. He turned toward the car again. "Well, are you going to help me find my phone or what?" he barked.

A car sped by. Maya had the window open. "I'm sorry, but I warned you," she said. She reached into her purse and dug out her cell phone. "Relax. I'm calling you right now. We'll see the phone light up and hear the ring. It's back a few more yards, I think . . ."

Maya punched in his number and counted two rings before an automated recording came on. It wasn't his regular message: *"The wireless customer you're calling is unavailable. Please try your call again."*

"I think we're out of luck," she announced.

"Well, you're the one who threw it out the goddamn window," he yelled. "I could use some help! I have stuff on that phone I'd rather not have some stranger looking at."

She stared at all the bushes and trees—and beyond, the shadowy, ominous woods. "I don't think you're ever going to find it, Liam. I'll chip in for a new phone. But you'll have to change some of your passwords. . . ."

"Those pictures I took of you naked are on that phone," he said.

"Oh, shit," she whispered, opening the car door. "All right, I'm coming!"

Maya got out of the car and teetered down the ditch at the roadside. Using the light on her cell phone as a makeshift flashlight, she nervously explored the brush. She could hear things shifting around in the woods. Maybe it was just the sound of tree branches rustling or raccoons. Whatever it was, it made her uncomfortable. Every once in a while, she lost track of where Liam was, and she'd panic. Then she'd realize, there was just a tree between them, or he'd stepped into the shadows. So—she kept talking to him and listened for him to grunt a response every minute or two.

They'd been searching for at least ten minutes when she snagged her new sweater on a thorny bush. Then she noticed her favorite Cole Haan casuals were caked with mud. A car sped by on Silverdale Way, the first one in a long while, and she wished she were in it.

"You know, at this point, Liam, I don't care who finds your phone and sees me naked," she announced. "I say we give up the search. I'll buy you a new phone—a better phone, okay?"

No response.

"Liam?" she called. She felt a pang in her stomach. "Liam, where are you?"

Maya glanced around to make certain a tree or bush wasn't blocking her view of him. She didn't see him anywhere. It was as if she was all alone out there.

"Liam, if you're hiding to get even with me for the phone, it's not funny!" Her voice quivered, and she couldn't breathe right. "C'mon, please, enough already!"

Up ahead, Maya thought she saw something duck behind a tree. She stood there, frozen. She wasn't sure if she should move toward it or run away. Tears stung her eyes.

"Answer me, Liam! I've had enough of this! I mean it! I'm heading back to the car!"

She heard a twig snap behind her, and swiveled around. Maya didn't see anything, but she started to back away. Something caught her foot, and all at once, she fell. But Maya didn't hit the ground.

She landed on top of a slightly bloated corpse. Her hand hit the young man's cold, soft, clammy chest. He was naked. Someone had slashed him across the throat. The wound looked so deep, his head seemed barely attached to the rest of him.

Maya let out a horrified shriek.

It brought her boyfriend out of hiding. They were both so unnerved by their discovery, neither one recognized the sophomore from their high school who had been missing since the previous morning.

Later, the police discovered a cell phone about thirty feet away from Fernando Ryan's body. The phone belonged to Liam.

Eventually, they would come across Fernando's clothes and his backpack.

But they never found his phone.

CHAPTER THIRTEEN

Poulsbo—Wednesday, October 3, 8:40 a.m.

For a while, his grandfather did all the talking in the police lieutenant's office—and most of it was just friendly BS. He and Collin sat in hard-back chairs in front of the lieutenant's desk. Andy called him *Jim*. He was a lanky, balding man in a dark gray suit with an ugly salmon-colored tie. Collin wondered if he'd put on the tie for his grandfather. A stocky young tow-headed cop sat in the corner, behind Jim's desk, taking notes—except for the few minutes when he went to fetch Collin's grandfather some coffee. He came back with it in a Styrofoam cup. Old Andy took one sip and didn't touch it again.

Collin wouldn't exactly say the cops kissed his grandfather's ass, but it came pretty close to that.

They'd called last night at around eleven o'clock with the news about Fernando.

Collin had figured it was something bad as soon as the phone had rung at that hour. His grandfather had answered it in the bedroom.

Listening outside the closed door, Collin sank down on the carpet and tipped his head back against the wall.

Mrs. Ryan must have told the police that he was friends with Fernando. He figured the cops wanted to talk with him and find out if he knew anything.

"I'll bring my grandson to the station tomorrow morning at eight-thirty," he heard his grandfather say. "Now's not a good time. He's already had a rough day, and it looks like things just got rougher. He needs some rest. I'd look at it as a personal favor if you let this wait until morning. All right, Jim?"

A few minutes later, his grandfather stepped out of the bedroom with his robe on. Collin looked up at him from where he sat sobbing on the hallway floor. His grandfather didn't have to say anything.

His grandparents stayed up to keep him company. They gathered at the kitchen table—his grandfather with some scotch, and Dee with herbal tea. She kept asking Collin if she could fix him a sandwich, and he kept telling her no, thanks. At one point, Dee broke down and wept. After his initial crying jag in the up-stairs hall, Collin had become sort of numb and dazed.

His grandparents finally went up to bed around midnight. "Let me do most of the talking with the police tomorrow," his grandfather whispered, giving him a hug.

Collin stayed up another two hours, spending most of the time on his computer. Before turning in, he adjusted the webcam, switched it on *record*, and then crawled into bed. Once his head hit the pillow, the numbness wore off, and he fell asleep crying for his dead friends.

This morning, he'd played back the webcam recording—in fast motion. He'd tossed and turned some, but hadn't budged from his bed all night.

That didn't mean he wasn't tired and nervous as hell right now in the police office. Though his grandfather acted as if they were just dropping in on some old friends, Collin was completely on edge. He couldn't help thinking they were about to arrest him. Sitting there across from the two policemen, his leg shook.

The lieutenant asked him how well he knew Fernando, if Fernando had any other friends—or any enemies. How often had he hitchhiked? Did he have any favorite hangouts? Collin answered honestly, saying Fernando sometimes thumbed a ride to school and to the mall on weekends. "He thought it was a cool way to meet new people," Collin explained. "But I have to admit, I've always thought it kind of risky."

"What exactly do they think happened, Jim?" Collin's grandfather interjected.

"Well, Collin has helped confirm some things for us," the balding man said, shifting a bit behind his desk. A map of Kitsap Peninsula was on the wall behind him. "We're pretty sure on his way to school Fernando was picked up by some—" He shot a wary look at Collin.

"Go ahead," his grandfather prompted him.

The lieutenant sighed. "We're—um, still trying to determine if the boy had been molested or violated. The body was naked when it was discovered in a ditch along Silverdale Way last night. It looks like he was hit over the head at one point—"

"Was that the cause of death?" Collin's grandfather asked.

The lieutenant shook his head. "No, someone slit his throat. We'll know more after the coroner files his report." He straightened his salmon-colored tie, and glanced at Collin again. "Meanwhile, we're wondering if Fernando got in touch with you anytime Monday. He never made it to school. I understand from Mrs. Ryan you missed school on Monday as well."

"That's right," Collin's grandfather answered for him. "I was feeling under the weather Monday morning. Didn't even put in an hour on the golf course before I turned around and hightailed it home. I had some important errands to run in Seattle that day, and I sent Collin to take care of them. I called the school in the afternoon and talked to a nice lady, and explained it was my fault Collin was AWOL." Andy reached over and put his hand on Collin's knee—apparently to keep his leg from shaking. "He was off the island all day. Anyway, I hope you don't sic the truant officer on us."

The lieutenant seemed to work up a smile. Collin was waiting for him to ask what kind of *important errands* he'd run for his grandfather in Seattle, but he didn't. "So—just to double-check," he said. "Fernando didn't call you or leave a message any time Monday?"

Collin shook his head. "No, sir, the only person who called me was Gail Pelham, around six o'clock, when I was getting off the ferry. . . ."

His grandfather squeezed his knee. Collin could tell old Andy thought he was offering too much information. But the police certainly had to think it was one hell of a coincidence that his only two friends both died under different circumstances within twenty-four hours of each other. Collin kept talking. His stomach was in knots. "Gail called to tell me their house had been broken into. So I swung by—just to check in on her. Neither one of us knew Fernando was missing at the time. I got the call from Mrs. Ryan later that night."

"Must have been an awful shock to hear about Gail and her family," the lieutenant said.

He nodded. "Yeah, I was supposed to pick her up and take her to school yesterday. I came by and saw the policemen there, and the firemen cleaning up."

"You didn't talk to any of them?"

"No, but I talked to a neighbor on the street in front of their house—or at least, what was left of it. She said Mr. and Mrs. Pelham, and Chris, and Gail, all of them were—"

"He was pretty rattled when he came home and told me," his grandfather interrupted. "I had him lie down for a while. Poor guy, he hadn't slept well the night before, worried about Fernando. In fact, I couldn't sleep either on Monday night. I got up around two, and went downstairs and watched TV." He turned to Collin. "I heard you get up a few times. I don't know when you finally fell asleep—must have been a little before four in the morning. I peeked in on you at around four-fifteen, and you were snoozing. . . ."

"Four-fifteen," the lieutenant repeated.

Collin's grandfather nodded. It was all a lie. But old Andy had just given him a perfect alibi. "The last couple of days have been pretty tough," he went on. "Do they have any idea what started the fire? Do they think it had anything to do with the break-in earlier?"

"Possibly," the lieutenant said. "The fire department is still investigating it." His eyes narrowed at Collin. "Do you know if Gail had any enemies at school?"

"There are some girls in our class who are pretty mean to her," Collin admitted, shrugging. "But I don't really think they'd have taken it that far."

The police lieutenant asked for the girls' names. Collin reluctantly named three classmates who had made Gail's life miserable. He figured there was a slight, slight chance one of them had something to do with the break-in. But none of them had started that fire.

No. Starting fires had been Wade Grinnell's specialty.

Collin and his grandfather finally got out of the lieutenant's office around nine-thirty. But old Andy spent another twenty minutes roaming the City Hall corridors and dropping into one office after another to shake people's hands.

A young, uniformed policeman held the door open for him and his grandfather as they stepped out of City Hall. The morning was cloudy, gray, and cold. Collin quietly thanked the cop, but his grandfather stopped and shook his hand, too. Collin continued down the steps in front of the tall, modern, red-brick building. At the bottom step, Collin turned back and watched his grandfather still chatting with the young cop. "Oh, God, Grandpa," he muttered under his breath. "Can we please just get out of here already?"

His grandfather waved at him to come up. "Collin, this is Timmy Kinsella," he said. "His dad was one of the best foremen we ever had at the plant. . . ." Collin had to hear all about Timmy's mom and dad, retired and now living in Tampa. He kept telling himself he should be grateful to his grandfather, who had just lied for him. Behind that smile and his friendly BS, old Andy had to be hurting inside. Even with all his clout and all these people sucking up to him, he had to feel awful. His daughter had been a total screwup most of her life. And now there was every possibility his only grandson had started a fire, killing four innocent people.

His grandfather finally patted the young cop on the shoulder and said good-bye. Collin walked down the City Hall steps with him. Neither one of them said anything. His grandfather pressed the device on his car key chain, and his BMW beeped. Collin climbed into the passenger side while his grandfather got behind the wheel. He started up the car.

But he just sat there for a moment with his hands on the wheel.

"Grandpa," Collin said. "I'm really sorry you had to lie for me."

His grandfather just shook his head and started crying.

In the car, on the way home, he tried to convince his grandfather to let him go back to school today. He pointed out that if he left the house at 10:30, he could be there in time for third period. He really didn't want to sit around at home all day, and he knew his grandparents wouldn't want him going off on his own—not after what had happened to Fernando. He pointed out that if he missed any more school, it would be tougher for him to catch up. The sooner he could go back to a normal routine, the better his chances for actually feeling normal again.

His grandfather seemed skeptical. But by the time he pulled into the driveway, he had agreed to write a note for Collin's homeroom teacher.

"Promise me you won't go off on your own or take any chances. I know you don't hitchhike or anything like that. But let's not forget, there's someone out there, and the police haven't caught him yet." He switched off the engine to his BMW, and then leaned back in the driver's seat. "And just so we understand each other. There won't be any more secret trips. No obsessing about this reincarnation stuff and hypnotism and all that hocus-pocus . . ."

Collin shook his head resolutely. "No, sir."

"And I want you back home by four."

"Yes, no sweat, Grandpa."

While his grandfather tried to get Dee on board with this arguably premature back-to-school idea, Collin retreated up to his room and gathered his schoolbooks.

He couldn't help worrying something might happen to his grandparents while he was gone. It seemed everyone close to him—or at least, anyone who had spent time with him lately—wasn't safe. He thought about Mrs. Pollack-Martin. He'd been at her place for nearly two hours on Monday. Someone had left him that note on the ferry on his way back from that visit. Had the same person followed him all the way to Leavenworth and back?

It would be easy to kill an elderly lady in a rest home and make it look like an accident or natural causes. She could be smothered in her sleep or thrown down a flight of stairs, and no one would know what really happened.

Collin wished he could warn his grandparents and Mrs. Pollack-Martin. But how could he explain to them that they might be in danger? How could he make them understand when he didn't even understand himself?

With a sigh, he started to load up his backpack—even though he had no intention of going to school today. He held on to his spiral notebook for a moment. In the back of it he'd tucked away some printouts he'd made on his computer last night. He unfolded the first sheet of paper and stole a look at it:

DISCOVER THE INNER YOU THROUGH HYPNOTHERAPY!
sleep anxieties – weight problems – smoking
anger management – transitions

Explore Your Past Lives and Future Potential!

DR. DORIAN Provides Healing & Help with Hypnosis!

Make an Appointment Now!

Drdorianhypnosis@gmail.com 206-555-5239

Office Conveniently Located Near Downtown Seattle – E-Z parking!

It was the *Explore Your Past Lives* part that had really piqued Collin's interest. He'd gone online last night and, using a phony name, booked an appointment with Dr. Dorian at 12:15 today. Under *Reason for Visit*, he'd typed in: *To answer questions about my past life.*

He wasn't even a real doctor. His stupid initials were D.R., but it sure didn't look that way on his website. Collin figured he was about as phony as his name: Dante Reynaldo Dorian. His office was actually a dumpy, messy apartment on Eastlake that smelled like death. He had four cats, one of which was mean and kept taking claw-swipes at Collin's leg. Every piece of furniture in the place had been scratched to shreds. D.R. was a large man in his mid-forties with receding flaxen hair. He wore a poncho. He spent the first twenty-five minutes of their session bragging to Collin about his *gift* for tapping into people's past lives.

Collin tried to cooperate when he sat in the torn-to-ribbons easy chair and focused on the pendant that D.R. dangled in front of him. But he didn't get sleepy or tired. He couldn't get past the feeling he was wasting his time—and money. Collin was still awake and frustrated when D.R. announced he was making contact with the young Native American warrior from Collin's past life. Collin told him, "I'm sorry, this just isn't working."

D.R. insisted that all his sessions were two hundred dollars each—even if they didn't last the full ninety minutes. That was a total rip-off as far as Collin was concerned—especially since he'd only been there forty minutes.

"Here's eighty," he said, tossing the bills on the scratched-up coffee table. Then he ran out of the apartment and took the stairs down to the lobby. Once outside, he kept glancing over his shoulder to see if D.R. was following him. In the car, he checked his rearview mirror. Just moments after pulling out of his parking spot on Eastlake, he noticed a black Saturn peel out after him.

At first, Collin thought the Saturn was tailing him, but after a few blocks, another car got between them, and then another. Eventually, he lost track of the Saturn and focused on getting to his two o'clock appointment in Ballard with Claudette, who offered *"Psychic Counseling & Hope thru Hypnosis!"* She also did psychic readings. When he phoned to bump up their appointment to one-thirty, she was okay with it. He also noticed her heavy French accent.

Claudette lived in a semi-modern, tall apartment building near the Ballard Bridge. Her cramped little unit was full of antiques. With the lacy curtains drawn, the place seemed a bit gloomy. Confined to a wheelchair, Claudette had bluish-white hair, and was at least ten years older than Collin's grandfather. He figured

she was around Mrs. Pollack-Martin's age, but definitely more frail. She had one milky blue eye that
looked damaged or dead. It was hard for Collin to look
at her, even when she was smiling at him sweetly. She
wore a black pantsuit with a blue blouse. She seemed
like a very nice lady, and Collin wanted it to work.
He'd told Claudette in his email that he had trouble
sleeping.

She had him sit down on her sofa, which had a knit-
ted throw draped across the back. "Oh, so many bad
dreams," she said, rolling her wheelchair closer to him.
"I can see that already. No wonder you cannot sleep."

He nodded. "I was hoping you could heal me
through hypnosis."

Claudette used a little hand mirror and had him
focus on the reflected patch of light it made on the
flocked wallpaper. Collin had told her that his name
was Rusty, so she kept telling him in her heavy French
accent, *"Roosty, you get very, very tired. . . ."*

Instead of getting tired, Collin just became panicky.
What if Wade came out and hurt this poor, old crippled
woman? Across the room, Collin spotted her purse on
a lace-covered table. Collin imagined Wade taking her
money, then setting the apartment on fire.

This whole experiment seemed ill-conceived. If
Claudette met up with Wade Grinnell, the best Collin
could hope for was her telling him what transpired
while he was under. The session wouldn't do him much
good unless it was recorded—and the hypnotherapist
knew the right questions to ask.

"You resist," she said, setting the mirror down in her
lap. She pushed her wheelchair closer and studied him
with her one good eye. "Roosty, it's not your real
name."

He shook his head. "It's Collin."

Her frail hand patted his arm. "Not each time does the hypnosis work with people. I won't charge you."

"Well, I—I'm sorry I took up your time," Collin said. He was thinking he should at least give her twenty-five dollars for the aborted session. He was about to reach for his wallet in his back pocket, but she clung to his shirtsleeve.

"I'm psychic, you know," she whispered.

He nodded. "Yes, you said that in your ad online."

She pointed to her own arm. "The woman who has scars here, you need to warn her."

Collin squinted at her. "What?"

Claudette let go of his sleeve, then sat back. "You wished you had warned your friends," she said. "You need to warn the woman with the scars."

"Warn her about what?"

The old woman stared at him for a moment. Finally, she shook her head. "I do not know. But perhaps what happened to your friends is going to happen to her. Is that any help? Do you know a woman with many scars?"

Collin nodded. "Yes, but I don't understand how you'd know something like that—"

Smiling, she touched her forehead with her bony finger. "On some level you were thinking it, and I just picked up on it. That's all. You go with your instincts, and warn the woman with the scars."

Collin got to his feet. He reached back for his wallet and took out three twenties. "Listen, I'd like to pay you for at least part of the session. You've been a lot of help. In fact, I'd like to come back here and . . ." He trailed off when he noticed her shaking her head.

"I cannot hypnotize you, Collin. I saw you were

afraid for me. You know it yourself. It won't work with me. You need someone who is strong and young to help you—at least, younger than this old lady in the wheelchair." Gently, she pushed away his hand with the bills in it. "Keep your money for the other hypnotist."

Collin thanked her. Before he left, he managed to slip the folded-up sixty dollars onto a table by her door. He figured she'd find the money later and think she had misplaced it or something. Then again, maybe Claudette would know it was from him.

After all, she was a very smart lady.

"Hi," he said, after he heard the beep from her answering machine. "Um, this is Collin—you know, from the other day? I don't know how to tell you this without sounding crazy. But, well, you might want to go stay with a friend someplace. I think there's some people who—"

There was a click on the other end. "Hello?"

"Hello, Mrs. Pollack-Martin?" he said. "This is Collin. . . ."

"Well, hello, Collin," she said. "Let me make sure this old answering machine is switched off. . . . There. How's your English composition coming along?"

"Um, okay," he lied. Collin sat in his car with the windows rolled up to block out the noise. He was parked in line at the ferry terminal. Some passengers stood outside their vehicles, talking to each other—or on the phone. Security guards with their scent dogs on leashes walked up and down the rows of cars. The ferry was due in twenty minutes, and the terminal lot had started to fill up.

"Do you have some more questions about my

books?" Mrs. Pollack-Martin asked. "I'm sorry about the other day. I kind of went—what do they call it? I went *off-topic*."

"No apologies necessary." Collin shifted a bit in the driver's seat. "Actually, I'm calling about another thing. I know this sounds crazy, but I'm worried something might happen to you."

"Really?" she asked.

"See, two of my good friends were killed yesterday. One died along with her parents and kid brother. They were all killed when their house caught on fire. It happened just hours after I talked with you—"

"I don't think that's the least bit funny—"

"Neither do I," Collin said. He knew it had to be awful for her to hear about another deadly fire. "I'm serious, Mrs. Pollack. My friend's name was Gail Pelham. It happened in Poulsboro yesterday morning. You can check. My other friend's name was Fernando Ryan. He was hitchhiking to school Monday. Somebody picked him up and killed him, slit his throat. They found his body last night." Collin's eyes filled with tears and his voice started to shake. "They were my only friends. I think they might have been killed because someone knew they were close to me. This person—or maybe it's a couple of people—they must have thought I'd told them something. I—I'm not explaining it right. . . ."

"Well, if what you say is true, I'm really very sorry," she said soberly. "I haven't looked at the newspaper today, except for the crosswords. I didn't hear anything about it. You—you must be devastated. . . ."

"It's pretty awful, yeah," he said, wiping his nose with the back of his hand. A woman waiting for the ferry walked by his car. Collin turned his head away from the window so she wouldn't see him crying. "But right now I'm worried that something might happen to you," he explained. "I think some people have been following me around. I'm afraid they'll go after you next. Maybe just to be safe, you could go stay with some relatives for a while. . . ."

"Oh, honey," she said with pity in her voice. "Don't worry about me. I'll be fine where I am. Listen, are you getting any help—grief counseling through school or something like that?"

Collin took a few deep breaths. Obviously, she thought he was crazy. And why wouldn't she? He cleared his throat. "Yes, in fact, I went to a therapist today. I just came back from seeing her. It's why I'm calling you. She's a psychic, too, and she described you to me. She said that after what happened to my friends, I should warn you. Anyway, ma'am, the thing is, you're a really nice lady. I don't want anything bad happening to you. . . ."

There were a few seconds of silence on the other end. Through his windshield, he could see the ferry in the distance, a speck on the water for now.

"Okay, Collin," she said finally. "I'll be careful. I won't take any chances. I doubt anyone will come after a dotty old lady like me. Just the same, I'll keep a look-out and lock my door—if that makes you feel any better."

"It does—a little," Collin told her. "But I really wish you'd take me seriously."

"Okay," she said. "But you need to promise you'll talk to your parents about how you're feeling right now. If your parents can't help you, maybe there's a teacher or counselor at school you're close to—someone older than you. Talk to them, confide in them, okay?"

Collin was about to reply, but hesitated. He was thinking that just hours after he'd confided in Gail, she and her family had perished in a fire. He sighed. "I will, ma'am. Thank you. Good-bye."

As the ferry made its crossing, Collin stayed in the car. He didn't want to risk having another one of his grandfather's friends spot him on the deck or in the cabin seating area.

It was ironic that Mrs. Pollack-Martin had recommended he talk with a counselor. He had six printouts from hypnotherapist-counselor websites in the pocket of his jacket. He'd already seen two of them. He wondered if the four others would be as awful as D.R. Dorian.

Collin decided to go to his morning classes tomorrow. But at lunch, he'd take the ferry back over to Seattle and see these other hypnotists.

Sitting at the wheel, he called in appointments with three of them. He said his name was Russell Leander, after a character he'd played in his second film, *Honor Student*, which had tanked at the box office. He told the therapists he had sleeping issues. Once he found a hypnotist he trusted, he'd ask them to record the session on his cell phone. If Wade came out, then he and the hypnotist could hatch a plan for the next session. He got the first three therapists to agree to forty-five-minute sessions at a reduced fee.

He'd spent a hundred and forty dollars in just three hours today—and most of that had been a total waste. His grandfather had been footing the bill for his mom's life insurance for years, and now it was paying back in annuities. Old Andy had insisted he take the money and save it for his living expenses during college. Collin had collected three thousand dollars so far. He didn't intend to go through a big chunk of it visiting a bunch of bogus hypnotists.

The fourth one of the group didn't impress him at all. For starters, her ad was awfully similar to "Dr." Dorian's:

HEAL YOURSELF THOUGH HYPNOSIS!
Let Olivia Be Your Guide to a Better You!

*Lose Weight, Quit Smoking, Conquer Fears
and Phobias,
Increase Self-Esteem, Break Bad Habits
& Build a Happy Tomorrow!*

Olivia could only squeeze him in at 4:45 tomorrow, which meant he wouldn't be home from school until seven. He'd have to make up some excuse in advance for his grandparents. Plus she charged one hundred dollars a session, and wouldn't budge when he asked about reducing the rate if he didn't stay for the full hour. Finally, for some reason, when she asked about why he needed help, instead of insomnia Collin said he had a drinking problem.

"Well, I'm not qualified to handle people with alcohol issues, Russ," she said on the other end of the line. "I can't promise results the way I can with clients who want to lose weight or quit smoking or sleep better. I recommend you check out your local AA chapter—"

"I drink to fall asleep most of time," Collin said. "It started out as kind of an insomnia cure, and I've been drinking pretty heavily for almost two years now. I'm a student and it's really starting to affect my grades. I want to quit, but I can't seem to. Anyway, I'm hoping you can help me. Maybe we can discuss it when I see you tomorrow. If it doesn't work out, it doesn't work out. No harm done, y'know?"

"All right, then we're on for four-forty-five tomorrow, Russ. And you have the address in Madison Valley?"

"Yes, thanks, Olivia. See you then."

Clicking off the phone, Collin figured seeing this Olivia woman would be pointless. But if there was just a tiny chance she could reach Wade Grinnell, then it was worth a shot.

He slipped the folded printouts in his pocket and thought about what Mrs. Pollack-Martin had said. He needed to talk with someone older. He needed a friend right now.

Even though he'd never called it, Collin had Ian Haggerty's number programmed in his cell phone. He brought it up, and hit the SEND button. While it rang, Collin squirmed in the driver's seat. On the fourth ringtone, it went to a voice mail greeting: *"Hey, it's Ian. Sorry I missed you. You know the drill. Leave a message. Thanks."*

Collin waited for the beep, but then he balked and hung up.

He felt stupid calling someone he hadn't spoken to in almost three months. Ian hadn't even been a real friend. He'd been assigned to guard the house and protect him. That had been the extent of it.

No one was protecting him anymore.

Four cars behind him and one lane over, the man in the black Saturn watched Collin Cox in the front seat of his Taurus.

He'd been following Collin ever since he and the old man had returned home from their visit to City Hall. The kid hadn't stayed long at either the Eastlake address or the place by the Ballard Bridge. So it was likely neither one of the hypnotherapists had worked out for him. Collin probably wouldn't be going back to either one.

That was lucky for them.

For a while, shortly after the Eastlake excursion, he'd had a feeling the kid had caught on he was being followed. But the man in the black Saturn had hung back for a while and tailed him all the way to Ballard. The only problem he'd encountered had been later, at the ferry terminal lot with those goddamn scent dogs. They were supposed to sniff out bombs. But these two German shepherds seemed to detect something in his trunk.

The man thought he'd cleaned it out. But that Fernando kid's corpse had been in there for at least two hours. There was blood and shit and soiled clothes. Maybe he hadn't washed out the trunk thoroughly enough, because those damn dogs had sure picked up on something.

The security guys had asked him to pop the trunk for them. He'd stayed in the car and held his breath while they'd poked around back there. He'd been parked far enough away from Collin's car that he'd figured the kid wouldn't notice. But other people had been staring, and he'd started getting tense—until one of the security guys had shut the trunk and waved at him. "Thanks!" he'd called.

Now he listened to the announcement over the ferry's loudspeaker, telling people to return to their vehicles and get ready to disembark. He glanced at his wristwatch. It was almost four o'clock. The next ferry back to Seattle would be at 4:45. He hoped the kid would go straight home to Grandma and Grandpa.

Then he could make the return ferry. He still had a hell of lot of driving ahead of him tonight—all the way to Leavenworth and back.

Leavenworth—Wednesday, 9:20 p.m.

As Leonard Bernstein's soundtrack swelled to a stirring crescendo, a priestly Karl Malden and a winsome Eva Marie Saint smiled at each other. They watched a beaten, battered, but determined Marlon Brando staggering toward the waterfront warehouse.

It was Best Picture Night at Riverview Manor Retirement Center, and residents had gathered in the lounge to watch *On the Waterfront* on the big-screen TV. Only a few of them had fallen asleep during the movie, which was something of a record at Riverview Manor. Irene Pollack-Martin was very much awake and joined in on the applause as the movie ended.

The film took her mind off her troubles for a while. Mostly, she was concerned for that young man from Poulsbo whose two friends had been killed. She'd gone onto her computer and found the news stories—first, about the fire that had taken four lives; and second, about a boy who had been abducted and brutally murdered. It seemed like too much of a coincidence. Just hours after she'd told Collin about the hotel fire that had destroyed her family, someone close to him had died in another blaze. He'd seemed like such a good-hearted young man. At the same time, he'd looked too much like the cruel-eyed teenager she'd seen running away from the Hotel Aurora Vista the night of the fire.

It had been hard to get past how he'd looked. But as someone whose body was half-scarred, she'd long ago learned how to do that. Irene liked him. She hoped he found someone to help him deal with his loss.

She'd tried to go back to her crossword puzzle, but hadn't been able to concentrate. She'd thought about Collin's warning. It seemed a bit crazy, but she'd made sure to lock her door when she'd gone down to the lounge to watch the movie tonight.

"I forgot how sweet some of those romantic scenes were between him and the girl," her neighbor Roseann pointed out as they rode back up in the elevator together. A tiny, feisty woman of eighty, Roseann lived down the hall from her.

Irene and Roseann mentioned getting together for breakfast, and then went their separate ways after the elevator let them out on the fourth floor.

Stopping in front of her door, Irene took out her keys. Suddenly, she felt something push against her leg, and she recoiled. Her cat, Smike, let out a startled screech and raised his back. A hand over her heart, she stared down at the silver tabby. "What in the world are you doing out here?" she whispered. She never let him out of the apartment.

Irene bent down and scooped him up in her arms. Then she managed to get her key in the lock. She gave it a turn and realized it was unlocked. Was she getting senile? She was almost positive she'd locked it. Opening the door wider, she hesitated at the threshold. She couldn't help remembering Collin's warning that someone might want to kill her.

Nothing looked disturbed in the apartment. The kitchen light and one lamp in the living room were on—just as she'd left them two hours ago.

Smike jumped out of her arms and raced toward the kitchen, where his food dish was. He usually got some kitty treats at this time of night.

Irene closed the door behind her and locked it. Everything looked fine. She told herself she was being silly.

But all at once, Smike let out another screech and darted back to the living room. From where she stood, frozen, Irene saw only part of the kitchen. She noticed a shadow rippling across the cabinets.

Her cat scurried behind the sofa.

Irene froze. Her first inclination was to get out of there—just as soon as she could move. But Smike was like her family. She inched toward the sofa. "Smike?" she called to him nervously. "Come here, sweetie. . . ."

She eyed the kitchen. The shadow moved again—over the wall. From where she stood, Irene saw the refrigerator—and the blurry reflection on the stainless-steel door. A dark figure backed away. Now she knew for sure—someone was in there, waiting for her.

"Smike?" she said, her voice quivering.

The cat finally came to her and Irene snatched him up.

Swiveling around, she hurried for her door. She didn't dare look back, but she was convinced the intruder was coming up right behind her. With a shaky hand, she unlocked the door, swung it open, and raced down the hallway to Roseann's apartment. Smike squirmed in her arms, but she held on to him. She pounded on the door and repeatedly rang the bell. Her friend was hard of hearing.

Irene glanced back toward her own unit. She'd left her door open. But from this vantage point, it looked as if the door was opening even wider.

She rang her neighbor's bell again and again. At last, Roseann opened the door. "Good God, Irene, what's—"

She rushed inside, almost knocking down her friend. Then she turned around and shut the door. Smike flew out of her arms as she twisted the lock and the dead bolt. Irene couldn't get her breath. She thought her heart was going to explode in her chest. "Call the front desk," she gasped. "There's someone in my apartment. . . ."

At least twice a week, one of the residents needlessly called 911 or the fire department. Irene didn't want to be one of those panicky, senile people. That was why she had Roseann call the front desk instead of the police. She'd never really seen the man who had broken into her apartment, so she couldn't describe him. But she knew someone had been in there.

Roseann remembered to hide Smike in her closet while one of the staff people came up to investigate. "Responding to a potential intruder in apartment 405," was how the husky young Latino security guard referred to it while talking to someone on his cell phone. Irene and Roseann followed him down the hallway to Irene's unit. A few neighbors stood in their doorways to see what the fuss was about.

Irene had a feeling they wouldn't find anyone in there, and she was right.

The guard was more concerned about the water dish and cat toys. Irene lied and told him they were for a cousin who visited last week and had brought along her cat. He didn't seem to take her very seriously about the break-in.

She could have told him that a young man from Poulsbo had warned her something like this might happen. In fact, if Collin hadn't called to warn her, she very well could have walked into the kitchen and gotten her throat slit—like Collin's poor friend.

But Irene didn't say anything, because it sounded

crazy. The security guard was already treating her like just another one of those panicky, senile people.

After he'd left, and after Roseann had smuggled Smike back to her, Irene thanked her friend. Obviously, Roseann had her doubts about this intruder as well. "It was probably nothing," she said at her door. "But better be safe than sorry, right?"

"Right," Irene allowed. "See you at breakfast tomorrow."

She felt a little foolish double locking the door and leaving a light on in the living room. But that was what Irene did before getting ready for bed. She wondered if the security man and Rosie had a point. Maybe she'd been a bit too jumpy after that call from Collin—and reading about those deaths. After all, she hadn't actually seen anyone—just shadows on the wall and a blurry reflection on the refrigerator.

She switched off the kitchen light and gave the room one last look. The light from outside came through the window and shone across her breakfast table, where she'd left her newspaper. She wandered to the table and glanced down at the *Wenatchee World*, folded over to her favorite page.

All at once, Irene knew she hadn't imagined the intruder.

He was real. And he was a very smart and patient man.

While waiting here in the dark for her to come home, he'd finished her crossword puzzle.

CHAPTER FOURTEEN

Seattle—Thursday, October 4, 4:40 p.m.

Collin stood in the atrium of the building, which had a fancy, high-priced antique store on the street level. On his way into the little lobby, Collin noticed some crappy-looking lamp in the front window selling for eight hundred and ninety-nine dollars. As if.

He was in a lousy mood. He'd shown up to his classes this morning. Luckily, his grandfather hadn't dated the note he'd given him to cover his absence "for the last few days." His friendship with Fernando and Gail had slipped under the radar at school. No one had seemed to know he'd been particularly close to them. So no one had treated him any differently this morning. He'd remained the invisible man, sadly listening to classmates speculate on whether or not Fernando had been raped. He'd even heard some stoner asshole telling a horrible joke: "Hey, what's the difference between Gail Pelham and a marshmallow?"

Right then, Collin had decided to leave for Seattle a little early. He'd been wrong assuming he might start to feel normal again by going back to school.

It had just made him feel bad.

Since one o'clock, he'd been to three hypnotists and spent two hundred and twenty dollars—not counting gas and ferry tickets. None of the hypnotherapists had been able to put him into a trance. Hell, they hadn't even made him sleepy with all their incantations. And they kept acting like it was his fault. He wasn't trying hard enough. He was trying too hard. He wasn't relaxing. He wasn't focusing. He was resisting.

Yes, and he was pissed off and discouraged, too.

Collin stood near the foot of the lobby's stairway. On the wall was a glass-encased, black, grooved velvety sign with white plastic letters that fit in the grooves. Among two lawyers, an accountant, a chiropractor, two psychologists, and a massage therapist, he spotted her:

OLIVIA BARKER, HYPNOTHERAPY – Rm. 304

He couldn't help feeling this would be almost as bad a rip-off as that antique lamp in the window next door. But at least she had an office, which gave her a professional edge over most of the other hypnotists he'd seen in the last two days. Only one of the others—his first appointment today—had had an office, and that gray-haired guy had been a jerk. Cold, clinical, and impatient to the point of grouchiness, he'd been the one who had said Collin wasn't focusing.

As he walked up the two flights of stairs, Collin told himself to keep an open mind. He found the door marked 304, along with a computer-printed, laminated sign:

PLEASE COME IN & HAVE A SEAT
Someone Will Be With You Shortly

He stepped into the small waiting room and sat down on the yellow Ikea-looking sofa. There was another door across from the one he'd just come through. He gave her some points for the framed Edward Hopper sailboat print on the wall. At least she had nice taste in art. Some of her periodicals were a few months old. He spotted the *People* with Kate Middleton wearing that big blue hat on the cover. It was the issue that featured his mother's murder—three pages of THE REAL-LIFE NIGHTMARE FOR THE NIGHT WHISPERER CHILD STAR, with a few photos of him, old and current. There was also a candid shot of his mother and Chance at some party. He didn't even have to open the magazine, because he practically knew the article by heart. Under that headline, it said in big, bold print:

> Former child actor Collin Cox, 16, is back in
> the public eye after the grisly murder of his
> mother and her lover. While he slept, just one
> floor below him the carnage was happening . . .

Collin wasn't sure why he felt compelled to do it, but he took the magazine and slipped it to the bottom of the pile on the end table.

Picking up another issue of *People,* he nervously thumbed through it. He heard a click, and looked up just as the door opened.

The pretty, auburn-haired woman wore black slacks and a dark blue blouse. Standing in the second doorway, she looked perplexed to see him. Still, she kept a polite, pleasant smile fixed on her face. Collin figured she had been expecting someone older. There was something about her that he immediately liked. She seemed normal, nice. He remembered Claudette's advice, and figured this thirty-something Olivia person had the smarts and inner strength to take on Wade Grinnell if she had to.

She was also the last hypnotist on his list. It had to work with her.

Clutching the doorknob, she stared at him. "Russ?"

Olivia glanced out her office window. The light rain showers had turned into a torrent. She noticed the downpour against the streetlights, practically coming down sideways. But she couldn't see Collin Cox anymore. Nor was there any sign of the man who had been skulking behind him.

Everything about this situation looked bad.

She'd started her hypnotherapy business so that she wouldn't have to deal with patients whose problems were in any way life-threatening. Some genuinely troubled people had come to her, and she'd wanted to help them. But after Layne, she just couldn't risk it again. So if a potential client had a severe addiction or mental condition, she always gave them her list of qualified therapists and psychologists—and refused to take money for the introductory session.

She'd read about Collin Cox and his horrible stage mother, who had been murdered along with her boyfriend. Obviously, his problems were even worse now. If ever there was the perfect candidate for her referral sheet, Collin Cox was it. She was enough of a film fan that it was tempting to help this vulnerable onetime child star. But she couldn't risk getting involved.

The lights in her office flickered.

"Shit," Olivia muttered. She'd had more than her share of excitement for one evening. She didn't need the power going out right now, not when she was the only one in the building. She opened the bottom left drawer of her desk and grabbed a flashlight. She set it on top of the desk, so it was nearby—just in case.

She collected her coat and purse, but then she heard a click from the cordless phone on her desk. The light on the recharger cradle started blinking. She had another call. Olivia saw the caller ID: *STAMPLER, C*—again.

"Oh, for God's sakes . . ." She swiped up the cordless and clicked it on. "You're going to have to stop calling me," she announced.

"I know I'm pushing my luck, and I'm sorry," he said. It sounded like he was talking to her from inside a drum with all the tapping in the background. Olivia realized it was the rain. He was probably sitting in his car. "Did you get my last message?" he asked. "Do you know who I really am? If you don't believe me, I'm in an issue of *People* in your waiting room—"

"Yes, Collin," she said. "I got your message. And yes, once you told me who you were, I recognized you. But it doesn't change anything. I can't help you."

"But you already have," he said. "I've learned a lot after watching that one session with you. This Wade guy, I'd never heard of him until last Saturday night, when my friends recorded me while I was hypnotized. Wade Grinnell is a real person who's been dead for fifty years. You can look him up on Google. He did some awful things—"

"This isn't some character you're playing in a movie?" she asked skeptically.

"No, I'm not doing any acting right now," he replied. "I'm living with my grandparents in Poulsbo and going to school. That 'chubby girl' and 'the Mexican guy' he mentioned, they were my friends. They were the ones who hypnotized me, and now they're both dead." He let out a half-laugh, half-cry. "I guess that's hardly an incentive for you to see me again. But you should know why I can't go back to her to hypnotize me anymore. None of the other hypnotists I've seen could get me into a trance. You're the only one. I need you to talk to this person inside me. I need to find out why this is happening—and if he had anything to do with my mother's murder."

"Collin, I can't—"

"Please. You can charge me double your usual fee. If you could just see me a couple of times, and put me under. I'll write out the questions you can ask. I—I saw how he was with you. That was somebody else. That wasn't me—"

"I understand that, but—"

"If you need to restrain me for the next session, that's fine. Tie me to a chair if you have to. I'll go along with whatever you say. You call the shots. I don't want to hurt anyone. . . ."

The lights flickered again. She heard a click on the line.

"Are you still there?" he asked, sounding panicked.

"Yes, I'm here," she said. "But I need to go. The lights keep blinking. I'm worried the building might lose power. We could get cut off at any minute. Listen, Collin, I'd like to help you, but you're underage. I can't do anything without permission from your legal guardian. That's the first hurdle. Second, if this is a true case of multiple personality, I don't have the expertise to help you. On that list I gave you, there are several highly qualified therapists. I think you're much better off going with one of them."

"Just see me one more time," he said. "Then you can pick the therapist I should see—and I'll go see them. Okay? Please?"

He wasn't giving up.

Olivia sighed. "Let me think about it." It seemed like the only way she could get him to leave her alone for now. "Give me the weekend, and I'll get back to you. In the meantime, I want you to make an appointment with Marlys, on the top of that referral list. She's good, and very compassionate. But she'll insist on clearing all sessions with your grandparents. The same goes for me, Collin. I can't see you again without your guardian's permission."

"But you don't understand—"

"That's non-negotiable," she said, cutting him off. "And no more calls. I'll get in touch with you on Monday. Okay? Is it a deal?"

"Okay, thanks."

When she hung up the phone, Olivia glanced at the caller ID again. She scribbled on her notepad:

Collin Cox – 206/555-5028
Stampler—Poulsbo—Grandparents?

If she couldn't make Collin back off, she'd get in touch with his grandparents herself. In the meantime, she scribbled: *Call Marlys* on the same piece of paper. If Collin did indeed contact the therapist at the top of that list, Olivia needed to warn her exactly what she was in for.

Before slipping the piece of paper in her purse, Olivia wrote one more thing on it:

Google <u>Wade Grinnell</u> RIP – 50 yrs.

The lights suddenly went out, and a panic swept through her. Outside, the rain subsided—and the streetlights were on. The lights remained on in the storefronts across the street, too. It was just her building.

Olivia thought about that man who was following Collin. She wondered where he'd disappeared to.

There was enough light from outside for her to see her way around the office. She picked up her coat and purse again, then grabbed the flashlight.

With a flicker, the power came back on. She wasn't sure how long it would last this time. All she wanted to do was get out of there while the lights were still on.

The phone rang, startling her. The brief blackout must have tripped the silent ring setting. Without thinking, she picked up the cordless and clicked it on. "Collin, I told you, you can't keep calling me. . . ."

There was silence on the other end. Olivia glanced at the caller ID: *Unknown.*

"Hello?" she said.

She heard nothing, and then there was a click on the line.

Frowning, she hung up the phone. Stashing the flashlight in her purse, she headed toward her office door. She was about to switch off the lights when the phone rang again. "Oh, give me a break already," she muttered, returning to her desk. She clicked on the cordless. "Hello?" she said impatiently.

"Olivia?"

It had been weeks since they'd spoken. Most of their correspondence had been through their attorneys. "Clay?" she murmured.

"Hi, your dad gave me your office number," he said soberly. "I didn't want to leave this on your voice mail. It's—well, it's pretty horrible news."

"What's going on?" she asked warily.

"It's Susan and Jerry," he said, his voice a bit shaky. "Their house caught on fire in the middle of the night.

The police still aren't sure exactly how it happened. Anyway, Olivia, they're—they're all gone, Sue, Jerry, Gail, and Chris. . . ."

With the phone to her ear, Olivia moved to the other side of the desk and sank down in her chair. It was like someone had just punched her in the stomach. She liked Clay's sister—and her family. She thought of the email from Gail last week: *My mom would kill me for telling you this,* she'd written. *But I've heard her say the same thing. I think Uncle Clay is a huge dope.*

"When did it happen?" Olivia heard herself ask.

"Early Tuesday morning, while they were all asleep," he said. "Someone broke into the house on Monday afternoon. The police think there might be a connection, but they're not sure yet."

Olivia said nothing. She felt the tears starting.

"I keep thinking that in the last conversation I had with my sister, she told me how disappointed she was in me—for what I did to you."

Olivia sighed. "I don't know what to say to that."

He'd disappointed her, too. But now wasn't the time to go into it.

"There's going to be a memorial service Saturday, in Poulsbo," he said. "I'll email you the details. I really hope you can make it. At the same time, I totally understand if you decide not to attend."

She didn't ask if Corinne would be there. She just assumed he'd be bringing her.

Olivia sniffled. "Let me think about it."

"Of course," he said. "Listen, do me a favor and don't bite my head off. But I just need to say it. I've missed you, y'know?"

Olivia took a deep breath. "I—I'm really sorry about Sue and Jerry and the kids."

Then she hung up.

She leaned over her desk and cried—dark, inconsolable sobs. She wasn't sure how long it went on, but she went through several Kleenexes, which were usually for her clients. Then the lights flickered again.

Unsteadily, Olivia got to her feet. She grabbed her purse and headed for the office door. Switching off the lights, she stepped out to the waiting room and locked her door. She was about to head out to the hallway when she heard a door shut somewhere downstairs.

Olivia froze. She didn't think anyone else was in the building. She listened for another moment, and didn't hear anything, not even the rain. She opened the waiting room door and found the third-floor hallway almost completely dark. If not for the light in the waiting room behind her, she wouldn't have been able to see her hand in front of her face.

"Is—" Olivia hesitated. She was about to call out, *Is anyone there?* Then it occurred to her that it was a pretty stupid question. Anyone quietly standing there in the pitch blackness wasn't likely to answer her. She thought once again about the man who had been following Collin Cox.

Olivia reached into her purse and took out the flashlight. Switching it on, she directed the beam along the hallway—and the different doors. The light was wobbly, because she couldn't keep her hand from shaking.

Reluctantly, she set the lock catch and closed the door to the waiting room. She was swallowed up in darkness now. With the flashlight as a guide, she made her way toward the stairs. She spotted the light switch on the wall—at the top of the staircase. Olivia flicked it up and down. Nothing.

Someone must have gotten into the electric room and tinkered with the power.

She hurried down the stairs as quickly as she could.

The flashlight made frenzied shadows on the steps and the wall.

At the second-floor landing, she could see some light from the street coming through the window in the lobby door. Olivia raced down to the first floor. She shined the flashlight down the shadowy hallway, and didn't see anyone.

As she turned around again, a man on the sidewalk hurried past the door. Startled, Olivia let out a gasp. She almost dropped the flashlight. It took a few moments to get her breath back—and find her key for the street door. Her heart was still racing. She took one last look toward the stairs. She noticed that the glass door encasing the building directory was ajar. Someone had managed to unlock it.

Olivia ran the flashlight beam over the directory— with the white lettering fixed in the grooved black velvet. Everything was the same, except for her name.

All the letters had been turned upside down.

CHAPTER FIFTEEN

She couldn't stop staring at the back of Corinne Beal's head.

Clay's girlfriend—and the mother of his baby, which she'd be popping out in five months—hung all over him in the front pew. She kept wailing and sobbing at full volume every few minutes, while everyone else in the Stone Chapel at Cherry Grove Memorial Park grieved quietly. It seemed as phony as it was distracting.

The clean-lined, modern chapel seated about a hundred and fifty mourners and was packed to full capacity. At the front of the sanctuary—above a cherrywood crucifix—was a large screen for video and pictorial tributes to the deceased. Over to one side was a podium, where one speaker after another shared a special sentiment about Jerry, Sue, Gail, and Chris. An assortment of sweet, evocative images of the Pelhams was displayed on the screen during the readings. It was really heartbreaking—especially when one of Chris's fifth-grade classmates came up to talk about how much he missed his best friend. But every memorial homily was interrupted by a mournful yowl from Corinne in the first pew.

The North Kitsap High School girls' choir stood in front of the chapel, on the other side of the pulpit. They provided beautiful hymns between the speeches. It was pointed out early in the service that Gail had auditioned for the girls' choir only a week before her death. All twenty or so of the choir girls wore black. No one stood out—not the way Corinne seemed to scream for attention in her silky, slinky royal-blue number with black polka dots. It showed off her baby-bump. Her blond hair was swept up and she'd pinned some black netting in it—with dark blue sequins, no less.

There weren't any caskets at the front of the chapel. The four bodies were still with the county coroner while an investigation into the fire continued. Jerry's brother, Mike, had decided along with Clay that there would be a quiet burial later—attended by family only. Mike and his wife, Cathy, had arranged the memorial. Olivia knew them from several different family functions over the years.

Cathy had greeted her in the reception room before the service. "Now is probably not the time to be catty," she'd whispered. "But really, what's the deal with Clay's supposedly grief-stricken girlfriend? Sue and Jerry met her once—back when they were in Portland last month. They couldn't stand her. And she's acting like she's just lost her best friends. Oh, and wait until you get a load of what she's wearing. It's like something from the Lady Gaga funeral collection. Everyone misses you, Olivia. Of course, you know that Sue, Jerry, and the kids adored you. You're coming to the reception afterwards, aren't you?"

Olivia had always liked Cathy. But she'd already

made up her mind to catch the ferry back to Seattle right after the service.

Sitting in a pew in the back, she'd been so consumed with grief and distracted by Corinne's shenanigans that she hadn't really paid much attention to anyone else in the congregation. It wasn't until she stepped out of the chapel and opened her umbrella that Olivia spotted Collin Cox among the mourners. Her first thought was that he might be stalking her. But he was dressed for the memorial service in a tie, blazer, and khakis. He filed out along with the others—toward the parking area and the chapel's lush, green grounds. The rain fell lightly, almost a mist. He didn't open his umbrella until an older couple came out of the church. Then he held the umbrella over them as they headed toward the row of cars along the side of the road.

"Collin?" she called.

He glanced toward her, and his mouth dropped open. He looked stunned to see her.

Olivia started toward him.

He quickly hustled the older couple toward a BMW.

Olivia stopped abruptly at the edge of the parking lot. She could tell he didn't want to introduce them to her. She remembered writing that note to herself the other night: *Stampler—Poulsbo—grandparents?*

Standing beneath her umbrella, she watched him hold the door open for his grandmother. He said something to his grandfather, who was climbing behind the wheel. Then with his umbrella overhead, Collin trotted toward her. "What are you doing here?" he asked, out of breath.

"I was about to ask you the same thing," Olivia said. She glanced toward the BMW. "Are those your grandparents?"

He nodded. "Listen, I'd rather we not talk here, at least not in front of them." He looked back over his shoulder at the car. "I tried to explain to my grandfather about what's happening to me, and he's totally in denial. He figures if I just stay away from therapists and hypnotists, my problems will all go away. He'd be really pissed off if he found out I went to see you on Thursday. Can we meet later—in town? How did you know I'd be here anyway?"

"I didn't," Olivia said. "Sue Pelham was my husband's sister."

Collin just stared at her and blinked. "Wait a minute," he whispered. "You're the aunt who taught Gail how to hypnotize people. No wonder you had the same technique as her. Gail was like practically my only friend here—her and Fernando."

Olivia started to put it together in her head. Collin was Gail's blue-eyed crush, the one who had acted "weird" last Saturday night. Gail had always struggled to lose weight, and Collin's other friend was named Fernando. Now it made sense that Collin's loutish alter-ego had emerged during their session on Thursday night and asked, "So where's the fat girl and the Mexican guy?"

Collin had told her to Google the name Wade Grinnell, and Olivia had even written it down. But she hadn't researched this Wade person. Instead, she'd looked up Collin Cox, expecting to find something about him having a breakdown after his mother's death. But there was nothing. Then again, she hadn't researched him very thoroughly. She'd still been in shock over news of the fire that had killed Clay's sister and her family. The brief talk with her estranged husband—especially the part when he'd told her that he really missed her—had been on her mind, too. In fact, she'd almost forgotten about the power outage in the hallways on Thursday night—and the bizarre rearrangement of her name in the building directory.

She shifted her umbrella a bit, and her eyes searched Collin's. "The other night, after you left the building, you didn't come back, did you?"

He shook his head. "No. Why?"

Olivia thought about the man who may or may not have been following Collin. She studied the vulnerable expression on Collin's handsome young face. Should she warn this already troubled kid that someone *might* be following him? Dare she risk unnecessarily messing him up even more? She hesitated, and then shook her head. "Nothing, I think someone was just playing a practical joke on me. Forget it."

Craning his neck, Collin glanced past her umbrella and gave a little wave.

Olivia looked over her shoulder and saw his grandfather standing outside the car. He had the driver's door open, and the windshield wipers were going. He held a program from the memorial service over his head. He gave his grandson an impatient, exasperated look.

Collin turned toward her again. "Listen, I gotta go," he whispered. "But to be honest with you, I didn't call your friend Marlys. And I can't get my grandfather's permission to see you. Do you really need his consent? Couldn't you see me at least one more time? None of the other hypnotists I saw needed permission from a guardian."

"I'll bet none of the other hypnotherapists knew they were dealing with someone who may have multiple personality disorder. I'm sorry, but if this *Wade* persona is real—and he's clearly real to you—then this is serious, Collin. And it's way beyond my level of expertise."

"Please," he whispered, "just one more session. No one has to know."

Olivia felt so torn. Part of her longed to help this poor kid, but she knew it would end up getting her into a hell of a lot of trouble. She looked over toward the chapel again, and saw Clay in a black suit—and a black-and-maroon tie she'd bought him for his birthday two years ago. He held up a big umbrella, and Corinne was hanging on his arm. Corinne didn't seem to notice her, but Clay had. He was staring at her with a forlorn look on his face.

"Please," Collin repeated.

Olivia turned to him. "You need to give me some time. I have your phone number. I'll call you." She noticed his grandfather over by the BMW, glaring at them. "You better go now. Tell your grandfather that I'm Gail's aunt, and that we've met before. You won't be lying."

Collin glanced over his shoulder, and then leaned in toward her. "Thanks," he whispered.

He turned and started for the car. His grandfather ducked back inside. Collin was about to reach for the back passenger door when someone else approached him. It was a handsome, lean, thirtyish man with wavy brown hair and a dark blue suit. He didn't have an umbrella.

Collin didn't look happy to see him.

"Well, hi," he muttered, stopping a few feet away from the BMW. "What's going on? What are you doing here?"

"Didn't you get my emails?" Ian Haggerty asked. "I sent two."

Collin shook his head. He nervously glanced back at the car.

"Well, it's not the first time that's happened with my server," Ian said. "Anyway, I saw you called and hung up the other day. I also read that two of your classmates had died. I wasn't sure how close you were to them—"

"They were my only friends here," Collin said, his voice cracking a little.

"Then I guess I was right to be concerned about you." Ian shrugged. "I would have called, but all I have is your grandparents' home line, and I wasn't sure how my calling to chat you up would go over with your grandfather—or my boss. I'm already in enough trouble at work. Anyway, I read about the memorial service, and took a chance you'd be here."

"So you came all this way?" Collin asked.

"Sure, I didn't have anything else going on. Plus, like I said, I was concerned. . . ."

"Well, thanks," Collin said. He shot another look toward the car.

Ian stepped closer to him. "So—am I still *persona non grata* with your grandfather?"

Collin shrugged evasively. *Persona-non-whatever* sounded like one of his grandparents' expressions. "I'm not sure what that is," he said under his breath. "But if it means my grandfather probably isn't thrilled I'm talking with you, then yeah."

Ian nodded. "Well, I guess my timing here sucks. If you ever want to get together for an old bull session, just give me another call and leave a message. You can . . ." He trailed off as the BMW's driver's door opened and Old Andy stepped out.

Collin sheepishly glanced at his grandfather. He was

about to apologize for keeping him waiting. But to his utter surprise, his grandfather broke into a friendly smile and approached Ian. "Well, hello. How've you been?" He put his hand out for Ian to shake.

"I'm fine, thanks, Mr. Stampler," Ian said, pumping his hand. Then he waved at Dee in the passenger seat. She waved back.

"I tell you, my friend," his grandfather said. Collin could see he'd forgotten Ian's name. "We could sure use you looking after the house again what with everything that's been going on around here. It's a sad, scary state of affairs. These poor folks—first their house gets broken into, and then the fire. At the same time, Collin's other good friend got picked up by some . . ." He trailed off, shook his head and sighed. "Anyway, it's been awfully rough. Tell me, are the Seattle police interested in either case? Do they have any leads?"

Ian shook his head. "I wouldn't know, Mr. Stampler—"

"Andy," he said.

"I wouldn't know, Andy," he continued. "I'm not here on business. I have friends on the Peninsula, and their daughter—my godchild, in fact—she was singing in the choir today. She wanted me to come listen to her."

"Well, those girls did a lovely job. Be sure to tell your goddaughter that for me. What's her name?"

"Brooks, Amanda Brooks." He turned toward Collin. "In fact, we were—um, thinking of grabbing something to eat at Crepes Nuevo. Collin, you're welcome to join us."

Collin realized Ian was suggesting a rendezvous place if he needed to talk with him. He automatically glanced at his grandfather for his approval. But he got a furtive, sour frown.

Ian must have seen it, too. "Then again, it might not

be the right time," he said, patting Collin's shoulder. "It was a pretty emotional service for everybody."

Collin shrugged awkwardly. "Yeah, thanks for the offer, but maybe another day."

"Listen, Collin, we should skedaddle," his grandfather said. He grinned at Ian and pumped his hand again. "Nice running into you again, my friend."

"You, too, sir," Ian said. Then he shook Collin's hand and held on to it for a moment. "It was good to see you, Collin. I'm really sorry about both your friends. Feel free to ring me up anytime, okay?"

"Thanks," Collin said.

He felt defeated as he climbed into the backseat of the BMW. He couldn't help resenting his grandfather for that one little frown. He really needed a friend right now. And Ian would have listened to him. He couldn't discuss anything with his grandfather. And right now, he wasn't sure if Olivia Barker would even see him again.

His grandfather got behind the wheel and shut his door. "What's his name again?"

"Ian," Collin said.

"This goddaughter, Amanda, do you know her?"

Collin hesitated. He wasn't completely sure whether or not Ian had been telling the truth about his Bainbridge Island friends. "I don't know her very well," Collin lied. "She's a senior."

"Who was the pretty woman you were talking to?" Dee asked, squirming a bit in the front seat.

"Oh, she's Gail's aunt," Collin said. "I met her a while back."

His grandfather started up the car. But Dee was shaking her head. She patted Old Andy's hand on the steering wheel. "You're going to hate me, but I don't think I'll make it for the drive home. I better go visit the ladies' here."

Collin climbed out and got the door for his grandmother. He opened the umbrella, and handed it her. As she headed back to the Stone Chapel, he looked over at Olivia Barker. She was talking to a man in a black suit. Collin realized she probably knew a lot more people here than he did. After all, she was family.

He turned and watched Ian wander back toward his Honda Civic.

"You might as well get in from the rain and sit up here," Collin's grandfather said. "You know your grandmother. She's going to be a while."

Collin sat in the passenger seat and closed the door. His grandfather still had the car on, and the wipers were sweeping across the windshield.

"So what were you and this Ian fellow talking about? Was he asking about the fire? I mean, are the Seattle Police investigating this now or what?"

"I don't think so, Grandpa. I think it's just like he said. He's here because Amanda—"

"Bullshit," his grandfather grumbled. "Where is she? Why is he getting into the car by himself if they're going out for crepes together? He's sniffing around here about something. You can bank on that. Did he ask about where you were on Monday or Tuesday? Because if he's trying implicate you in anything . . ."

"No, I don't think it's like that at all," Collin said. "He was just being friendly."

"That's what he wants you to think," his grandfather said. "I've dealt with a number of guys like that in business. They act like your friend, and all the while they're planning to screw you. We haven't seen him in over two months, and suddenly he shows up again—

right after you lose your two friends. There's a connection here, I can tell." Old Andy nodded to the black Honda Civic pulling out of the Memorial Park's lot. "See, there he goes, all by his lonesome. Where's the niece?"

"Maybe she drove in a separate car," Collin said. "The choir probably had to get here early. Grandpa, I know you've never liked him much, and thought it was weird we were friends. But Ian's a good guy. I remind him of his kid brother. It was nice to have somebody kind of older I could look up to. I sure never got that from any of Mom's boyfriends. . . ."

"Well, I still don't trust him, Collin," his grandfather said. "You watch out for that guy. Let me know if he comes poking around again. What's his last name?"

Collin hesitated. If he made something up, his grandfather was bound to figure out the lie sooner rather than later. He already felt he was on borrowed time with this Amanda Brooks he'd never heard of. "Haggerty," he said finally.

With a frown, Collin stared out the rain-beaded window at Olivia Barker and the man in the black suit. He wondered if the guy was a relative of Gail's. He looked a bit like Mrs. Pelham.

It had been over two months since she'd seen him in person.

Olivia wondered if he remembered that she'd given him the tie he was wearing. Had he put it on thinking of her? She wished like hell it didn't still matter to her what Clay was thinking.

He was just as attractive as ever as he stood in front of her. The light rain matted down his dark blond hair, and the drops cascaded along his handsome face. All the moisture made his long eyelashes stick together. Most devastating of all was the wounded, vulnerable, apologetic look he gave her. "I've got to tell you, Olivia," he whispered. "I don't know what I was thinking. I'm absolutely miserable."

"Good," she said. She held her umbrella directly overhead—and didn't allow an inch of it to shield him.

He smiled sadly and nodded. "I deserve that." He shrugged. "I don't know how it happened that I started up with Corinne. Maybe it was all the pressure I felt to make a baby. That really took the romance out of everything. And I kept thinking I was failing you, because you weren't getting pregnant. I hated letting you down. So much of my self-worth is wrapped up in you—and it still is. But Corinne made me feel as if I—"

"I don't give a shit how she made you feel," Olivia said, cutting him off. "I'm not interested in analyzing what you were going through. I was there, and got hurt a hell of a lot more than you did. I'm sorry about Sue and Jerry and the kids. I've been crying about it for the last two days. I feel horrible for you right now. But don't expect me to give you a break for the terrible way you treated me before all this happened."

"That's fair enough," he said, looking down at the ground. "I guess I deserve that, too. If it's any consolation to you, every single one of my relatives thinks I'm an idiot for letting you go. Plus you already knew this, but Corinne's crazy. . . ."

Olivia glanced over at Corinne, standing near the doorway of the church. She held an umbrella over her head and glared at them.

"I'm living with a crazy woman," he continued. "It's a horrible thing to say about the mother of my unborn child, but it's true. I can't handle her. These last few days, since we found out about Sue and Jerry and the kids, she's been totally off the wall. She barely knew them, and you'd think it was *her* sister's family who died. She's angry as hell one minute, and all weepy the next. We came up to Seattle on Thursday morning and checked into a hotel. When I told her I was going to call you, she went ballistic. She wouldn't listen to reason. I told her how Sue and Jerry were family to you. But that didn't matter to her. She got so upset she jumped in the car and drove away. She left me stranded in this hotel on Lake Union—and I had a bunch of things I needed to do for this service. I'd promised Mike and Cathy I'd—"

"This was on Thursday?" Olivia cut in. "How long was she gone—from when to when?"

"From around four until almost eight. And I was supposed to go pick up memorial programs from the printer that afternoon. Plus I had to—"

"Did Corinne say where she went?"

Clay shrugged. "She said she went for a drive. I was worried about her in all that rain."

Olivia frowned. "I have a feeling she swung by my office."

He winced. "Jesus, don't tell me she screwed around with your car again."

"No, there wasn't any property damage this time. She just tried to spook me out, that's all."

"I'm so sorry," he muttered.

Olivia looked over at Corinne again, and glared right back at her. "Listen, Clay," she said, her eyes still narrowed at his girlfriend. "Tell the mother of your child if she comes near me again, I'll get the police on her so fast, it'll make her crazy head spin. And you won't be able to protect her this time. Make sure she knows that."

"I will," he whispered. "Please, Olivia, I'm trying to

tell you that I'm sorry. I didn't realize how much I needed you."

She looked at him, and took a deep breath. "I'm really sorry about Sue, Jerry, and the kids," she said steadily.

Then Olivia turned away and started for her car.

More than anything, she wanted a cigarette. But she didn't have any in her purse or in the car, and smoking wasn't allowed on the ferry. So Olivia settled for a turkey and Swiss on wheat bread from the assorted plastic-wrapped cold sandwiches in the cafeteria's refrigerator case. She got a bag of SunChips and a Diet Coke, too. She was in line for the cashier when she spotted the handsome, brown-haired man who had approached Collin after the memorial service.

Grabbing a box of popcorn, he smiled at her.

Olivia quickly looked away. Collin had seemed pretty uncomfortable when this man had come up to him outside the Stone Chapel. She didn't want to encourage the guy to come up and make her uncomfortable, too. Besides, she had enough on her mind after talking with Clay.

She paid for her food and took it to one of the booth-style seats by the windows. She set everything down on the Formica table.

Clay hadn't exactly said it, but he'd given her every indication he was ready to come crawling back to her. Now—while his insane girlfriend was pregnant? Was he crazy, too?

Olivia was thinking about that as she unfolded her napkin.

"Is it all right if I sit here?"

She glanced up at the man in the dark blue suit. With

his box of popcorn and a can of Hires root beer, he nodded at the empty bench across from her.

"Help yourself," Olivia said, putting her napkin in her lap. She tried to look terribly interested in her food.

"Didn't I see you at the memorial service for the Pelham family?" he asked.

With a mouth full of turkey sandwich, Olivia nodded, and left him hanging for a few moments. "Yes, Sue and Jerry were my in-laws," she finally said. "Were you a friend of theirs?"

"No, I never met them." He set his box of popcorn on the table.

"But you know Collin Cox," Olivia said.

"Yes. I guess you know Collin, too. At least, I saw you talking with him."

"That's right," she replied over her Diet Coke. She didn't say anything more. She suddenly felt protective of Collin. After talking with Clay, she was almost certain Corinne had fiddled with the lights and the directory sign in her office building on Thursday night. But she still wondered about the man who had been following Collin after he'd left her office. Could this be him?

"He's a nice kid," the man said. "By the way, my name's Ian Haggerty."

"Olivia," she said. "Do you live in Seattle?"

He nodded. "Madison Park."

Olivia nibbled on a SunChip. If he was telling the truth, he lived only a few blocks from her office in Madison Valley. She gave him a wary sidelong glance. "So tell me, what brings you all the way to Poulsbo— and a memorial service for a family you've never met?"

"I guess it does seem a little strange," he admitted. "I knew Collin was friends with—well, I guess Gail Pelham was your niece. I'm awfully sorry, by the way. Anyhow, I went there for Collin. I don't know if he told you, but he lost another friend the very same day as the fire. It was a homicide. After everything he's been through, I just wanted to offer my support."

Olivia sat back. "Are you with the police?"

He chuckled. "Yeah, I'm a Seattle Police detective. How did you know?"

"Just a guess," she said. "You sound like a policeman. Not too many civilians refer to a murder as a *homicide*. Which are you investigating, the fire or the murder?"

"Neither. I wasn't there on police business. Like I said, I was there for Collin."

Olivia couldn't help frowning. She wanted to say, *And yet he didn't look all that pleased to see you.* Instead, she took another bite of her sandwich.

"Do you know Collin well?" he asked, nibbling on some popcorn.

"Actually, I've met him only once before today," Olivia answered. "He seems like a great kid. But now I'm not so sure. I told him to look me up next time he's in Seattle. If the police consider him a murder suspect, I'd really like to know—I mean, just in case he takes me up on the offer."

"I don't think you have anything to worry about with Collin," he said. "You're right, he's a great guy. It's just that he's had some real bad breaks lately. . . ."

Olivia's cell phone rang in her coat pocket. She took it out and checked the caller ID:

BISCHOFF, CLAYTON
503/555-8982

"I'm sorry, but I have to take this," she said. She clicked on the phone. "Hi, could you hold on, please?"

"Sure," she heard Clay reply. She started clearing her food from the table.

"It's okay," the cop said, getting to his feet. "I can move. After all, you were here first."

"No, I'm fine, really. Sit there and finish your popcorn. It was nice meeting you."

He nodded. "Nice meeting you, too, Ms.—I'm sorry . . ."

"Barker, Olivia Barker," she said.

He nodded. "I'm sorry for your loss, Ms. Barker."

"Thank you," she murmured. She hurried to the nearest trash can and threw out the food. She didn't want the cop spying on her while she was on the phone with Clay. He'd never explained how he knew Collin. She had a hard time believing they were really friends.

It was still drizzling outside, and windy on the deck. So Olivia headed for the stairwell to the parking level. "Are you still there?" she said into the phone.

"Yeah," Clay said. "Listen, did I get you at a bad time?"

"I'm on the ferry, heading down to the car, where it's quieter. Keep holding, okay?" She didn't wait for him to answer before putting him on hold again.

She probably could have talked with him while she walked, but part of her wanted to keep him waiting. It was strange, talking with Collin after the memorial, and then Clay—two different people telling her how much they needed her right now.

The one who seemed to need her more, the one who seemed genuine, was Collin. Even with the crazy way he'd acted when she'd hypnotized him on Thursday night, he seemed less capable of hurting her than Clay.

On the parking level, she found her car and unlocked it with a beep. Then she climbed in behind the wheel. "Thanks for waiting," she said into the phone. "What's going on?"

"I'm at Mike and Cathy's," he whispered. "I'm in one of the kids' rooms upstairs. Corinne's down at the buffet. . . ."

"Well, thanks for the update," Olivia said dryly.

"I'm just saying, in case I have to hang up suddenly."

"Did you talk to her about her little visit to my office building on Thursday night?"

"Yeah, and Corinne says she doesn't know what you're talking about. She doesn't even know where your Seattle office is."

"She figured out where I worked in Portland, and where I parked my car," Olivia said. "She can be quite resourceful. Is this why you're calling me now—to tell me that I've got it all wrong about your sweet, unassuming girlfriend?"

"God, no," he sighed. "I didn't mean—"

"A little over an hour ago, you were telling me that she's a raving lunatic."

"I'm not siding with her or anything. I just thought you should know it's possible she didn't do what you said she did. Please, babe, this is all coming out so wrong. It's not why I phoned you. . . ."

Olivia felt a little heart-flutter when he called her *babe*. It had always gotten to her when he'd used that term of endearment—especially while making love. She hated that the sound of his voice saying that word still had an effect on her.

"You lost the right to call me *babe* three months ago," she said evenly.

"I'm sorry, it just slipped out."

"So—why exactly did you call me?"

"It was awkward after the memorial—what with

Corinne in front of the church, watching us like a gargoyle the whole time. We'll be here in Poulsbo until Monday morning, and then we're spending the night in Seattle. Corinne is seeing some friends at four-thirty Monday afternoon. I'm wondering if I could meet with you around five o'clock."

"I'm sorry, I can't," Olivia heard herself say. "I have to meet a client at five on Monday."

"Can't you cancel or rearrange it?" Clay asked.

"No, he's a special client," she said. "And right now, he needs me a hell of a lot more than you do, Clay. Have a safe trip back to Portland."

Olivia clicked off before he had a chance to say anything.

In her purse, she found the piece of paper with the phone number on it. She punched in the number, and counted four ringtones before his recorded greeting answered: *"Hi, this is Collin, and I'm sorry I can't pick up right now. So please leave a message after the beep, and hopefully we'll connect later. Thanks for calling!"*

He didn't sound like a goofy teenager in the recording. He sounded like the professional actor he was. But the greeting was interrupted by a couple of static breaks. One glance at the phone told her that *Bischoff, Clayton* was trying to call her back.

Olivia ignored him. She waited for the beep, and left a message for Collin Cox: "Hi, this is Olivia Barker. I can see you Monday in my office at five o'clock. Let me know if that works for you. Also, I need to find out if you're friends with someone named Ian who claims to be a cop. He came up and spoke with you after the memorial service this afternoon. Let me know, okay? We can talk about it when we get together. You have my number. Give me a call and let me know if you can make it. Take care, Collin."

She switched off her phone and stashed it in her purse. Then Olivia sat back and drummed her fingers on the steering wheel.

She desperately wanted a cigarette.

Inside the idling black Saturn, he lit up a cigarette and watched Olivia Barker across the street.

She emerged from a cheesy little convenience store not far from her office, Madison Val-U Mart. Just outside the glass door, she unwrapped something and tossed the wrapper in the trash. He could now see she'd bought a pack of cigarettes. She took one out and lit it. She stayed under the store awning, but wandered closer to her car in the small lot. It was still raining lightly. She really seemed to be enjoying that cigarette.

He chuckled and took another drag from his Winston. On the seat next to him, he had half a box of popcorn from the ferry ride this afternoon. In the backseat he had an overnight bag. For now, he wasn't putting any of his personal items in his trunk—not until he gave it another thorough cleaning. Those scent dogs at the Seattle ferry terminal the other day had obviously picked up some remnants of the dead Ryan kid. Maybe it was a bit OCD, but he didn't want anything from that kid rubbing off on his stuff.

The overnight bag was there in case he decided to spend the night in Central Washington. He had to make a return trip to Leavenworth before dark so he could finish the job he'd botched the other evening. He figured he might want to grab a shower and some shuteye—after he'd killed the old lady tonight.

Right now, he was focused on someone about fifty years younger. He watched Olivia Barker finally toss the cigarette on the pavement and grind it out with her shoe. She fished the pack out of her purse and went over to the trash can again. She looked like she was about to toss the new pack into the garbage, but hesitated. After a moment, she shoved the cigarettes back in her purse and walked back to her car.

He waited until Olivia's VW turned left onto Madison. Then he slowly pulled out and followed her. Someone cut him off, darting into the space between him and the VW. But he didn't mind. It would be harder for her to spot him now.

She continued down Madison and took a right onto Lake Washington Boulevard. He knew where she was headed—to her father's house on Alder Lane in the Denny-Blaine neighborhood, where a lot of cake-eaters lived. He guessed Walter Barker's classic two-story colonial was worth about 1.5 million. Surrounded by trees and lush gardens, the house was nestled along a narrow, hilly side street and had a majestic view of Lake Washington and the mountains. He'd already scoped the place out this morning while Olivia Barker slept. He'd even taken a little stroll around the garden after her father had left to play golf—at 6:45 on a cool, drizzly October morning. *Another fanatic.* Collin Cox's grandfather was the same way. What was with these retired guys and their golf?

Walter Barker was seventy-one. He'd been a marketing big shot for KOMO-TV before retiring six years ago. The wife, Jane Gallagher Barker, had croaked two years later at age sixty. According to the obit he'd read, they had three kids and two grandchildren at the time. The married one with the kids lived in Pittsburgh. Next in line was Olivia, and then a brother, Rex, several years younger. He was away at college right now.

A few online articles about a shooting at the Portland Wellness Cooperative in July included the wounded therapist's maiden name. Otherwise he might not have made the connection between Olivia Barker the hypno-therapist and Olivia Bischoff the shooting spree survivor. It gave him a better understanding of her background and her vulnerabilities.

What a funny coincidence, the name *Bischoff* had come up in the obituary for the Pelham clan. Earlier today, after the service, he'd watched Olivia talk to that blond guy who looked like an ex-jock. He knew it must have been her husband. And the ditzy blonde in the blue and black polka-dot dress hanging all over him earlier was probably Corinne Beal—and the reason Olivia had moved in with her daddy. He'd read a short article online from *The Oregonian* about how Corinne Beal had wrecked Olivia Bischoff's car—as well as her marriage.

He followed Olivia until she turned onto Alder Lane. He knew she was going home. There was no need to tail her any farther, though she did intrigue him.

He had the old lady to take care of in Leavenworth.

Even if he could linger here, Olivia Barker would certainly notice if he followed her on that little, wind-ing street. With cars parked along one side, it was al-most like a narrow alley.

A fire truck would have a tough time getting down there.

The thought of that made him smile.

CHAPTER SIXTEEN

The *Seattle Times* article she read online was ten years old. Celebrating the fortieth anniversary of the Seattle World's Fair, it featured a *Century 21 Exposition Timeline*. The article was the only search result Google listed for the Wade Grinnell, who had died fifty years ago—the same Wade Grinnell she'd supposedly met through Collin Cox on Thursday night.

She sat in front of her laptop at a little desk space at the end of the long, dark granite countertop in the kitchen. Six years ago, her dad had had the kitchen remodeled: stainless-steel appliances, granite countertops, black-and-white tiles, a butcher-block island that doubled as a breakfast bar, and a big picture window that looked out at the garden and patio. One wall was covered with menus from different restaurants where Olivia's parents had eaten in the thirty-eight years they'd known each other. This little desk area, looking out at the garden, used to be her mother's writing nook. Her mother had gotten to enjoy the new kitchen for only about sixteen months before she'd passed away.

Olivia had R.E.M. on her brother's old boom box in

the corner of the counter. Soon her father would be back from the supermarket, and he'd start dinner on the grill outside. Olivia had the house to herself for now. On a yellow legal pad, she'd scribbled down some notes from the timeline snippets she'd read:

7/9/62 – Ronald & Betty Freitag murdered @ El Mar hotel. 2 kids killed. Less than $100 stolen.

8/8/62 – Five die in fire @ Hotel Aurora Vista. Brandon & Irene Pollack (Irene survived) & kids.

10/11/62 – Wade Grinnell killed by train, running from police. No arrest, no conviction.

The El Mar murders reminded Olivia of the Clutter family killings in Nebraska in 1959, the case Truman Capote wrote about in his book *In Cold Blood.* It was the same sort of bizarre, senseless tragedy—an entire family tied up and executed for less than a hundred dollars.

But Olivia was more concerned about the deadly fire at the hotel, which seemed too similar to the blaze that had killed her in-laws just days ago. Obviously, Collin was concerned about it, too. She remembered back when Collin Cox was in *The Night Whisperer,* there had been stories about a curse that had plagued the film set. One of the main actors had died, and a house they'd used for several scenes had mysteriously burned down.

Olivia didn't believe in curses. Bad luck and bad judgment, yes, but not curses.

Every explanation for what was happening to Collin Cox seemed far-fetched. She didn't know a single therapist who had encountered a patient with multiple personality or dissociative identity disorder. The most famous cases, which had influenced the books and movies *The Three Faces of Eve* and *Sybil*, had since been determined to be faked or fictitious. Some experts regarded Albert DeSalvo, the Boston Strangler, as a true case of multiple personality disorder. But that was up for debate. She only knew a few basic things about dissociative identity disorder. One of them was that people with DID were supposed to be highly susceptible to hypnosis—more than any other clinical patients. Hadn't Collin told her that he'd been to five hypnotists before her—with no results?

In Monday's session, she'd have to ask him about some of the DID symptoms: memory loss, childhood traumas, and frequency of headaches. She'd need to find out if he was ambidextrous, and if he had a history of childhood abuse—sexual or physical.

She didn't think he had dissociative identity disorder, but then, if he did, she was way out of her league. All the other explanations seemed even weirder.

Wade Grinnell had died long before Collin Cox was born. Olivia didn't believe the dead could come back and take possession of the living. And she wasn't much on reincarnation either. She couldn't think of any grounded, logical explanation for what was happening to Collin—which brought her back to her very first assessments of his case, before she'd even known he was Collin Cox. Was it possible he hoped she'd help him come up with some kind of psychological excuse for something terrible he'd done? Was he trying to lay the groundwork for an insanity plea? He'd been associated with several grisly deaths recently. It was possible he'd set fire to Sue and Jerry's house. Who better to provide him with a defense than a relative of the victims?

Meanwhile, the police were still looking for clues in his friend Fernando's murder. And though the case seemed closed, there never had been any arrests or convictions for the murders of Collin's mother and her lover.

She didn't want to believe that Collin was a murderer. She hoped to God he wasn't manipulating her that way. But it was quite possible.

After all, he had been a very good actor once.

Olivia stared at the computer screen. The trouble with Google was sometimes it didn't pick up old newspaper and magazine articles unless they'd been archived. If she wanted to read more about Wade Grinnell, she'd have to go to the library and look through microfiche files of old *Seattle Times* and *Seattle Post-Intelligencers*.

She looked up the Seattle Public Library hours for Sunday. The downtown branch was open from noon until six tomorrow.

She heard the front door open and automatically sprung up from her chair, almost tipping it over. She hadn't realized how jumpy she was until just now.

"Pop?" she called, hurrying toward the front of the house.

"I have hunted and gathered," he announced, stepping into the foyer with two bulging cloth grocery bags. Despite a slight potbelly and his thinning gray hair, her father was still dashing. He dressed sharp and was always very personable. At church and the supermarket, Walt was a regular Beau Brummell with the widows in the over-sixty set.

He'd be grilling chicken breasts and vegetables for dinner tonight. He asked Olivia if she could make her "special wild rice recipe."

"Pop, it's Rice-A-Roni," she said, sitting back down in front of her computer. "Sure, I'll fix some. . . ."

Keeping his jacket on, her father stepped outside to the patio and started up the grill. Olivia leaned back in the desk chair. It looked like she had yet another exciting Saturday night ahead of her. At least it was better than last week, when her dad had had a date with one of the widows—and Olivia had stayed at home alone.

Her father stepped back inside and started to unload the groceries. "Is that the same thing you were working on when I left for the store?" he asked.

"Yes," she said, typing in the words "reincarnation, past lives," for a Google search. "It's research for a new client. You don't believe in reincarnation, do you, Pop?"

"I don't know, sometimes, I guess." He put some beer in the refrigerator. "The older I get, the more I wonder about stuff like that. Why do you ask? Does this new client think she was Cleopatra or something?"

"It's a young man," Olivia said. "I hypnotized him, and while he was under, he turned into someone else. His voice, his looks—he just sort of morphed into this person. And it's a real person who has been dead fifty years. By the way, for the record, we aren't having this conversation. . . ."

Her father took a stainless-steel bowl from the cabinet. "I thought it was only when you were a licensed *therapist* that you couldn't talk about your patients."

He was right. Olivia didn't have any confidentiality requirements as a hypnotist. But in this case, she knew it was more than just hypnotherapy. She was going out on a limb for Collin Cox. Her father didn't know her new client was a onetime movie star. And he shouldn't know. She'd probably said too much to her dad already.

"Sounds like a Bridey Murphy thing," he mused.

Half-turned in her chair, Olivia squinted at him.

"Why does that name sound familiar? Didn't she have something to do with ghosts?"

"Oh, it's right up your alley, sweetie." At the butcher-block island, he tossed the chicken breasts and some marinade in the bowl. "It happened to this house-wife from Colorado, back in the early fifties. Someone hypnotized her to make her remember things from her childhood. . . ."

"Hypnotic regression," Olivia said.

He nodded. "I'll take your word for it. Anyway, this Colorado woman started talking in an Irish brogue. She said she was Bridey Murphy of County Cork, and she'd died in the 1850s or thereabouts. I think she even did an Irish jig for him—or so the story goes. Well, this woman had never been to Ireland, but as Bridey, she re-membered places and people from the old sod way back when. And they found out later that a lot of the stuff she recalled was genuine."

He started cutting up carrots and zucchini. "All this went on when I was a teenager. It became a big fad. There was a Bridey Murphy book and then a movie. They had songs about her on the hit parade. There were even Bridey Murphy parties where people dressed up as whoever they were in their past life. Folks had séances, and all sorts of crazy things." He picked up the bowl with the chicken and the plateful of vegeta-bles. He nodded toward the patio and the grill. "Could you get the door for me, sweetie?" he asked.

Olivia stood up and opened the door for him. "So what happened with this Bridey Murphy case?" she asked.

The bowl and plate in his hands, Walt hesitated in the doorway. "I think it turned out to be a hoax or something," he said. "How long do you need to make your special rice?"

Olivia stared at him for a moment, and then she worked up a smile. "The Rice-A-Roni takes twenty-five minutes, Pop."

"Well, if you don't mind getting started on it now, that's perfect."

She nodded. "Will do."

Olivia left the door ajar after her father stepped out to the patio. She wandered over to the laptop and the notes she'd scribbled on the yellow legal pad about Wade Grinnell, the long-dead teenage murderer from Collin Cox's past life.

Her father's words still echoed in her ears: *". . . it turned out to be a hoax or something."*

Frowning, Olivia was about to turn away and start the Rice-A-Roni. But something in her notes caught her eye:

8/8/62 – Five die in fire @ Hotel Aurora Vista.
Brandon & Irene Pollack (Irene survived) &
kids.

She couldn't help wondering if Irene Pollack was still alive.

Leavenworth—Saturday, 11:18 p.m.

Mrs. Pollack-Martin's apartment was in the east wing of Riverview Manor. So he picked a vehicle on the west side of the parking lot, near the front. He didn't want the car alarm to wake her up. He just wanted it to distract the young, dumb-looking desk clerk for a few minutes.

It was so quiet and still as he worked his skeleton key in the lock of the Lincoln Town Car. For a few mo-

ments, he thought he'd actually break into it without
any problem. But then the alarm suddenly went off
with a shrill, piercing wail. He saw several lights go on
in windows on the west side of the big chalet. He raced
for the bushes along the front of the building. He wore
a black running suit so he easily blended in with the foliage. Catching his breath, he waited until the desk
clerk hurried out with his cell phone. "Yes, yes, I'll see
what I can do," he was saying.

While the clerk headed for the Town Car with its
lights blinking, the man ducked into the front lobby.
He heard several phone lines ringing as he hurried for
the stairwell. Outside, the siren-like wail of the car
alarm became an incessant *beep-beep-beep*. But it
seemed to fade as he made his way up the steps in the
cinder-block stairwell.

The old lady lived four flights up, so he took his
time. He'd come with nothing—except a knife and his
skeleton keys. From the other night, he already knew
the layout of her apartment and the locks on her door.
Even if she had the door double-locked, breaking in
would be a cinch. He'd decided to suffocate her with a
pillow. His knee on her chest would keep her from
moving, and cut off the breathing, too. He needed to
make sure it looked like she'd died in her sleep. There
couldn't be any sign of a break-in. He'd been hiding in
the bushes minutes ago, and now made a mental note
to take off his shoes once he got into her apartment.

At the top of the stairs, he pulled a pair of surgical
gloves from his pocket and put them on. Stepping into
the fourth-floor corridor, he listened for the car alarm,
but couldn't hear it anymore. Someone down the hall
had a TV on. Otherwise, it was deathly quiet. He
skulked down the hallway to unit 405, and took out his

skeleton keys. They hadn't changed the lock, which meant if she'd reported a break-in Thursday night, no one had really taken her seriously. He found the same key he'd used last time, and unlocked the door.

Inside the darkened apartment, he hesitated and looked around for the cat. It was nowhere in sight. He figured the old lady might sleep with it. Gently closing the door behind him, he slipped off his shoes and crept toward the bedroom. The door was closed. He slowly turned the knob, and the door squeaked on its hinges as he opened it. A streetlight from outside filtered through the sheer curtain, enough for him to see the full-size bed.

"Shit," he hissed.

It was neatly made—and empty.

He checked the bathroom, just in case she was hiding. No sign of her, no sign of the damn cat either.

Returning to the living room, he switched on the light.

On her desk, he noticed an old answering machine by her telephone. The message light was blinking. He pressed the *Play Messages* button. *"You have five messages!"* the automated voice announced. *"Tuesday, nine-fifty . . ."*

"Hello, Mrs. Pollack-Martin, this is Ruby at the Safeway pharmacy—"

He clicked on *Next,* and got the automated voice again: *"Wednesday, five-forty-two . . ."*

"Um, this is Collin—you know, from the other day? I don't know how to tell you this without sounding crazy. But, well, you might want to go stay with a friend someplace. I think there's some people who—"

There was a beep, cutting him off. It meant she must have picked up when he was in the middle of leaving his message.

The automated voice came on once more: *"Thursday, ten-thirteen . . ."*

"Hello, Mrs. Martin, this is Harold at the front desk. I've received a call from Ms. Stella down the hall from you. I'm sending up Claudio, our security man. He should be there in a minute. He's ringing me right now. I think he's found you. Never mind. Good-bye."

There was a beep, then: *"Friday, one twenty-two . . ."*

"Hello, Mrs. Martin, this is Magic Carpet Travel, calling about your plane ticket. Though it was so last minute, it still ended up working in your favor. . . ."

A beep cut her off, too.

The last message was yesterday evening: *"Friday, six-forty-one . . ."*

"Hi, Irene, it's Rosie. Are you there? Okay, well, I don't mind looking after Smike for however long you'll be gone. Boy, this trip was sudden! Anyway, I'll swing by tomorrow morning and pick up Smike and all the kitty things. You sure you don't want me to water your plants? It almost sounds like you don't want me going into your place. . . ."

Mrs. Pollack-Martin must have picked up the phone at that point, too, because there was another beep.

"End of messages!" announced the automated voice.

Obviously, the smart old biddy had taken Collin Cox's advice and gotten out of town this morning. It sounded like she didn't even want her friend snooping around in the apartment on the off-chance that she might get mistaken for her.

With a little investigating, he could probably hunt her down. But it was quite apparent she didn't want to make any trouble. She just wanted to disappear. She probably didn't even know why her life was on the line. Certainly, that chubby girl and the Latino kid had been clueless as to why they'd had to die.

Right up to their last breaths, they'd had no idea.

He switched off the light, put his shoes back on, and locked the door after himself. He'd avoid the front desk and climb out a window on the first floor.

He told himself the old lady would come back eventually.

Then so would he.

CHAPTER SEVENTEEN

Seattle—Sunday, October 7, 4:50 p.m.

At 8:20 on the morning of July 9, 1962, Maria Ramirez, a housekeeper at the El Mar Hotel in Capitol Hill, ran screaming from room 20. It was a second-floor unit of the small, two-story rambler-style hotel. The entrances to all the rooms were from the outside.

A young couple in the hotel's parking lot heard the shrieks. They looked up to see Maria as she clung to the walkway railing. "They're dead!" she cried. "They're all dead in here!"

Olivia read six different articles in *The Seattle Times* and the *Post-Intelligencer* about the murders of Ron and Betty Freitag and their two children. Bound, gagged, and stabbed repeatedly, Ron and Betty had been found on top of their bed with the sheet half-covering them. In the connecting room, their children's bodies had been similarly tied and tucked in their respective beds. Olivia knew more details about the murders than she cared to. Stab wounds to the children had been deadly and few. Early reports from the coroner indicated that they'd died quickly. But Ron Freitag had been stabbed twenty-three times. Betty had nineteen stab wounds.

Because all the bodies had been found in their beds, each one partially covered with a sheet, someone in the Seattle police force had dubbed them the *Rockabye Killings*.

Investigators had concluded the killer must have had a gun and surprised Ron and Betty while they were sleeping. He'd forced one or both parents to tie up the children, and then tie up each other. They'd assumed Betty was the last to be bound, lying on her stomach with her hands behind her. The rope secured around her wrists had been tighter than any of the others—and the only one with a sailor knot. They'd figured it was the only knot actually tied by the killer that night.

Other guests at the El Mar had been questioned. According to a follow-up article, *"a dark-haired man with an olive complexion and a crew cut, between 25 and 30, wearing a red T-shirt and jeans"* had been seen in the parking lot late on the night of the murders. One witness had said he looked intoxicated.

Olivia studied the crude police sketch, which made the suspect look like a flat-faced zombie. He didn't resemble Collin Cox in the least.

Apparently, the sailor knot had led the police to the local Maritime Union and several taverns frequented by seamen. But from what Olivia could tell, there were no significant developments in the case until two months later, when the police went after seventeen-year-old Wade Grinnell.

She figured somewhere along the line, the investigators must have changed their minds about the dark-haired man in the red T-shirt. The newspaper accounts of Wade Grinnell's involvement in the El Mar murders were frustratingly vague. They merely pointed out that the teenager was a suspect, and the police had already questioned him once in connection with the slayings. On the afternoon of October 11, 1962, two detectives had arrived at the hotel-kitchen apartment Wade shared with his older sister, Sheri. They had a warrant for his arrest.

Wade slipped out a back window. The detectives chased him on foot several blocks to Interbay Railroad Yard. By that time, several patrol cars joined in the pursuit. It seemed as if they'd trapped their suspect. But Wade Grinnell was struck and killed by a speeding train in a last-ditch effort to elude the police.

The newspaper articles portrayed Wade as a juvenile delinquent with a four-time arrest record. Olivia figured the newspapers didn't list the arrest charges or carry a photo of him because he was a minor.

For the past two hours, she'd been sitting at the microfiche viewer, near the racks of magazines and newspapers in the downtown branch of the Seattle Public Library. The vast room's modern, glass-and-steel walls looked out at the surrounding buildings, the Sound, and the darkening skies.

So far, Olivia had gone through about twenty microfiche files and an entire roll of Butter Rum Life Savers. She stretched, and rubbed her neck. Her auburn hair was in a ponytail. She wore a striped long-sleeved tee and jeans. Her comfy black cardigan hung on the back of her chair.

Collin had returned her call last night and left a message that he'd be at her office at five o'clock Monday. He'd also confirmed that Ian Haggerty was indeed a cop and he'd guarded his grandparents' house for a month. But Olivia still wondered what this policeman's angle was and why he'd been grilling her about Collin on the ferry yesterday.

She'd come here to the library to prepare for the appointment tomorrow. If Wade Grinnell emerged again, she wanted to know who she was dealing with.

In addition to the El Mar murders, she'd also read several accounts of the fire at the Hotel Aurora Vista, which had wiped out Irene Pollack's family. All the news stories blamed the fire on a stray cigarette. It didn't make sense to Olivia that in the Century 21 Exposition timeline she'd read yesterday, Wade Grinnell was named as a suspect in this fire—when there was nothing connecting him to it in any of these older articles. Obviously, that timeline didn't have the complete story.

Then it dawned on her. The timeline had been compiled forty years after the fact. Sometime between 1962 and 2002, something must have happened to implicate the late Wade Grinnell in that fire—as well as the El Mar murders.

Olivia took the microfiche files back to the desk, where a neatly coiffed, forty-something woman had been helping her—and begrudgingly so. She wore a Ralph Lauren blouse and a tan skirt. She also had a superior, *I-can't-be-bothered* attitude that didn't go well with her job helping people. When Olivia asked for the *Times* and *Post-Intelligencer* microfiche index files for 1963 through 1968, the lady seemed annoyed. "This is going to take me a few minutes, you know," she muttered, pushing the request form at Olivia.

"That's fine, thank you very much," Olivia said— though the woman had already turned away. She filled out the form and waited five minutes for Ms. Attitude to retrieve the files. Returning to the viewer, Olivia didn't find anything for Wade Grinnell or Sheri Grinnell for 1963. But they both had a listing for page three of *The Seattle Times* on 9/20/64. There was nothing else for either newspaper through 1968.

She filled out the request form for the September 1964 microfiche file. Once again, the snooty librarian acted as if it was a big imposition. Once again, Olivia thanked her.

Back at the viewing machine, she scanned down the file until she found the front page for Sunday, September 20. Olivia inched the viewer lever down to page three and saw the headline:

SCREAMS UNHEARD: THE SEATTLE WORLD'S FAIR MURDERS
Kept Under the Radar, and Never Officially Solved,
Grisly "Rockabye" Killings Claimed the Lives of Several Families

"What?" she murmured, hunched close to the monitor.

According to the article, from June through late September 1962, three different families—including a pair of newlyweds—were tied up and slaughtered in their Seattle hotel rooms. Two more families died when their hotel suites caught fire. It broke Olivia's heart to see the photographs of the victims, the young parents and their children—a total of eighteen lives snuffed out.

The 1964 article used a then-current serial killer's reign of terror to point out the relevance of these murders from two years before. She was pretty sure the term *serial killer* hadn't even been coined yet:

In Boston, women have been alerted to the strangler who has held the city in the grip of fear since last year. However, two years ago, while hundreds of thousands of visitors poured into Seattle to attend the Century 21 Exposition, a killer preyed on tourists in several local hotels, and very few people knew about it. Police investigators worked diligently to track down this maniac, but they also put an enormous effort into keeping news of the murders from the general public. Fearing World's Fair attendance numbers might plummet if the grisly killings made headlines, the press (including this newspaper) cooperated. The murders were reported, but never made the front pages. The notion that a mass murderer was haunting Seattle hotels was never introduced to an unsuspecting public.

The news story pointed out that the only suspect in the murders had been killed—and had never been formally charged. Seventeen-year-old Wade Grinnell and his sister, Sheri, had lived in the Gilbert Arms Apartments before the place had been converted into the Gilbert Arms Hotel for the World's Fair. The Gilbert Arms was also where the first victims, Stuart and Tracy Compton, newlyweds from Bowling Green, Ohio, had been bound, gagged, and stabbed to death on the evening of June 23, 1962. Stuart's wrists had been tied together behind him with a traditional double knot. The rope around Tracy's wrists was secured with a sailor knot.

Investigators didn't begin to suspect Wade Grinnell until the Holleran family of Denver was murdered in the King's View Hotel on September 29. The Hollerans were attending the fair with friends, who said the Holleran sisters, Rebecca, sixteen, and Patricia, twelve, spent some time at the fair with a local teenager who called himself Wayne. The other couple from Denver later identified Wade Grinnell, from a 1961 arrest mug shot, as the young man named Wayne.

Olivia studied Wade's mug shot on page four of the article. With his hair slicked back in a pompadour, the teenager could have passed for someone in his mid-twenties. He wore a T-shirt that showed off his wide shoulders. For the camera, he had a defiant smirk. Collin Cox didn't resemble him—except for the cocky grin that had emerged while he'd been in the trance. The expression was almost exactly the same.

A quick look at Wade Grinnell's background explained why the Seattle Police thought he might be responsible for the murders and the deadly fires. At age eleven, he'd burned down a neighbor's doghouse. One of his arrests, at age fifteen, was for malicious mischief after starting a fire in a wastebasket at a five-and-dime store. He'd also tried to steal several items from the store. His father was a seaman, and hot tempered. Before dying in a knife fight, Wade Senior could have taught his son something about knives, and how to tie a sailor knot. But it was the police interview—in which Wade contradicted himself one too many times—that really raised the investigators' suspicions.

"My brother had his problems and his scrapes with the law," Sheri Grinnell had said. She was twenty-two at the time of the article. *"But Wade wasn't a monster. He couldn't have murdered those families."*

Olivia pulled out two quarters and put them in the slot on the side of the machine to copy both pages of the article. Then she scribbled a note along the side of the paper:

Sheri Grinnell—married? Alive or dead?

She'd noticed that in three cases out of five, a teenage girl had been among the victims. Loretta Pollack—who died in the Hotel Aurora Vista fire along with her older brother, nieces, and nephew—had been seventeen. Rebecca "Becky" Holleran had just had her Sweet Sixteen party a week before she and her family were butchered in the King's View Hotel. And Cynthia Helms was about to start her freshman year at the University of Washington. Her parents had accompanied her by train from Redding, California. They were staying at the Pioneer Motor Inn when a blaze swept through their connecting rooms on the night of August 31. All three perished.

Olivia circled the names and wrote another note on the margin:

Ask Collin/Wade if he remembers these girls.

The witnesses from Denver had said they'd seen Wade hanging around with Becky and her kid sister. Had he gotten to know the other two teenage victims as well?

Olivia had already read about the El Mar murders and the fire at the Hotel Aurora Vista. But the other Rockabye Murders were news to her. She wanted to find out as much as she could about the other two hotel murders and the second fire. Returning the microfiche files to the librarian, Olivia filled out the request form for files covering June, August, and September 1962.

The woman rolled her eyes and then went to retrieve the files. She took longer this time. She finally came back to the counter and shoved the files toward Olivia.

"The library's closing in a half hour, you know," she said.

"Thank you, I'll keep that in mind," Olivia said, gathering up the microfiche envelopes.

With a sigh, she sat down at the viewing machine. She took out the file for June 1962 and flicked on the switch at the side of the machine. Nothing happened. The light didn't go on. The fan in the machine wasn't humming. Had she broken it?

She reached over and flicked the switch on the viewing machine next to it. Nothing. It was dead, too.

"Crap," she muttered under her breath, standing up again. The last thing she wanted to do was ask that sourpuss woman for more help. She plodded back to the reference desk. "I *really* hate to bother you," she said.

The woman behind the desk glared up at her from her chair.

"I went back to the machine to view the files you just gave me," Olivia explained, "and suddenly the machine isn't working—and neither is the one next to it."

Getting to her feet, the woman came around from the back of the desk. "What did you do to it?" she asked.

"I didn't do anything to it," Olivia replied defensively. "It was working fine when I finished up with the last batch of files. Then I came back—and nothing."

They walked past the periodical shelves, to the desks with the viewers. The woman flicked the switch on the side of the machine—and then tried the next machine over. Nothing happened. She walked around in back. "Well, here's the problem," she announced, holding up the plug. She raised an eyebrow. "Did you unplug this?"

"Of course not," Olivia sighed. She walked around near the back of the machine, where she saw a tangled mess of cords on the desk—and a power strip on the floor. The woman crouched down on one knee to plug in the machine. Olivia noticed the other end of the cord drop from the twisted heap and land on the floor. Someone had cut it.

"No, wait!" Olivia yelped.

The woman balked and dropped the plug. Wide-eyed, she gaped up at her. Then she seemed to notice the cut cord she was about to plug in. "Did you do this?" she asked, bracing herself with one hand on the floor. "This is dangerous! If I'd plugged this in, I could have . . ." She trailed off, and put a hand over her heart. She looked a little wobbly.

Olivia noticed people on the other side of the room staring at them.

It took her ten more minutes to convince the lady and the maintenance man that she hadn't sabotaged the machines.

"Somebody could have gotten killed," the librarian had muttered.

Stepping outside, Olivia lit up a much needed ciga-rette—her first today. The sidewalks were practically empty on this chilly Sunday night. She trudged uphill on the steep sidewalk to where she'd parked the car on Sixth Avenue. She never got to read about the two other murders and the second fire. But she had the scanned copy of the article from 1964.

The librarian had kept asking, "Well, if you didn't cut those cords, then who did?"

"I have no idea," Olivia had told her again and again.

Olivia spied the darkened doorways of the buildings. She nervously glanced down an alleyway as she hurried by. The wind blew a piece of paper past her. She kept looking over her shoulder for whoever was out there.

As she'd told the librarian—she had no idea who it was.

But Olivia had a feeling he knew her very, very well.

CHAPTER EIGHTEEN

Poulsbo—Sunday

"Seven-thirty on a Sunday night," announced his grandfather—over the ringing telephone. He hit the pause button on the TV remote. He was ensconced in his favorite chair with a TV table in front of him. "I'll bet it's some stupid telemarketer."

The cordless was on the table lamp beside him. Dee had made stuffed pork chops for dinner, and TCM was showing *Doctor Zhivago*. For the last forty-five minutes, Collin hadn't been able to figure out what the hell was going on in the Russian epic, but he'd fallen in love with Julie Christie. She'd helped him take his mind off his troubles for a little while. Then the phone had rung, and he was back to reality again.

His grandfather checked the caller ID. "So—does anyone know who Olivia Barker is?"

Collin hesitated, and then watched his grandfather click on the cordless. "Hello," he grumbled into the phone. He was dead silent for a few moments.

"Who is it?" Dee asked. With a TV table in front of her, she sat on the other end of the sofa from Collin.

Old Andy waved her question away. "Uh-huh," he

said into the phone. "He's here right now. He's been here all day. We're just finishing up dinner. I'll hand you off to him. . . . Well, yes. It's been nice talking with you, too." He held the cordless out to Collin. "It's Gail's aunt."

Moving the TV table aside, Collin got to his feet and took the phone. "Um, you guys keep watching the movie. I'll see it some other time. I've still got homework to do." He headed into the kitchen and heard them start the movie. "Hello, Olivia?" he whispered into the phone.

"Hi, Collin. Your grandfather says you've been home all afternoon. Is that right?"

"Yeah, I've been here."

"You haven't had an extended memory lapse or anything like that today?"

"No. Why?" He headed for the front door. "What's going on? Did something happen?"

"I—I was at the library today, and thought I might have seen you. Never mind."

Stepping outside, Collin left the front door open a crack. The night air chilled him, but he walked down to the driveway—just to make sure his grandparents didn't hear him. "Are we still on for five o'clock tomorrow?"

"Yes," she said. "Listen, just to double-check on that policeman, Ian Haggerty. You said he's a friend of yours. Is that right?"

"Yeah, he's a nice guy. He's cool."

"You didn't seem too happy to see him at the memorial service."

"Oh, I was just surprised he was there. Plus, my grandfather doesn't like him much. So it was kind of awkward."

"Why doesn't your grandfather like him?"

"I'm not sure, really. When the cops were guarding

the house for the first month after my mom was killed, Ian was the only nice one. I used to smuggle him Cokes and snacks, and we'd talk. He was like my only friend for a while. My grandfather found out, and put a stop to it."

"Why'd he do that?"

"I guess he thought it was *inappropriate*, which is a crock. Anyway, my grandfather doesn't trust him. By the way, you never explained. How do you know Ian?"

"I don't," Olivia said. "He came up to me on the ferry yesterday on the way back from the service. He asked a lot of questions. He said he was your friend."

"What kind of questions?"

"Oh, how I knew you, that sort of thing. Don't worry. I didn't tell him anything. I didn't talk with him very long. But I have to agree with your grandfather. I don't quite trust him."

"Ian's okay, really," Collin said. But suddenly he wasn't so sure.

"Well, maybe it's my suspicious nature," Olivia sighed. "Before I forget, could you email me that recording you made of our session on Thursday night? I'd like to look it over before we meet tomorrow."

"Sure, no problem, I'll do it right away."

"Good. See you tomorrow at five. Good night, Collin." She hung up.

Clicking off the phone, Collin stepped back into the house and returned the cordless to the family room. His grandfather put Julie Christie on pause again. "So what's going on with Gail's aunt?" he asked.

Collin collected his grandfather's dinner plate and silverware. "She wanted to thank me again for coming to the memorial." He grabbed his grandmother's plate and then his own.

"Thanks, honey," Dee said. "Just leave those by the sink. I'll wash them later."

Retreating to the kitchen, he set the dirty plates in the sink. He glanced back toward the family room, and quietly slipped out the front door again. He took his iPhone from his pocket and composed an email:

Dear Olivia,

Thanks again for agreeing to see me tomorrow. Attached is the video of our last session. It was good talking with you tonight.

He started to type, *I think you're wrong about Ian,* but erased it. He signed off, *Take Care, Collin.* Then he attached the file for the video and sent it.

He rubbed his arms to fight off the chill, and gazed at the shadowy driveway ahead. He couldn't see the gate. Everything turned to black after a curve in the gravel trail. Collin clicked on his phone again, pulled up Ian's number, and dialed it. He figured he was standing far enough away from the front door—and the intercom by the gate—so his grandfather wouldn't overhear.

Ian answered on the third ringtone. "Collin?"

"Hi. Did I get you at a bad time?"

"No, not at all," he said. "What's going on?"

Collin wandered down the driveway. "Sorry I couldn't get together with you yesterday."

"No sweat. Bad timing on my part. Your grandfather seems to have come around a little. He certainly was friendly enough. Or maybe he was just putting on a good front."

"To tell you the truth, he hasn't changed much," Collin admitted. "He doesn't trust you. He thinks you might be trying to pin something on me for what happened to Gail and Fernando—like I might have been responsible for them getting killed."

"Well, he's wrong. I'm just concerned about you, that's all."

"Gail's aunt called. She says she met you on the ferry yesterday. She says you were asking a lot of questions."

"Yeah, I was curious about how she knew you. Collin, what are you getting at?"

"Well, what are *you* getting at?" he retorted. "I'm sorry, but you showed up out of the blue at the memorial—based on a hunch that I might have been friends with Gail? Don't get me wrong. I was glad to see you. But it's just kind of weird. I don't know. . . ."

Collin turned toward the house again. He saw something dart between two trees by the living room window. It kept moving. Bushes rustled, and suddenly a tall man's silhouette emerged from the darkness. He wove through the trees and bushes along the driveway. He was coming toward him.

Collin's heart stopped.

The front door swung open. Collin's grandfather appeared in the doorway. "Collin, are you out there?" he yelled. There was panic in his voice. He had the cordless phone in his hand. "Get in the house, right now!"

The man disappeared behind the brush, but Collin could still hear his footsteps and twigs snapping. He was paralyzed. The steps were coming closer. He heard the man breathing—and then he seemed to pass him.

"Collin!" his grandfather called again.

All at once, his feet started working, and Collin sprinted toward the house.

His grandfather opened the door wider for him.

"Were you meeting somebody out here? Who was that?"

Out of breath, Collin staggered inside. "I don't know. . . ."

His grandfather slammed the door shut and locked it. "Son of a bitch came right up to the window, scared the wits out of your grandmother. . . ."

Wringing her hands, Dee stood in the front hall. "Where did you go off to?"

Collin shrugged. "Nowhere, I just stepped outside for a sec." He glanced down at his iPhone, and realized he'd hung up on Ian.

"Hello, 9-1-1?" his grandfather was saying into the cordless. "This is Andrew Stampler at 27 Skog-Strand Lane. We have an intruder on the premises. . . . No, he didn't get into the house. I think he ran away. But I'd like you to get a patrol car over here as soon as possible. . . ."

Dee put a hand on his arm. Collin could feel her trembling. "Your grandfather and I didn't get much of a look at him," she whispered. "Did you?"

Collin shook his head again. "No, I couldn't even see what he was wearing."

His grandfather clicked off the cordless. "Who were you talking to out there?"

Wide-eyed, Collin stared at him. He was too frazzled to make up a good lie. And it was too late to hide the cell phone in his hand. Just then, as if on cue, it rang.

"Who is it?" his grandfather demanded to know.

Collin looked at the caller ID. "It's Ian Haggerty," he admitted. Turning away, he clicked on the phone. "Hi, sorry we were cut off," he muttered.

"What happened?" Ian asked. "Are you okay?"

"Yeah, I think so. We had a prowler sneaking around outside the house. But I think he's gone now. We called the police. They're on their way. In fact, I should go. I'll call you later or shoot you an email."

"All right, do that, because it sounds like we need to talk. Are your grandparents there with you now? Are you sure you're safe?"

"Yeah, we're fine. Talk to you later." Collin clicked off the line. He sheepishly looked at his grandfather, who still glowered with disapproval.

Collin could hear a police siren in the distance. He wondered if the cops might spot the prowler somewhere alone Skog-Strand Lane. The guy was sure running pretty fast.

He didn't say anything to his grandfather, and he didn't want to overthink it. But he could have sworn when he was talking on the phone just now, Ian had sounded like he was out of breath.

Three flashlight beams cut though the darkness, rippling over the trees and bushes in his grandparents' front yard. In addition to the three cops combing the woods around the house, two more were out in patrol cars, checking Skog-Strand Lane and Viking Way for the would-be prowler. Collin stood outside the front door with his grandfather watching the eerie light show. Dee was in the kitchen, washing the dinner dishes.

"I made a few calls after we ran into your friend Ian yesterday," his grandfather said.

At his side, Collin glanced down at the ground. He should have seen this coming.

"First of all," his grandfather continued, "there isn't a senior at your school named Amanda Brooks. In fact, there's no Amanda Brooks at North Kitsap High at all.

So—your pal was lying to me, and you were backing him up."

"I'm sorry," Collin murmured.

"Did Ian mention in your brief conversation yesterday that he's on suspension from the police force?"

Bewildered, Collin gazed at him and shook his head. "What are you talking about?"

"He was suspended for two weeks. He beat up a kid—not much older than you. He has one more week to go before he's allowed back." His grandfather sighed, and put a hand on Collin's shoulder. "The point is, you don't really know him. You only know him from what he's told you—like that business about you reminding him of his little brother. Well, Ian Haggerty doesn't have a little brother. He has an older sister and a widowed mother, both in Pittsburgh—but no little brother."

Collin winced. "Are you sure?"

"Like I said, I made some calls." Old Andy squeezed his shoulder. "Now, I want you to be honest with me. Have you told him about any of your crazy reincarnation theories?"

Collin shook his head. "No. I swear I haven't, Grandpa. Yesterday was the first time I saw him or heard from him since they stopped guarding the house in August. I almost called him last week, but I got his machine and hung up. That's the closest I've come to talking with him in months. In fact, I was just out here calling him to find out why he showed up yesterday like he did."

"And what did he tell you?"

Collin frowned. "He said he was concerned about me, that's all."

His grandfather said nothing for a moment. He just stared out at the policemen with their flashlights, searching the woods near the end of their driveway.

"Son," he whispered finally. "Take it from me. He's not your friend."

The police continued to search the area for another hour, but they didn't find the prowler. They assured Collin's grandfather that they would put an extra patrol on the cul-de-sac for the next few nights.

Collin was glad to hear that. After what had happened to Gail and Fernando, he was worried about his grandparents' safety. He'd been worried for Mrs. Pollack-Martin, too. Following the service yesterday, he'd tried to phone her several times, but kept getting her answering machine. He'd finally phoned Riverview Manor and asked if she was all right. The operator had told him Mrs. Pollack-Martin had gone out of town, and would be away for several days.

He wondered if anything had happened to make her change her mind and take his advice. Or was this "gone out of town" story concocted by someone as an explanation for her disappearance? Was she ever coming back?

Sitting at his desk, he looked out at Liberty Bay. There was no sign of the boat tonight. He read over an email he'd just composed:

Hi, Ian,

Sorry about the weird phone call tonight and the interruption. Sorry also that I never called you back. It was crazy here for a while, and then it got late. Everyone is okay. We just had a little scare. The police looked around for a long time and didn't find anyone.

It was thoughtful of you to come to the memorial yesterday and to be concerned about me. But I'm okay. Anyway, don't worry about me.

Thanks again for thinking of me. Hope you're doing fine. Yesterday, you mentioned maybe getting together sometime soon. But I don't think that will work out, because I'm super busy with school and will be for a while.

Take care.

Collin

He decided it wasn't worth asking Ian about his suspension from the police force or his fictitious kid brother. Collin didn't plan on seeing him again. He'd made that pretty damn clear in the email. He clicked on the SEND icon.

Sitting back in his desk chair, he gazed out at the bay again. He really missed those nights he used to keep an eye out for skinny-dippers.

From his computer, he heard a click, and saw the NEW MAIL icon was highlighted. He wondered if Ian had gotten back to him already. Collin brought up his email, and looked at the line along the top of the list:

10/7/2012 – arealfriend43@humblelo . . .
Sympathies

Collin didn't recognize the sender, but he clicked on the *Read* icon anyway:

Dear Collin,

I am sorry to learn about the deaths of your friends Fernando Ryan and Gail Pelham. They were very lucky to be close to you—if even for

**just a short while. Now they're with the angels
and they live on in your heart. Remember, you
are always in my prayers.**

You looked so sad tonight.

☺

"Jesus," Collin muttered. Flustered, he clicked on
the REPLY icon. His fingers raced over the keyboard:

Who are you?

He quickly clicked on SEND.

Gnawing at a fingernail, he waited for the response
he knew would come. Sure enough, Collin heard a
click signifying a new email. He checked the line on
the top of the list and frowned:

10/7/2012 – MAILER-DAEMON . . . Returned Mail

"Who the hell are you?" he whispered.
But he knew he was talking to no one.

CHAPTER NINETEEN

Their logo was a silhouette of a tall man, wearing a hat and trench coat. It stood six feet tall on the marquee above the entry to Caffe Ladro on Fifteenth Avenue. The coffeehouse was on the corner, along a strip of old neighborhood stores and restaurants at the top of Capitol Hill. Olivia had a date there.

With the microfiche machines temporarily out of order at the library's downtown branch, she'd tried in vain to get more information about the World's Fair murders from the Internet. But the old articles weren't archived, and nothing had been written in the last twenty years about the murders—except that hopelessly incomplete piece with the Century 21 Exposition timeline.

Still, Olivia had the *Seattle Times* feature from 1964 that linked Wade Grinnell to three mass murders and two deadly hotel fires. She searched Google for an update on the author of the 1964 article. He was Orin Carney, a *Seattle Times* correspondent since 1961. Later, he'd become an editor. Four years ago, he'd celebrated his seventieth birthday, picked up an award from the city, and retired. There was an article about it on-line.

It took Olivia a while to track down his Capitol Hill address and a phone number. But once she'd gotten him on the phone and asked about Wade Grinnell, it had only taken a minute to set up a time to meet for coffee. She figured anything he could tell her would be useful. The more information she had, the better to handle Collin Cox—and his second personality—during their appointment this afternoon.

Olivia passed under the marquee with its trench-coat-man logo and stepped into the cafe. The coffee smell—along with a hint of chocolate—filled the air. There were about twenty customers, sitting at the tables or on the stools along the window counter. The walls were deep red with artwork on display. Cookies, scones, croissants, and other baked goods filled the glass case by the counter.

A tall, handsome silver-haired man in an argyle sweater and khakis rose from one of the window tables. He took off his sunglasses and smiled at her. "Olivia?" he asked.

They shook hands. At the counter with her, Orin Carney insisted he pay for her coffee and scone. "It's been a long time since I've had a rendezvous with a beautiful young woman," he told her, cramming two dollars inside the tip jar. "Allow me to treat you."

As they sat down at the table with their orders, Olivia wondered if he was just being sweet. Or did he really consider this a date? Sitting across from him, with the light coming through the window, she could now see that his full head of silver hair was a toupee.

"I'm really grateful for your help on my thesis," she said, over her coffee cup. "Except for your article, I couldn't find much out there on Wade Grinnell."

"And you won't," Orin said. "He's a well-kept, dirty little secret here. After our talk last night, I got out my scrapbook and read that old article again. That piece landed me in some hot water back in sixty-four. The people running this city then weren't happy with me. They'd pretty much swept the whole Rockabye Killer business under the carpet. During the fair, they were worried news of these hotel slayings would hurt the tourist trade—and believe me, Seattle had poured a ton of money into the World's Fair. The future of this city depended on it. After the fair, they still didn't want to talk about the murders. They didn't want it to seem like they weren't warning people of the danger. The truth is—they weren't. Like lambs to the slaughter, these families were checking into these hotels, and they had no idea that someone was out there, preying on them. Maybe some of the victims would have been a bit more vigilant about locking their rooms. I mean, if you're staying in a hotel and step out for ice, you might leave your door open a crack. Or if someone knocks on the door and says they're with the hotel to check the plumbing or the air conditioner, you might not think twice about opening up for them. These tourists in town for the fair didn't think they had a reason to be extra-cautious."

"Is that how he got into the rooms?" Olivia asked.

"It's an educated guess from police investigators at the time," he said over his coffee. "Calling the desk clerk away for a spell so he could steal a hotel room key was another ploy."

"Your article pointed out that some of the families had teenage daughters," Olivia said. "You made it seem like Wade might have tried to pick them up at the fair. . . ."

Orin nodded. "That's right. There's no way of knowing for sure, but I think he might have scoped out his victims early—either at the fair or the hotels. From Brandey and Bronson Faurot, who were friends with the Holleran family, we know that Wade tried to pick up Rebecca Holleran at the fair's Science Pavilion. And in police interviews after the fire at the Hotel Aurora Vista, Irene Pollack said that her teenage niece, Loretta, was approached by a young man at the fair's amusement park." He picked up his croissant. "You know, I tried to interview Irene Pollack for that piece, but she didn't want to participate. I guess I can't blame her."

"Do you know if she's still alive?" Olivia asked.

"I'm not sure."

"What about Wade's sister, Sheri?"

Orin sighed. "I seem to recall that she got married shortly after I wrote that article. But I never got in touch with her again. So I don't know if Sheri's still alive."

Olivia picked at her scone. "Why do you think he killed all those families?"

"Well, the detectives I interviewed believed it had to do with the first murders—at the Gilbert Arms Hotel. Wade and Sheri had lived at the Gilbert Arms for three years. They were among the hundreds of tenants forced to move from their apartments before the fair. You see, a lot of landlords hoped to cash in on the tourist trade by turning their apartment houses into hotels. So they gouged prices and evicted tenants *en masse*. For a while, the city council allowed it, too. They even let the landlords collect their rents in shorter terms. In some buildings, rents went from eighty-five dollars a month to one hundred a *week*. A lot of people became homeless. And a lot of people were angry. One of those people was Wade Grinnell."

Olivia pushed her half-eaten scone away and sat back. "These hotels where the murders and fires occurred, were all of them former apartment buildings?"

He shook his head. "No, just the Gilbert Arms and the King's View. The others were new hotels, built for the fair. But he probably blamed the tourists as much as he did the landlords for displacing him. My theory is it wasn't just revenge. No landlords were murdered, just hotel guests. They were all seemingly happy families, and believe me—with his history of abuse—Wade had no idea what a happy family was. I think he was jealous and angry. Unlike most serial killers, who stick to one method of murder, Wade switched back and forth. So there were the mass 'Rockabye' killings—and the fires, which were just as lethal. For a while there, the police didn't connect the two."

He crumpled up his napkin and set it on the table. "Some serial killers really enjoy the notoriety. They almost want to get caught—for the recognition. The cops questioning Wade said he seemed very full of himself and almost gleeful during the interrogation. But until they're caught, a lot of these murderers get off on reading about their crimes and seeing the news reports on TV. Imagine how frustrating it must have been for Wade to see his murders relegated to page two or three of the local papers and have the fires he set deemed as accidents. I think he might have been testing which methodology of murder got more attention."

Orin shrugged. "Of course, back in sixty-two, we didn't even have the term 'serial killer.' That came later—and so did the research into the minds of these murderers. I was going to do a follow-up article in 1966, but there was already way too much killing in the news that year—the University of Texas shootings and that creep who murdered the nurses in Chicago.

Plus I wasn't getting any cooperation from the police or the city. So—I dropped the idea. . . ."

He leaned forward. "Say, I just remembered, I tracked down Wade's sister for that follow-up piece I never wrote. She'd gotten married and had a new last name. I'm pretty sure I wrote it down. It's probably in my Wade Grinnell file."

"You have a whole file on him?" Olivia murmured.

"Oh, yes, I kept files on all my stories. Each article has a file full of documents, research notes, receipts, you name it. It'll take me a little while to find it. But I have it at my house, three blocks away. Did you want to see Wade's file?"

The old-world charmer of a Craftsman house had a covered front porch. Inside, there were built-in china cabinets, leaded glass windows, and dark hardwood floors. As she followed Orin Carney to the kitchen, Olivia noticed the place was slightly messy with furniture that could have used some re-covering or re-varnishing. Dirty dishes were piled in the kitchen sink. The cabinets were eighties oak, and all the appliances were avocado green. Orin stopped to toss out a Coke can that had been left on the counter. Then he put away a box of Corn Chex in the cabinet. "Sorry about the way the place looks," he said. "This is what happens when a twenty-six-year-old moves back in with his widower dad."

"I can sort of relate," Olivia said quietly.

"My son's at work. I would have cleaned up if I'd known I'd be taking home a pretty young lady today." He opened the basement door. "Are you married?"

She hesitated. "Not for very much longer."

"Well, his loss." Orin switched on the basement

light. "All my files are stored down here. It's pretty much of a mess. I apologize in advance."

Olivia glanced at the dirty gray plank stairs that led down to the unfinished cellar. He took a few steps down, and the floorboards creaked. She stood by the kitchen door, staring down at the hairpiece on top of his head. She knew he was just trying to be nice, but she wished he hadn't given her that *pretty young lady* routine and then asked if she was married. It made following him down into his gloomy basement all the more forebidding.

"I have an office on the second floor where I used to do my writing." He stopped in the middle of the staircase to gaze back up at her. "I keep my scrapbooks of clippings there. But I've covered several murder cases, and never wanted the kids poking into all the unpublished photos and data. There's some pretty nasty stuff in those folders. So—I kept it all locked in my storeroom down here. Are you still game? You look a little apprehensive."

Olivia quickly shook her head. "No, I'm fine. I—I really appreciate this, Mr. Carney."

"Oh, call me Orin. You've seen my dirty dishes. We can drop the formalities." He continued down the stairs.

Olivia took a deep breath and followed him down to the cluttered, dismal basement. It smelled musty. Piles of clothes were heaped on top of the washer and dryer, near the bottom of the stairs. There was a series of rooms off a poorly lit hallway. All the doors were open. Some of the rooms remained dark while others seemed to be on the same light circuit as the hallway.

"Welcome to the Carney dungeon," Orin said cheerfully.

Olivia managed a weak chuckle.

"I don't know why I even bothered to lock my file room for so many years," he said, heading to a shadowy annex at the end of the corridor. "The kids were terrified to come down here on their own until they were teenagers."

Olivia understood their trepidation.

Orin turned a corner and disappeared into the alcove.

She heard the squeaking sound of a door opening on rusty hinges. Then a light went on. But it was hardly reassuring. The bulb must have been dangling from a cord on the ceiling, because the light threw off shadows that crazily swayed back and forth along the cellar walls.

Olivia inched toward the alcove and saw the open chain-link door to the little room. It was more like a gate. The lightbulb, with a pull-string by the socket, was still swinging on the cord. Four tan metal file cabinets along one wall took up half the room. Stacks of folders were piled on top of the cabinets. More folders covered the card table in the corner of the room. It also held an aqua-colored radio, a relic from the sixties that was plugged into a socket on the wall. There was an old tilt-back desk chair by the table. The seat padding was ripped and losing its stuffing. On the cellar wall was a poster of Steve McQueen on a motorcycle. Olivia recognized the still from one of her dad's favorite movies, *The Great Escape.* Somehow, it made her feel better. She realized that Orin Carney must have put the poster up in an effort to make this dingy little room more habitable while he'd been working down there.

She stood in the alcove, watching him search through the file cabinet. She thought she heard something upstairs. It sounded like a few footsteps, and then, nothing.

"Is—is someone else home?" she asked.

"Nope, just us," he said, his nose in the file cabinet.

"I thought I heard somebody upstairs."

"Probably just the house," he said, thumbing through the files. "Built in 1911, and it's still settling. Jesus please us, I can't believe the Wade Grinnell file isn't in here." He nodded toward the stack of folders on the card table in the corner of the tiny room. "You want to try there? I hope it's not too dusty. It's been ages since I've been down here."

Olivia hesitated in the doorway. She didn't want to walk into that little storage closet, where he could slam the gate and lock her in.

"Ah, wait a second, here it is!" he said. He pulled out the folder and tossed it on the card table. He had a thin, square box in his other hand. "And I think you might be interested in this, too." He nodded toward the card table again, and then brushed past her as he stepped out of the room. He took the slim box with him. "Have a look there. I need to check something. . . ."

Olivia watched him duck into another one of the rooms, where the overhead light was already on. With trepidation, she stepped into his file room and flipped open the folder on the card table. The first document in the thick pile was a negative copy of an arrest record for fifteen-year-old Wade Grinnell. He'd been charged with housebreaking and assault. From the comments, which were illegible in spots because of the primitive copy, it looked as though Wade had climbed into the kitchen window of a house where a classmate had been babysitting. He'd tackled her and tied her up—along with her charge, a five-year-old boy. A neighbor had

seen him skulking around outside the house and tele-
phoned the police. When the cops arrived, Wade had
maintained it had all been a prank. But the traumatized
girl hadn't thought it was too funny. From what Olivia
could tell, it looked like the charges had been dropped.

A yellowed index card was stapled to the arrest report. On the card was a handwritten list of names with
phone numbers and job titles—like *Seattle City Coun-
cilman*, *Assistant Chief of Police*, and *Police Lieutenant*. One name in the middle of the list didn't have a
job title:

Sheri Grinnell <u>Morrow</u> – KL5-6754

Olivia pulled a pen and an old envelope from her
purse, then copied it down. Of course, this contact list
had been created back when Orin had considered writing that follow-up article in 1966. So this *current*
information was older than she was. Still, it was something.

"I should warn you," Orin called from down the
hallway. She heard him shifting and dragging things
around in the neighboring room. "That file might have
some pretty gruesome photos in it. What is it they say
on TV? *Viewer discretion advised. . . .*"

"Okay, thanks," she replied. Olivia looked back over
her shoulder toward the dark alcove beyond the doorway. "What's going on over there anyway?"

"I'm just trying to get something to work here," he
replied, his voice slightly muffled. "Give me another
couple of minutes."

She thought about checking in on him, but got distracted by some old postcards and mini-brochures of
the hotels where the Rockabye Killings took place.

Each one featured a photo of the hotel, of course—but some also had pictures of their pool, or their Space Needle view:

Comfort & Quality
THE EL MAR HOTEL

Easy Access to the World's Fair!
—Be Our Guest for Your Trip of a Lifetime!—

Beneath the brochures, Olivia found the photographs he must have been talking about. They were black-and-white eight-by-tens. The first one showed a teddy bear with SEATTLE WORLD'S FAIR emblazoned across its chest. The stuffed animal was on the floor by a bed—with rumpled bloodstained sheets. At the bottom corner of the photo, someone had written in block letters: BED OF KIM FREITAG, 5 YRS OLD – EL MAR HOTEL 7/9/62.

The next photo made Olivia gasp. It showed a woman lying facedown on a blood-soaked bed. Her nightgown was torn and covered in blood. The close-up shot went from her shoulders down to the top of her buttocks—and focused on her hands, tied behind her back. SAILOR KNOT, it said. BETTY FREITAG, 31 – EL MAR HOTEL 7/9/62.

While her host kept moving things around in the next room, Olivia forced herself to look at some more of the awful pictures. They included shots of the charred, burnt-out suites at the Hotel Aurora Vista and the Pioneer Motor Inn. There was also a high school portrait of Wade Grinnell at age fifteen. He had slicked-back hair and half-closed eyes. He wore a bolo tie with a jacket. Olivia studied another photo of him—

with a brunette who had a big beehive hairdo. A cigarette dangled out of his mouth, and he had his arm
around her. They posed in front of a Seattle restaurant
that had closed ages ago, the Twin Teepees. Olivia
turned the photo over and saw someone had scribbled
on the back:

Wade Grinnell, 17 & sister, Sheri Grinnell, 20.
(May 1962)

Then Olivia came across some postmortem photos
of the naked, slain newlywed couple in the morgue.
That was too much. She closed the folder. She wanted
to run upstairs and be outside again—in the fresh air
and daylight.

Suddenly, it turned quiet in the next room.

"Mr. Carney?" she called nervously. "Orin, are you
still there?"

She heard a click, and then a weird humming sound.
Olivia poked her head out the doorway and stared down
the hall. A shadow spilled across the floor—two doors
down. There was another click, and someone talking.
The sound of his voice made her shudder: *"Yeah, well,
dig this, I've seen that crummy hotel, but I've never set
foot in it, man. You've got the wrong guy. . . ."*

Olivia hurried to the doorway to find Orin in a small
storage room. Folding chairs leaned against shelves
full of boxes. There were old lamps, stacks of magazines, and even an old dollhouse. He had an archaic
reel-to-reel tape recorder propped on a small steplad-
der. The reels turned and squeaked as the young man
continued to talk in a defiant, self-satisfied tone. The
machine was plugged into the base of the light fixture
overhead.

"This is the second half of the police interrogation

of Wade Grinnell," Orin explained, over Wade's voice. "The interview took place the day before Wade was killed running from the police. I had a friend on the force who copied the recording for me. Between you and me, I don't think they were even supposed to be recording him—without a lawyer or an adult guardian present. That part you heard earlier, where he says he never set foot inside the hotel—well, he's going to contradict himself later and mention something about the 'ugly blue bedspread.' Like I told you earlier, it's almost as if he wants to give himself away. Just listen. . . ."

Olivia braced a hand against the doorway to the storage room. "This is crazy," she whispered. She couldn't breathe right. She wasn't listening to what the young man was saying. She was listening to his voice.

She'd heard that exact same voice talking to her in her office last Thursday night.

CHAPTER TWENTY

Seattle—Monday, 4:51 p.m.

"What the hell is with the parking around here this afternoon?" muttered Olivia at the wheel of her VW. She searched for an open spot along a side street three blocks from her office. After all her prep work for her session with Collin Cox, she'd be late for it now. She hadn't counted on spending over two hours with Orin Carney. Any initial strangeness she'd felt about him had evaporated by the time he'd walked her to his front door. He'd been incredibly helpful.

She found a parking spot at last, locked the car, and hurried toward her building. It was dark, and the streetlights were already on. Outside the antique store, she glanced at her wristwatch. She still had two minutes until her appointment time with Collin. Pushing open the glass door to the vestibule, Olivia suddenly stopped.

Someone was waiting for her in the small lobby.

"Clay?" she murmured.

He wore the tan jacket she liked. "I'm sorry to ambush you like this. But I really had to see you."

She let the door close behind her. "I—I have to meet

with a client. He's probably in my waiting room right now."

Clay shook his head. "I was just up there five minutes ago, and the place was empty."

"Well, I guess you figured out where my offices are. What do you want, Clay?"

"Corinne's not pregnant."

Olivia numbly stared at him. "What?"

"She says she miscarried. She told me after the service on Saturday. She says it happened right before we got the news about Sue and Jerry—only she wanted to give us both a few days before telling me." He shook his head. "I have a feeling she was never really pregnant. I think she might have had a hysterical pregnancy. Or maybe she's just been lying through her teeth all this time. I never got to see a sonogram."

"Why am I not surprised?"

Neither one of them said anything for a few moments. Olivia finally sighed. "Well, I'm sorry about Corinne and the baby—if—if there actually was a baby."

Clay took a step toward her. "Don't you see what this means?" he whispered. "It means she doesn't have a hold on me anymore. I'm not under any obligation to stay with her. Technically, you and I are still married."

"Yes, so?"

He gently touched her face with his hand. "Olivia, I've been an idiot. Don't you see? There's nothing keeping us from being together again—except maybe some bad history and the horrible way I treated you. I'm asking you to think about us for a while, look into your heart and see if you can't forgive me. I swear, I'll spend the rest of my life trying to make it up to you. . . ."

He leaned in like he was going to kiss her. She could feel his warm breath on her lips.

But Olivia pulled away. "This is all coming at me a

little too fast," she said. Her heart was pounding wildly. "In practically the same sentence you tell me Corinne isn't pregnant and that you want me to take you back."

"I know. I'm sorry. It's just that I've wasted so much time."

The door opened slightly behind her.

Turning, she saw Collin. He had his school backpack slung over one shoulder, and wore a navy-blue hooded sweater. His wavy black hair was sort of a mess.

She quickly stepped aside so he could come into the lobby.

"Hi," he said, eyeing Clay—and then her.

She worked up a smile. "Hi, Collin. Why don't you go ahead upstairs? I'll be with you in a couple of minutes."

He nodded. "Okay, thanks." He shot another look at Clay and lumbered up the stairs.

Clay watched him, and then turned to her. "Isn't that the same kid you were talking to after the memorial service?"

"That's right. He was friends with Gail. Now he's a new client."

Clay glanced toward the stairs again. "Why does he look so familiar? I was wondering that on Saturday."

"Beats me," Olivia lied. He probably hadn't yet figured out that he'd seen Collin in the movies. "Anyway, he's waiting for me. So I should get going."

Clay took hold of her arm. "Olivia, I want you to think about what I've told you."

"Yes, I'm thinking about it, and it's pretty disgusting," she said, pulling away from him. "I can't believe you're talking about ditching your girlfriend less than two days after she told you about her miscarriage."

Clay frowned. "I don't think she was ever really pregnant—"

"It's awfully convenient for you to think that way, isn't it?" Olivia said. "But it's possible she's telling you the truth about losing the baby. And all you can think about is how that gives you license to dump her now. I don't care how crazy she is. It's still a lousy way for you to treat a person—any person. I'd say I didn't know you could be so selfish and uncaring, Clay. But I *do* know." She sighed, and then patted him on the shoulder. "Now, you need to leave me alone. And I need to see my client."

She turned away from him and started up the stairs.

"I'm not giving up that easily," she heard him say.

Olivia said nothing, and just kept walking up the stairs—one step at a time.

Corinne Beal sat in the lounge of Gene Juarez Salon. Thumbing through an issue of *Vogue*, she wore a smock with the GJ logo emblazoned all over it. The woman behind the desk had just set a cup of herbal tea in front of her.

She'd told Clay that she was seeing friends this afternoon. But as soon as she'd found out they were coming to the Seattle area for the memorial, she'd made this appointment. She knew after a weekend with Clay's relatives, she'd be ready for some "me" time. She'd scheduled a manicure, a pedicure, and facial.

Corinne figured the sooner she started feeling good about herself again, the sooner she'd drop the extra weight from her hysterical pregnancy. She'd known for six weeks now that it had all been a false alarm. But she'd managed to make it work to her advantage.

Now that she had Clay, she wasn't letting go. She had to think of other things—besides the promise of a baby—to help her hold on to him. There was always sex, of course. Maybe while she was here she'd get a bikini wax—and then surprise Clay with the Brazilian look. The thought made Corinne smile.

Her cell phone rang. Tossing *Vogue* on the glass top table, she reached inside the pocket of her smock. She glanced at the ID screen. It was an unknown caller.

Corinne ignored it. She took a sip of the tea and picked up a copy of *W* from the table. She flipped through it until her phone chimed to signify she had a text message waiting. Corinne checked it. The message had a photo attachment.

She frowned at the text that popped up:

CLAY IS A DIRTY DOG SNIFFING AROUND HIS OLD BITCH

An image came up on the screen. It was a slightly blurred photo—but unmistakably Clay, and he was about to kiss his soon-to-be ex on the lips. They were in a vestibule someplace—standing by a glass door. The bastard wasn't exactly discreet about it. The photo looked like it might have been taken across the street from wherever they'd had their rendezvous. The date and time were in the lower right corner of the grainy photo: *10/8/12 4:59 PM.*

Tears stung Corinne's eyes as she gazed at the photo—taken exactly six minutes ago.

"Who was that guy in the lobby with you?" Collin asked. He pulled off his backpack, set it on her sofa, and then sat down. "He was at Gail's memorial service, too, wasn't he?"

Olivia switched on the desk lamp and tossed her coat over the chair. "Yes, he's Gail's uncle. Mrs. Pelham was his sister. And he's soon to be my ex-husband. 'It's a small world after all.' "

She was still rebounding from the episode with Clay down in the lobby. When had he become such a jerk? How had it happened? He hadn't been that way when she'd married him. She had to remind herself to focus on Collin.

Hunched forward on the sofa, he seemed nervous. He was so gangly-handsome and sweet-looking. After just seeing the handiwork of Wade Grinnell, she couldn't fathom how Collin could have this other persona inside him.

"Sounds corny," he said. "But I was thinking about it on the way here. It's almost like you were meant to help me out. One of the last things Gail told me was that I should see you and get some therapy."

Olivia grabbed her notepad and sat down. She had a brief flashback to the summer before last, when Gail had stayed with her and Clay. The three of them had eaten out at Stanford's in the Lloyd Center mall. Their cute server had flirted with Gail, and while waiting for dinner to arrive, Olivia had started to teach her niece a little about hypnosis. She hadn't realized at the time just how happy they'd been.

"Yes, she was a sweet girl," Olivia said, a little tremor in her voice. Then she cleared her throat and looked at the notes she'd been writing over the weekend. "Okay, Collin, let's get started. Have you ever been to a counselor or therapist before?"

He shook his head. "Nope."

"And the only time you've been hypnotized before was with Gail?"

"Right."

"You said you saw some hypnotists before you came to me. How many? And were any of them able to put you in a trance?"

"There were five, and none of them worked."

Olivia consulted her notes. "Are you a righty, lefty, or both?"

He shrugged. "Lefty. What does that have to do with anything?"

"According to some studies, people with multiple personality disorder tend to be ambidextrous, and they're said to be easily hypnotized, too. I'm trying to determine if what's happening to you is some type of multiple personality disorder. Play along with me here, okay?"

He nodded. "Okay, sure."

She asked if he had any history of substance abuse or seizures or blackouts.

Collin just shook his head.

Did he recall any childhood abuse—sexual or physical?

"My mom wasn't exactly a candidate for Mother of the Year, but she never let anything like that happen to me," Collin answered. "Nobody while I was modeling or acting ever tried anything weird with me. Everyone was pretty nice."

"How often do you get headaches?" she asked.

"Once in a while, I guess. I take an aspirin and the headache usually goes away."

"Did you have any imaginary friends when you were a child?"

Collin nodded. "Dave. He and I were outlaws to-gether—like Butch Cassidy and the Sundance Kid.

Only we were Dastardly Dave and the Shilshole Kid. Shilshole Bay is where we had our hideout—this shack in the woods by the beach. In fact, the last time you hypnotized me—and when Gail hypnotized me—that was my safe place. It's where I went in my head. . . ."

"Yes, I remember. Let's get back to Dave for a minute. How real was he to you?"

Collin shrugged. "I always sort of knew he was made-up. But I still pretended Dave was around when I was alone or scared. I guess that sounds kind of psycho, huh?"

"Not really," Olivia said. She decided—with the possible exception of Dave—he showed no signs of dissociative identity disorder. "Having fantasy friends during childhood is a fairly normal thing."

Frowning, he shifted a bit on the sofa. "I don't know if this is important or not. But the night my mom and her boyfriend were killed, I had a dream with Dave in it."

"How often does he show up in your dreams?"

"I can't remember any other times—at least, not recently. Do you think it means anything that I dreamt about him that night?"

"Possibly. It's really too soon to deduce anything from it." Olivia scribbled in the margin of her notes. "Okay, Collin, moving on. You said in our first session that you'd never heard of Wade Grinnell until Gail hypnotized you. How much do you know about him now?"

He sighed. "Well, I went online, and read this article about the World's Fair from ten years ago. It had a timeline of events—"

"Yes, I think I read the same article," Olivia cut in. "It had little paragraphs explaining what happened on certain dates, right?"

He nodded. "Yeah, that's the one. Plus I drove to

Leavenworth last Monday and talked with Mrs. Pollack-Martin, who survived the hotel fire."

"She's still alive?"

Collin nodded again. "She was last Monday. I hope she still is. After what happened to Gail and Fernando, I'm not so sure about anything—or anyone."

"Was Mrs. Pollack-Martin able to tell you something about Wade?"

"Just that he flirted with her seventeen-year-old niece at the fair—and then she spotted him again at the hotel, right before the fire broke out." He leaned forward on the couch. "But here's the thing you should know. She said I looked just like him. In fact, she almost fainted when she first set eyes on me."

"Really?" Olivia murmured, staring at him. "Collin, have you seen a photo of Wade? Do you know what he looks like?"

He shook his head. "All I know about him is what I read in that timeline article."

Olivia decided not to say anything to him for now. Obviously, he wasn't aware of the two other hotel murders and the second fire. And he had no idea Wade didn't resemble him at all physically. She wondered what Mrs. Pollack-Martin had seen in him that had almost made her faint.

"What can you tell me about the 1962 Seattle World's Fair?" she asked.

"Well, I know from the timeline article that Elvis Presley visited—"

"No, before you read that piece, what did you know about the Seattle World's Fair?"

"Not much," he replied, shrugging. "I knew it was a very big deal fifty years ago, and they built the Space Needle for it. But that's all."

"No one in your family or extended family told you about attending the fair?"

"No. My grandfather was away at military school when the fair was going on, and my grandmother is from Houston." He straightened up a little. "But you just made me remember something that happened when I was a kid, visiting here with my mom. I think she was here for another stint in rehab. It was about a year before I made *The Night Whisperer*. My grandparents took me to the Seattle Center, and I asked my grandfather why the Space Needle wasn't orange. He told me, no, that it had been white for years."

"Well, it was originally orange-gold," Olivia said. "Maybe you saw a photo of the Space Needle from 1962, and that was how you still thought of it."

"Or maybe that's how Wade Grinnell remembers it," Collin said.

"Should I ask him?"

Gaping at her, Collin nodded. He grabbed his backpack and unzipped it. "I dug these out of storage last night," he said, showing her a pair of handcuffs. "Just to make sure he can't do anything like last time. They're real. We used them in a cable movie I made about six years ago. The cops slapped them on Harry Hamlin when they arrested him at the end of the movie. The prop man let me keep them." He glanced around the room and pointed to a radiator pipe in the corner. "You can cuff me to that." Standing up, he reached into his pocket. "Here's the key." He handed it to her.

Ordinarily, Olivia would never restrain a client, but considering what she knew about the real Wade, she wasn't giving Collin an argument. She took the key, and then moved a hardback chair over to the corner of her office. Collin set his iPhone on her desk and looked through it to make sure he had the area in frame. He didn't seem to like the height of the camera phone, and retrieved some books from his school bag to prop the phone up higher.

He joined her in the corner of the room, then cuffed his wrist and slapped the other cuff around the radiator pipe.

"It's not too hot, is it?" she asked, positioning her chair so it was out of his reach.

"No, I'm fine," Collin said, breathing harder now. He seemed nervous again. He sat down in the chair with his right arm outstretched.

"Are you comfortable? Are we filming?"

He nodded a few more times than necessary.

Grabbing her notebook again, Olivia sat down in front of him. She glanced back to make sure she wasn't blocking the camera. Suddenly she was nervous, too. "All right, Collin," she said, trying to steady her hand as she held it in front of his face. "I want you to think about that little shack near Shilshole Bay. . . ."

It took longer than last time to work him into a deep sleep. Olivia figured he couldn't have been very relaxed with his hand cuffed to the radiator pipe. But now he was slouched in the chair, with his eyes shut. His breathing was steady and deep.

"Collin, can you hear my voice?"

"Uh-huh," he grunted, barely nodding.

"I'm talking to the man inside Collin right now," she said.

A low, menacing cackle came from his mouth. "You make it sound like I'm fucking him," he said. It was the same voice she'd heard on the old tape two hours ago—the voice of the young sociopath who had murdered eighteen people.

"Wade?"

He opened his eyes and grinned at her—but only for a second. He noticed his shackled hand. He gave it a tug, and the metal handcuff clanked against the radiator pipe. "What is this shit?" he growled.

"You weren't very gentlemanly toward me last time," Olivia said. "So we took some precautions. I'll consider taking off the handcuffs if you answer some questions for me."

"Goddamn you, bitch," he muttered, glaring at her. He rattled the cuffs again, and then glanced around. Olivia wasn't sure what he was looking for—maybe something to break the handcuffs or something to throw at her. She wasn't sure.

"This will only be for a little while, Wade," Olivia said. She wondered if that was what he'd told his victims while tying them up—before he'd killed them. "First, you need to know that you're under hypnosis right now, and you can't lie. With that understood, did you set fire to the Pelhams' house last Tuesday morning?"

"I'm no firebug," he grunted. "I didn't set fire to any houses. Who the hell are the Pelhams?"

"Gail Pelham was the girl who hypnotized you last time, the girl you spoke with."

"The fat girl?"

Olivia sighed. "Yes, she was a big girl. She and her family were killed in a house fire early Tuesday morning."

He laughed like he knew some dirty little secret. "Well, don't look at me, honey."

"So you had nothing to do with the fire?"

"Nope."

"And I suppose you had nothing to do with the fires

at the Hotel Aurora Vista or the Pioneer Motor Inn," she said.

He chuckled again, and then straightened in his chair. "Well, that's a different story."

"What about Collin's friend, Fernando?" she asked.

He squinted at her.

"Collin's Latino friend, he's dead, too. Someone slit his throat."

He burst out laughing, and slapped his knee with his free hand. "Shit, no, that's news to me. I had nothing to do with that."

"Why is it so funny?" Olivia asked.

He smiled—the same smirk from the mug shot. "I'm just surprised, that's all. Could I have a glass of water?"

"In a minute," she said. "You said you've known Collin for a long time. Did you know his mother, Piper Cox, and her boyfriend, Chance Hall?"

He frowned. "Nope, don't know them."

"Then you don't know who killed them?"

His eyes narrowed at her. "You're asking the wrong guy, honey. Maybe the kid did it, and he's pretending he doesn't remember."

"You mean, you don't know everything Collin does?" she asked. "You aren't aware of his actions? What is it—like you're asleep inside him while he's awake?"

He slouched lower in the chair, and scratched his crotch. "I can't answer," he whispered. "My throat's too dry. I need some water."

"Last time, when I asked why you were doing this to Collin, you said something about wanting to drive him crazy—before killing him. Why? What has Collin done to you? Who is he to you?"

Shaking his head, he pointed to his mouth. "Wa-wa . . ."

"All right, I'll give you some water," she said. "But you have to answer some questions first. They're easy. You can keep the answers short—so as not to strain your parched throat. What color is the Space Needle?"

"They say it's gold, but it's really orange."

"What color was it before?"

"Before what? They painted it orange when they finished building the stupid thing earlier this year."

Olivia bit her lip for a moment. She scribbled a note down:

W thinks it's still 1962

She glanced up at him and caught him trying to manipulate the lock to the handcuffs. It dawned on her that she and Collin hadn't tested them.

"Don't bother trying to do that," she said coolly. "I've got the key and I'll unlock the cuffs in a couple of minutes. You'll get your water, too. Just a few more questions—and they're easy. Who is the president of the United States?"

"Kennedy. Duh."

"Who's the vice president?"

He tapped his foot and had to think for a moment. "Nixon."

Olivia didn't let on that he was wrong. "What's the last movie you saw in the theater?"

"*Lawrence of Arabia.*"

"What's today's date?"

He rolled his eyes, and then twisted around in the chair. His cuff knocked against the pipe. "October something. How the hell should I know? I don't have a calendar with me."

"Okay, just give me the year."

"1962," he growled. "Now when the fuck are you gonna take these cuffs off me, bitch?"

"In a minute. Do you know who Loretta Pollack is?"

"Never heard of her," he grunted.

"How about Rebecca Holleran—or Becky? Did you meet her at the fair, Wade?"

"You've got nothing on me," he muttered, eyes narrowed at her.

"What about Cynthia Helms? She came up here from California with her parents. She was a freshman at the University of Washington. Are you going to tell me that you've never heard of her either?"

"I want some goddamn water. . . ."

"Why won't you answer my questions?"

"Screw you, bitch!" he yelled. Suddenly, he kicked and his shoe flew off. It sailed right past her head.

Startled, Olivia dropped her notebook.

He lunged at her, knocking his chair out from underneath him. His free hand swiped at the air just inches away from her face. Grunting, he tugged and tugged at the handcuff. It made a loud clatter against the radiator pipe.

Reeling back, Olivia tried to keep calm. "Collin?" she called in a shaky voice. She spoke over all his clanking and cursing. "Collin, I'm talking to you now. When I snap my fingers, you'll wake up. Collin?" She snapped her fingers three times. "Collin?"

He suddenly stopped and slumped down to the carpet. The cuff made a scratchy whine as it slid down the radiator pipe. He leaned back against the wall with his eyes closed.

All at once, everything seemed so quiet.

"Collin?" she whispered. "Can you hear me, Collin?"

"Yeah," he murmured, opening his eyes. He started to move his shackled right hand and winced in pain.

Grabbing the key off her desk, Olivia crouched down beside him and unlocked the cuff.

Suddenly, his other hand grabbed her arm.

She screamed and fell on the floor.

"What?" Collin asked, panicked. "What'd I do?"

It took her a moment. "Nothing," Olivia said, catching her breath. "You just scared the hell out of me, that's all. I thought you were still him for a second."

Olivia picked herself up. She put a hand over her heart and felt it pounding furiously. "Are you all right?" she asked him.

Still sitting on the carpet, Collin rubbed his right wrist and grimaced again. He nodded.

She helped him to his feet. "We should get some ice on that wrist right away," she said. "Otherwise, it'll be black and blue and all swollen tonight. There's a convenience store across the street that sells their version of Big Gulps. We can get some ice from them."

Collin picked up his chair. "Good. Maybe I can get something to drink, too. I—I'm so thirsty."

Olivia retrieved her notebook. She looked at him and nodded. "So was he."

"I didn't take you for a smoker," Collin said, sitting beside her on one of the benches in Knudsen Park. The fenced-in, small urban park was tucked away one block behind all the stores and restaurants along Madison Street. An artful balance of pavement, trees, and plants, it had become Olivia's own peaceful safe place. She often took her lunch from the Essential Baking Company or the teriyaki joint nearby and ate it in this little oasis. She'd never come here at night before. The park was well lit, and empty—except for them. Collin had Madison Val-U Mart's version of a Big Gulp in his left hand. The guys behind the counter knew her by now and gave them free ice. Olivia had loaded it in a handkerchief, which she'd tied around his wrist.

"Aren't you supposed to help people *quit* smoking?" Collin asked.

"Okay, so I'm a big phony," Olivia grumbled, puffing gratefully on her first cigarette of the day. "I'm trying to cut back. I only had six cigarettes yesterday. Between my dealings with Wade Grinnell and my soon-to-be-ex-husband, I'm finding it harder and harder to give it up."

"Sorry," Collin muttered, sipping his drink through a fat straw.

She nudged him with her elbow. "Don't sweat it." Taking a final drag from her Virginia Slim, she carefully put it out and tossed the extinguished stub in the trash can.

She hadn't let Collin watch the video of the session yet. "Okay, first the good news," she said. "Wade—and therefore you as his host—didn't have anything to do with the fire that killed Gail and her family. And he wasn't involved in Fernando's death either. Subjects under hypnosis usually can't lie, so I believe him. But you'll see in the video that he seems to think it's all kind of amusing—and I'm not sure why."

"Did he say what he was doing right before dawn on Tuesday?" Collin asked anxiously. "Did he explain where he'd been? I mean, why were my shoes all muddy? Why did my clothes smell like gasoline?"

Olivia shook her head. "I didn't ask him about that. I'm sorry. But you can let yourself off the hook about your friends—and about your mother and Chance, too. He didn't know them and didn't know about the murders."

With a sigh, Collin sagged against the bench-back. He took another sip of his Big Gulp.

Olivia reached into her purse and fished out a copy of the 1964 *Seattle Times* article. "Now brace yourself," she said, handing him the two pieces of paper. "That's an old newspaper feature. As you can see, Wade was a lot busier than we thought. His picture's there on the second page. I don't see any resemblance. So I'm not sure what Mrs. Pollack was talking about."

"My God," Collin murmured, staring at the article. "You know, he hinted in the second session with Gail that there were others. But I had no idea. He killed all these people?"

Olivia allowed him some time to skim over the feature. "I'm not sure why they didn't mention the other fire and the other murders in the timeline. Maybe it was a mistake or it was intentionally buried. Who knows? The author of that article you're looking at, he gave me access to his files this afternoon. I also heard a tape of Wade being interviewed by the police. And it's the exact same voice coming out of you when you're in a trance."

Collin looked up from the news story.

"I'd like to try a little experiment," Olivia said, taking out her iPhone. She pulled up Google and carefully typed in "Lawrence of Arabia, Premiere." "I want to ask you some of the questions I asked Wade. It's just a comparison thing."

"Go ahead," he said.

"This is right up your alley. It has to do with movies. What year did *Lawrence of Arabia* come out?"

Adjusting the ice on his wrist, Collin nodded immediately. "1962, it won Best Picture."

"Who was the president that year?"

"John F. Kennedy?"

She nodded. "Who was vice president?"

He squinted at her. "Nixon?"

"Actually, it was Lyndon Johnson," Olivia said. "Wade made the same mistake."

Collin frowned. "So what does that mean? Do you think I'm faking?"

"I don't think you're faking, Collin." She glanced at the top search result on Google and clicked on it. "From what I could tell, Wade still thinks it's 1962. And when he was alive, I'm assuming he was no brain trust. So—maybe he didn't know who the vice president was at the time. But the thing is, you both made the same mistake." She glanced at her iPhone again.

"What are you looking up anyway?" he asked.

"Something else Wade got wrong," she said. "He told me the last movie he saw was *Lawrence of Arabia*."

"Yeah, well, it came out in 1962, I'm almost positive."

With her eyes on the phone screen, she nodded. "It says here the film had its royal premiere on December 10, 1962, and its U.S. premiere on December 16, 1962."

"So?"

She gazed at him and slowly shook her head. "Collin, by then, Wade had already been dead for two months."

CHAPTER TWENTY-ONE

Bainbridge Island ferry—Monday, 6:21 p.m.

Collin studied the mug shot of Wade Grinnell again. Sixteen years old and the guy looked practically thirty. Of course, teenagers looked older back then. He and Fernando had found online a sex education video from the mid-fifties about VD. Between laughing hysterically, they'd also marveled at how all the teenage girls resembled mousy housewives, and the guys looked like doofus junior executives. Or maybe they just couldn't cast anyone under eighteen in those things. Whatever, Wade Grinnell didn't look like a juvenile delinquent. Instead, he could have passed for someone who had already done hard time in prison.

In fact, he looked like someone who might have murdered eighteen people.

Sitting in the car, waiting in the ferry terminal parking lot, he had the interior light on. He kept looking at the photo, and then at the rearview mirror—to see if there was any resemblance at all. He didn't know what Mrs. Pollack-Martin had seen—except possibly something inside him.

He was supposed to meet Olivia again at the same

time tomorrow. He'd have to make up yet another lie to explain to his grandparents why he wouldn't be home until dinnertime. It was worth it. He couldn't believe Olivia refused to take his money.

Switching off the interior light, Collin looked in the rearview mirror again, and gasped.

About five cars behind him, a man stood outside his vehicle, holding a pair of binoculars up to his face. He looked like the man from the boat at night behind his grandparents' house. He wore a navy-blue Windbreaker and khakis.

His cell phone rang. Ignoring it, Collin opened the door and jumped out of the car. He turned around and the man with the binoculars was gone.

Collin started down the aisle between the rows of waiting cars. All the while, his phone kept ringing. He finally dug it out of his pocket and saw it was his grandparents' number. He let it go to voice mail, and kept walking down the aisle, eyeing people inside their cars. After passing by nine vehicles, he still hadn't spotted the man in the blue Windbreaker.

Collin realized the guy must have left his car in another aisle. He heard the boat horn blowing as the ferry came into the terminal. He started back toward his Taurus, but kept glancing around for the blue-Windbreaker man. Was it possible he just looked familiar because of the binoculars? The body type seemed the same.

Climbing behind the wheel, Collin shut his door. He was about to retrieve the message from his grandparents when his cell rang again. It was their number.

Clicking on the phone, he glanced in the rearview mirror again. "Grandpa?"

"Collin?" It was his grandmother, sounding frazzled. "Where are you right now, honey?"

"Um, the—the school library," he lied. "Why? Did

something happen? Did that prowler from last night come back?"

"No, it's your grandfather. He had a little spell about a half hour ago—and he refuses to go to the hospital. . . ."

"Where is he?" Collin heard his grandfather yell in the background.

"He's at school, Andy," she answered, her voice slightly muffled. "Listen, sweetie," she said. "I think you should come home and try to talk some sense into him. He won't let me call the doctor. He doesn't want to go to the emergency room—"

"I had a dizzy spell!" his grandfather barked in the distance. *"It's no big deal!"*

"And your speech was slurred!" she shot back. Then she spoke into the phone again: "I'm worried he had a ministroke or something."

"Call his doctor. If Grandpa won't budge, get the doctor to come over."

"I'm going to do that right now. In the meantime, hurry home, okay?"

Collin glanced ahead at the ferry docking. "Um, I'll be about an hour. I'm sorry, I—"

"An hour? Whoever's keeping you there, tell them you have a family emergency. . . ."

"Actually, I—I loaned my car to someone," Collin lied. "They won't be back for another forty-five minutes. But as soon as they get back, I'll . . ." He trailed off. He could hear Dee talking to his grandfather.

"He let a friend borrow the car," she said.

Collin squirmed in the driver's seat at his grandfather's response: *"WHAT?"*

A moment later, Old Andy came on the line. "What is this I hear about you letting a friend use the Taurus?" he asked hotly. "And you're not in the car with him? Collin, we aren't insured for that kind of thing. What in the name of all that's holy are you thinking? What if he has an accident?"

"It was kind of an emergency," he lied. He thought his grandfather might have another ministroke right there. "Grandpa, let Dee call your doctor. I'll be there as soon I can. Okay?"

There was no response.

"Grandpa, are you still there?"

"Collin, honey," his grandmother said. "He just handed off the phone to me. He's okay, just upset. Come on home as soon as you can. Okay?"

"Okay," he said. Then he listened to the click on the other end.

Sitting at the wheel, he listened to all the car doors shutting. The din echoed in the ferry's tunnel-like parking level. Collin kept looking around at the passengers getting out of their cars. He still didn't see the man in the blue Windbreaker. Maybe the guy had pulled into one of the other two parking areas.

The boat started to pull away from the terminal. It looked like most everyone who was getting out of their cars had already gone up to the main cabin. Collin thought about making a car-by-car search—for a pair of binoculars on someone's front seat. But there were hundreds of vehicles, and scores of tourists took the ferries every day—half of them had binoculars.

Collin decided instead to go upstairs to the restroom. After that Big Gulp in the park, he really had to go. Climbing out of the car, he looked over at the stairwell access, and he froze.

A dark-haired man in a blue jacket hovered in the alcove doorway. All at once, he quickly ducked toward the steps. Collin didn't get a look at his face.

He shut his car door, made sure it was locked, and started toward the stairwell access. He was shaking. An announcement came over the loudspeaker: *"Welcome aboard Washington State Ferries. Please listen to these very important announcements. . . ."*

Approaching the stairwell access, Collin peeked around the corner toward the stairs. Near the top of the steps, he saw a shadow sweep across the wall—then ripple down the stairs. It stopped suddenly. He couldn't help thinking someone was up there waiting for him.

"For security reasons, we ask passengers not to leave any backpacks, luggage, packages, and any other personal belongings unattended during this crossing. . . ."

With a glance over his shoulder, Collin noticed the access to the other stairwell, closer to the bow. He took one more look at the shadow overhead. It moved, swaying back and forth a little. Whoever was up there, they seemed impatient.

"In the event of a shipboard emergency, signals will be sounded on the ship's general alarm. . . ."

Collin turned and ran to the other stairway access. He hurried up the narrow staircase to the main cabin. Weaving around other passengers, he rushed down the aisle to the front stairwell. The swinging door at the top of it was still moving back and forth a little.

Catching his breath, he looked around at the other passengers in the vicinity. He didn't see anyone wearing a blue Windbreaker in the crowd.

With a sigh, Collin retreated into the men's room. The place smelled so gag-awful he tried to hold his breath while peeing. He didn't see anyone in a blue jacket. Quickly washing his hands, he wiped them dry on the front of his pants and hurried out of the restroom. Then he finally took a big breath of air.

He glanced around at the other passengers once

more, looking for that man in the blue Windbreaker. No luck.

Collin headed to the stairwell again. He wanted to get an update on his grandfather. But he needed to phone his grandparents from inside the car, where it was quieter. He had to keep up the pretense that he was calling from the school library. He didn't even want to think about how he'd cope if his grandfather's condition was serious. Old Andy was just about the only stable force in his life right now. Even though Collin was doing things behind his grandfather's back, he'd come to depend on him, too. He didn't want to think about him becoming sick and feeble.

With a sad, scared pang gnawing at his stomach, he plodded down the stairwell to the parking level. He saw a man in a blue Windbreaker prowling among the cars.

Collin stopped in his tracks and watched him. He couldn't see his face, but the guy was headed toward the Taurus. He took a piece of paper out of his pocket.

Quickly glancing around, Collin noticed some people still in their cars. He wasn't totally alone down here with the man. He swallowed hard, and took a few steps forward. "Are you leaving me another note?" he called in a shaky voice.

The man swiveled around and stared at him. He was tall and thin, with black hair and a slightly pinched look to his face. Collin guessed he was about forty. He looked familiar.

"Well, hello, Collin," the man said, smiling at him. He furtively slipped the piece of paper back inside the pocket of his Windbreaker.

Threading around a couple of cars to get closer, Collin recognized Rick, the weirdo who had cornered him in the alley behind Hot Shots Java three months before. Ian had said the guy was stalking him. He'd even been poking around the rental house where his mom and Chance had been murdered.

"I know you," Collin said, stopping between the bumpers of two parked cars.

The man laughed. "Well, I'm flattered you'd remember me."

"Yes, your name's Rick, and you've seen all my movies and TV appearances. And for a long time now, you've been following me around. . . ."

Rick shrugged, and stepped toward Collin. The trunk of a parked Camry was between them. "I wouldn't say I've been *following* you. We just happen to travel in the same circles."

"But don't you live in Seattle?"

He laughed again. "Wow, you know where I used to live? I really am flattered. . . ."

"Ian told me. He said you were stalking me. He told me a lot about you."

"Well, I wouldn't believe everything that hotheaded cop has told you. Talk about a stalker. It's a good thing me and my family moved to Poulsbo two months ago— so I could keep an eye out for you occasionally." He looked around, and then smiled at him. "Look, Collin, this is silly, standing here talking and choking on gas fumes. Why don't we go upstairs and chat where it's warm and comfortable?"

"I'd rather choke on gas fumes," Collin muttered.

Rick sighed. "I should be hurt, but you really don't know me that well, not the way I know you. So I don't blame you. You probably think I had something to do with your friends getting killed. But I didn't, Collin. I wasn't jealous of them or anything, honest. In fact, I was glad to see you making friends. You don't believe me, do you?"

Collin stared at him. He wasn't sure.

Rick took a step toward him. "You were right earlier. I left a note on your car last Tuesday. Imagine my surprise when I was coming back from my skin doctor's appointment in Seattle and spotted you on the ferry—instead of in school. I almost came up and talked with you while you were on the outside deck, but you looked so pensive. I decided to leave you a note instead. If you want, I can dig up the receipt from my skin doctor showing the time of my appointment. That would put me in Seattle the afternoon your friend, Fernando, was murdered and when the Pelham house was burglarized. My wife, Michelle, could tell you, we had another incident with Kelsey. He's five and still wets the bed. It happened around four in the morning on Tuesday. Isn't that around the time the newspapers said your friend's house caught fire?"

Collin nodded. A part of him believed the guy, but he was still wary—and put off. "Where are your binoculars?" he asked pointedly.

"In the car," Rick replied, half-smirking. "You must have spotted me earlier at the ferry terminal in Seattle. I thought you had."

"I've seen you at night, too—on the bay, on that boat behind my grandparents' house."

Rick shook his head. "I don't own a boat, Collin."

"Right," he replied sarcastically. "And you didn't send me those emails either, the ones with the smiley face."

"I don't know what you're talking about."

"Bullshit! The way you're talking right now—those emails are just like something you'd send! It's the same tone and everything."

Rick let out a bewildered laugh. "I've never emailed you, Collin. I don't know anything about a boat. . . ."

"You were sneaking around outside my grandparents' house last night, weren't you?"

"I wouldn't do anything like that."

"What's the new message?" Collin asked hotly. "You admitted you left me a note last time we were on the ferry together. You had a piece of paper in your hand earlier. You were going to leave it on my car. What does it say?"

Rick turned away and walked between the vehicles to the railing. Collin followed him. In the night darkness, he could see only the silvery ripples on the black water below. Rick took his hand out of his pocket and offered him the folded piece of paper.

Collin unfolded the note:

SOMEONE'S WATCHING YOU. BE CAREFUL.

He frowned at the man. "I know someone's watching me. You are."

Rick suddenly seemed nervous. "I wanted to keep the warning anonymous," he said. "I don't know for sure who killed your friends. And I really don't want the police grilling me about how I know you're being followed. I'm simply watching out for your well-being, and will not have that be misconstrued. Don't you see what would happen to me if it came out I might know something? I can't get involved. I have a wife and family to worry about. I don't want my house burned down in the middle of the night, too."

Collin looked at the note again and shook his head. "What are you getting at? Who's following me besides you?"

"I saw your cop friend, Ian, parked outside your school two weeks ago," Rick said. "Classes were getting out, and you were outside with your two friends.

He'd parked across the street and watched you from his car. I thought he might be back on surveillance duty, but I did a little research. Turns out he was on temporary leave from the force. They were deciding how to reprimand him for beating up a teenage suspect during an arrest. So—when you say he's accused me of stalking you, I can't help being amused."

"Is that all?" Collin asked.

"There's someone else. I don't know if he's working with your cop friend or not—"

"Stop calling him my *cop friend*," Collin interrupted. "Who is this other guy? What does he look like?"

"I've never seen his face. For all I know he could be your cop—" Rick stopped himself and smiled condescendingly. "He could be *Detective Haggerty* in disguise. He's very skilled in his elusiveness. Mostly, he stays in his car, a black Saturn. I don't think he's paparazzi or police. He started showing up last week. At least, that's when I first noticed him—on the ferry Wednesday. I wasn't sure if he was watching me or you. Since then, I've seen him outside your school, on Skog-Strand Lane and here on the ferry again. Just an hour ago, he was in front of that woman's office building, sitting in his car." Rick gave Collin a sidelong glance. "Who is she, by the way? I looked at the directory in the lobby. Is she one of the psychologists in that building? If you're seeing a psychologist, Collin, I think it's a mistake, because—"

"That's private," he said, cutting him off.

Rick raised his eyebrows, and then seemed to work up a contrite smile. "Of course it is."

"Did you ever get a license number off the black Saturn?"

Rick sighed. "I tried to. I only caught the first three

letters—WJO. Then, the next time I saw him, I tried to get a better look at the plate. It started out with the letters DJK. He's switching license plates. And for all I know, he's switching cars, too." He leaned in close to Collin, and glanced over toward the rows of parked vehicles. "For all I know, he could be watching us right now. . . ."

He touched Collin's shoulder. "I'm probably putting myself at risk, standing here talking to you." He stroked his upper arm.

Collin stepped back. "Well, then you better stay away from me," he said. "And stay away from my grandparents' house. If you don't leave me alone, I'll call the police. I really will."

He turned away, and threaded his way through the cars toward his Taurus.

"I'm trying to help you!" Rick called, his voice echoing. "Ask yourself what might have happened if I wasn't around looking out for you! You need me, Collin!"

Collin ducked inside his car and shut the door.

He hated to think that what Rick said might be true.

CHAPTER TWENTY-TWO

"I tried phoning you at the hotel around five o'clock, but there was no answer."

"I decided to go shopping at REI," Clay said. "Why didn't you call me on my cell?"

"I tried," Corinne lied. "But I kept getting some recording saying the party I was calling was unavailable. What did you buy at REI?"

"Nothing. So when do you think you might be back from this hen session? Should I order dinner for myself or what?"

"I'll be there in an hour," Corinne said. "I need to make a stop on the way."

She was sitting at the wheel of their Lexus, parked at the end of Alder Lane. She and Clay had both been lying to each other. The difference was Clay really believed she'd been with her girlfriends this afternoon. And she knew where he'd been, the son of a bitch.

At the reception desk at Gene Juarez, she'd canceled her salon appointment and borrowed a phone book. She'd looked up the address of Olivia's father, Walt Barker. She didn't have the GPS take her directly there.

She'd made a side trip to Lowe's. With a little assistance, she'd found what she was looking for in the vast home improvement warehouse.

The recent purchases were now in a bag beside her on the passenger seat.

"One of the girls this afternoon was talking about having a chemical peel," Corinne said into the phone.

"Really?" Clay didn't sound too interested.

"Yes. She was trying to talk me into getting one. Your ex, she doesn't have much going for her, but she does have very pretty skin. I'll grant her that much. Wouldn't you agree?"

"Jesus, Corinne, I don't want to get into anything with you right now."

"I'm just saying, she has a smooth complexion. I won't bite your head off if you agree with me."

She heard him sigh. "All right, I agree with you."

"Did she ever have a chemical peel?"

"I don't think so," he replied. "And listen. If you're thinking of getting a chemical peel, you don't need it."

"You're probably right," she said. "Listen, I should scoot. See you soon, honey."

Clicking off the line, she reached over and fished the pair of thick work gloves and safety goggles from the bag. Then she took out the quart container of concentrated muriatic acid. The label had a long list of warnings. The acid-based corrosive usually came diluted in gallon jugs. It was for big jobs, like cleaning scum off swimming pools or dirt from bricks and cement.

Corinne just needed it for a small job tonight.

At the stove, she gave the spaghetti sauce a quick stir. Then Olivia hurried back to the laptop at the writing nook. She wore jeans, a white long-sleeved tee, thick gray socks, and no shoes. The kitchen smelled of Italian chicken sausage, garlic, and French bread baking.

She plopped down on the chair in front of the laptop screen—and page seven of the Google search results for Sheri Grinnell Morrow. None of the links seemed to be about Wade's sister.

Olivia heard a knock. It sounded like someone at the front door. Her dad was upstairs taking a shower.

She headed to the front of the house, and switched on the outside light. Smoothing the hair back from her face, she glanced through the peephole in the door. She didn't see anyone on the front stoop. She unlocked the door, opened it a crack, and peered outside.

No one was out there.

Olivia opened the door wider and glanced around. She didn't see anybody—or any movement, except for the tree branches and bushes rustling in the wind.

She felt a chill. Stepping back inside, she closed the door and locked it again.

Upstairs, the shower water turned off with a squeak. "Dinner's on in fifteen minutes, Pop!" she called, rubbing her arms.

"Okey-doke!" he replied from upstairs, his voice muffled.

Olivia headed back to the stove, where she tossed some pasta into the boiling water. Then she checked page eight of the search results on Wade's sister. She found something:

TACOMA WOMAN DIES IN APARTMENT FIRE

www.tacomanewstribune.com/local.news/10/29/99.html

Sheri Albertson, 57, perished in the blaze, which is believed to have started . . . Albertson is survived by Troy **Morrow**, 33, her son from her first marriage . . .

"Another fire," Olivia murmured, clicking on the link to the story.

The short article was dated October 29, 1999. A divorcee, Sheri Albertson was the same age as Wade's sister. Sheri had been twenty in 1962, according to the note on the back of that snapshot of her and Wade in front of The Twin Teepees. Orin's notes had her married around 1965, which meant Troy could have been born just a year later. This had to be her: *Sheri Grinnell Morrow Albertson*.

According to the article, she'd burned to death in her small one-bedroom apartment. It appeared the fire had started in the bedroom. A neighboring apartment had some minor smoke damage. In the final paragraph of the article, it said: *The cause of the fire is still under investigation.*

"Of course it is," Olivia muttered, frustrated.

She clicked back to the Google home page, and typed in: *Troy Morrow.*

The first page of results focused on a champion fisherman. Olivia looked up his age—just to be sure he wasn't Sheri's son. He wasn't. She was moving on to page two when she heard a loud thump outside. Startled, she gaped out the big picture window at the back patio.

The wind must have knocked over one of the plastic recycling bins. Empty, it rolled around the leaf-littered patio. Getting up, Olivia headed to the back door and stepped outside. The concrete stoop was cold against her stocking feet. She padded toward the fallen bin, but she heard leaves rustling and stopped. She stared over toward the tall, shadowy bushes alongside the house.

"What's going on?"

Olivia swiveled around toward the door, where her father stood.

All at once, something behind the bushes scurried away. Olivia saw the shrubs moving, and she heard twigs snapping.

Her father switched on the patio lights. "I think we just scared away Rocky Raccoon."

Olivia caught her breath, worked up a smile, and nodded. She tiptoed over to the bin. "I got this, Pop. Can you check on the pasta?" She picked up the plastic bin, and then the lid. "Don't we usually weigh these down when they're empty?" she called.

Her dad answered back from inside the kitchen. "Yeah, looks like we had a very determined critter tonight. The pasta's sticking to the wall!"

Olivia returned the bin to its spot alongside the house, between two other bins. She noticed two bricks strategically placed on either side of the lid handles of both receptacles. For some reason, the *very determined critter* had picked this middle bin to knock over. But the two bricks that had weighed it down were on the ground, side by side.

It was as if someone had carefully taken them off the container lid and set them down. No unthinking animal could have done that.

Olivia nervously glanced at the shrubbery and lush garden alongside the house. She didn't see anything. Whoever had been there had disappeared. She decided not to say anything to her father. He'd want to know why someone would throw a recycling bin across their patio, and she wouldn't have any explanation for him. She just knew something was wrong.

Her feet were cold again, and she hurried toward the kitchen door.

* * *

"Goddamn it," Corinne hissed, out of breath.

Inside her car once again, she set the plastic container of muriatic acid concentrate on the passenger floor. Tugging off the gloves, she tossed them on the passenger seat. Then she took off the safety goggles.

Sitting at the wheel, she waited to see if the police showed up. She didn't think Olivia or her father had spotted her, but she needed to make sure. She was so mad at herself for not dousing her at the front door when she'd had the chance. She'd had such a clear shot, too. But she'd lost her nerve. The second opportunity had been blown when the father had come to the back door.

Corinne glanced at her wristwatch. She'd decided to give it another ten minutes. If a police car didn't come down Alder Lane in that time, she'd give it another try. She was determined to get Olivia tonight—one way or another.

Poulsbo—Monday, 7:25 p.m.

The garage door opened with a mechanical hum, and Collin carefully steered the Taurus into its spot. He shut off the engine, grabbed his backpack, and opened the car door.

"Hey, kiddo . . ."

He turned and glanced over at the door into the house. His grandfather was standing at the threshold. He wore a button-down yellow shirt and khakis. He looked a bit pale.

Collin slung his backpack over his shoulder and looped around in front of the other two cars—toward his grandfather. "Did the doctor come by?" he asked anxiously.

"He left about fifteen minutes ago," Old Andy sighed. "He was barely here a half an hour, and I'm sure he'll charge me four hundred bucks for this little house call."

"What did he say?"

His grandfather didn't move from the doorway. He patted Collin's shoulder and frowned. "He thinks it was a ministroke. He's scheduling me for some tests on Friday. It sounds like an all-day ordeal. If I don't die before that, the tests will probably kill me. In the meantime, he's putting me on some blood-thinner stuff. I'm supposed to take it easy, not get riled, and not play golf—for crying out loud."

"I'm sorry about the golf part, Grandpa," he murmured. "I know that's killing you."

"Well, as for the *not-getting-riled* part, I don't know what you were thinking—lending your car to a friend. That was really careless. You know we're not insured for that. You're lucky I don't take the car away or suspend your driving privileges. I should be really upset with you, Collin, but I'm not supposed to get riled, so that's all I'm going to say."

"Sorry," he muttered.

His grandfather sighed and leaned against the doorway frame. "I didn't want to mention anything in front of your grandmother, because I don't want her to think I'm worried. But for the rest of the week, I'd like you to come home right after school. If I need to write a note to get you out of these after-school projects, so be it. With everything that's happened lately—including this little scare today—I'll feel better with you around."

Collin stared up at him. He was thinking about his appointment with Olivia tomorrow.

"Is that going to be a problem? This isn't a punishment, kiddo. I'm asking for your help. It's just for the rest of the week."

Collin shook his head. "No, it's not a problem at all," he lied.

His grandfather patted his shoulder again. "Good. Let's go. Dinner's ready."

Following his grandfather inside, Collin noticed he'd lost a little spring in his step. He suddenly seemed slow and feeble. Collin's heart ached. He felt horrible. It was because of him that Old Andy was under so much extra stress lately. But he didn't say anything.

He didn't want his grandfather to know he was worried.

"Anyway, I can't make it tomorrow at five," Collin said on the other end of the line.

With the cell phone to her ear, Olivia stood outside the front door. She'd put on some slippers and an old cardigan. She was having a Virginia Slims break, her second cigarette of the day. She could hear a football game on the TV in her father's study.

Since that weird incident with the recycle bin, she'd been a bit on edge. There hadn't been any more strange occurrences, thank God. Still, she warily eyed the bushes and trees in the front yard. The branches stirred in the night's gentle breeze, occasionally shedding a leaf.

"I'm sorry to hear about your grandfather," Olivia said, puffing on her cigarette.

"I might be able to cut school tomorrow at lunchtime and then catch the ferry—"

"No, I won't have you ditching school to meet with me," she said. "Besides, it's just as well you're canceling tomorrow. I still have some research to do before we meet again. Maybe I can take the ferry over on Wednesday and meet you at school around lunchtime. We'll figure something out. Why don't you call me to-morrow night?"

"What kind of research, stuff about Wade?"

"That's part of it. By the way, how's your wrist?"

"Kind of sore—bruised," he said.

"Well, keep icing it, and get some sleep tonight. We'll talk tomorrow."

"Okay," he said. "And thanks, Olivia. Thanks for everything."

"Take care," she said. Then she clicked off and took a long drag from her cigarette.

Olivia figured it was just as well she wasn't meeting Collin tomorrow. She still needed to figure out how to restrain him while he was under so he wouldn't hurt himself again. She also needed the extra time to track down Troy Morrow and see if he could tell her some-thing about his uncle. Or had Sheri kept Wade a secret from her son?

After washing the dinner dishes, she'd gone back to her online search for Troy Morrow. A call to the only *Morrow, Troy* in the Seattle phone directory had been a bust. She'd gotten an old man who had yelled at her for waking him up "in the middle of the night." She'd made the call at eight-fifteen, for God's sakes.

The online White Pages had shown two more Troy Morrows in Washington state. She'd tried the first Troy on the list—a number in Spokane—and talked to a col-lege student at Gonzaga, who had kept calling her "dude."

Olivia finished her cigarette, stepped on the butt, then carefully peeled it off the front stoop and took it inside. She wet the butt under the kitchen faucet and tossed it in the garbage. Sitting at her mother's desk, she grabbed her cell and tried the second and last *Troy Morrow* listed in the White Pages for Washington State. This one was in Centralia. If this wasn't him she'd try the Oregon White Pages.

It rang twice before a woman answered, sounding lethargic. "Hello?"

"Hi," Olivia said. "Is Troy there, please?"

"Who's this?"

"My name's Olivia. I'm trying to track down a Troy Morrow whose mother's name was Sheri. This Troy Morrow would be around forty-five or forty-six years old."

"Troy's not here. What do you want with him?"

"Well, I—I'm an old friend of his mother's—"

"Troy's mother is dead," the woman grumbled.

"Yes, I know. She died in a fire several years ago. Do I have the right Troy Morrow?"

"No."

There was a click.

"Hello?" Olivia said, hunched over the desk. "Are you there?"

The woman had hung up on her.

With a sigh, Olivia clicked off the phone.

"The Seahawks are getting creamed," her father announced, shuffling into the kitchen. He had his slippers on—along with a pair of ill-fitting jeans and a gray sweatshirt. He was carrying an empty glass, a crumpled napkin, and a bag of Chips Ahoy. "It's hopeless. I'm hitting the sheets."

She leaned back in her mother's chair and watched him put the cookies away. "G'night, Pop," she said, working up a smile.

He glanced toward her as he refilled his glass at the water dispenser in the refrigerator door. "Are you still researching stuff for that reincarnated, secret client of yours?"

Olivia nodded wearily. "Though I'm pretty sure he's not reincarnated."

He moved over to the butcher-block counter with his glass of water. "I'd rather you were on that computer checking out one of those dating sites. You ought to be cooking spaghetti dinner for a boyfriend, not your dad."

"The divorce isn't even final yet," she said. "I'm just not ready to start dating anybody. Why do you ask? Tell me the truth, Pop. Am I in your way here? Am I cramping your style?"

"Lord, no," he said. He stepped up to her and put a hand on her shoulder. "I love having you here. You can stay as long as your heart desires. I only want you to be happy."

"Well, would you settle for *not miserable*?" she asked.

"Nope, and you shouldn't either." He bent down and kissed her forehead. "Don't stay up too late, honey."

"G'night, Pop."

With his water glass in hand, her father headed out of the kitchen. A moment later, Olivia heard his footsteps on the stairs.

She told herself she was doing all right—at least, a hell of a lot better than she had been two months ago. Though lonely, she was finally getting over Clay. She certainly didn't want him back. And now she was trying to help someone. She had a sense of purpose.

Taking a cigarette and some matches, she got up and wandered to the front of the house. She stepped out the door, left it open a crack, and then lit up another Virginia Slim. From the front stoop, Olivia cautiously surveyed the grounds. She couldn't help remembering some of those grisly photos she'd seen in Orin Carney's basement. For a moment, she imagined someone pointing a gun to her father's head and making him tie her up on her bed. Would he cooperate—as Wade Grinnell's victims had? Would she?

In those situations, she always used to think she'd be brave and resourceful. She couldn't see herself kowtowing to some gunman and going down without a real fight. But when it had happened to her with Layne, she'd just stood there, paralyzed.

Her father had a gun hidden in his bedroom closet. If someone broke in, could he get to it in time?

Olivia thought of the Rockabye murder victims again. She made a mental note to bring a piece of rope next time she met with Collin. She'd ask Wade to tie a sailor knot, and then see if Collin knew how to tie one. She'd already confirmed today that Collin's situation wasn't anything supernatural. He wasn't possessed. The real Wade Grinnell wasn't dwelling inside him. At best, Collin was acting out or channeling his impression of the dead serial killer—though only God knew why. Collin had the voice down, but his facts were slightly muddled. Whether he remembered it or not, somewhere along the line, he'd heard about Wade Grinnell, and he knew his voice. Collin Cox was a good actor. He was able to mimic the way Wade spoke, the intonations, everything.

Olivia figured if the *Wade* part of him was able to tie a sailor knot and Collin couldn't—then she might have to rethink her theory. But she had a feeling neither Collin nor his other personality would know how to make the knot Wade Grinnell had tied around his victims' wrists fifty years ago.

Past the wind stirring the tree branches and bushes, she heard her cell phone ringing. Olivia dropped her cigarette, stepped on it, and hurried back inside the house. In the kitchen, she snatched up the phone before it went to voice mail. She didn't recognize the number on the caller ID. "Hello?" she said, a bit out of breath.

"Yeah, hi, um, is Olivia there?"

"Speaking."

"My name's Troy Morrow. I think you tried to call me earlier. . . ."

"Yes, I did," she said, sitting down in the desk chair and grabbing a pen. "Thanks for calling me back."

"Dawn said you're a friend of my mother's?"

"Ah, well, if your mom was Sheri Grinnell, then she was friends with my mom back in the sixties."

"Well, Grinnell was her maiden name, yeah. But if you're trying to get ahold of her, she's been dead for several years."

"I know," Olivia said. "I heard about the fire. I'm sorry. Do you—do you happen to have some time tomorrow afternoon? I'd really like to talk with you."

"What about?"

Olivia was stumped for a moment. She couldn't come out and ask about his serial killer uncle—or about what had started the fire that had killed his mother.

"You still there?" he asked.

"Yes. My mom died recently, and she wanted me to make sure I tracked you down and paid you back some money your mom loaned her decades ago."

"Yeah?" he said, sounding interested. "How much?"

"Well, it was originally a hundred and fifty dollars, but my mom wanted to make sure you got three hundred."

"Huh, I didn't think my mom had a hundred and fifty bucks she could spare back in the early sixties."

"I believe she scraped it together as a favor to my

mother, who was—ah—in trouble, if you get my drift. Anyway, I have a check for three hundred dollars I'd like to give you."

"Well, I'll be damned," he said. "Listen, could you give it to me in cash?"

With her hair swept back in a ponytail, Olivia brushed her teeth over the bathroom sink. She wore sweatpants and an old T-shirt with Chris Isaak on the front. It was almost midnight.

Troy Morrow had given her directions to his farm near Centralia. She'd said she would come by around noon tomorrow. She hoped this wouldn't be a total waste of three hundred bucks—and her time. She also hoped her dear, Catholic mother wasn't rolling over in her grave after that lie about her getting into "trouble" back in the early sixties.

Olivia had spent the last two hours following her father's suggestion and browsing an online dating site, Meet-a-Mate.net. She'd gone through two glasses of merlot and come up with absolutely no prospects. Nearly every guy around her age whom she'd found attractive was seeking a girl in the twenty-one-to-twenty-six age bracket. Even if a man had seemed pretty decent, all Olivia saw were red flags.

She still had a lot of Clay damage. It would be a while before she could trust a guy again. Hell, she'd probably be here cooking spaghetti dinners and Rice-A-Roni for her father until she was fifty.

Olivia put her toothbrush away. She was reaching for the Neutrogena bar to wash her face when she heard footsteps in the hallway. She shut off the water.

"Olivia?" her father called. "Honey, did you burn something in the kitchen?"

She opened the bathroom door and stared at her father. He was wearing his flannel robe and slippers. His thinning hair was all mussed.

"What's going on?" she asked. Then the sharp waft of smoke hit her. She glanced up at the hallway light and saw a gray haze.

"Did you leave a cigarette burning?" her dad asked.

"No," she murmured. She ran to the top of the stairs and switched on the front hallway light. The smoke loomed heavier down on the first floor. Shadows flickered against the wall. She immediately thought of Jerry and Sue and the kids. This was how it must have happened to them. A panic swept through her.

Olivia rushed down the stairs and felt the heat building. The smoke became denser, but she still couldn't tell where it was coming from. Something outside the front door hissed and crackled. The two tall thin windows bracketing the door showed utter blackness. Then flames suddenly flared out on the other side of the glass. The blistering wood let out a loud pop.

"Get back!" her father yelled, brushing past her. He flung open the hall closet door.

Olivia hadn't even realized he'd followed her downstairs. Covering her mouth from the smoke, she stepped back and watched him haul a fire extinguisher from the closet. He struggled with the lock, and then yanked the door open. A wall of flames filled the entryway. Bright orange sparks glowed on the blackened door, spitting pieces of fiery debris. Thick smoke billowed into the foyer. She heard her father coughing. For a moment, he was swallowed up by the black haze.

"Poppy!" she shrieked.

All at once, there was a hiss and an explosion of white clouds that plumed through the front hall. Blinded, Olivia staggered back and waved her hand in front of her face. She screamed out for her father again.

In all the chaos and smoke, she realized the crackling sound had stopped.

"Sweetie, are you okay?" her dad finally called out.

"Yes. How about you? Are you all right?" Through the smog that filled the hallway, she could just make out his silhouette in the doorway.

"No injuries!" he replied, clearing his throat. "Better open some windows. I'll get the garden hose and wet everything down."

Olivia stood there for another moment. She was thinking about that weird little incident with the recycle bin earlier, and now this. She was thinking about her in-laws, too. Had the fire started at their house the same way?

Heading across the smoke-filled living room, she unlocked all three windows and opened them. The room turned cold, but the haze started to dissipate.

CHAPTER TWENTY-THREE

Seattle—Tuesday, October 9, 7:20 a.m.

S he heard voices downstairs.

Olivia rolled over in bed and squinted at the alarm clock on her nightstand. She couldn't believe she'd actually fallen asleep—after so much tossing and turning under her old *Titanic* poster last night.

Her father had hosed down the outside of their house around the burnt, blistered front door. The actual damage seemed surprisingly minimal. The front door would have to be replaced, and the surrounding area needed to be cleaned and repainted. Olivia had managed to air out the downstairs. They still weren't sure if the front hall would need repainting.

After downing a bourbon and water, her dad had announced there would be no golf for him tomorrow, and he'd shuffled off to bed around 2:15. Olivia had shut and locked the last window an hour later. Then she'd dragged herself upstairs.

Considering he believed she'd caused the fire with a stray cigarette, her dad was pretty sweet and forgiving. His assumption seemed pretty far-fetched, but possible. After all, she'd been smoking there earlier in the evening. She was usually so careful about picking up the butts after extinguishing them. But she remembered her last cigarette break had been interrupted by the phone call from Troy Morrow. She'd put out the cigarette in a hurry and rushed inside to grab her cell. Maybe the butt hadn't been completely extinguished.

And then two hours later, it had become a small inferno?

No, it just wasn't likely. But she wasn't ready to tell her father that. She didn't want him to think she was trying to shirk responsibility for the fire. She also didn't want to tell him all the possible explanations that had come to mind. She kept thinking of Jerry, Sue, and the kids—and of those hotel fires fifty years ago.

Olivia wished it were merely her stupid cigarette butt—and nothing more—that had caused this whole flaming mess. How she'd managed to nod off was a mystery—but somehow she must have.

She rolled over on her left side, tugged her sheets around her neck, and listened to her father's muffled voice downstairs. Was he on the telephone? Or was someone else with him downstairs? After a few moments, it grew quiet. But then she heard footsteps on the stairs.

There was a knock on her door. "Olivia, honey?" her father gently called.

She sat up in bed, and rubbed her eyes. "Yeah, Pop, come on in. . . ."

He opened the door and ducked his head in. "Sweetie, the police are here. Could you get dressed and come on downstairs?"

"What's going on?" she murmured. "Is it about the fire?"

"That's part of it," her father answered grimly. "I don't think your cigarette caused the fire after all. It was no accident. And neither was what happened to your car."

"My car?"

He nodded. "Somebody really went crazy and trashed it last night."

"Her name is Corinne Beal," Olivia said evenly. "She's my—*estranged* husband's girlfriend. This is her work. There's absolutely no mistaking it. . . ."

With her arms folded, Olivia stood in front of her car—parked in the carport beside the garage. She'd thrown on a pair of jeans and wore a jacket over her T-shirt. Tears of anger filled her eyes as she gazed at her poor little VW bug—once again splashed with acid. The black-rust blotches and crusted-over bubbles covered the hood—for the second time. The front tires had been slashed.

"She did the exact same thing to my daughter's car—this same car—three months ago," Olivia's dad told the cop. "I'm not kidding. The woman's got a screw loose. She's dangerous."

Olivia was furious, but also slightly relieved to see Corinne's trademark work. At least now she knew who was behind all the strange things that had been happening lately.

Her father—in plaid slacks, a button-down shirt, and a fall jacket—stood behind her, along with one of the two cops who had responded to his 911 call forty minutes ago. Her dad had been on his way to his car for a coffee and donuts run when he'd noticed the damage to her VW. The cops were a man-woman team, both uniformed. The woman was about twenty-five, and skinny with brown hair. She looked like a neophyte, but seemed to overcompensate with a brisk, no-nonsense attitude. She was examining the charred front door—and talking a lot into her shoulder mic. Her partner was forty and mustached, with a macho swagger. He stood by Olivia's dad with a pen and notepad. He'd already said something about getting a police photographer there to take snapshots of the property damage.

"Obviously, it wasn't enough just messing up my daughter's car again," Walt went on. "She had to torch the house. What a nutcase!"

"Corinne was in town last night, staying at a hotel with my husband," Olivia said, still assessing the damage to her VW. "They were supposed to return to Portland today. You might catch them before they leave. I'm not sure which hotel they're at. But you can reach my husband on his cell phone. His name is Clay Bischoff, and his number is five-oh-three-five-five-five-eight-nine-eight-two."

"In Portland, this girl broke into my daughter's house," Walt was saying. "She made one hell of a mess. . . ."

Olivia's cell phone rang, and she pulled it out of her jacket pocket. She checked the caller ID: *Leroy Swanner*. He was the chiropractor whose office was down the hall from hers.

"Who is it, honey?" her father asked.

"Someone from my office building." She clicked on the phone. "Hello? Leroy?"

"Hi, Olivia," he said. "Are you okay?"

She shrugged, and let out a bewildered little laugh. "Yeah, I guess. . . ."

"That's a relief. I was worried something had happened to you. I came in a little early today, and noticed—well, I think somebody broke into your office. They really tore the place apart, too. I called the police. They're on their way. . . ."

*   *   *

"Looks like they stole your hard drive," said one of the cops. He was checking under and around her desk, which was a mess.

"Shit," Olivia muttered, rubbing her forehead. She had billing information on there for her regular clients—and God only knew how much more confidential information.

She'd never had so many people in her little office at one time. All five of them were policemen—two plain-clothesmen (one of whom was on his cell phone), two more uniformed cops, and the policewoman from the team that had shown up at the house earlier.

Olivia had splashed some water on her face and thrown on a black V-neck sweater. With the police-woman driving, she'd ridden to her office in the back of the squad car. The cop's partner had stayed behind with Walt to wait for the police photographer to show up.

Olivia figured this ought to be the photographer's next stop. The damage here was just as bad. It felt as if the business she'd worked so hard to get off the ground had been destroyed in one fell swoop. Her throat tight-ened and tears brimmed in her eyes as she stared at the slashed sofa and chairs. The white foam stuffing spilled out of the cushions. The framed Monet print over the sofa had been smashed—along with a lamp and her computer monitor. There was glass every-where. She heard a crunch every time she took a step. Her rock-sculpture fountain had been toppled over. Amid the scattered pieces, a puddle of water drenched the tan carpet.

"We got ahold of your husband and Corinne Beal at the Hotel Deca in the U-District," announced the plain-clothesman. He still had a cell phone to his ear. "She claims she has no idea what's happened here—or at your house."

Olivia didn't even look at him. She was still gazing at the destruction to her office. "That crazy bitch did this," she heard herself say. "I'm pressing charges. Ever since she and Clay got into town on Thursday, she's been following me around, trying to scare me one way or another. She fooled with my name in the directory downstairs and shut off the power the other night. Then on Sunday, she must have been stalking me in the library downtown, because the microfiche machine I was using got sabotaged. And a couple of hours before she set fire to our front door last night, I could tell someone was sneaking around outside the house. . . ."

"Your husband and Ms. Beal have agreed to come to the East Precinct station for an interview," the detective said.

"Are you really so sure she's responsible for *every-thing*?" someone asked. It was a new person in the room.

She swiveled around to see Ian Haggerty in the doorway. He wasn't wearing a suit today. He was slightly rumpled in jeans and a beige fisherman's sweater. He had a bit of beard stubble, and his brown hair was messy. But he still looked handsome.

Olivia narrowed her eyes at him. "I beg your pardon?"

"Are you certain this Corinne person is behind all the strange things happening to you since Thursday?" he asked.

Olivia nodded. "Corinne or maybe someone she hired, yes. It's Ian, isn't it?"

"Yes, hi," he said, still lingering in the doorway. "Nice to see you again."

The other cops seemed baffled by his presence there.

"Have you been assigned to this case?" she asked.

He shrugged. "Actually, I happened to be driving by, and saw the police cars. I was concerned. I knew you worked in this building."

"Really? How did you know that?"

"You told me—when we were talking on the ferry Saturday," he said.

"I think I mentioned my office was in Madison Valley. I don't believe I gave you the exact address."

"What's going on, Haggerty?" one of the plain-clothesmen asked. "You have no business here. You're on a leave of absence."

"Yeah," one of the uniformed cops chimed in. "Beat up any sassy third-graders lately?"

Ian glared at him for a second. Then he turned to her and seemed to force a smile. "Could I talk to you out in the hall?"

Olivia nodded. She brushed past the policewoman near the doorway and walked through the waiting room with Ian. They stepped out to the hallway together. "What is it?" she asked. "What were they talking about in there—'beating up third graders?' "

He took her arm and started to lead her farther down the hall.

Olivia stopped and pulled her arm away. "I didn't give you my address here."

"You're right, you didn't," he whispered. "After I met you on the ferry, I looked you up on Google and found your hypnotherapy site. I did some more searching and got your address."

She let out a stunned, little laugh. "I'm not sure if I should be flattered or take out a restraining order. Why do I get the feeling you didn't just 'happen to drive by' here this morning?"

"That part's true," he said. "I live in Madison Park. I drive by this building at least twice a day. They know me at the Madison Val-U Mart. I'm a regular there. Anyway, when I saw the squad cars outside your building, I thought something might have happened to you."

"Why's that?" she asked.

"Collin Cox hasn't made a lot of friends since he moved to the Kitsap Peninsula. And two of them were killed last week. I have a feeling you're closer to Collin than you let on the other day. So—when I saw two prowlers and one unmarked car parked outside here . . ."

"I don't think what happened here or at my house has anything to do with Collin."

"Did he mention to you that they had to call the police because someone was sneaking around outside his grandparents' house on Saturday night?"

"No," Olivia murmured. She thought about the man she'd spotted tailing Collin after he'd left her office Thursday night.

"You'll say it's none of my business. Still, I have to ask. Are you working your hypnotherapy on Collin to help him recall things from the night his mother was murdered?"

She nodded. "You're right. That's none of your business."

"Here's why I'm asking. I think the murder of Collin's friend Fernando Ryan wasn't a random thing. And I don't believe the fire that killed your in-laws was an accident. I'm pretty certain they were killed because someone thought Collin told them something—something about the night his mother was murdered. I don't mean to scare you, but it's possible the same people might be after you now. Did I hear Detective Yeager right? Did they make off with your computer's hard drive?"

"Yes, but that's not so unusual, is it? There are a lot of things on a hard drive that thieves can use—credit card information, passwords, Social Security—"

"Back there in the office, you said this Corinne person was responsible for everything. Now you're talking about a theft."

Olivia scowled at him. "Okay, what exactly are you getting at?"

"About twelve hours before their house burned down, the Pelhams were burglarized—"

"Yes, I know. . . ."

"They stole Gail's computer. They didn't touch Jerry's laptop or Chris's Xbox. But they stole Gail's computer and rifled through her journal. They were after whatever Gail might have recorded or emailed—to see how much she might know. So—let me ask you again. Do you still think your *husband's girlfriend* stole your hard drive?"

Olivia couldn't answer him. She wasn't sure anymore. "What about Fernando?" she asked. "Was his computer stolen, too?"

"The Ryans have one ancient computer for six kids. Fernando used the computers at school and the library whenever he had a paper due. For everything else, he used his iPhone. He had it with him when he disappeared last week. Since then, the Kitsap Police have recovered Fernando's books, his backpack, and his clothes. They even found part of his lunch that didn't get eaten by four-legged scavengers. But they never found Fernando's phone."

"I'm not sure I understand," Olivia said. "On the

ferry Saturday afternoon, you told me that you weren't at the memorial on any kind of police business."

"That's right. This is my own independent investigation. Mrs. Ryan was nice enough to answer some questions. And I made a friend or two on the Kitsap force while I was on duty there. I'm doing this all on my own. I'm on a leave of absence from the force right now."

"What for?" She folded her arms. "Does it have something to do with that business about beating up a third grader?"

Ian's jaw seemed to tense up, and he nodded. "He was a seventeen-year-old. I'd responded to a gay-bashing on Capitol Hill outside the Egyptian movie theater. This guy and his buddies beat the hell out of this poor kid who was walking home from a midnight movie. I was there when they were putting him in the ambulance. I don't know how he could even talk. His face was all swollen and bloody. But he gave me a description of the ringleader. They were in school together. He knew the kid's name, the car they were driving, the plate number—everything. My partner and I tracked them down in about ten minutes. They were cruising around the gay bars, probably looking for more people to beat up. We pulled them over, and I approached the vehicle. The ringleader was at the wheel. He rolled down his window, and I could see his knuckles were still bloody. He was grinning from ear to ear, and his friends were laughing. Then he made some filthy joke about the kid they'd just pummeled—and I lost it. I punched him square in the face, broke the little bastard's nose."

"Good," Olivia murmured. She hadn't meant to say anything. It had just slipped out.

He rolled his eyes. "It felt great for about five seconds. But it was really uncool of me. I blew the arrest. The kid and his fellow assailants walked. Plus his dad's a big shot over in Bellevue, and he raised holy hell. Anyway, it was stupid of me. I'm lucky I didn't get sacked."

"Hey, Haggerty . . ." The uniformed cop who had made the third-grader crack stuck his head out of the waiting room doorway. "I thought maybe you'd kidnapped our witness. You know, this isn't your call. You can't be conducting any police business here. . . ."

"Do you still have some questions for me?" Olivia asked.

"Not right now, but—"

"Well, we're not discussing police business," Olivia said. "And if you don't have any questions for me right now, would you please leave us alone? We're almost finished here."

The cop grumbled something under his breath and retreated back into the waiting room.

She turned toward Ian again, and he was looking down at the floor with a smile on his face. "Thanks for that."

Olivia just nodded. She still didn't completely understand Ian's interest in all this. "When I asked Collin about you, he said you two were friends—until his grandfather put the kibosh on it. If I understand correctly, you guarded the house in Poulsbo until mid-August. Were you still communicating with Collin after that?"

He shook his head. "We emailed back and forth once, but that was it."

"In his email, did he tell you about his friends Fernando and Gail?"

"No. The emails were back in August. He hadn't started school yet."

"Then how did you know Collin was friends with them? It wasn't mentioned in any of the newspaper accounts."

He scratched his beard stubble. "Well, it's hard to explain. I really like Collin. He's a sweet kid. Ever since *The Night Whisperer*, he's reminded me of my kid brother, Joey, who died from leukemia ten years ago. He would have been around Collin's age. Anyway, it was my job to protect Collin for five weeks. So after I got into trouble for being such a stupid hothead, there was a week of limbo when I was waiting to hear if I was in, out, on suspension, or whatever. So I came back to the island and checked on Collin. I guess I felt like I needed to look after somebody—besides myself, I don't know. . . ."

"I think I know what you mean," Olivia said. "You needed a sense of purpose?"

He nodded. "That's right. Anyway, I drove by his school when classes were letting out. I wanted to see if he was making any friends. Back when I was on guard duty, he'd told me that he hadn't been very lucky in the friends department. Anyway, I saw him hanging out with Fernando and your niece. I followed them and watched them horsing around at Muriel Williams Park. Then they went to the bookstore, and I went home. It felt good to know Collin had friends, and that he was okay."

Ian let out a long sigh. "Then a few days later, I was online checking out some of the local police bulletins, and I saw a photo of a missing high school student in North Kitsap. I recognized Collin's friend. The next day, I read about a deadly fire that killed an entire family in Poulsbo, and I recognized your niece. I knew something was wrong. Collin *wasn't* okay. The next day, I got a hang-up on my cell. The caller ID showed it was Collin. I knew his grandfather didn't approve of our friendship, so I emailed Collin and asked how he was doing. He never replied. So that's why I went to your in-laws' memorial service. I needed to check up on him. I was worried. Collin said he never got the email. Anyway, I'm still worried. You see, there's still a part of me that needs to protect him. I could be all wet with my theories about why Fernando and your niece were killed. Maybe I'm merely grasping at straws there. But I know something's terribly wrong—and poor Collin is in the middle of it."

Olivia leaned against the corridor wall. "You may be right," she said. "I mean the number on my car, that's classic Corinne stuff. But the other strange things that have happened, it's almost like a campaign to discourage me from helping Collin. When I first smelled the smoke from the fire last night, I immediately thought of my in-laws trapped in that burning house."

Ian gently took hold of her arm. She didn't pull away this time. "You said all these things started happening on Thursday when Corinne and your husband came to town. Did anything else happen that day—any other thing that may explain these occurrences?"

Olivia looked him in the eye and nodded reluctantly. "I—I met Collin for the first time on Thursday afternoon," she admitted. "I guess it really started then—right after that session."

Seattle—Tuesday, 11:20 a.m.

"I can't believe you're telling me this now," Clay said.

Dressed in a black suit with a blue shirt and no tie, he stood in the parking lot of the Hotel Deca, a tall, art-deco throwback from the thirties located in the University District. They were parked in a handicapped spot. Corinne had insisted on it, since they were loading up the car. As far as Corinne was concerned, designated handicapped zones were her personal loading, unloading, and temporary parking spaces. It was another bugaboo of hers that Clay tolerated—just barely.

The sun was out, but an autumn chill crept through the air. Clay looked at their luggage in the open trunk of his Lexus—and then at Corinne. She wore the same slinky black-polka-dot-on-blue dress she'd worn to the memorial—except without the black net sequined hat. Her blond hair was down around her shoulders, and her lipstick was on a bit crooked, which made her look even crazier.

"Did I hear you right?" he asked.

Staring at him from behind a pair of sunglasses, she sighed. "I didn't do any of that other stuff she's accusing me of. I didn't even slash the tires on her stupid car this time. All I did was pour some acidy shit on the hood. She's damn lucky I didn't do more. I wanted to throw it in her face, but lost my nerve. . . ."

Clay ran a hand through his hair. "Jesus, so that's why on the phone last night you went on and on about chemical peels. That's why you wanted to know if I thought Olivia had a pretty complexion. You're sick, you really are. . . ."

"I was angry!" she yelled, her hands at her sides—in fists.

"I can't believe you're telling me this now. Two hours ago, you swore you were innocent. I didn't think the police had a case. We were together all of last night.

I've told the cops and our attorney you had nothing to do with it. When did you pull off this cute stunt?"

"Around seven o'clock," she said. "I don't know what happened after that, but I'm sure the bitch had it coming."

Clay shook his head in exasperation. His lawyer in Portland had arranged for an associate in Seattle to represent them during the police interview. They were headed off to meet him and review their strategy before the session with the police.

"We've packed our bags and checked out of the hotel," he said, waving a hand in front of their luggage in the trunk. "Do you really think the cops will let us go back to Portland tonight? I can't believe this. What the hell were you thinking when you trashed her car?"

Corinne whipped her cell phone out of her purse. "This!" she screamed, her thumbs rapidly working the phone's keypad. "This is what I was thinking about, you asshole!" She shoved the phone in his face.

Clay stared at the slightly blurred photo of him and Olivia in the lobby of her building. It was from late yesterday afternoon, and appeared to have been taken by someone across the street with a zoom lens. In the picture, he was leaning in close to Olivia, about to kiss her. "Where did you get that?" he asked. "Did you have some private detective following me around?"

"No, goddamn it, but maybe I should have!" she bellowed. "I don't know who sent it, maybe some friend of your skanky wife. . . ."

Clay noticed other people around them in the parking lot stopping to stare. A bellman from the hotel came out the door and squinted at them. Clay shut the car trunk, walked around to the passenger side, and opened the door for her. "Okay, okay, just get in the car," he muttered.

Corinne climbed into the front of the Lexus. She showed him the photo on her phone again. "Look at the date and time," she said. "It's yesterday—at 4:59. That's when you were supposed to be at REI—or so you said. Where were you two? Was this in the lobby of some crummy hotel or something?"

"Oh, give me a break. It's not how it looks." He shut the car door. Then he went around to the driver's side, climbed behind the wheel and buckled his seat belt. "I'd still like to know who sent that picture to you," he grumbled, starting up the engine.

"It came in a text—from an unknown sender," Corinne said.

"Well, I don't like being set up," he mumbled. "Nothing happened there, Corinne. In the picture, we're in the lobby of the building where Olivia has her office. We're just talking—"

"Yeah, with your faces about a fucking inch apart!" she retorted. "What exactly were you talking about?"

He pulled out of the hotel parking lot and into traffic. "Are you sure you don't know who sent that to you?"

"Yes, goddamn it! You keep avoiding the subject and turning this around like you're the wounded party here. You're the liar! What were you doing with her yesterday?"

Stopping for a traffic signal, Clay turned to her. "I needed to talk with her, that's all."

"What did you two discuss? I have a right to know. . . ."

He took a deep breath. "I told her you weren't pregnant, and that I had my doubts you ever really were."

"What?" she murmured.

"You heard me, Corinne. Were you ever pregnant—or did you just think you were for a while?"

She slowly shook her head at him. "How can you even ask me such a thing?"

He sighed. "You had the exact same reaction when I asked if you'd vandalized Olivia's car, home, or office last night."

"What's that supposed to mean?"

"It means I'm not sure I believe anything you tell me." The light changed, and someone behind them honked.

Clay turned down Roosevelt Way and headed toward the city. "Lately, I haven't liked myself very much for how I treated my wife," he admitted, watching the road ahead. "And then there's the shit you pulled on her. I still haven't been able to forgive myself for how I handled that. But I thought you were pregnant—"

"I was!" she cried. "I was carrying *our* baby! Now I'm not anymore, and my heart's broken. So you're dumping me, aren't you? You're going back to her. That's why you snuck off and met with her last night, isn't it? Did you ask her to take you back?"

He kept his eyes forward. They were approaching the University Bridge—the four-lane, double-leaf drawbridge over Portage Bay. He swallowed hard and tightened his grip on the wheel. "Yes," he whispered.

"Then it's true?"

"Yes, I'm sorry," he said. "I've been trying to make it work with you, because of the baby. But I can't anymore."

"You son of a bitch . . ."

"I'm sorry, Corinne. I'll pay for this lawyer to help you out. If you really did miscarry, maybe it'll elicit some sympathy, and they'll be able to cut you a break. But I can't be a part of your craziness anymore. . . ."

He heard a clink, and realized she was unfastening her safety belt. They'd just passed the bridge tower. The tires made a loud humming sound as the paved road beneath them became grid. Clay shot a look at her. Corinne threw off the safety belt sash. For a second, he thought she was going to open her door and jump out of the car.

Instead, she lunged toward him and grabbed the wheel.

The tires screeched as they swerved into the oncoming lane in the center of the bridge.

Clay hit the brake, and the Lexus spun out of control on the grid road. Screaming, Corinne fell back against her door.

Out the passenger window, he saw the front of a green SUV barreling toward them.

He shut his eyes. But Clay heard the deafening crash at the point of impact.

Then the screaming stopped.

From a small, semitropical garden, a floodlight shone on the side of the rambler-style building. It illuminated the metal scripted sign mounted on the white brick veneer. The aqua-blue-painted letters spelled out: EL MAR HOTEL.

Among the cars in the parking lot, he noticed a shiny new Impala, a Thunderbird, and a Fury. Somewhere—maybe in one of the rooms—someone was playing Del Shannon's "Runaway" a bit too loud.

He came closer, and peered into a window on the corner of the building. There was a tiny gap where the closed curtains didn't quite come together. He saw two children in their pajamas, sitting on the floor in front of a black-and-white TV, mesmerized by a *Yogi the Bear* cartoon. The father was sitting on top of the double bed in a T-shirt and tan slacks, smoking a cigarette and reading a copy of *Look* magazine. The blond wife, who looked just like a character out of *Mad Men*, was in a silk robe. She stood at a sink—just outside the bathroom. He noticed the hotel ice bucket and the glasses on the counter. She was rinsing out some nylons.

"Wait 'til they're asleep," he said. It was Wade's voice.

All at once, he was inside the room. There was a frantic whimpering, which seemed to get louder and louder. He stood over the blond wife. Her hands were tied behind her, and a rope was tightly wound around her ankles. The woman rolled back and forth on her bed. Her robe had opened up in front, and he saw her black bra and half-slip. She was trying to scream past the washcloth crammed in her mouth. Next to her on the bed, the husband was similarly bound and gagged. He lay on his side, motionless. His white T-shirt was soaked with blood.

The muffled whining became louder and louder.

"Fucking kill her already!" Wade whispered. "She's making too much noise!"

Collin woke up, startled.

He realized he was in a small lounge area in the corner of the school library. Tucked behind the American history shelf were three stuffed chairs. It was quiet there. He sometimes napped in one of the chairs during his free period or lunch. He hadn't had much of a lunch—just a Rice Krispies Treat. Then he'd come here. He hadn't counted on having a nightmare—or an audience. Sitting across from him in the alcove was a red-haired girl named Jodee from his English lit class. She had a biology textbook in her hands, and stared at him. "Who were you talking to in that weird voice?" she asked.

Rubbing his eyes, Collin realized Wade must have been talking out loud. "What did I say?" he whispered.

"Something about 'kill her, she's making too much noise,'" Jodee explained, scowling at him. "What were you dreaming about?"

"I don't remember," Collin lied. But he remembered all of it now. He had been Wade, and he'd been killing that family at the El Mar Hotel fifty years ago.

Collin asked himself the same question the girl had asked.

Who had Wade been talking to?

CHAPTER TWENTY-FOUR

Centralia, Washington—Tuesday, 12:11 p.m.

"We have a traffic advisory," the radio announcer said—on the oldies rock station her father usually listened to in his silver Mercury Sable. Ninety miles south of Seattle, Olivia was starting to get some static on the channel.

"*If you're headed in or out of the U-District, traffic on University Bridge is at a standstill, due to a head-on collision. All lanes are closed. Police and medical aid units are on the scene. At least one fatality has been confirmed—along with some injuries. Traffic is being rerouted. So avoid the University Bridge. Tune into 102.5 for all the latest traffic bulletins. . . .*"

Olivia was lost.

She was on Centralia Alpha Road, looking for the turnoff to Troy Morrow's farm. She had a feeling she'd passed it already.

Earlier, she'd thought about canceling with Troy. After everything that had happened this morning—including her car getting trashed—she hadn't exactly been up for a three-hour wild-goose chase to Centralia and back. Besides, she'd wanted to be there when the police questioned Corinne. Hell, she'd have bought tickets to watch them put the screws to her.

But one of the plainclothesmen had advised her to wait at home for their call. Ian had offered to drive her, which would have been fine with Olivia. But the same bossy detective had said Ian shouldn't involve himself in police business any further. So the policewoman had driven her home.

Fortunately, Olivia had had only one client scheduled this morning—a regular, whose number was on her speed dial. She'd managed to catch the woman at home and reschedule.

She'd borrowed her dad's car, swung by the bank and withdrew three hundred dollars, then started off for Centralia. The long drive gave her time to think about her conversation with Ian Haggerty. Maybe she'd been wrong about him. To her surprise, she liked him— and he seemed to care about her. He wasn't hard on the eyes either. Still, a part of her felt compelled to push him away. She didn't trust her own judgment as far as men were concerned.

Maybe it wasn't just men. Here she was, trying to find a remote farm for an assignation with a total stranger. The only thing she really knew about him was that he had a serial killer for an uncle. This guy had Wade Grinnell's blood coursing through his veins, for God's sake. She hadn't brought along anything to defend herself, not even pepper spray. On top of that, no one else knew where she was.

At this moment, she didn't know where she was either.

Olivia pulled over to the side of the road. She read the directions again, and realized she had to make a U-turn and backtrack a couple of miles. Since she had already pulled over, she took out her cell and phoned home. It rang twice before her father answered.

"Hi, honey," he said.

"Hi, Pop, how are you?" After the talk with Ian, she didn't like the idea of her dad being alone in the house all afternoon. "Are the police still there?" she asked.

"They left about a half hour ago—just about the time your friend, Ian, showed up."

"Ian?" she said.

"Yeah, he came by to make sure you were okay. He's right here. Want to talk with him?"

"Sure, I guess," she replied, a bit baffled. "But let me talk to you afterward, okay?"

"Okey-doke. Here he is."

"Hello, Olivia?" Ian said.

"Yes, hello." She let out a surprised laugh. "Ah, why are you at my father's house?"

"Like your dad said, I just wanted to make sure you were okay. I'm sorry I missed you. But your dad's been very nice."

"How did you get our address?" Olivia quickly shook her head. "Never mind, forget it. So what's going on? Do you plan to stay the afternoon? Or are you moving in permanently?"

"I know you think I'm pushy, but I'm concerned about you. And to answer your question, in your office, I overheard one of the other cops mention your home address. I'm leaving soon. I promise not to darken your already darkened front door again—at least, not without an invitation."

"I'm sorry if I sound ungrateful," she said. "It's just that—"

"It's okay. You don't know me very well, and I'm

coming on pretty strong—showing up in your office, dropping by your house. I get it. I'm just concerned about your safety."

"Did you tell my father about Collin? That's confidential stuff, and he doesn't know."

"Well, he knows now. I'm sorry, but you both need to be extra cautious until this thing is resolved. By the way, where are you? Your dad said you borrowed his car for the afternoon, but you didn't say where you were going. Until this blows over, you really should let someone know where you are at all times."

"Hey, I've already got a father," Olivia said with an edge in her voice. "He's right there in the room with you. I don't need two fathers, thanks. And you are pushy, you really are. Can I talk to my father again, please?"

"Sure," he said. "Here's your dad. . . ."

"Hi, honey," her father said.

"Listen, I'm sorry I didn't tell you about Collin Cox. I was just trying to keep it professional, you know?"

"That's fine. But your friend Ian here warned me there might be some risks involved. I don't want you taking any chances, sweetie. He's right. You really should keep me posted on where you're going and what's happening."

"Okay. But first, I hardly know Ian," she said. "He's not my friend. Before today, we met only once, very briefly. I'm not sure I even like him. Anyway, I'm outside Centralia, trying to find a farm belonging to a Troy Morrow. It's supposed to be somewhere past milepost eight off Centralia Alpha Road. I'm doing some research. I should be finished there within the hour. I'll call you when I'm done." Drumming her fingers on the steering wheel, she rolled her eyes. "Meanwhile, can you do me a favor and tell Ian I didn't mean to be rude and fly off the handle? I've just had a rough morning, that's all."

"Do you want to tell him yourself?" her father asked.

"No, thanks, just pass that along, please. One more thing, Pop, before I forget. Did the police call about Corinne? Have they talked with her yet?"

"I'm not sure," he said. "They haven't called here."

"Well, I'll give you a shout in about an hour or less, Pop. Take care."

"Be careful," he said, and then he hung up.

Ten minutes later, Olivia turned down an unmarked dirt road in front of the milepost sign. The car rocked and wobbled over the crude path. White-knuckled, she gripped the steering wheel and prayed she didn't get a flat. Clumps of trees and tall bushes along the trail limited her view. The road seemed to go on forever. Olivia was starting to wonder if she'd taken the wrong turn when she spotted a clearing ahead. She saw a sprawling, dilapidated ranch house—and beside it, a garage and a tall barn that looked as if it were ready to fall apart. A strange symbol was painted on the barn: a circle within a triangle—and a slash through it. Olivia had no idea what it meant, but it was prominently displayed. She came closer to the house, and noticed three women dressed in rags, tilling a vegetable garden. One of them was heavily pregnant. All of them stopped working and stared as she pulled up in her father's car.

"God help me," Olivia muttered, shutting off the car engine. She took a deep breath, grabbed her purse, and opened the car door.

She saw a man step out of the ramshackle house. He let the screen door slam shut behind him, but he didn't move from the front stoop. He seemed to be staring at her. Barefoot and shirtless, he wore jeans that were unfastened in the front. With his receding gray hair in a ponytail and his paunchy body, he looked like he might be in his late forties. He puffed on a cigarette, and quietly called to one of the women. She dropped her hoe and immediately ran to him—like an obedient servant. He whispered something to her, and she nodded. He planted a sloppy kiss on her mouth. As she turned away, he seemed to stare at Olivia for a moment. Then he ducked inside the house, letting the door slam behind him again.

Olivia stood by the car, fighting the impulse to jump back inside and get the hell out of there. The woman was coming toward her with a wide-eyed, manic grin on her face. Her brown hair was in dusty-looking dreadlocks, and she had a nose ring. She wore a tattered sweater with army-fatigue cutoffs. "Welcome!" she called.

"Thank you, hi," Olivia said, working up a smile. "I'm here to see Troy Morrow. He's expecting me. My name's Olivia."

The woman came closer and reached out to take her hand. Olivia noticed a tattoo on her forearm—the same cryptic symbol that was painted on the barn. Her hands were filthy from working in the garden. She had the sort of burnt-out, dried-up look that came from too many drugs or too much sun. On her chin were several long whiskers that managed to catch the midday sun every time she tilted her head in a certain way.

"Troy wants me to take care of you," she said. "He's still kind of getting his shit together. It's like his morning. Come into the house, Olivia. I'll make you some tea."

"Well, thanks," she said, heading toward the ranch house with the woman. Olivia noticed her friends in the garden were still glowering at her.

Some wind chimes played outside the front door. A sick-looking old collie hobbled up to meet them inside the house. The place smelled like burnt soup—or maybe it was the poor dog that stank. Olivia wasn't sure. She patted the dog's head, and it wandered away. The furniture in the main room looked as if it had been collected off people's front curbs. The woman told her to have a seat, and then she ducked into the kitchen.

Olivia remained standing. All she could think about were bedbugs and lice. Past the wind chimes, she heard the woman whispering to someone. After a few moments, a man wandered out from the kitchen wearing only a pair of torn, dirty white briefs. Unshaven, and with his curly long hair in his eyes, he looked about twenty-five. On his chest was a tattoo with that same strange symbol. "Hey, is that your car in front?" he asked.

Olivia nodded. "Yes, it is."

He scratched his hairy stomach. "Can I borrow it? I only need it for—like—an hour."

She shrugged. "Ah, you know, I'd like to help you. But it's not my car to loan out. Besides, I won't be here that long. I'm probably leaving as soon as I finish up some business with Troy. I'm sorry."

"C'mon, really?" he pressed. He plopped down in one of the eight mismatched chairs around an old picnic table. "That sucks. I mean, you say you want to help me, and then you give me all these lame-ass excuses . . ."

"No means no, Bobby," said the gray-ponytail man as he wandered in from the kitchen. He'd donned an old flannel shirt and some boots—along with his jeans.

Passing his friend in the chair, he grabbed him by the scalp and playfully shook his head a little. This close, Olivia saw a resemblance to Wade Grinnell, especially when he smirked. She also saw the tattoo on the side of his neck—that same obscure symbol again. "Do me a favor and get lost so I can talk to this pretty woman alone," he said, rubbing his friend's shoulder.

Wordlessly, the younger man got to his feet and wandered back into the kitchen, tugging his underwear down in back to scratch one butt-cheek.

"Welcome, I'm Troy." The gray-ponytail man smiled at her. He seemed friendly enough. He pulled out a chair for her. It made a scraping sound against the wood floor.

"Hi, I'm Olivia," she said, sitting down. "Thanks for agreeing to see me, Troy. My mom never really talked about your mother, not until the last few weeks of her life. I guess I'm just curious to know more about my mother's friends. I think maybe—"

"Did you bring the three hundred bucks?" he interrupted. He sat down at the head of the table—next to her.

Olivia worked up a smile and nodded. "Yes, I did. If it's okay with you, I wanted to find out something about Sheri. I think there's a whole chapter of my mother's life that's missing."

"What was your old lady's name?"

"Corinne Beal." For some reason, she didn't want to give him her mother's real name.

He shook his head. "Never heard of her."

"Well, they were friends before you were born."

"She never talked about her, sorry."

The dreadlock woman came in with two mugs and set them on the table. Troy took one and put it down in front of Olivia.

"Would you like some honey with that?" the woman asked, with her slightly crazy smile. "We don't have any cream here, but we have goat's milk."

"Straight from the goat," Troy added.

"Oh, this is fine," Olivia said. "Thank you very much."

"Enjoy!" the woman said. Then she retreated toward the front door.

Olivia jumped a bit as the screen door slammed. She glanced down at the pale brown tea—with little black bits still swirling in it. She couldn't help thinking it might be drugged. Everything about this place was a little off. She'd read *Helter Skelter* in high school, and this place reminded her of the Manson gang's hangout, Spahn Ranch. She was curious about the symbol all of them had, but was afraid to ask.

She lifted the mug to her mouth and blew into the tea. It had an underlying funky odor. She put the mug down again. "My mom passed away a month ago— cancer," she said. "She told me your mom died in an apartment fire. Did they ever find out how the fire started?"

He shrugged. "It started in her bedroom. The insurance company was pretty sure this old space heater she used went haywire or something. She didn't even make it out of bed. My guess is she was shit-faced. Mom drank a lot." He slurped some of his tea. "Can't blame her. She had a pretty crappy life. She used to tell me that her stint on this farm was the only time she was ever really happy. And man, that's rough, because she lived here—like—only two years. This was my dad's farm. He dropped dead about twenty years ago, and I inherited the place. Now, I have my own family here, a family of friends."

"It's very nice," Olivia lied. She heard gunshots in

the distance. She looked out the window. There was an old, rusty VW minibus on bricks, and beyond that, some woods.

The old dog whimpered, then got up and waddled over to Troy. She put her head on his knee. "Old Bernice always gets nervous when she hears us hunting for dinner," he explained, stroking the dog's head. "Anyway, my mom and good luck were always strangers. She never had any money, which is why I was surprised she'd scraped together a hundred and fifty bucks for your mother way back when. Funny thing though. I remember about a week or two before the fire, she started talking like she'd be coming into a lot of cash soon—big money, too. But she wouldn't say how. . . ."

Olivia shifted in the hardback chair. She wondered if the fire might have been an insurance scam that went awry.

"Didn't your mother have a younger brother?" she asked.

He chuckled. "Yeah, Bad Boy Wade. What did your old lady say about him?"

"Just that he was in some kind of trouble with the police," Olivia said. "I guess he was hit by a train or something when they were trying to arrest him."

"Do you know what they were arresting him for?" Troy asked.

Playing dumb, Olivia shook her head.

"Let's just say he may have killed a few people back in 1962, and we'll leave it at that. I got some of the details from my dad. My mom didn't talk much about Wade—not until the last year of her life. She claimed the police never knew the whole story about Wade and these murders. Mom told me on the hush-hush that she was one of two people who knew the truth behind these killings—and no one else would ever find out. She said the two of them would carry it to their graves. I can tell you, she was at least half-right—maybe completely right, if the other person's dead, too."

"So—you have no idea who this other person might have been?"

"Haven't got a clue," he replied, stroking the dog's head. "You don't suppose it was your mother, do you?"

"I don't think so."

"Huh, maybe there wasn't anybody or any big unknown truth about her kid brother's killing spree," he grumbled. "My old lady could be pretty full of shit at times. 'I'm gonna get a lot of money. . . . I'm gonna quit drinking. . . . They'll be sorry they ever tangled with me. . . . Blah, blah, blah.' She wasn't past making up stories and telling lies. Like I say, the reality of her life wasn't very happy."

Olivia gave him a sympathetic smile. She had a feeling there was nothing more Troy Morrow could tell her.

He nodded at the mug. "Aren't you going to drink your tea?"

"No, thanks," she said, opening her purse. "I have a long drive back, and I don't want to make any stops." She took out the three hundred dollars and set it on the table. "Anyway, there's the long-overdue thank-you from my mother. And thank you from me, too." She got to her feet.

Troy quickly totaled up the bills and shoved them in the pocket of his jeans. He smiled up at her. His expression reminded her of Wade Grinnell's mug shot. "Hey, y'know, I'll bet you'd be interested in what I've got in the garage," he said.

Olivia hesitated. "Oh, thanks, but I've already taken up too much of your time."

He gently pushed the collie's head off his thigh and

stood up. "No, I think you ought to see this. After all, you came all this way. . . ." He took hold of her arm.

Olivia felt her whole body tense up, but she let him lead her to the front door. Stepping outside, she breathed the fresh air again, but it felt good for only for a fleeting moment. He still had ahold of her arm. Past the wind chimes, she heard some more gunshots in the distance. She looked over at the women in the garden. The dreadlock woman smiled at her and then whispered something to the others.

Troy led her toward the two-car garage, between the house and the barn. Olivia stole a glance over at her car. She wondered if she should break away and make a run for it. Or was she being paranoid? No one had done anything threatening yet.

There was a padlock on the handle to the garage door. Troy finally let go of her arm to reach into his pocket. Pulling out a set of keys, he found the one for the padlock and opened it.

"You know, I should really get going," Olivia said, taking a step away.

The door made a loud squeak as Troy opened it. "You sure?" he asked. "I have a bunch of my mom's old letters in here—along with some audiotapes she made. They got left behind back when my parents split up. Maybe you'll find some letters from your mom—or maybe your mom's on one of the tapes. Sure you don't want to check it out?"

With uncertainty, she looked past Troy, into the dark, cluttered garage. He reached around the doorway and switched on a light. Inside, along with a trio of motorcycles in various stages of repair, Olivia noticed a few bikes, some machine parts, hoses, and yard equipment.

Troy stepped inside, and moved a plastic kiddy pool

turned on its side so he could get to a tall wooden ladder. "The boxes are up in the attic space here," he said. "I don't know why I've held on to this shit. It's not worth anything. Guess I was just waiting for someone like you to show up."

Olivia glanced over her shoulder at her car again. She took a step closer to the garage and saw the trapdoor in the ceiling. Troy set up the ladder beneath it. She noticed the one and only garage window had bars on it. "You know, I—I'd love to see what's there," she said. "But I'm not good in attics and confined spaces. I'm claustrophobic." It was a lie, but she didn't completely trust him—or his friends.

"It's only a couple of boxes. If you hold the ladder, I'll bring them down to you."

Nodding reluctantly, Olivia stepped into the garage and over to the ladder. She held on to it while Troy made his way up to the trapdoor. "I really appreciate this," she said nervously.

With a grunt, he dislodged the trapdoor and pushed it aside. Olivia turned away as a few little flecks of debris and dust fell from the hole in the ceiling. Troy continued on up into the dark loft space. After a moment, a light went on up there. She heard his footsteps and things being dragged across the floor. Another cloud of dust wafted down from the ceiling as he dropped something heavy. Olivia turned her head to the side and fanned the air. Troy seemed to be taking an eternity up there.

Outside, she noticed a man shuffling toward her car. It was the underpants guy, Bobby, now in jeans and a jacket. His hands in his pockets, he walked up to the driver's door and peered into the window. Olivia couldn't remember if she'd locked it earlier or not.

She glanced up at the cobwebs and rafters beyond

the trapdoor above her. "Are you having any luck find-ing it?" she called.

"Not yet," he grumbled. She heard something shift-ing up there.

Biting her lip, she checked on the car again. The seedy young man circled around the Mercury Sable. He ran a hand along the roof, then down the wind-shield and over the hood.

Olivia reached into her purse and found the car keys with the automatic locking device on the chain. She pressed the *lock* button, but nothing happened. She was too far away.

The guy was standing by the driver's door again. With one hand on the side mirror, he was peeking into the car once more.

"Hey, Troy?" Olivia called timidly. "I'm sorry, but you know your friend from earlier? I think he might—"

"Found 'em!" he yelled. There was more rumbling and creaking from above.

Olivia looked over toward her father's car again. Troy's friend was walking away from it. But he had a sudden bounce in his step—as if he'd just found a dol-lar on the sidewalk or something. He headed off toward the woods.

"Coming down," Troy announced.

Olivia tightened her grip on the ladder as he climbed down the rungs—one at a time. He balanced a box with a Smirnoff Vodka label on it—and a smaller box on top of that. As he made his way down to the last rung, the smaller box started to tilt. Olivia got on her tiptoes and managed to grab it. The box was heavy—and old. She recognized the Frederick & Nelson logo on it from when she was a kid. The store had closed decades ago.

"Thanks," Troy gasped, stepping away from the ladder. He dropped the Smirnoff box on the garage floor. Then he nodded to the box she was holding. "Those are her letters, and in here . . ." He gave the container on the floor a little kick. "These are the tapes, about twenty of them. It's all old reel-to-reel shit. Christ knows why I saved it."

Olivia thought about the reel-to-reel tape from Orin Carney's basement. She set down the box of letters and looked inside the liquor store carton. Some of the tapes were in boxes with labels like *Music Mix, Jim Munchel's Birthday Party—May 3, '63, Xmas Carols, Beach Boys,* and *Jam Session—June 7, '62.* Several of the boxes were unlabeled, and about a dozen tapes didn't have boxes. She wondered if Wade was on any of those recordings.

"If you don't mind parting with these for a while," she said, "I might be able to take them to a place in Seattle that could transfer these onto a disc for you."

"What for?" he asked. "So I could listen to the Beach Boys or a bunch of people getting drunk at a birthday party? No thanks." He climbed back up the ladder and struggled to pull the trapdoor back in its place.

Olivia moved over to the ladder and held it for him.

He finished with the trapdoor, and started climbing down the rungs again. "Take'm, keep'm," he said, collapsing the ladder and lugging it back to its spot against the wall. "Take the other box, too. It's nothing but a bunch of cards and letters and old recipes she clipped out of magazines—just crap. It's not like we can get any money for that stuff. You're welcome to it."

"Well, thanks," Olivia said. She picked up the Frederick & Nelson box.

Troy grabbed the carton of tapes and hoisted it up on his shoulder.

As they stepped out of the garage together, Olivia noticed the women had stopped working in the garden. They stood stationary with their hoes and spades, looking toward the woods. Bobby came into the clearing with his two hunter friends. One was skinny with a beard. He wore an army fatigue jacket and a knit stocking cap. As he walked, he had a rifle slung across his shoulders with his hands dangling on each end—as if crucified. The third man was bald and stocky, with a long-sleeved T-shirt and sunglasses. He carried a shotgun at his side.

Approaching her dad's Sable, Olivia quickened her pace. It looked like Bobby and his friends were headed toward the car as well.

Olivia set the smaller box on the vehicle's hood. Then she reached into her purse and anxiously searched for the car keys.

"Hey, Troy!" one of them called. "Troy, hold up, man!"

Olivia finally found the keys and hit the *unlock* button. She realized the car was already unlocked. She quickly opened the door and set the Frederick & Nelson box on the passenger seat. Olivia took the Smirnoff box from Troy, who was distracted by his friends. "Thanks," she said, a little breathless. She stashed it on the passenger side floor, and then shut the car door.

"Hey, don't let her leave," the bald one called.

"What's going on?" Troy asked.

The three of them stopped just a few yards away from the car. Bobby motioned for Troy. "Come here for a sec. . . ."

Scratching the back of his neck under his ponytail, Troy sauntered over toward them.

Olivia glanced at the three women in the garden, all

of them still watching. They seemed to know something was about to happen with the men in their impromptu powwow. The scrawny guy with the knit cap kept looking at her while the others muttered something to Troy.

She started to back away—around the front of her dad's car.

"Hey, girlie, stick around!" the scrawny one grinned.

With the keys clutched in her fist, Olivia froze.

The bald one raised his voice: "You can't just let anyone in here to snoop around. . . ."

"Hey, she's cool, man," Troy assured him.

The skinny guy took the rifle from across his shoulders and now held it one hand. With his eyes fixed on her, he started to sway from side to side.

"What are you talking about?" she heard Bobby say loudly. "We could get some good money for it, man. . . ."

Olivia knew he must be talking about the car. She had a feeling they weren't going to let her leave—ever. Suddenly she bolted for the driver's door and pulled it open. Jumping into the front seat, she slammed the car door shut and locked it. With a shaky hand, she jammed the key into the ignition.

"Hey!" she heard one of them yell.

Olivia started up the car. The skinny one banged his fist on the hood. She hit the gas, wrenched the steering wheel to one side, and peeled away. The tires spewed out clouds of dirt and dust behind her. She couldn't see anything out the rear window. Speeding down the bumpy, potholed, dirt road, she expected to hear gunshots at any minute. But all she heard was the engine's roar—and the sound of pebbles rattling against the underside of the car.

Her heart racing, Olivia clutched the wheel and took

a turn in the road. She almost expected the car to tip over. But the wheels stayed on the ground. Plumes of dust swelled behind her. Up ahead, she saw the highway—level and clear.

Olivia was third in line for the drive-thru car wash attached to a 76 station north of Centralia on Interstate 5. She couldn't very well return her dad's Sable to him filthy with an empty tank.

She'd gotten gas, made a much-needed stop in the restroom, and now sat in the front seat with the window rolled down. She really wanted a cigarette, but resisted. Instead, she sipped the Diet Coke she'd bought inside the station. She took out her cell. She'd told her father she'd call him in an hour—and that was over ninety minutes ago.

She called home, and her father answered on the third ring. She raised her window so she could hear him over the droning and churning of the car wash.

"Did you have any luck digging up whatever it was you went there to dig up?" he asked.

"Yes, I got a couple of boxes of junk that may or may not lead to something. We'll see." She figured he didn't need to hear the details about how she'd gotten the materials. "I'll be diving into this stuff tonight, which includes some old tapes. Didn't we have one of those reel-to-reel tape recorders ages ago?"

"Yeah, I think it's still somewhere in the attic under a mountain of dust."

Olivia hoped it still worked. She moved up in the car wash line. "Did Ian leave?"

"Yeah. We went out to lunch, and he dropped me off here about twenty minutes ago."

"You had lunch with him? What did you two talk about?"

"I'll tell you when you get home," he answered. "What's your estimated arrival time?"

"Oh, I'll probably be there in about an hour and a half. By the way, Pop, did you hear anything from the police about Corinne?"

"Um, yeah, I—I'll tell you about that when you get home."

"You sound funny," she said. "What's going on? What did she tell the police?"

"I'll explain when you get here, honey. You just be careful and take your time."

Olivia heard a click on the other end. Her father almost never hung up first—not without her saying good-bye or take care.

She knew something was wrong.

CHAPTER TWENTY-FIVE

Seattle—Tuesday, 7:52 p.m.

"I know I should feel sorry for her, but I don't," Olivia's dad said. He sat at the island counter in the kitchen, trying to thread one of Sheri Grinnell's tapes through the ancient reel-to-reel player. He'd dug the machine out of the attic and dusted it off. Olivia couldn't believe the thing had actually started up again after thirty years. Her father had dabbed a bit of Vaseline on the turning mechanisms to keep them from squeaking.

While he fiddled with the tape player, Olivia sat at her mom's writing desk, going through Sheri's old letters and cards. There were also yellowed newspaper clippings of recipes and cartoons that she'd saved, along with the occasional Polaroid or graduation photo of someone. The names scribbled on the back in faded pen didn't mean anything to Olivia.

She'd been relieved to learn that she hadn't been the main topic of conversation between her dad and Ian over lunch at the Attic Ale House in Madison Park this afternoon. According to her dad, Ian was a "terrific guy," and they'd talked mostly about the Seattle Sea-

hawks and local politics. Then Ian had driven her dad
to Broadway Video on Capitol Hill. Walt had decided
to rent two Collin Cox movies, *The Night Whisperer*
and *Honor Student*. He hadn't seen either one. Both
DVDs were now in their cases on the kitchen counter.

The lights in both the front and back yards were on.
The police had promised to beef up their patrol on
Alder Lane. Neither Olivia nor her dad felt like cooking. So they'd ordered a pizza from Pagliacci. It hadn't
arrived yet.

Hovering over the tape recorder, which was the size
of a shoebox, her father went on about Corinne. "The
cop I talked to said she grabbed the wheel and the car
went out of control right in the middle of the University Bridge. That poor guy in the SUV. And on top of
everything, just think about all those poor people
stranded and rerouted, too—all because of her. I can't
understand it. Crazy, selfish . . ." He shook his head.

"I'm not giving you an argument, Pop," Olivia said,
glancing at a birthday card with a cartoon donkey
wearing a sombrero on the cover. *I feel like an ass I
forgot your birthday!* it said inside. It was signed, *Lots
of Love, Bill & Judy.* Olivia tossed the card aside in a
pile with the other junk. Maybe Troy had been right.
Maybe all this stuff was totally worthless.

"Okay, I think I got this thing figured out," her father
announced. "Cross your fingers. . . ." He pressed a button on the recorder, and nothing but a static-laced
humming noise came over the built-in speaker. Olivia
could hear some music starting up, but it was muted
and scratchy. Her dad fiddled with the volume.

"I keep waiting for that thing to start smoking," she
said.

Then she heard a man's voice: *"Throughout history,
there've been many songs written about the eternal tri-*

angle. This next one tells the story of a Mr. Grayson, a
beautiful woman, and a condemned man named Tom
Dooley. . . ."

"Well, this is sure a blast from the past," her father
said. "I loved this tune. . . ."

On the tape, The Kingston Trio broke into "Tom
Dooley." Olivia was glad at least the recorder worked.
Her dad glanced inside the liquor store box. "There
must be about thirty hours' worth of tapes in here. I'm
still not sure what you're hoping to find."

Olivia sat back in the chair, and sighed. "Neither am
I," she admitted. It was a long shot, but she hoped
somewhere along the line Sheri Grinnell might have
bared her soul on tape.

Her dad poured himself a beer and wandered toward his study. Olivia continued to dig into the Frederick & Nelson box. She found an old Seattle First
National Bank book from June through December
1961. She saw the notation *Rent* by Sheri's first-of-the-
month withdrawals. Orin Carney was right. In October
1961, just six months before the fair had started, Sheri's
rent jumped from $95 a month to $275. She never had
much money in her account.

Olivia remembered what Troy had told her about his
mother in her final days. She'd predicted she would be
coming into a large amount of cash soon. She'd also
talked about someone else knowing the whole story of
Wade and the Rockabye Killings. She'd spoken more
about her dead brother in those last weeks of her life,
too.

The police had kept the grisly killings off the front
pages of the newspapers during the run of the World's
Fair. What if Wade hadn't been *accidentally* hit by a
train while escaping from the police? What if it had
just been made to look that way so they could blame

him for the El Mar killings and then sweep everything else under the rug?

Olivia wondered if Sheri had been killed because she'd tried to blackmail some old city official. It didn't make sense that she'd wait until 1999 to extort money over something that happened back in 1962. Or had she stumbled onto some information very late in the game?

She heard her father turn on the TV in his study. Then the doorbell rang.

"Pizza guy's here!" her father announced.

Olivia put down Sheri Grinnell's bankbook and got to her feet. "Pop, check before you open the door!" she called. She hurried toward the front of the house and heard the click of the door lock. Nearing the foyer, she saw her father opening the door. She stopped in her tracks.

Her dad merely nodded at the person on the front stoop. Then he looked at her, sighed, and retreated to his study.

Olivia numbly gazed at Clay at their threshold. He wore a wrinkled black suit and a blue shirt stained with blood. There was a bandage on his forehead, and already one of his eyes was blackened. His right hand was wrapped in an ACE bandage. "Hi," he muttered.

She'd talked with him on the phone earlier. Corinne was at the UW Hospital with a broken arm and multiple lacerations. The doctors were trying to determine the extent of injuries to her spine—and whether or not she'd walk again. The driver of the SUV, a stay-at-home father of two, had been killed instantly. He'd been on his way to pick up his toddler son from a swimming lesson.

Clay had told the police why he'd lost control of the car. He'd also told Olivia on the phone that Corinne had confessed to pouring acid on her VW. But his girl-friend had insisted she hadn't done anything else.

Her arms folded, Olivia stared at him. He looked so pitiful. He nodded at the burnt, blackened exterior of the door. "If she did this, I'm really sorry," he said. "Can I come in?"

Olivia nodded. "Sure." Then she called to her father: "Pop, we'll be in the kitchen."

"Fine," he grumbled.

Clay followed her into the kitchen. Olivia didn't have to show him the way. He'd been here countless times. Yet it felt strange to have him in her dad's house again. She wondered if he noticed the photos of him and of them together were no longer on the refrigerator door. "Do you want a beer?" she asked.

"That's okay," he said. "I won't stay long. I know I'm not very welcome here."

Olivia turned down the volume of the reel-to-reel player. The Kingston Trio was singing "Greenback Dollar."

His eyes narrowed at the tape player, the box of tapes, and Sheri Grinnell's pile of keepsakes from the old Frederick & Nelson box. "What's going on?"

"It's just something I'm working on for a client. How are you? How are you feeling?"

He let out a pathetic laugh. "Like somebody worked me over. You know what this black eye is from? The air bag, the damn thing gave me a bloody nose. . . ."

Olivia sat down at the island counter. She figured he was trying to make light of the situation. But she couldn't work up a chuckle or even a smile. Like her dad, she was thinking about that poor guy in the SUV. "How's Corinne?" she asked.

"The same, still in Intensive Care." He leaned back against the cabinet counter. "They've got her on a ton of medications and painkillers. She's totally out of it, sleeping most of the time. When she's awake, she doesn't even know I'm there."

"So you came here," Olivia said. "What for?"

"I need to find out who's responsible for this," he said resolutely.

"You mean there's someone else responsible—besides your girlfriend in the ICU?"

He nodded. "Some asshole sent Corinne a text—with a highly incriminating photo of you and me yesterday in the lobby of your building. That's what set Corinne off. She saw the photo and went nuts. In the picture, we were about to kiss. . . ."

"If I remember correctly, you were about to kiss me, and I had the good sense to shoot you down," Olivia said.

"Yeah, okay, whatever. The thing of it is someone was watching us. They took our picture and sent it to Corinne—just to stir up trouble. Well, I'm sorry, but I don't like being set up. The picture—I saw it—it was obviously taken by someone parked across the street from your building. I don't know if they were following me or staked out there or what. I thought it might have been someone Corinne had hired. But she didn't know a thing about it, and I believe her. So—do you have any idea who it was?"

Olivia shook her head. "No, I'm sorry, I don't."

"What about that kid who had the appointment with you? Who is he? First he was at the memorial, and then he was at your office. It's like he's following us around."

"I told you, he was a friend of Gail's," Olivia said. "And he isn't following us around."

"How do you know for sure? That picture was taken

just seconds before he came through the door. That's awfully convenient, isn't it? Who is he? You called him *Collin*. Why does he look so goddamn familiar?"

"He came in when he did because that was his appointment time, Clay."

"Tell me the truth." He stepped toward the island counter. "Is that kid working for you?"

"No," she said. "I'm working for him. He's my client."

"Olivia, somebody set us up. That kid was right outside the door when they took our picture. If he didn't snap the photo, the little shit must know who did—or at the very least, he must have seen them. That Collin kid has something to do with this, I know he does. So why the fuck won't you tell me his full name?"

Olivia saw her father step into the kitchen. Clay must have followed her gaze, because he turned around toward Walt.

"Clay," he said quietly. "Nobody talks to my daughter that way in my house. Unless you want another black eye, you'd better leave right now."

Clay cleared his throat. "I'm sorry, Walt." He glanced back at her. "Sorry, Olivia, I didn't mean to be rude. Chalk it up to a really crappy day."

"You better go," she said.

He nodded. "Okay, but I'm not giving up on this." He turned and took a step toward her father, but then froze. His back was to Olivia, and she watched him—just standing there. He seemed to be looking at something on the counter. Clay finally reached over and picked up the DVDs her father had rented. He turned toward her. He was grinning. "*Collin Cox*," he said. "Goddamn it, that's why the kid looked so familiar. What's his business with you?"

"That's confidential," Olivia said.

"So—you have this washed-up kid actor following me around, is that it?"

"He has nothing to do with you, Clay."

"Bullshit," he grumbled. He turned toward her father and shook his head. "I apologize, Walt. I'm leaving." He tossed the videos on the counter and brushed past her dad as he stomped toward the front of the house.

"I'm not letting this go," he called over his shoulder. "Somebody tried to screw me, and I'm going to find out who it was if it's the last thing I do."

Olivia heard the front door open and then slam shut.

Poulsbo—Tuesday, 8:55 p.m.

"You're awfully sweet to help out." Dee stood at the kitchen sink, scrubbing a saucepan. She wore a chef's apron over her lavender pantsuit. "When you head off to college in a couple of years, I'll have to learn all over again how to wash the dishes by myself."

Collin was at her side, drying a baking dish. He'd come home from school at 3:45, acting like it had been a normal day. But he couldn't stop thinking about his dream. It had seemed so real. He still wondered who Wade had been talking to in the dream. Himself?

For the rest of the day, Collin couldn't shake the feeling someone was watching his every move. He kept looking over his shoulder, expecting to see Rick or maybe Ian. Rick had claimed a black Saturn had been tailing him. Collin wasn't sure he believed him. Yet he'd been on the lookout all day for people sitting alone in vehicles parked outside the school.

It had almost been a relief to come home—away

from crowds and cars. But his grandfather had been in a restless, grumpy mood. He'd even snapped at Dee during dinner, something about hating lima beans. Usually, he'd make a joke about stuff like that. But tonight he'd been dead serious.

"I'll bet you'll be happy when the doctor lets Grandpa play golf again," Collin said, working the dish towel over a spatula.

"I'm concerned about him." Dee frowned. "Your grandfather wants the three of us to take off for a couple of months and travel through Europe—or maybe Australia."

"When? In the summer?"

"No, soon. He wants to go sometime next week—if the doctor says it's okay for him to travel. He thinks we need a change of scenery after everything that's happened."

Collin put down the dish towel. "But what about school?"

She shrugged. "He said it wouldn't hurt for you to take a year off. You could start as a junior again next year."

"I'm not sure I like that idea," Collin murmured.

"That makes two of us." Dee shut off the faucet. "The man just had a ministroke, and he's talking about packing up and traveling for two months. It's crazy."

Collin figured his grandfather was hoping this "scenery change" would make all their problems go away. It was Old Andy in denial again.

Dee took off her apron, and started to fold it up. "I know you're in some kind of trouble, honey," she said.

Collin stared at her. He was about to shake his head, but he hesitated.

She gave him a sad, shrewd smile. "I'm not sure why you and your grandfather want to keep me in the dark about it. But I'm a lot stronger and smarter than you might think. If there's a problem, I say we stay put and all face it together. Gallivanting through Europe isn't going to solve anything." She reached up and smoothed down a cowlick in his hair. "That's what I'm going to tell your grandfather. And I hope you'll back me up on it."

Collin wrapped his arms around her, and he got a waft of her lavender perfume. "I will, Grandma," he whispered. "Thanks."

She kissed him on the cheek. "He's probably snoozing in his chair right now. So it'll have to wait until tomorrow." She gently pulled away and gave his shoulder a pat. "Anytime you want to tell me what's going on, sweetie, I'm ready to listen and help all I can."

He worked up a smile and nodded. "Thanks," he said again.

Dee headed toward the family room—and the Food Network channel on TV.

Collin wandered over to the sliding door to the patio. A fog had rolled in off the bay. A mist hovered over the black water, but he could still see a solitary light from one small boat.

"Damn," he muttered. He lowered the binoculars and let them dangle from the cord around his neck. He stood on the bow of his sixteen-foot Com-Pac Legacy, which swayed from side to side a bit. He held on to the railing. He didn't mind that the water was a little choppy tonight. What annoyed him was the lousy fog obscuring his view of the Stampler house.

Rick Jessup figured the visibility would only get worse by the time Collin went up to his bedroom. Like it or not, he'd have to turn back toward the dock. He lingered for another few moments at the front of the small vessel. He took one last look at the big house on the hill.

For weeks now, the subject of his near-nightly vigils had kept a pair of binoculars on his bedroom desk. Rick doubted Collin's binoculars were as sophisticated as his. Some evenings, there was enough moonlight for him to make out Collin in his darkened bedroom, staring back out at him.

He knew he'd been spotted long ago—but not yet identified. Collin had confirmed that when they'd met on the ferry yesterday. It was a gold star day. He'd actually spoken at length with Collin Cox—and he'd gotten the last word in, too. Rick knew Collin would come around and eventually realize he only had the young film star's best interests in mind. So what if he'd fibbed a little, pretending he didn't know anything about a boat on Liberty Bay behind Collin's grandparents' house? As for his smiley face emails, those had been sent to comfort Collin, not torment him. How could Collin have misconstrued his intentions there? And Sunday night, he'd merely been checking up on Collin when the boy's grandparents had spotted him outside the house. He'd done it before countless times—once those cops had stopped guarding the house. *Someone* had to look out for Collin.

He knew it would take a while before Collin appreciated everything he was doing for him—and at his own peril, too. He wasn't just thinking about how he'd managed to elude the police on Sunday night. It was a lot more serious than that. Someone else was watching and following Collin—and he *didn't* have the boy's best interests in mind. Rick didn't know if it was that cop, a friend of his, or somebody else entirely. But whoever it was, they'd almost certainly killed Collin's two friends. Rick knew the closer he got to Collin, the more he was putting his own life in jeopardy—maybe the lives of his wife and children, too. But he couldn't help it. Watching over Collin Cox had become his calling.

The fog had gotten so thick that he no longer saw the lights on the first floor of the grandparents' house. The mansion had become a blurry silhouette on the hill above the beach. He heard the water lapping against the side of his boat, but now it sounded like it was in stereo. Was there another boat nearby somewhere in this fog?

Rick gazed around, and could only see the whitish mist rolling over the black water. He was engulfed in it. He reminded himself that fog could play tricks with sound.

He had to turn the boat around and get back to the dock before it got any worse.

All the moisture left the deck surface slick, so he held on to the railing as he made his way starboard to the small cabin. Except for some equipment and an ice chest, he hadn't bothered to decorate the small space— which had two benches and a table with fold-up flaps. He went to retrieve a flashlight from the storage bin.

Suddenly, something slammed into the boat with a clatter. It threw Rick off balance. He fell down and landed on all fours. The flashlight rolled on the cabin floor as the boat rocked from side to side. He heard the floorboards creaking and water splashing. He felt some of the drops on the back of his neck. Stunned, Rick remained crouched on the floor until the boat stopped swaying.

He had a feeling another boat had bumped into his.

And it sounded like someone had climbed aboard his Legacy. "Who's up there?" he called in a shaky voice. "Haggerty, is that you? Damn it, who's there?"

Grabbing the flashlight, Rick got to his feet. He usually kept only one light on while watching Collin. But now he reached over and switched on all the lights—including the cabin interior. Stepping out of the cabin, he was swallowed up by the white, moving mist. He tried to see if another boat had come alongside him. But the flashlight was just a bright beam in the haze. He couldn't see if anything was on the water.

The sound of the folded sail flapping in the slight breeze spooked him. He shined the flashlight over the deck.

"Haggerty?" he said.

If it wasn't the cop, it could be the elusive, faceless driver of the black Saturn.

He heard the floorboards squeak again, and the boat rocked. He knew he wasn't alone. The damn fog was throwing everything off. One minute it sounded like someone was at the bow—and the next, they seemed to be starboard. The boat started to pitch from side to side again.

He shined the flashlight toward the bow and the cover to the Tohatsu motor, which he'd left on the floor of the deck seating area. He gave the plastic material a kick. No one was hiding beneath it.

He heard the folded-up sail shifting behind him. "Who's there?" Rick yelled nervously. He started to turn around. "Who—"

Rick didn't finish. He didn't even get a chance to turn around. Someone grabbed him by the scalp. Rick realized they must have been lying alongside the folded-up sail.

The boat lurched again as he started to struggle. The binoculars flopped and thumped against his chest. He thought the guy was going to tear his hair out by the roots. It hurt like hell.

But Rick barely felt the ice pick entering the back of his skull.

CHAPTER TWENTY-SIX

"Oh, Clay, I'm so sorry," Cathy said on the other end of the line. "I hope Corinne gets out of the hospital soon. Please, give her our best."

"Thanks, but like I say, she's been pretty out of it," he replied. "She's sleeping right now. There's nothing I can do for her over there."

He was sitting at the desk in his room at the Commodore Inn, near the Space Needle. He'd showered and then changed into a T-shirt and sweatpants. He was waiting for a room-service French dip to be delivered. "Listen, while I've got you here," he said to Jerry's sister-in-law. "Did you and Mike get the guest book from the funeral home yet?"

"Yeah, but don't worry. They gave us a bunch of preprinted thank-you notes. We'll take care of the guest thank-yous. You've got enough on your plate."

"Oh, good, thanks." He hadn't even thought of that. "Well, as long as you have it, could you check one of the names in there for me?"

"Sure, hold on for a sec."

There was a pause, and Clay frowned at his slightly swollen hand in the ACE bandage.

"Okay, got it," Cathy said. "What's the name?"

"Collin Cox."

"As in little Collin Cox, the actor? Are you serious?"

"Yeah, he was there with an older couple. He was talking with Olivia for a while."

"Oh, yes, I remember. He was in the pew right behind Tom Hanks. Clay, are you sure you didn't get a head injury?"

"Just check it for me, please," he said. "Okay?"

"Hmmm," Cathy said. "Well, I don't see his name. Closest I have to it is a Collin *Stampler* on 27 Skog-Strand Lane, Poulsbo."

"Like I say, he was there with an older couple. They drove away in a BMW."

"Well, in the space above him are Andrew and Dee Stampler—same address. Wow, I didn't know they attended the service—not that I would have recognized them."

"What are you talking about? Who are they?"

"Andy Stampler's a big name on the Kitsap Peninsula. Makes sense he'd be driving a BMW. He used to employ half the people here in town. He's retired and, I'm sure, a multimillionaire. He's always good for a couple of grand whenever there's a fund-raiser."

"How old is he?"

"I'm guessing he's in his seventies. How do you suppose they knew Jerry and Sue?"

"Can you spell that last name for me?" Clay asked, grabbing a pen with his bandaged hand. "And what's that address again?"

* * *

The pipes squeaked as Collin shut off the shower. As he reached for a towel, he thought he heard the home line ringing. He stepped out of the tub and opened the bathroom door. Steam escaped to his bedroom. He listened to the phone ring once more—and then nothing. He figured one of his grandparents must have picked it up in their bedroom.

Squinting at the digital clock on his nightstand, he wondered who would be calling at 10:15 at night. He remembered the last time the home line had rung after 10 PM. It had been when they'd found Fernando dead.

He ducked back into the bathroom, then quickly toweled off and dressed in jeans and a sweatshirt. Opening his bedroom door, he peeked down the hallway. He thought he heard his grandfather murmuring. After a moment, it was quiet. Then the master bedroom door opened and a shaft of light poured into the darkened hallway. With his hands in the pockets of his robe, Old Andy slowly walked up the corridor toward him.

"Who called?" Collin asked, running a hand through his still-damp hair.

"The husband of some hypnotist you've been seeing—behind my back," he replied, glumly.

Collin grimaced. He moved aside as Old Andy stepped into his bedroom.

"Better close the door," his grandfather said.

Halfway through the theme from *Exodus*, there was a click on the recording—and then a voice. For a moment, Olivia thought it was Collin in a trance. Then she realized it was Wade.

"Hey, is this on? Is this working?" he asked.

Sitting at her mother's desk, Olivia put down another birthday card from the Frederick & Nelson box. She turned toward the tape recorder on the island counter. It had been playing for the last two hours. She'd listened to the Kingston Trio, the Beach Boys, and then an extremely tedious recording of people at a birthday party, occasionally and quite drunkenly belting out a song, one of which was "Hello Muddah, Hello, Fadduh." This latest tape was a vast improvement, with movie music like "Moon River" and the theme from *The Apartment*.

"Testing, one, two, three," Wade said.

"Hey, you idiot, that's my Ferrante and Teicher tape!" someone yelled. Olivia figured it must have been Sheri. *"Get away from there!"*

"Shit, you don't have to bite my head off!"

"Stupid—"

There was another click, and then it went back to the *Exodus* theme.

The interruption gave Olivia a spark of hope that listening to these tapes wasn't an entire waste of time. She'd just heard an unscheduled interruption from Wade and Sheri Grinnell. It wasn't much, but there could be something more substantial and revealing on another tape.

In the box, amid Sheri's mementos, she'd found two cartoon birthday cards from Wade. He wasn't much for words. He'd signed both cards: *Happy Birthday, Sis – Love, Wade.*

Olivia had set both cards aside, and made a note to herself to have Collin write down the same words while in his Wade persona. She had a feeling his penmanship—unlike his voice—wouldn't be a match.

As the *Magnificent Seven* theme came on the tape, Olivia found something else near the bottom of the box: three more bankbooks, all bound together in a rubber band. The dried-up rubber band broke apart as soon as she pulled out the first book. It was Seattle First National again, with *Sheri Grinnell* in slightly girlish script on the front page. The book covered her transactions from July through December 1962. Wade had been killed on October 11, 1962.

Olivia flipped to that date. On October 15, Sheri withdrew six hundred and twenty dollars, practically draining her account. Olivia figured it must have gone to help pay for the funeral. Then on November 29, Sheri made a deposit of nine thousand, nine hundred dollars—an extraordinary amount, especially for someone whose deposits rarely exceeded a hundred dollars at a time.

Olivia wondered if Sheri had received some sort of payment for what had happened to Wade. Was it part of an inheritance or an insurance compensation? Or was it hush money? Sheri claimed to know some big secret about the Rockabye Murders and her brother's death. Had someone connected to the World's Fair or the police paid to keep her quiet?

Olivia started to jot down a note to herself:

Ask Orin Carney if Sheri Grinnell received any kind of comp—

Her cell phone rang, interrupting her. As Olivia reached for it, she glanced at the clock on the microwave: 10:39 PM. The caller ID showed: *Collin Stampler*. She clicked on the phone. "Hi, Collin," she said. "I was supposed to call you tonight, wasn't I? I'm sorry."

"It's okay," he said, sounding a bit stiff.

"It's been a crazy day here." She got up to switch off the reel-to-reel tape player. "How are you?"

"I'm all right. Um, you said you might be able to see me tomorrow."

"That's right."

"Well, my grandfather wants to come with me to the appointment."

"You told him?" she asked, sinking back down in the desk chair.

"Well, not really. Your husband thinks I took his picture and texted it to somebody or something. I'm not sure what's going on. But he called my grandfather, all bent out of shape. Anyway, your husband told my grandfather that I was seeing you for hypnosis therapy."

"Oh, Collin, I'm so sorry," she murmured. "But you know, maybe this is a good thing. You were going to have to tell your grandfather eventually. The fact that he wants to come to the appointment with you, that's a positive sign—at least, I hope it is."

"Well," Collin sighed. "Here he is. He wants to talk with you."

Now she realized why Collin sounded so strange. The grandfather had been standing beside him all the while. He came on the line. "Hello?"

"Hello, Mr. Stampler," she said, straightening up in the chair. She wasn't sure why, but she suddenly felt intimidated.

"What time were you planning to see my grandson tomorrow?" he asked abruptly.

"We hadn't arranged a time yet. My schedule is pretty open."

"Well, I don't like taking him out of school, but I don't want to drag this out any longer then we have to. How about ten o'clock tomorrow morning?"

"That works for me," she said. "Would you like me to come there to Poulsbo?"

"No, we'll see you at your office. Collin knows the way."

"Actually, my office is—well, it's under repair right now. But you could come to my father's house. It's off Lake Washington in the Denny-Blaine neighborhood—182 Alder Lane."

"182 Alder," he repeated. "All right, Collin and I will see you at ten o'clock. Meanwhile, please tell your husband not to call my house again."

"I will," she said. "I'm sorry about that, Mr. Stampler."

"Good night, Ms. Barker," he said. Then he hung up.

Olivia clicked off the phone. After that conversation—and before calling Clay—she desperately needed a cigarette.

Her father had just gone to bed. So she tried to be as quiet as possible stepping out the front door. She lit up a Virginia Slim. She still couldn't get used to the burnt, crusty exterior of the door. Clutching the collar of her sweater around her neck, she gazed out at the bushes along the border of the front lawn—and the street beyond it. All at once, she saw someone dart between two trees on the parkway.

A panic swept through her. "Who's there?" she cried.

"It's me, Ian!" he called back softly. He waved at her and came up to the front walkway. "I'm sorry, did I scare you?"

She held a hand over her heart. "What are you doing here?"

He shyly approached the front stoop and shoved his hands in the pockets of his jeans. "I know they're supposed to put an extra patrol on this street, but I needed to make sure you're all right. I saw you come outside. I thought you might be investigating a noise or something."

She puffed on her cigarette. "No, I just stepped out to satisfy my filthy habit."

"I didn't take you for a smoker."

"I'm trying to quit. This is my third cigarette today."

The light went on in the window upstairs.

Ian glanced up. "I think I woke your dad."

"It's okay," she said, flicking an ash. "Dad won't be upset. He thinks you're a great guy."

Ian gave her a crooked smile. "So how am I doing with his daughter? I mean, my pushiness and borderline-stalker behavior aside, what do you think of me?"

"To be honest, not too long ago, I got burned as badly as this door here. I'm still kind of getting over it. So if you're interested in me, I'll probably be a lot of work." She dropped her cigarette and ground it out. "All that said, in answer to your question, I think my dad might be right about you."

Ian took a step closer to her. "Really?"

Olivia heard a car engine purring, and she looked toward the street.

A patrol car cruised up the narrow road and stopped in front of the house. A stocky young cop climbed out and came to the start of the walkway. "Haggerty," he said. "They just radioed this to me. . . ."

Olivia thought it might be some new, startling development.

"I'm the third guy who's seen you out here and almost mistook you for a prowler. Unless the nice lady invites you in, they want you to go home and let us do our job here. Otherwise, I'm supposed to haul you in for loitering."

Olivia laughed. "You better go home," she said to Ian.

He smiled at her and nodded. "Sleep tight."

She picked up the cigarette butt, stepped back inside, and locked the door.

Before heading home to his apartment in Madison Park, Ian pulled into the small parking lot of Madison Val-U Mart—near Olivia's office. The place was open until midnight. Right now, there was only one other car in front of the store—a black Saturn with two people in the front seat. The way the store light reflected on the windshield, Ian couldn't see their faces. It looked like two men in there. But he wasn't sure.

He stepped into the store, and got the familiar smells of coffee, stale popcorn, and jumbo hot dogs that had been on a rotating spit since six o'clock this morning. Sanjay, the thin, twenty-something East Indian, worked the counter tonight. He was a good-looking guy, but the ugly blue vest he was forced to wear made him look like a nerd. "Oh, it's the cop coming to shake us down!" he announced in his clipped, precise accent. "How are you doing, Serpico?"

"I'm great, Sanjay," he said. "In fact, in just a week or two, I may not be coming in here so often anymore."

"Well, then it can only be a woman—or one of those inflatable sex dolls."

Ian chuckled. " 'Tis the former, my good man," he replied, heading down the aisle to the frozen foods. He'd gotten to be a regular at the Madison Val-U Mart shortly after the breakup with Janice. He'd worked a lot of late shifts, and always swung by the store to get a snack or last-minute item before returning to his empty apartment. It had gotten so he couldn't pass the place without dropping in. They were always nice to him.

Tonight, he needed half-and-half and paper towels,

and he wanted to treat himself to an ice cream sandwich. Near the end of the aisle, Ian noticed something in one of the store's security mirrors. Someone else was coming into the store.

"Oh, shit," he heard Sanjay mutter.

He swiveled around, and saw two men rushing toward the counter. They had ski masks pulled over their faces and guns in their hands. One of them suddenly turned and hurried down the next aisle—while his partner held Sanjay at gunpoint. "Okay, asshole," he growled from behind the mask. "Slowly reach into the register and take out the money. . . ."

Ian didn't have his gun on him. But before he could even move, the second gunman was already down the next aisle and coming around behind him. Ian turned and started to raise his hands in surrender. The man pointed his gun at him. "What—are you trying to be a hero? You're off duty. . . ."

Ian didn't understand. How did the guy know he was a cop?

Baffled, he glanced up at the security mirror, and noticed the first gunman at the counter had turned away from Sanjay at the register. He aimed his gun at him as well. In a split second, Ian realized these two guys weren't here to rob the store. They were here to kill him.

All at once, Ian grabbed a can of peaches off the shelf and hurled it at the gunman directly in front of him. He lunged at the guy. At the same time, he heard four loud shots go off.

Ian felt a burning sting in his lower back. His legs suddenly gave out and he collapsed to the linoleum floor.

The gunman closest to him turned and ran toward the door. He repeatedly fired at Sanjay. With a gun clasped in both hands, the clerk fired back. The loud shots reverberated through the store. In the cross fire, glass jars exploded and cans ricocheted off the shelves. Sanjay ducked as the holdup man paused at the doorway and fired at him one last time. Then the gunman fled.

His partner was sprawled on the floor by the display of candy and magazines at the checkout counter. He was totally still. The only thing moving was the expanding pool of blood on the dirty floor.

Ian could hear the car engine start up and the screeching tires as the holdup man made his getaway. But everything was getting dark. His back was wet, and he realized he was lying in his own blood. It felt cold.

The last thing he heard was Sanjay, in his precise English, calling to him: "Hey, Ian? Buddy, are you okay? Ian. . . ."

CHAPTER TWENTY-SEVEN

"Listen, I don't know if you're the one behind this or if it's your has-been child-star grandson," Clay said hotly. "But somebody set me up. It's beyond me why they wanted to piss off my girlfriend, but they sure as hell did. They set off this whole chain of events. That's why I'm here at the hospital with my girlfriend, who's now fighting for her life. It's why a third motorist is dead. I swear to God, I'm going to get to the bottom of this. . . ."

He stood by the garden near the drop-off loop in front of the hospital. Behind him a big blue sign with white letters spelled out: UNIVERSITY OF WASHINGTON MEDICAL CENTER. Some bitch of a nurse had told him he couldn't talk on his cell phone in the lobby. So now he was freezing his ass off outside, talking over car engines, and holding a tall Starbucks latte in his good hand. His bandaged wrist hurt like hell as he clutched the phone to his ear, but he had no choice.

"I don't know what you're talking about," Andrew Stampler grumbled on the other end of the line.

"Well, I'll bet your grandson knows," Clay argued.

"He was right there when someone took that picture and texted it to my girlfriend."

"I thought I made it very clear to your wife that I don't want you calling me."

"Yeah, well, she doesn't tell me what to do anymore," Clay shot back.

Olivia had phoned him late last night, swearing up and down Collin Cox had nothing to do with that incriminating photo. But Clay didn't believe her. She was hiding something.

"Listen to me," he continued. "At the very least, your grandson must have seen who took my photo the other day. I want to talk to that kid. If not, I'll go to the newspapers and TV. I'll raise all sorts of hell if I have to. No one sets me up and gets away with it."

"All right," Stampler said with resignation. "Let me talk to Collin about this. He's been under a lot of strain lately, and I don't anyone harassing him. I—I'll get to the bottom of it. If he has any information about this picture-taking incident, I'll let you know. And if—if you're seeking any kind of compensation, then we'll work something out. Where are you? Is there somewhere I can meet you tonight?"

"I'm staying at the Commodore Inn," Clay said. "There's a small bar off the lobby. I'll meet you there at seven-thirty."

"All right," the old man said. "In the meantime, could you please not tell anyone about this? You'll understand why when I talk with you tonight. And if you need to call me, please, don't phone me here at my house anymore. My cell phone number is 206-555-1450."

Clay repeated the number. "All right," he said. "I'll see you tonight. And you better have some answers for me."

As he clicked off his cell phone, Clay had a triumphant smile on his bruised face.

Collin could hear his grandfather murmuring to someone on the phone in his study. He sat at the breakfast table with Dee. The *Today* show was on the wall TV in the breakfast nook. His grandmother was unusually quiet this morning. Collin figured she saw through their lie about where he and his grandfather were headed today. He felt bad about it, especially after their talk last night.

Supposedly, he was missing school to accompany his grandfather to Seattle, where Old Andy had an appointment with a neurologist. "He's reputed to be the best on the West Coast," his grandfather had claimed. Of course, Dee had wanted to go, too. "I'm sorry, but I don't want you there, honey," his grandfather had told her. "Every time you come with me for some medical thing, you get all nervous and weepy. It sends my blood pressure right through the roof."

Collin figured telling her the truth would have been easier and, in many ways, more respectful. It was kind of ironic that his grandfather had been so disappointed in him last night when he'd found out about the hypnotherapy sessions with Olivia. And yet, here he was lying to his wife about what they were doing today. Even if it was supposed to be for her own good, it still didn't seem right.

His grandfather hadn't made it very clear to him exactly why he wanted to come along for this session with Olivia. Obviously, he had every intention of putting an end to it. In Old Andy's mind, a long trek through Europe or Australia was a better solution.

He'd been on the phone for about ten minutes now.

He'd taken the call in the kitchen. Dee had asked who it was, but he'd waved the question away and retreated into his study with the cordless.

His grandmother sipped her coffee—her third cup this morning—and stared at the TV. Collin hoped she'd be all right in the house alone all morning. Even with the extra police patrols in the area, he couldn't help worrying about her. Nothing seemed certain anymore.

His grandfather finally emerged from the study. He looked tired. "You two will have to eat your dinner without me tonight," he announced, rubbing his forehead. He set the cordless back in its cradle on the kitchen counter. "They need me to help pitch this new proposal to the city council. It's a big dinner meeting. I'll be gone from six until at least nine."

Dee frowned. "Well, I don't like it. When you're talking with this specialist today, you ask him if it's smart for you to be going out to business meetings where there's lots of drinking, cigar smoking, and fatty food."

He patted her shoulder. "Oh, now, calm down. . . ."

Staring at the tabletop, Collin didn't say anything. But he had a feeling his grandfather was lying about where he'd be tonight.

He waited until they were in the BMW together, on their way to the ferry. Then he'd asked, "Do you really have a dinner meeting with the city council tonight? Or is something going on that you don't want Dee to know about?"

With his hands on the wheel, Old Andy gazed at the road ahead. "It's just what I said it was."

Collin turned his head away and stared out the window.

He couldn't get past the feeling that he'd just been lied to.

Seattle—Wednesday, 10:12 a.m.

"Collin, I want you to think about your safe place," she said.

Olivia glanced over at Andrew Stampler. With his plaid pants, and a blue cardigan over a polo shirt, he looked like he bought his clothes at the pro shop. His arms folded, he sat on the edge of the desk in her father's study. He rolled his eyes a little. She definitely saw Collin in him—and in his expressions. Obviously, he thought *safe place* was a new-age term deserving of a good eye-roll. But at least he remained quiet for the session with his grandson.

Collin sat in her dad's recliner. Olivia was in front of him in a straight-back chair from the dining room. He'd been concerned about her safety—in case Wade became violent again. But she'd wanted his hands free, and explained that between her and his grandfather, they could restrain Wade. In RECORD mode, Collin's cell phone was propped up on a nearby TV table.

The room was the coziest in the house—with a fireplace in one corner, the TV in another, and built-in shelves full of books, DVDs, and family photos. A big picture window looked out at the front yard. Olivia figured it would be easy for Collin to relax in here. She didn't want anything distracting him. So when he and his grandfather had noticed the burnt front door earlier, Olivia had shrugged it off as an "accident."

Making himself scarce, her dad had taken the car to run some errands. He'd tried to get ahold of his new best friend, Ian, to go out for brunch. But Ian hadn't returned his call.

As she'd prepped Collin for hypnosis, she'd told him to pretend his grandfather wasn't in the room. She'd told herself the same thing.

But she could tell Collin was still nervous. Olivia

moved her hand toward his face and back again—more slowly each time. "Think about your safe place, Collin. It's a shack in the woods—somewhere near Shilshole Bay. Focus on it. Describe it to me. Take me there."

Collin's eyes started to glaze over as he stared at her hand. "I end up on the number sixty-one bus in Ballard," he murmured. "I get off on Fifty-eighth, a few blocks before Ray's Boathouse. You know—the restaurant? There's a big white stucco house at the top of the hill, overlooking the beach. Right by the chain-link fence at the side of the house, I head down a path. The fence ends about a quarter of the way down, and I follow the trail to the right. By now, I can smell the beach and hear water lapping on the shore. It's fall, so I can see the bay through the trees. I look around the big pine, and just off the path, there's the little shack. It's safe. No one can find us there, Dave and me . . ."

Olivia glanced over at Collin's grandfather, who seemed to hang on his every word.

"Collin, I want you to stay focused on my hand," Olivia said. "You're very sleepy. I'm going to count backwards, and when I get to 'one,' you can close your eyes. Then you can go to sleep in your safe place. Five . . . four . . . three . . ."

She watched his eyelids flutter as he sank back in the recliner. His breathing became deeper. "Collin, can you hear my voice?" she asked.

"Yeah," he murmured, barely audible. His eyes were closed.

"I'm talking to the person inside you now. If you hear me, you too are hypnotized. You will remain seated and answer my questions truthfully. Do you understand me?"

A low growl seemed to come from deep within him.

Olivia stole a glance at Mr. Stampler, who was staring at his grandson.

When Olivia turned to Collin again, his eyes were open—with that same cold, dull, cruel look Wade had. He grinned at her. "Hey, it's you again," he said in Wade's voice. He raised his hands off his lap. "And lookee here, no handcuffs. You still got them? Maybe you'll let me put them on you this time."

"My God," Mr. Stampler whispered.

Collin glanced over at him. "Who's this, your old man?"

"He's just here observing," Olivia said. "Could you tell him your name?"

"My name José Jiménez," he said in his bad Spanish accent. Then he cackled.

"Seriously, okay?"

"I'm Wade Grinnell."

"What year is it?"

"1962," he answered impatiently. "Shit, we've been through this before."

"I thought we'd talk about the hotel murders and the fires," Olivia said.

She glanced over at Mr. Stampler, who kept shaking his head. Collin had told her that his grandfather had viewed the videos Fernando had shot. But obviously it was a shock for him to see it happening right in front of him. His face was ashen. "Sir, are you all right?" she asked.

"Yeah, daddy-o, you don't look so hot," Collin said. "Call Ben Casey, call Dr. Kildare!"

"Excuse me," Mr. Stampler murmured, heading out of the TV room. "Keep going. I—I'll be okay. . . ."

Olivia got to her feet. She wanted to make sure he was all right. But she remembered Layne Tipton—and what had happened when she'd left him alone for a minute while he'd been in a hypnotic state.

"Where the hell do you think you're going?" Collin growled.

She stopped in the doorway and turned toward him.

He sat up in the chair; his hands gripped the armrests. "Don't you want to hear a confession? That's what you've been bucking for, isn't it, bitch?"

She glanced back at Mr. Stampler, who hurried into the kitchen. "Are you sure you're all right, sir?" she called.

"Thanks, I'm fine!" she heard him reply—a bit feebly. "I'm just getting some water."

She turned to Collin again. He shifted in the chair. "That old fart, he's a cop, isn't he?"

"No," she said, stepping toward him. "I told you—he's just here observing."

Slouching back, he slung a leg over the chair's armrest. "You probably want to ask me the same things the police did. Do you want to know how I managed to tie them up?"

Olivia looked him in the eye. "I'm assuming you held them at gunpoint, and made them tie each other up."

Smiling, he gave a little shrug. "Maybe."

Olivia heard the refrigerator dispenser going, and knew Collin's grandfather was filling a glass with ice water. She took him at his word that he was all right. She moved over to the desk, where she had a pen and notepad ready—along with a piece of rope. "On the subject of tying people up," she said, lowering the rope into Collin's lap. "I understand your dad was a sailor. Can you show me how to tie a sailor's knot?"

He seemed amused. He took the rope and started to manipulate it.

Olivia stepped back. It occurred to her that she'd just given him something with which he could strangle her—or at the very least, tie her wrists together. She remembered Orin Carney's files, and the close-up photo she'd seen of Betty Freitag, facedown on a hotel bed—with her bloodstained nightgown torn and her bound wrists in back of her. SAILOR KNOT, said the handwritten caption. BETTY FREITAG, 31 – EL MAR HOTEL, 7/9/62.

He tied a knot in the rope, and then tossed it back at her.

Olivia caught the rope and inspected it. As far as she could tell, it was an ordinary knot. "Nice," she said. "Can you do something else for me?" She returned to the desk and retrieved the notepad and pen. Then she handed them to him. "Could you write this down for me? 'Happy Birthday, Sis—Love, Wade.' "

"It's not Sheri's birthday," he muttered.

"I know. Just humor me."

He scribbled on the notepad and handed it back to her. Olivia glanced at the message. His handwriting didn't match Wade's messy scrawl on the birthday cards. Collin had finally put to rest any far-fetched notions about the dead Wade Grinnell invading his body and psyche. There was nothing supernatural about this. There was a rational explanation.

Olivia set the notepad and pen back on the desk. When she turned around again, she caught him checking out the desk and the bookcase. From the recliner, he seemed to be assessing if there was anything in the room worth stealing. She sat down across from him once more. "You were saying earlier that you were ready to give me a confession."

He shook his head. "I didn't say that. I asked, 'Don't

you want to hear a confession?' There's a big difference."

"Well, in answer to your question, yes. I'd like to hear your confession. I know you didn't admit anything to the police, but you did inadvertently give yourself away a few times. I listened to part of the police interview. They had you on tape."

He glared at her. "Well, those sons of bitches don't know shit. Only two people know the whole story—and one of them is me."

"Is the other person Sheri?"

He shook his head again. "Sheri doesn't know—not yet."

"What do you mean, 'not yet'? Are you planning to tell her?"

He slid his foot across the floor so it touched hers. "I've already told her. But Sis just doesn't know yet."

Olivia moved her foot away. "What do you mean?"

"I know the cops are coming after me soon," he sighed, looking down at the carpet. He seemed disappointed she wouldn't play footsie with him. "It's only a matter of time before they arrest me. But I won't let that happen. I'm getting out of town tomorrow. I'll die before I let them throw me in jail. Either way, after I'm gone, Sheri's gonna know the whole story."

"Did you send her a confession in the mail?" Olivia asked.

He nodded. "Go to the head of the class. It's on tape."

Olivia stared at him. All this was new. Where did he get this? She hadn't told him about her talk with Sheri's son. She hadn't mentioned anything to Collin about the keepsakes and the tapes she'd been going over. She'd stashed the boxes and the reel-to-reel player before they'd come over—to make sure it didn't influence him during this session.

"So you have a tape-recorded confession?" she asked.

"I sent it out this morning," he said. "By the time Sheri gets it, I'll be long gone." He glanced over at her father's desk again.

Olivia followed his gaze. She realized what he was looking at. Her dad had a perpetual calendar facing out—a set of faux gold blocks with black lettering that snugly fit into a holder. Changed daily, it gave the date and day of the week: 10 – OCTOBER - WED.

But it didn't give the year. Wade still thought it was 1962. And fifty years ago, on Thursday, October eleventh, Wade Grinnell was killed running from the police. In his mind, this was the day before.

Olivia leaned forward in the chair. "You said someone else knew the whole story behind the murders. Who is it?"

He looked her up and down. "Well, now, pretty lady, I might just tell you—if you made it worth my while. What are you willing to do for the information?"

"I'm not willing to do what you have in mind. However, I'm a therapist with some expertise in psychology. I might be able to help when the time comes for you to plead your case—"

"It won't get that far. I told you, the cops aren't going to catch me." He chuckled. "And I've got news for you, sweetie. If you aren't willing to give it up, that won't stop me. I just take what I want." He grabbed the recliner's armrests and started to pull himself toward her.

"All right, Collin," Olivia said, trying not to shrink back. "Collin?"

He stood up. "I've got nothing to lose, you know.

Hell, the cops want me for a lot worse than rape. I don't give a shit about chalking up another crime. I'm disappearing tomorrow. . . ."

"Collin, I want you to wake up!" she said. "Collin . . ."

"Don't scream," he whispered, standing directly in front of her now. "I'll bash that old man's head in if he tries to stop me. You better not try to stop me either. . . ."

He grabbed hold of her hair.

"Collin, wake up!" she screamed, wrenching away from him. Her chair fell out from under her, and Olivia felt a clump of her hair torn out by the roots. She toppled to the floor. He stood over her. "No, Collin, stop it!" she cried.

"Collin, what are you doing?" It was his grandfather's voice.

Collin stopped. He was still for a moment. Olivia watched him stagger back and flop down in the recliner. She swiveled around to see Mr. Stampler in the study doorway.

Horrified, he gaped at his grandson.

Getting to her feet, Olivia grabbed the dining room chair and set it upright again. She warily looked at Collin, slumped in the recliner. His mouth was open and his eyes rolled back.

"Collin?" she said, trying to catch her breath.

He moaned and shifted in the chair. Then at last, he seemed to focus on her. "What happened?" A worried look came to his gawky-handsome face. He glanced down at his fist and opened it up. Several strands of hair fell out of his grasp. "What did I do?" he asked.

She knew Collin was back.

"I need to apologize to you," Mr. Stampler whispered.

He and Olivia stood in the doorway of her father's study. Collin was in the kitchen, watching the recorded session on his iPhone. She'd already told him about some of what had transpired—like his handwriting not matching Wade's scribbling on the birthday card, and how he hadn't been able to tie a sailor's knot.

His grandfather still seemed shaken by the whole experience. "I saw the recordings his friends made with him talking like that," Mr. Stampler continued. "I thought it was something they'd coached him to do while he was in a trance—you know, like in those hypnotists' nightclub acts? I didn't realize until I saw it myself how serious this is. Please, I want you to keep seeing him. I think you're helping him. Collin likes you, too. He told me that you've refused to take his money. Well, I want to pay you."

Olivia patted his arm. "Let's worry about that later. Mr. Stampler, eventually Collin will need to see someone a lot more qualified than I am. I have a list of therapists—"

"No, no, no, you're the only one I trust with him," he interrupted. "He's been through so much. Please, stick with him. Can you see him tomorrow—at this same time?"

Olivia nodded. "Certainly."

"Thank you." He glanced toward the kitchen. "Why was he talking in that—that voice?"

"I've listened to Wade Grinnell on tape, Mr. Stampler. And that's how he sounds. I'm convinced sometime in his life—maybe when he was just a toddler—Collin heard a recording of Wade's voice. Maybe he even heard Wade's confession. Do you know any way that could be possible?"

He rubbed his forehead. "I couldn't say. His poor mother, she hung around with some pretty disreputable types. Maybe one of them had a recording of this criminal. But Collin told me he'd never even heard of this Wade character until his friends hypnotized him."

"If he heard something that scared him, Collin may have suppressed it," she said. "He seems to have the sixties references down pat. Did he ever show an interest in that period?"

Mr. Stampler shrugged. "Well, he likes that show about the ad men."

"*Mad Men*?"

He nodded. "When he was a little boy, his mother used to park him in front of the TV all the time. He'd watch the old shows on that Nickelodeon channel. You know, *Dick Van Dyke, Dobie Gillis*, and *I Love Lucy*? Whenever he stayed with us, that was all he ever wanted to do. And he's a born mimic. I think it's what made him such a good actor. . . ." He noticed Collin emerging from the kitchen and fell silent.

Slump-shouldered, Collin approached them. He grimaced as his eyes met Olivia's. "I'm really so sorry about what I did in there."

"That's all right," she said, patting his shoulder. "We know it wasn't you. I think we made some real progress today."

Collin nodded. "I emailed you the session so you can look at it again if you want."

"Olivia says you must have heard a recording of this Wade character at one time," his grandfather chimed in.

Collin shrugged. "Maybe, but I don't remember."

"Well, we'll work on it tomorrow," Olivia said.

Collin looked at his grandfather, who nodded in agreement.

"I think we ought to start paying her, don't you?" Mr. Stampler asked.

Collin didn't say anything. He just buried his face in his grandfather's shoulder and hugged him.

A few minutes later, Olivia watched them from the doorway as they started down the front walk toward the street, where the car was parked. Mr. Stampler put his arm around Collin's shoulder. They were just about to get inside the BMW when Collin whispered something to his grandfather. Then he turned and ran back to her.

"Are you okay?" Olivia asked. "What is it?"

"Something in that session," he said, a bit out of breath. "Before I went under, I said something about Dave and me."

She nodded. "Yes, your imaginary friend—from when you were little."

"Grandpa said I must have heard a recording of Wade's voice at one time or another. Well, *Wade* and *Dave*—they kind of sound alike, don't they? We were outlaws together. Do you think that's how it started—I heard his voice and made him my imaginary friend?"

"It's possible," she replied. "It's definitely possible. We'll look into it tomorrow."

He started to turn toward the car, where his grandfather was waiting. But he hesitated. "There was something else in that session," he whispered. "You asked Wade how he tied them up. Then later, he said somebody besides him knew the whole story about the killings." Collin sighed. "Yesterday, I fell asleep during study period, and I had a dream. I was Wade, and I was killing this family in a hotel. In the dream, I was talking like Wade. I stood over the woman, who had her hands tied behind her. She was trying to scream out past a gag in her mouth. And I said—in Wade's voice— I said, 'Fucking kill her already. She's making too much noise.' "

Olivia gazed at him, and a chill raced through her.

"I can't help wondering who he was talking to," Collin whispered. "And now I think I know. Wade Grinnell didn't kill all those people by himself. I think he had a partner."

The BMW started down Alder Lane and disappeared around the corner.

Standing on the front stoop, Olivia was still trying to process what Collin had just told her. It made sense. The second person who knew the truth about the killings was a second killer.

I'm no firebug, Wade had told her. Had that been his cohort's specialty? Had they helped each other out? Had one liked to start fires while the other bound, gagged, and executed his victims? Olivia glanced at the charred, black front door. She thought about her dead in-laws, killed in an inferno, and Sheri Grinnell, swallowed up in a blaze before she could even get out of bed. Olivia realized there was every possibility the firebug was still alive.

Her cell phone rang, and she headed back into her father's study. She grabbed the phone from his desk and glanced at the caller ID: *Harborview Hospital.*

She wondered if they'd moved Corinne from University of Washington Medical Center. She clicked on the phone, expecting Clay on the other end. "Hello?"

"Olivia?" the man said. He sounded half-asleep.

"Yes?"

"Hi, it's Ian Haggerty," he murmured. "Somebody shot me after I left your place last night. I—I'm at Harborview. Could you maybe come see me?"

CHAPTER TWENTY-EIGHT

"I was set up," Ian said, sitting in the elevated hospital bed. He wore an ugly pale green gown, and had a pulse oximeter clipped on his index finger. He looked tired and scruffy. He'd admitted to being a little out of it, because of the painkillers they'd given him. The doctor had said he was lucky the bullet hadn't struck any vital organs. They were keeping him in the hospital tonight to make sure the stitches held and he didn't develop an infection. They were letting him go tomorrow afternoon.

"What do you mean you were 'set up'?" Olivia said. She sat on a hardback chair at his bedside. "From everything you've told me, it sounds like a holdup."

"No, that's how they wanted it to look for the security cameras," Ian said, his voice scratchy. "It was an ambush. They—they were sitting in the car when I pulled up to go into the store. They were waiting for me. When they came in, I didn't react. I was still trying to figure out what was going on. All at once, one of the gunmen was coming at me, and he said, 'Are you trying to be a hero? You're off duty.' "

Olivia squinted at him. "How did he even know you're a cop?"

"That's my point, exactly," Ian said, coughing a bit. "It was a setup. The other one by the counter completely turned away from Sanjay and had his gun aimed at me. They didn't come in there to rob the place. They came in there to kill me."

"But how did they know you'd be in the Val-U Mart at that particular time?"

"Because I'm in there practically every night around the same time." Ian let out a weak chuckle. "I never realized how pathetic that sounded until just now—admitting it to a woman I'm trying to impress."

"I sleep in the room I thought I'd left behind at age twenty-two," Olivia said, patting his shoulder. "There's a poster from *Titanic* hanging over my bed. I'm in no position to judge."

"Thanks," he replied, reaching for his water glass. He took a sip through the straw. "They must have been watching me for a few days to get down my routine. Don't you see? It's the same way they tried to make it seem as if your husband's girlfriend trashed your office and set fire to your house."

"Of course, the photograph," Olivia murmured—almost to herself. Now it made sense that someone had taken the "intimate" photo of her and Clay, and then sent it to Corinne. They'd wanted to get a reaction out of her—and certainly they had. Clay had said Corrine confessed to pouring acid on the car. Olivia had been ready to blame everything from that night on her—until Ian had planted the seeds of doubt in the hallway outside her office yesterday.

Olivia shifted restlessly in the chair. "There's a glitch to this. I mean, the police might get Corinne for dousing my car with acid. But for the other things, there's no guarantee their case would stick. The evidence against her is just circumstantial."

"It doesn't matter. If you and your dad had died in that fire, the police would still have a suspect—and a distraction from the real reason you were targeted. See what these people are trying to do? You die because your husband's crazy girlfriend set fire to your house. I'm shot to death in a convenience store holdup. Your niece and her family died in a house fire, because her father smoked. And while hitchhiking, Fernando Ryan was picked up by some psycho, who slit his throat. Corinne is just part of the smoke and mirrors. She'd only have to be a suspect for a while—to keep people from seeing that all these deaths have one thing in common. All the victims got close to Collin Cox—too close as far as someone is concerned."

He started coughing again, and took another swig of water. "You think I'm crazy, paranoid—or maybe it's the painkillers talking. But the holdup guy who was killed last night didn't have any ID on him at all. My friends over at the East Precinct have been comparing his postmortem photos to some mug shots. They're pretty sure he's a hit man with underworld connections and several aliases. He's not just some schmuck who tried to hold up a convenience store. Someone hired him and his friend to do a job—on me."

"I don't think you're paranoid, Ian," she assured him. "What you were saying the other day seems to make even more sense now."

"Then you won't object to what I've done."

She gave him a wary look. "Well, that depends on what you've done exactly."

"I've asked a private detective friend of mine to look after you and your dad for the next few days. His name's H. M. Langely—Hank. I used to work with him, and when the department got downsized, Hank got laid off. He's trying to make a go of it in the private detective business, but times are tough, you know? Anyway, he's a nice guy, and good with a gun. Would you object if he stayed with you and your dad for a few days? It would sure make me feel better, knowing you have someone watching over you."

She smiled. "You really are looking out for me, aren't you?"

He nodded, and then tipped his head back on the pillow.

Olivia took his hand in hers. "If it's okay with my dad, it's okay with me. Thanks."

A squat, fifty-something, copper-haired nurse came to the door with a vase full of flowers. "Excuse me, these just arrived for you, Ian. And you have another visitor waiting."

She set the flowers on the table at the foot of his bed. Then she headed out the door.

"I guess I'll leave you to your other visitor," Olivia said.

"Can you see who the flowers are from?" he asked. "Is there a card?"

Olivia found the card—amid the bouquet. "It says, 'I knew this would happen when you joined the police force. Are you sure you don't want me to fly in? Love, Mom.' "

He chuckled feebly. "Be careful going home. I'll send Hank over this afternoon."

She nodded, but then hesitated before turning to the doorway. "Yesterday, you said all of this might have to do with Collin's mother and her boyfriend getting killed. You were saying the people close to Collin are

being targeted because he might have told them something about the Friday the thirteenth murders. Is that
right?"

Ian shrugged. "At least, that's my theory, though I'm
sure it's got some holes in it. I still can't figure out why
they haven't actually gone after Collin."

"Ask yourself this," Olivia said. "You got close to
Collin back in July when you were guarding the house.
Why did they wait until yesterday to go after you?"

"What are you trying to say?"

"I have a feeling this doesn't have anything to do
with the murders on Friday the thirteenth. All of this
started ten days ago, when Gail and her family died in
that fire."

"Well, if it's not about the murders of Collin's
mother and her boyfriend, what do you think it is?" Ian
asked, almost sitting up in the hospital bed.

Olivia didn't answer.

He studied her. "You can't tell me, because it's confidential. It's something between you and Collin—isn't
it?"

Olivia took a deep breath and nodded. "I'm sorry.
Take care. I'll be back tomorrow." Then she hurried out
the door.

Heading down the hospital corridor, she spotted
Sanjay from the Madison Val-U Mart. He was in the
waiting area, holding on to a foil balloon with *Get Well
Soon* on it. He didn't notice her. Olivia was glad, because she couldn't talk to anyone right now. She just
kept walking toward the elevators.

She remembered what Orin Carney had told her—
about how the police and certain people in power back
in 1962 had done their best to bury any news of the
Rockabye Killings. And now, fifty years later, some-

body was trying to eliminate everyone who knew that
Wade Grinnell had returned—through Collin Cox.

Olivia thought about her poor, sweet niece, unwittingly hypnotizing Collin for the first time. How could
she have known the chain reaction she'd initiated?

How could she have known the killings were about
to start?

Seattle—Wednesday, 7:46 p.m.

"Where the hell are you?" Clay growled into his cell
phone.

Noshing on pretzels and nursing a vodka and tonic,
he sat at the bar in the small, dark lounge off the lobby
of the Commodore Inn. Though the woman behind the
bar was all smiles, she was too scrawny and mannish
for him. On the TV behind the bar, they showed a soc-
cer game on mute, and old music from *Saturday Night
Fever* played on the speakers.

Stampler had phoned about an hour ago, saying he'd
talked to his grandson—and maybe they could come to
an agreement about dropping this whole thing. He'd
bumped up their meeting time to 7:15. But when Clay
had shown up at twenty after, there had been no sign of
the old man. Had Stampler gone to the wrong hotel
bar?

"What happened?" he said on Stampler's voice
mail. "Did you get lost? I'll wait here for five more
minutes. Then I'm going back to my room. Maybe *The
Seattle Times* or KING-5 News would like to know
your famous grandson's involved in some kind of ex-
tortion or blackmail. I'm not going to be jerked around
here."

Clay clicked off. He ate a few more pretzels, finished his vodka and tonic, and listened to "Disco Inferno." He kept looking over his shoulder toward the lobby. "Screw it," he muttered under his breath. He paid his bar tab and headed back to his room on the first floor. As he stomped down the long, dimly lit corridor, he heard an ice machine churning. He pulled out his key card, slipped it in the slot under the knob, and opened the door.

Stepping inside the room, Clay felt a chill. He'd left a light on by the bed, which had an ice-blue, beige, and plum spread. The paisley pattern and colors matched the drapes. Clay let the door shut behind him.

Suddenly, the bathroom light went on.

Clay could only see the man's silhouette as he stood in the bathroom doorway.

"Sorry," the stranger said, stepping toward him. "I couldn't let anyone see us together."

Frozen, Clay saw it was Stampler, looking sort of feeble and sad.

"How the hell did you get in here?" he barked.

Collin's grandfather nodded toward the sliding glass door that led to the parking lot. "When I was a young man," he said. "I became very skilled at breaking into hotel rooms."

Clay squinted at the glass door—open a few inches. The paisley-patterned curtains fluttered a little. When Clay turned around again, he saw the old man with his hand up. He was holding something.

"Wait—"

That was all Clay could say—before the old man brought the policeman's nightstick crashing down on his head.

* * *

It was about two months too early for "The First Noel"—sung by Perry Como and a choir of backup singers—but Olivia let it play on the reel-to-reel box. There was always a chance that Wade or Sheri Grinnell might interrupt the Christmas music with some revealing announcement.

Her father and Hank Langely were in the study, watching a movie. The two of them got along great. Together, they'd grilled some steaks for dinner—all the while talking over each other about the best way to cook them. It had been amusing to see them out there, especially Hank, a sweet, harmless-looking, fifty-something guy with receding hair, hound dog eyes—and a shoulder holster. After dinner, Hank had called Ian, just to assure him everything was quiet.

Sitting in front of the laptop, Olivia pored over a 1999 *Seattle Post-Intelligencer* article she'd found on-line:

Industrialist Andrew Stampler,
'Mayor of North Kitsap,'
Retires with Honors and Awards

Now that Collin's grandfather was involved in his therapy, Olivia wanted to know more about Andy Stampler. The article focused mostly on his business ventures and civic contributions. But Olivia was more interested in the Wire and Cable magnate's personal life.

She found out he was younger than she'd thought. Born in 1945, he'd been the son of a dead war hero and his heiress bride. Andy—as the article referred to him—had lived with his grandparents and his mother in their estate on Shilshole Bay. Olivia wondered if it was the white house Collin had mentioned—the one up the hillside path from his "safe place" shack.

Andy started at Anderson Military Academy in Redding, California in 1962, but Olivia wasn't sure if that meant he'd actually missed the Seattle World's Fair—as Collin had said. He could have come home over the summer. He spent the Vietnam years stationed in Europe, where he met his French bride. He brought her and his father-in-law's cable manufacturing business to the States. He opened up a factory in North Kitsap, and business boomed.

In 1983, his thirty-two-year-old wife died of ovarian cancer. Olivia assumed that for the next eight years, Penelope "Piper" Stampler had been raised by a nanny or a series of nannies, which may have accounted for why she'd turned out so screwed up. Stampler remarried in 1991—to Dierdre "Dee" Hanna of Houston. Then he retired to much fanfare in 1999.

The article had been written before Collin Cox became famous. There wasn't much in there about Andy Stampler's grandson—or his wayward daughter, for that matter.

The Christmas tape ended and Olivia got up to put on a new tape. She'd become an expert at threading the tapes through all the little spools. As she turned toward the reel-to-reel player, something in the side window caught her eye.

Olivia froze.

She saw a man quickly duck back into the shadows, behind the foliage. Olivia gasped as a small tree branch slapped against the windowpane. She could hear his footsteps outside. "Hank!" she cried, her voice shrill. She raced toward the front of the house.

Ian's detective friend and her father were already in the foyer, heading for the door. Hank had his gun drawn. They must have heard the man out there, too. "Call nine-one-one," her father said. "Tell them we have a prowler. . . ."

He stared at Clay Bischoff, lying on his side on the beige carpet. Clay was beginning to stir. He moaned past the washcloth in his mouth. An old belt strapped his ankles together, and his hands were tied behind his back—in a regular knot.

Andy had always tied up the husbands and children, but Wade had liked tying up the wives. The sailor knot had been mentioned in one of the newspaper articles about the slayings. Wade had gotten a big kick out of that.

Clay groaned in agony. Andy remembered the same muffled moaning from some of those tourists. Wade had always whacked the husband over the head first, and then revived them when everyone else in the family had been tied up. Andy once suggested to Wade that they cover the children's heads with pillowcases so they didn't have to see their faces. But Wade wouldn't hear of it. Wade called all the shots.

He'd been the scrawny rich mama's boy, and Wade—a few months older—had been the swaggering hood who got into trouble all the time. They'd landed in the same class, because Andy's grandfather had figured a few years in a public high school would toughen him up. When Wade had first approached him after the last bell one day, Andy had figured the class hood was about to shake him down for some extra money. To his utter surprise, Wade just wanted to talk and hang out. They kept their growing friendship a secret. Andy couldn't let his grandparents know that he was keeping company with someone who had already been arrested several times before his sixteenth birthday. And Wade didn't want to be seen in public with the class wimp—a position Andy retained even after he'd started growing and filling out a little.

Wade was always daring him to do one risky thing after another. Who could stand on the railroad tracks longer—after the Northern Pacific line passed the crossing two blocks down? Andy never won the challenge. Wade had gotten him to shoplift everything from a six-pack of Hamm's to a $49.99 Timex at the Bon Marché counter. Then there was the time the two of them almost got caught peeking into homecoming queen Evie Caletti's bedroom window. It was all over the school the next day. Wade and Andy's hideout was the shack in the woods below Andy's grandparents' house. The place had a couple of sleeping bags rolled up. They kept it stocked with a transistor radio, several *Playboy*s, cigarettes, and an array of items they'd stolen.

One spring afternoon, Wade had talked him into giving a hot foot to a wino passed out in a brick-paved alley down near the waterfront. Always eager to impress his friend, Andy stole a can of lighter fluid at a nearby shop. He doused the sleeping man's dilapidated shoes with the fluid, then lit a match and threw it at him. Cracking up, they ducked into an alcove and watched. Andy had expected to see the shoes ignite, and then maybe the old derelict would leap to his feet and start dancing around to stomp them out. Instead the flames exploded from the man's shoes—and suddenly rushed up his pants leg to his waist. It happened so fast, the old rummy didn't even jump to his feet until he was half on fire. Screaming in agony, he did the funny little dance Andy had been expecting. But the blaze only swelled and his threadbare coat ignited, too.

Flames and black smoke swallowed him up. He staggered down to his knees on the pavement brick. The smell of his burning flesh was horrible. He stopped screaming and flopped facedown.

Andy and Wade tore out of there before anyone could see them. They didn't stop running until they were five blocks away—in a doorway in another alley. Shaken and trying to get his breath, Andy was horrified by what he'd done. How could the fire have consumed the man so quickly? Then he realized the vagrant must have spilled booze all over himself recently. His shoddy clothes were probably soaked in alcohol. Andy felt sick to his stomach.

But Wade started laughing. He imitated the way the vagrant had been flailing around. "I can't believe you killed him, man!" he cackled. "You're a goddamn menace to society! That was so great!" Wade laughed so hard, he lapsed into a coughing fit.

Andy realized he'd won Wade's respect. He also realized he'd never been so excited in his life. He started laughing, too.

Killing all those tourist families had been Wade's idea. He didn't think they had any right to be happy. Plus he and his sister had been evicted from a nice, affordable two-bedroom apartment on Capitol Hill so the landlord could turn it into a hotel for the World's Fair crowd. For their first kill together—the old rummy didn't count, his death was an accident—Wade made him knock on the newlywed couple's door at the Gilbert Arms Hotel. "You've got that respectable, boy-next-door look," Wade had explained. "They'll open the door for you. . . ."

And they did.

Wade had a gun that had belonged to his dead father. Not once in all the killings did he ever have to fire it. After the father had been knocked over the head, the families were always very cooperative.

"Just cooperate with me here," Andy said, standing over Clay Bischoff. He wanted to move him onto the bed.

But Olivia's estranged husband was anything but docile. He tried to scream out past the washcloth gag in his mouth. He struggled, kicked, and banged at the wall so the neighbors would hear him.

Fucking kill her already! She's making too much noise!

Andy remembered Wade whispering that to him when one of their victims had started freaking out. Her husband wouldn't die—no matter how many times Wade stabbed him. Andy usually just tied up the families and let Wade do his thing. That was the agreement. He did that for Wade, and Wade helped him set up the fires. Andy had become very skilled at making Molotov cocktails, strategizing exactly how to block all the exits, and initiating a deadly blaze without so much as burning his finger. But he wasn't used to killing this close. For a few moments, he didn't know what to do with the screaming, squirming woman. Wade had the knife. So Andy grabbed a pillow and held it over the woman's face. It was such a relief when she'd stopped struggling.

That had been the last family they'd killed together.

He had a knife with him now—in the pocket of his Windbreaker.

Clay Bischoff twisted and rolled around on the floor—like a little kid having a tantrum. Andy gave up trying to move him to the bed. He tugged at the belt around Clay's ankles, and pulled at his arm until he was able to turn him over on his stomach. It was a major undertaking. He narrowly avoided getting kicked.

At last, he had him facedown on the carpet. Catching his breath, Andy pulled the switchblade out of his pocket.

His screams muffled, Clay rocked back and forth on the floor. Andy stabbed him in the back—between his shoulder blades—again and again.

It was such a relief when the struggling stopped.

CHAPTER TWENTY-NINE

Seattle—Wednesday, 8:30 p.m.

The cop car in front of their house pulled away, leaving them on their own again. The two policemen had searched the yard and combed over the surrounding area: one from inside the squad car with the floodlight, and his partner on foot with a flashlight. They hadn't found anyone. But there were footprints in the damp ground around the outside of the house. After the reception their prowler had gotten, Olivia's dad surmised the guy was probably in another zip code by now.

He and Hank were once again in the TV room, watching their movie. Fighting the urge for a cigarette, Olivia returned to her mother's writing nook and the computer. On the reel-to-reel tape, Chubby Checker sang about the Twist. Blurry-eyed, Olivia was about to close the page on the *Post-Intelligencer* article covering Andy Stampler's retirement. But then she looked at the date again: October 17, 1999.

Rifling through the Post-its, printouts, and copies she'd accumulated regarding Wade Grinnell, Olivia found what she was looking for. It was a printout of the

article about Sheri Grinnell: TACOMA WOMAN DIES IN
APARTMENT FIRE. The date was October 29, 1999, just
twelve days after the story about Andy Stampler had
run.

Olivia wondered if Wade's sister had seen the story
about Andy Stampler eleven days before her death. She
remembered what Sheri's son had told her: *"Funny
thing though. I remember about a week or two before
the fire, she started talking like she'd be coming into a
lot of cash soon—big money, too. But she wouldn't say
how. . . ."*

It was almost too much of a coincidence about the
dates and the timing. She also had a feeling in her gut
that Andy Stampler was holding something back. Then
again, maybe she was just grasping at straws. There
was nothing connecting Collin's grandfather with
Sheri Grinnell.

She moved the cursor, pressed a key, and closed the
page to the article about Andy Stampler's retirement.

Suddenly, she heard a click on the tape, and Chubby
Checker stopped mid-song. *"Testing one, two, three. . . .
Testing. . . ."*

A chill ran through her at the sound of Wade's voice.
Olivia stared at the reel-to-reel player.

*"Sheri, this is Wade speaking. I have something im-
portant I need to tell you. . . ."*

Olivia slowly stood up.

There was a pause on the tape, and then she heard
Wade burp.

He cackled at his little joke. Another click followed,
and it returned to Chubby Checker.

Olivia sank back down in the chair.

Her father stepped into the kitchen and pulled a beer
from the refrigerator. "We really owe Ian Haggerty a
debt of gratitude for hooking us up with Hank."

She gave her dad a tired smile. "You can stop trying to sell me on Ian, Pop. I like him."

"Good," her father said. Then he headed for the TV room.

Olivia turned to look out at the patio. She couldn't help feeling someone might still be watching her. That prowler might have forced his way into the house if Hank hadn't been there with a gun. Obviously, the people who wanted Collin's friends dead weren't giving up after one try. Her father had been right—thank God Ian had gotten Hank to watch over them.

It suddenly dawned on Olivia. Who was watching over Ian?

Dressed in a surgeon's scrubs and cap, the man stepped off the hospital elevator on Ian's floor. A surgical mask was loose and down around his neck. He kept his arms folded, so no one could see he was holding on to a small box. Tucked under his bicep, it was a little kit that he'd used before several times—with great success. The box contained a hypodermic and a vial with a lethal mix of barbiturate, paralytic, and potassium solution.

He'd had to abort the Alder Lane job. They'd been expecting him. He wouldn't be able to go near that house again for at least a few more hours—when their guard was down.

But no one was expecting him here at the hospital.

He headed down the quiet, empty corridor toward Ian Haggerty's room.

Ian woke up in his room, lit only by the flickering TV screen and a small lamp in the far corner. It took him a moment to realize he'd drifted off. He'd been watching *Sweet Smell of Success* on TMC, but the painkillers had made him weak and drowsy. It looked like the movie was wrapping up, with Burt Lancaster yelling at Tony Curtis about something. Ian found the volume button on the remote and turned it down.

A shadow swept across the wall, and he turned to see a swarthy, fortyish man in pale blue surgical scrubs coming into the room. "It's time for another shot," he announced. Then he ducked into the bathroom on the right side of Ian's bed. The bathroom light went on, but Ian couldn't see what he was doing in there. "How are you feeling?" the man asked.

"A little out of it, I guess," Ian replied. He wondered why a surgeon was giving him a shot. Wasn't that the nurse's job? Ian knew he was loopy from the drugs they'd given him. But he couldn't get over the feeling that something wasn't quite right.

In a mirror on the wall across the room, he saw a reflection of the man's back as he hovered over something in the bathroom. Ian tried to sit up so he could see better, but he was too weak. "Um, what's the shot for?" he asked warily.

"Another painkiller," the guy answered from the bathroom.

"But I've already had one of those tonight."

"This one will send you to la-la land. What—are you trying to give me an argument?"

Ian knew his voice. He'd heard that voice last night, speaking to him from behind a ski mask: *"What—are you trying to be a hero? You're off-duty. . . ."*

His hand trembling, Ian reached over and pressed the call button for the nurse.

The man emerged from the bathroom holding the

hypodermic. "Relax. It's only going to hurt for a second. . . ."

Ian started to shake his head. He realized the guy wasn't even going to swab his arm first. He wasn't imagining things. This was no doctor. Ian tried to reach for the phone, but he knocked over his plastic water pitcher. It hit the linoleum floor with a clatter.

The man grabbed him by the wrist.

"No!" Ian yelled.

"What's going on in here?" the heavyset nurse asked in her crisp Jamaican accent. She stepped into the room and switched on the light.

"He's making a hell of a mess, that's what's going on," the bogus surgeon replied. "I'll get an orderly to clean it up. . . ." Brushing past the nurse, he hurried down the hallway.

"Please," Ian gasped. "Call hospital security—and the police."

Andy Stampler washed the blood off his hands. He watched the pink water swirling around the white sink. On the Formica counter, beside the hotel ice bucket, he'd laid out the knife and the policeman's nightstick—as well as Clay Bischoff's cell phone, his wallet, and the hotel room key card.

Staring at his pale reflection in the mirror, he saw the drops of blood splattered on his face. One big crimson glob dripped down along his right temple, mingling in his gray hair. Andy had thought it was sweat—until just now. He quickly rinsed off his face.

He wished he were more like his old friend. It never used to bother Wade when he'd gotten blood on himself. But Andy had preferred to keep his victims at a distance. Yards and yards away, he could still see the fire and smell the smoke. He could still hear the crack-ling sound—and the screams.

He remembered pulling into the lot of a Chinese restaurant a quarter of a block away when Irene Pollack had discovered her family trapped in the inferno he'd created. Just an hour before, he'd only gotten to second base with her sister-in-law, Loretta, in the back of his red '59 Chevy. Wade had been in the front seat, and Loretta had suddenly seemed more interested in him. She'd gone back to her room at nine. They'd been parked down the road from the sign by the hotel entrance. After they'd started the fire, it had been Wade's idea that they drive to Yum-Yum China for a better view of the fire.

"I'll bet you any amount of money the mother's gonna fry trying to get those kiddies out," Wade had said as they'd watched the blaze from inside the car.

Andy had hoped he was right. He hadn't been too concerned about Mrs. Pollack seeing him flirt with Loretta at the fair. But he hadn't counted on her—just minutes before—spotting him as they'd fled the blaze he'd created with two Molotov cocktails and a tin of charcoal starter. For the first time, he and Wade had left behind a witness.

Now, fifty years later, he stood in the bathroom of another Seattle hotel. In the mirror above the sink, he couldn't see the young man he used to be. Only when he looked at his grandson did he glimpse his former self.

It was his face Irene Pollack had seen in the Leaven-worth rest home.

It killed Andy to learn she was still alive—and to hear from his grandson that she still remembered. He wouldn't rest until she was dead.

Andy winced at the dark stain down the front of his

blue nylon Windbreaker. It was soaked. He carefully unzipped the jacket and took it off. He dumped it in the sink to keep the blood from dripping on the floor.

He'd smuggled two black garbage bags into the room earlier. One contained the clothes he'd been wearing when he'd left the house nearly three hours before. He'd changed out of them in the bathroom of a Shell Station near the hotel. The second bag held a gray sweatshirt and jeans belonging to his grandson. While Collin had attended his last three classes of the day, Andy had pilfered the clothes from his bedroom closet—along with a leather cowboy belt that had COLLIN stenciled on it. That belt was now wrapped around Clay Bischoff's ankles.

Andy dug the sweatshirt and jeans from the bag and dropped them on top of the blood-soaked Windbreaker. Then he started to get undressed.

Ten minutes later, he was in the hotel parking lot, wearing the "business casual" clothes he'd had on when he'd left the house earlier. He made certain no one saw him as he loaded the two garbage bags into the trunk of his BMW. Then he crept back into Clay's room—through the sliding door he'd jimmied open two hours before. This time, he locked it behind him. On his way to the door, he stepped around Clay's corpse and the puddle of blood on the beige carpet. He checked the peephole to make sure the hallway was empty. Quietly opening the door, he slipped out and hung the DO NOT DISTURB sign on the door handle.

Andy was pretty certain no one saw him leaving the hotel by a side door.

That had been something he and Wade had agreed upon a long, long time ago—always leave the hotel by a side door, not the lobby.

* * *

"I know it sounds crazy," Ian tried to explain. He was sitting up with his hospital bed elevated. "But that 'surgeon' was the holdup guy from last night. I recognized his voice. . . ."

At the other end of his bed stood the Jamaican nurse and a fifty-something security guard with a buzz cut and a sun-wizened face. Along with his modified gray policeman's uniform he had a belt that holstered his gun and a walkie-talkie. He and the nurse looked at each other as if they had a real nutcase on their hands.

"Did you recognize the guy?" Ian asked the nurse, trying to make his point. He was so drowsy from the medication. He talked loudly to keep himself awake. It was exhausting just getting them to listen. "You—you got a look at him. Does he work here? I mean, have you ever seen him before? I'm telling you, he wasn't a real doctor. And you guys let him get away. He's probably long gone by now—"

"Well, then he won't be coming back, will he?" the security guard said, with his thumbs in his gun belt. "You need to settle down, buddy."

Ian wished he knew the nurse by name. She must have worked the night shift, and just punched in. As for the guard, talking to him was useless. Ian had asked them to watch the hospital exits for a tall, thin, olive-skinned guy in surgical scrubs. But of course, they'd ignored him. They hadn't contacted the police yet either.

His tired eyes pleaded with the nurse. "Listen, please, if you don't believe me, ask yourself, why— why was a guy dressed like a surgeon giving me a shot? Isn't that your job? Is it on my chart that I was due for a shot?" Ian started coughing. It felt like his body was shutting down. "The guy was trying to kill me," he gasped. "He didn't succeed yesterday, so he came back to try again. Jesus, didn't you see the way he ran out of here—like he was escaping? He said he was getting an orderly to clean up the water. So where— where's the orderly?"

With one eyebrow raised, the nurse looked toward the door. Ian followed her gaze. Lingering in the hallway, outside his room, a stocky, baby-faced Latino orderly craned his thick neck to see what was going on.

"Are you here to clean up the water?" she asked him.

Gaping at her, the orderly shook his head. "I was wondering what the fuss was about."

The nurse sighed. "There's a puddle of water on the other side of his bed. Could you clean it up, please?" She gave the security man a look, and they both stepped out to the corridor. They spoke in hushed voices while the orderly ducked into the bathroom. He came out again with several paper towels.

"*. . . medication he's taking can cause some paranoia . . .*" Ian heard the nurse whisper.

"*I really don't have time for this,*" the guard muttered.

"*. . . give him a sedative,*" the woman said. Ian could only make out a few words here and there. "*I'll get the orderly. . . . We'll have to restrain him. . . .*" Then she raised her voice. "*Ricky, when you finish up in there, would you come out here? I need your help with something else. . . .*"

Ian glanced down at the orderly, crouched near the floor, wiping up the spilt water with the wad of paper towels. "Excuse me," Ian whispered. His body felt like so much deadweight as he tried to turn toward him. "Please, don't let them knock me out. . . ."

The orderly gave him a dubious look, and slowly

shook his head. Straightening up, he dumped the paper towels into the plastic pitcher, and carried it into the bathroom. Then he stepped out to the corridor.

The nurse poked her head back in the doorway. "Now, try to calm down, Mr. Haggerty," she said in a condescending tone. She switched off the overhead light, and the room was dim again—with just a small light on in the far corner. "We won't let anything bad happen to you. In fact, Ricky here will guard the door while I get something to help you relax. . . ."

"For God's sake, no," Ian cried. "Please, listen to me. . . . I'm not crazy. . . ."

He glanced over at the phone on his nightstand. He figured they probably wouldn't let him call anyone.

"Miss?" he heard the nurse say. Then her voice dropped to a whisper. *"Miss, you can't be here. Visiting hours are over. . . ."*

"It's okay. My father's down in the lobby talking to a Mr. Schlund. . . ."

He glanced over toward the doorway, and just saw shadows—and the back of the stocky orderly. "They'll be moving Ian to another room on a different floor," he heard Olivia say. "We'll have a bodyguard for him. They'll be calling you about it soon, I'm sure. If you'll excuse me, I'd really like to go in and see him. . . ."

Olivia stepped into the dimly lit room. She wore jeans, a sweater, and a navy pea coat. Her auburn hair was down around her shoulders. She was a beautiful sight. She came to his bedside and took hold of his hand. "We're moving you out of here," she whispered. "My dad's arranging everything. Hank's just down the hall. He rode up with me in the elevator. He's getting one of your buddies from your old department to keep you company tonight."

"I can't believe you're here," he murmured. "How—how did you know I was in trouble?"

"What do you mean? What happened?" She squeezed his hand.

"It doesn't matter now," he said weakly. "I'll tell you tomorrow. Just don't let Hank leave your side, okay?"

"I won't. But for now, I'm sticking close to you until your friend arrives. Then we'll get you into a different room." She touched his cheek. "Tomorrow, when they let you out of here, you're coming to stay with us, and I'll watch over you for a change. How does that sound?"

Ian wasn't sure if the drugs in his system were playing tricks on him. But it felt like he was dreaming. He just nodded, closed his eyes, and smiled.

On his way to the ferry terminal, Andy Stampler realized it was the anniversary of Wade's death tomorrow. Navigating through traffic downtown, he remembered back to that night exactly fifty years ago when Wade had called him from a pay phone. His friend said the police had taken him in for questioning. "The stupid cops don't have anything on either one of us—just a hunch about me. That family from Denver last week—you know, the King's View Hotel?—well, they had some friends who picked me out of a scrapbook of mug shots. They saw me talking with the daughter outside the Science Pavilion. So—suddenly, the cops are trying to connect me to the El Mar murders from back in July. It doesn't make sense. They're all over the map, and haven't got a clue. Anyway, we're in this together, Andy. Don't worry. I didn't rat you out. They have no idea about you. . . ."

Wade proposed that Andy steal some money from his grandfather, and then they'd meet at the shack.

They'd hop a train and ride the rails out of town together. He had some crazy idea about living in Las Vegas.

All at once, Andy didn't want anything more to do with him. But he didn't have the guts to say so. He made up a lie about his grandparents suspecting something and watching him very closely. Andy told Wade to call him once he'd settled down in a new city. "By then, the heat will be off me. I can get away from here with some cash and come meet you."

He didn't mean a word of it.

That night he'd skulked down the pathway through the woods and emptied out the shack of everything they'd accrued together: the sleeping bags, the *Playboys*, everything. It took four trips, carrying all that junk down to the beach. Andy piled it up and made a bonfire.

As far as he was concerned, he and Wade had never been friends.

Late the following afternoon, Wade was hit by a train while fleeing police.

Andy saw the story on the news that night. Until the late edition *Seattle Times* came out the next day, he was sick with worry the police would come after him, too. Was there anything at Wade and his sister's place to link him to his dead friend? He'd only met Sheri Grinnell once, and she hadn't seemed the least bit interested in him. He was terrified she'd suddenly remember him and tell the police.

Andy considered it divine intervention when the *Times* reported that the lone suspect in the murder of a tourist family at the El Mar Hotel had recently been killed himself. The case was closed. They didn't bring up the other murders or the hotel fires. They swept it all under the rug.

Shortly after that, Andy asked to go away to Anderson Military Academy in California. He didn't want to be around Seattle, and a part of him felt entering a strict military school was an appropriate self-punishment for what he'd done. Of course, his grandfather was for it, all the better to toughen him up.

It actually did toughen him up, and he thrived there.

Two months later, in early December 1962, Andy got pulled out of a class for a consult with one of his grandfather's attorneys. He was a thin, hawkish-faced man with wavy brown hair and a blue pinstripe suit. He introduced himself as Mr. Goldsmith. Except for a tiny, constipated smile Goldsmith gave while meeting him in the academy quad—"I'll tell your grandfather you looked impressive in your military uniform," he'd said—the guy snarled at him the entire time they walked around the campus together. Goldsmith explained that his grandfather had been approached by a certain Miss Sheri Grinnell. When Andy heard him utter that name, it felt like a sudden punch to his stomach. He couldn't breathe. He felt sick. It was all he could do to keep walking with his hands clasped together behind his back. He just stared down at the ground and nodded at what the man beside him was saying.

Sheri Grinnell had a tape, which had been mailed to her by her brother the day before the police had tried to arrest him for murder. She claimed that Andy had participated in these "thrill killings," and her brother had said so on the tape. On Andy's grandfather's instructions, Goldsmith gave Sheri Grinnell ten thousand dollars in exchange for the tape, which was immediately destroyed. Sheri was warned that if she tried to extort any more money from Andy's family, someone else less scrupulous than Mr. Goldsmith would deal with her.

"Your grandfather and I are the only people who know," the lawyer said. He and Andy stopped where they'd started their conversation—near the entrance to Andy's dorm. "Your grandfather has suggested that you spend your Christmas vacation skiing in Idaho. Maybe you can persuade some friends here to keep you company. You aren't welcome home. The reason why should be quite clear to you."

Andy couldn't say anything. He just stared at the man.

The attorney nodded at him. "Have a good holiday," he said. He turned and walked away to a nearby parking lot, where he climbed into a black Cadillac.

Andy remembered standing there and watching the car drive down the road to the checkpoint gate.

At the ferry terminal, he paid for his ticket and watched the crossing gate go up. He steered his BMW into the lane for the Bainbridge ferry. Shifting into park, he turned off the car. He could see the approaching ferry in the distance. Andy sat back and thought about what a son of a bitch his grandfather was.

He'd vowed to be a far better grandparent to Collin.

But then he thought of Collin's belt, now tied around Clay Bischoff's ankles. He thought about Collin's clothes, now stained with blood and tucked in a plastic bag in the BMW's trunk. When Collin woke up in the morning, he would find those bloodstained clothes and think he'd killed someone. It would be a repeat of last week, when Collin had woken up thinking he'd set fire to his friend's house.

How else could he get Collin to cooperate and shut up about Wade Grinnell? If he thought he'd killed someone, he wouldn't want to go to the police or a psychologist or a hypnotist. If he was anything like his grandfather, he'd distance himself from the situation the best he could. He'd be all the more motivated to get away—to Europe or Australia.

It was a horrible thing to do to his own grandson. But Andy told himself it was for the boy's own good.

Still, he felt like a son of a bitch.

"Hello?"

"You're probably wondering why a Mr. *Bischoff* is calling you," Andy said into the cell phone. He stood on the ferry deck with the night wind whipping at him. No one else was out there. Only about fifty cars had boarded the Bainbridge ferry.

"As a matter of fact, I was, sir."

"So—any chance you'll be calling me from the cell phone of Ms. Barker soon?"

"I ran into a little problem. She and her father have a babysitter. But I can promise results by noon tomorrow."

"Goddamn it," Andy muttered.

"It couldn't be helped."

He sighed. "What about our friend in the hospital?"

"I ran into a delay there, too. He switched rooms on me. But I can assure you by this time tomorrow, he'll still be in the hospital—but with accommodations in the basement."

"See to that," Andy grumbled. He clicked off.

He glanced at Clay Bischoff's cell phone for a moment. Andy dropped the phone into the Sound, and watched the tiny splash in the dark water below. He thought about the man he'd just spoken to. Back when he'd been running a business, dealing with union problems and underhanded competitors, he'd kept some unsavory characters on a private payroll. He hadn't been above making secret deals with a few mob types when necessary. He'd always hired reliable people to do his dirty work.

But times had changed. He'd gone through an old connection to find this man, and so far, he wasn't impressed. Of course, he'd never thought he would have to hire anyone like him again.

When Collin had first come to live with Dee and him after Piper's murder, Andy had been concerned his grandson might have adopted some of Piper's problems. Little Collin had never given them a moment's worry the many times he'd stayed with them while his mother was in rehab or off somewhere with a new guy. But Andy had just lost his only child—and in all likelihood, because of her boyfriend's drug connections. So he'd taken precautions with his grandson. He'd bought Collin a new computer and a fancy new iPhone, both with watchdog applications installed so he could monitor the boy's texts, calls, emails, and the sites he visited. He'd had his grandson's best interests in mind.

To his relief, for the first two months, Collin's phone and computer activity had been blessedly dull and predictable. Andy had noted a couple of free, soft-core porn sites his grandson had visited with the frequency of any healthy teenager. His only cause for concern was the close friendship he'd developed with Ian Haggerty. The late-night chats between his sixteen-year-old grandson and a man twice his age had seemed unhealthy to Andy. Then again, perhaps that closeness had been just a bit too reminiscent of his own friendship with the slightly older Wade Grinnell. He'd experienced firsthand what that kind of hero worship could lead to. Andy hadn't cared how innocent Ian and Collin's friendship might have seemed; he'd put an end to it.

Collin hadn't given him any other cause for concern. Andy had been happy to see his grandson making friends at school. But then ten days ago, on a Sunday morning, he'd checked the content of a grainy cell phone video Collin's friend Fernando had sent.

He was horrified to see his grandson in a trance— speaking in Wade's voice. He couldn't help thinking his old partner in crime had somehow come back from the dead and invaded his beloved grandson's body. What other explanation was there? In front of his two friends, Collin-as-Wade dropped all sorts of hints about his criminal past.

Monitoring Collin's computer activity, Andy watched his grandson get closer and closer to the truth. That was when he hired the hit man to eliminate the potential witnesses.

Once again, Andy became part of a killing team. He was riding in the passenger seat of the black Saturn when they picked up Fernando. He remembered the boy's angelic face lighting up with a smile as he recognized him: *"Well, hey, I was just heading for school. . . ."*

After they found out Fernando hadn't told anyone else about Wade Grinnell, the killer-for-hire slit the boy's throat. Andy waited in the car while it happened.

The same contract killer had done a thorough job breaking into the Pelham house that afternoon. Though Collin's girlfriend hadn't recorded anything about Wade Grinnell on her computer or in her journal, she'd still become a liability. Together, they set the Pelham house ablaze in the wee hours of Tuesday morning. Andy hated to admit it to himself, but the experience still thrilled him.

He had near-complete damage control. The two witnesses were dead. All tracks had been covered. And
Collin—unhinged that he might be responsible for the
deaths of his friend and her family—had promised not
to mention Wade Grinnell to another living soul. It tore
up Andy to see his grandson so tormented. But he was
fighting for his own survival.

Irene Pollack seemed like the only loose end, and it
might have ended with her, too, if Collin had kept his
word. But the very same night he learned of Fernando's
death, Collin was online, looking up hypnotists.

Andy sent his killer-for-hire to tail him, and gave
specific instructions:

1) *Find out where Collin went and how long he
   stayed with each hypnotist.*
2) *If Collin seemed to make a connection with
   one of the hypnotists, do everything in your
   power to discourage the hypnotist from seeing
   Collin again (intimidation, scare tactics,
   whatever works).*

Olivia Barker wasn't easily discouraged. Andy's
watchdog program on Collin's phone had picked up the
video of his session in Olivia office last Thursday.

He'd seen Collin reconnecting with Ian Haggerty—
even after Andy deleted an email Haggerty had sent to
his grandson.

Then his hired helper had even more bad news: he'd
been spotted by someone named Rick Jessup who was
stalking Collin.

Suddenly three more people had to be eliminated.
And only one of those three was dead now. It was a
pretty damn shoddy success rate.

Andy saw the lights of the Bainbridge ferry terminal

on the dark horizon. He'd already purchased three one-way open tickets (first class) to London on British Air. Even his doctor wasn't going to stop him. It was the only way to contain this Wade situation, no more police investigating, no more hypnotists, no more witnesses. He remembered how going away to military school had helped him forget. The change of scenery would do his grandson good. Hell, it would be good for all of them.

By this time tomorrow Collin would agree that a long trip abroad was their best option.

And by this time tomorrow, it would be three out of three.

CHAPTER THIRTY

A white minivan with DAN DINSMORE CONSTRUC-TION printed in red letters on both sides pulled up in front of Walt Barker's house on Alder Lane. Along with his scraper knife and a tape measure, Dan had his iPhone with him so he could take photos and record dimensions.

Tall and lean with short brown hair and a goatee, the thirty-seven-year-old contractor wore a beige zip-up jacket. His name was on a decal sewn on the left side—above his heart. Starting up the walkway to the classic colonial home, Dan studied the charred front door and the smoke damage to the frame around it. The door still looked functional, but it definitely had to be replaced. There was no way he could refurbish it.

He was taking measurements when someone came around from the backyard. Dan hadn't rung the bell yet. He smiled. "Hi, are you Mr. Barker?"

"That's me." The man gave him a wary look.

"I'm Dan Dinsmore," he explained. "I'm here to give you an estimate on the door. We talked yesterday.

I'm about twenty minutes early. I hope that doesn't screw you up."

"Oh, no, not at all," the man said, grabbing his hand and shaking it. "Thanks for coming. Is that your truck there?" He pointed to the minivan.

Dan nodded.

"I don't see your picture on it. I can't remember. Do you have your picture on your website?"

With a mystified smile, Dan shook his head. "No, but if you'd like to see some ID . . ."

"Oh, no, no, no, that's not necessary. We're all just a little nervous here. We're still trying to figure out who's responsible for this. Anyway, I can see on your jacket who you are. How are we doing?"

Dan sighed. "Well, Mr. Barker, I think you were right. We need to replace the door."

"I was afraid of that," he said, frowning. "Well, listen, before you get too caught up in this mess, I have something around back I'd like you to take a look at. Would you mind?"

Dan shook his head. "No problem."

He followed him around the side of the house. Trees and tall bushes provided privacy in the backyard. He noticed a patio directly in back of the house—and off to the side beyond that, a black plastic tarp held down by bricks covered some plants in a small garden.

"It's the bottom of the kitchen door here," the man said. "I banged it up the other day."

Dan glanced at the base of the door. He crouched down for a closer inspection. A shadow passed behind him. He didn't see anything wrong with the door.

He didn't see the ice pick in the other man's hand.

His cell phone rang. Dan reached into the pocket of his jacket. "Excuse me," he said. He looked at the phone, and then let out a little laugh. "Well, this is the damnedest thing: *Barker, Walt*. I'm getting a call from *you* right now!"

Before he could click on the phone, the ice pick was already rammed inside his ear.

The cell phone dropped to the ground. The contractor fell down beside it. His thin body convulsed with spasms, and blood gushed onto the patio pavement.

The man grabbed the phone on the fourth ring. "Dinsmore Construction," he said.

"Yes, hi, this is Walt Barker speaking. You have an appointment at our house in about fifteen minutes, and it totally escaped my mind this morning. Would it foul things up to push it back a couple of hours? We're trying to spring a friend out of the hospital, and I think it'll take at least another hour."

The contractor's body stopped twitching. He was perfectly still. A pool of blood haloed around his head.

"That's no problem at all, Mr. Barker," the man said. "I'll see you at noon."

Poulsbo—Thursday

Collin woke up to the sound of his grandfather clearing his throat in the hallway. He rolled over on his other side and tugged up the sheets. The throat-clearing ritual would go on periodically until midmorning. It was how he knew his grandfather was awake, home, and not clearing his throat on the golf course.

After a long, nervous evening alone with his grandmother, Collin had been so relieved to hear the BMW pull into the driveway around 10 PM. Dee had been dozing in front of *House Hunters*. Letting her sleep, Collin had hurried out to the garage to meet his grandfather. Old Andy had looked tired and a bit shaky as he climbed out of the car. Still, Collin had just been glad to have him home and safe.

About an hour later, after his grandparents had gone to bed, Collin had been startled by a knock on his bedroom door. His grandfather poked his head in. "Kiddo, could you do me a favor?" he asked. He was wearing his plaid robe and slippers. In his hand he had a pill. "Would you mind hitting the sack a little early tonight— maybe even taking this sleeping pill? It's Dee's prescription. It's perfectly safe."

Standing in front of him, Collin looked at the blue pill and then at his grandfather. "I don't understand."

"Well, for the last few nights—ever since your friend died in the fire—I haven't been able to fall asleep if I know you're still up. I'll go to bed, and just toss and turn. Then I get up and check for the strip of light under your door. I can't really relax until I see your light's off. I need to know you're okay before I can knock off for the night."

Collin bit his lip. He knew he was causing his grandfather some stress, but he hadn't realized until now how much of a burden he'd become. It was clear that Old Andy was worried he was going to sneak out and kill someone again. He felt horrible.

His grandfather extended his hand, palm up, with the pill in it. "Anyway, I'm awfully tired. If you take this now, we'll *both* be asleep within the hour."

Collin plucked the pill out of his hand, and studied it. *Ambien*. He hadn't taken Ambien since the night his mother and Chance had been murdered. He looked into his grandfather's weary eyes and nodded. He'd take the stupid pill if the old man wanted him to.

His grandfather retreated into the bathroom. Collin listened to the faucet. A few moments later, Old Andy returned with a tumbler of water and handed it to him. "Dee talked to you about this trip to Europe. It'll do all of us a world of good. We'll work out something with your school. Anyway, I want you to think about it."

Collin swallowed the pill and chased it down with a gulp of water. "I'll think about it, Grandpa," he said listlessly. "I better go brush my teeth and wash up. If this is anything like the pills Mom used to give me, it'll kick in fast."

His grandfather hugged him. "G'night, kiddo."

"Grandpa, I'm sorry for all the trouble I've caused you," he whispered.

"Stop it," he murmured, kissing him on the cheek. "You've always been a good kid." He patted his back a few times, then broke away and shuffled out the door.

By the time he'd crawled into bed a few minutes later, Collin had barely been able to keep his eyes open. For a few moments, he'd panicked, remembering what had happened the last time he'd taken one of these pills. But he'd given in to sleep, because that had been what his grandfather had wanted.

Collin heard him clear his throat again.

Rolling over, he squinted at daylight coming through the curtain crack. His desk lamp was still on. The digital clock on his nightstand read 10:01 AM.

He bolted up in bed. "Christ," he muttered. He couldn't believe it. He'd slept almost eleven hours. They were supposed to meet Olivia this morning—right now, in fact. Throwing off the sheets, he staggered out of bed and hurried toward the bathroom. He switched on the light, and stopped dead in the doorway.

Collin stared down at his jeans bunched up on the tiled floor. Smeared with brownish stains, his gray T-shirt was draped over the side of the tub. Collin took a closer look. The stains were dried blood.

Around the sink and the bathroom counter were crimson fingerprints. They were all over a key card for the Commodore Inn—and dollar bills sticking out of a wallet. In shock, Collin stared at the Oregon driver's license in the wallet window. He recognized the man in the DMV photo from Gail's funeral—and from the lobby of Olivia's office. It was her estranged husband: *Bischoff, Clayton Lawrence.*

Suddenly, Collin couldn't breathe. He felt as if his legs were ready to give out. He staggered over to the toilet. With a shaky hand, he lowered the lid and sat down. He couldn't believe this had happened again. As soon as he got a breath, he started to cry.

There was a knock on his bedroom door. "Kiddo, are you awake yet?" his grandfather called, his voice muffled. "I let you sleep in. I called Olivia and pushed our appointment back."

There was a click of the doorknob turning, and his grandfather called to him again. His voice was clear this time. "Collin?"

He listened to the floorboards creak as his grandfather walked across the room. "Collin, what's going on? Did you sneak out last night? I thought I heard. . . ."

His grandfather fell silent as he reached the bathroom threshold. He was dressed in a plaid shirt and khakis, and had a folded-up newspaper in his hand. "Good Lord, what happened in here?" he whispered.

Hunched forward with his arms crossed in front of him, Collin looked up at him and shook his head. He started to tremble.

Stepping over to the sink, his grandfather put down the newspaper and picked up the hotel key card. "What is this? Collin, what's going on?" He examined the wallet. "I saw this man at your friend Gail's funeral. He was talking to—your hypnotist, Olivia. Who is he?"

His mouth open, Collin just stared at him. He couldn't answer.

His grandfather glanced down at the bloody clothes. He quickly picked up the jeans. Collin watched him empty his change and his wallet from the pockets. Then he pulled out a set of keys. "These are mine. You took my car. . . ." With a sigh of exasperation, he shoved the keys in his own pocket. He tossed the jeans in the tub—along with the sweatshirt. Turning on the cold water, he grabbed a shampoo bottle and poured some over the clothes. Then he hurried out of the bathroom.

Collin couldn't stop shaking. Past the shower, he heard the bedroom door click—and his grandfather's footsteps again. It sounded like he was looking for something in the closet. After a few moments, he came back into the bathroom with a robe that Collin rarely wore. "C'mon, get up," his grandfather urged him. He held out the robe.

Collin couldn't move.

"Get up," he growled. He threw the robe over his shoulders, then grabbed him by the arms and pulled him to his feet. "Collin, try to remember what happened. . . ."

Suddenly, he slapped him across the face. It startled more than stung him. Wide eyed, Collin stared at him. In all the times he'd stayed with his grandparents, Old Andy hadn't laid a finger on him. "Who is this Clayton Bischoff person?" his grandfather demanded to know.

"He—he's Olivia's husband," Collin heard himself say. "They're separated. I've only met him once. I hardly know him. . . ."

"You don't remember getting in the car and driving someplace late last night?" His grandfather swiped the key card from the counter. "Commodore Inn, Seattle," he said. "You don't have any memory of taking the last ferry to Seattle? Think, Collin, you must have caught the last ferry, then driven back *two hours*—across the Tacoma Narrows Bridge. That's just crazy, you have to remember. . . ."

"I don't, I swear," he cried.

He suddenly thought of the webcam attachment to his computer. At least he could see himself climbing out of bed—and get a record of the time and how long he'd been gone. But the pill last night had knocked him out so quickly that he hadn't set the timer to record his activity.

His grandfather picked up Clay Bischoff's wallet again, and riffled through it. He took out a piece of paper. "A room service stub," he said, almost to himself. "He was in room one-seventeen. Does that sound familiar?"

Collin shook his head.

"Then I suppose it's pointless to ask if you remember leaving anything behind in the room," he muttered.

"I'm sorry," Collin whispered, clutching the robe around him. He stared down at the tiled floor. "I'm really sorry, Grandpa. I don't know how this happened. I don't remember anything about last night. I don't even remember *dreaming* last night."

His grandfather grabbed a washcloth and started to wipe off the counter. "Let's face up to this. There's every indication here that you—well, that you killed this Bischoff person. You said he's the estranged husband of your hypnotist. They're divorcing, is that right?"

Collin nodded.

"Well, something tells me she must have made some sort of posthypnotic suggestion or whatever it's called and gotten you to bump off her husband for her. . . ."

"No, Grandpa, Olivia would never do that. . . ." Still, Collin was thinking of Wade Grinnell, who had no problem killing—especially in hotel rooms.

"Get dressed," he heard his grandfather say. "You and I are going to Seattle. We're driving to the Commodore Inn, and we'll check out room one-seventeen. Maybe we're jumping to the wrong conclusion here. Maybe it's not as bad as we think. Say a prayer that's the case. . . ."

His grandfather was on one knee, crouched in front of the cabinet under the sink. He loaded up his duffel bag with two sets of rubber gloves from the supply Dee kept to wash dishes. He also grabbed a roll of paper towels and a plastic trash bag and shoved them into the duffel. From the drawer, he took a washcloth and two dish towels, then stashed them in the bag as well. He zipped up the duffel.

Dressed in jeans and a denim shirt and his red jacket, Collin moved over toward the kitchen table. His grandfather had left Dee a note:

D—

Off to the ferry with Collin. Be back this afternoon. Sorry we won't be here to help you unload all the Costco plunder! Feel free to leave the heavy nonperishables in the car for us to lug later.

Wish me luck at the MD's!

XXX – Me

"You know, eventually, we'll have to tell Dee what's going on," Collin said. "She knows something's the matter. She's just waiting for one of us to explain it to her."

"We can worry about that later," his grandfather grumbled, handing him the duffel. Old Andy wouldn't even look at him, he seemed so upset. "First, we need to figure out exactly what it is you did last night—and if there's any way to fix it."

With the bag in tow and his head down, Collin followed him through the vestibule to the garage door. A beep echoed inside the large garage and the car lights flashed as his grandfather hit the device on the keychain to unlock the BMW. Then his grandfather opened up the driver's door to the BMW. "Oh, Lord," he muttered, glancing inside the car.

Collin opened the passenger side door. On the floor in front of his seat were a switchblade knife and a policeman's nightstick. Both had blood on them.

"Christ, where did you get those?" he heard his grandfather ask.

He shook his head. "I've never seen them before, I swear."

With a grunt, his grandfather climbed into the driver's seat and started up the car. Collin slipped into the passenger side. Grimacing, he moved the knife and the nightstick aside with his foot. He set the bag in his lap and shut the car door.

"Ah, goddamn it!" his grandfather barked, jerking his hands away from the wheel.

Collin gaped at him. He saw the blood smeared on his grandfather's hands.

"In the glove compartment," he growled, nodding at the dashboard. "Get me the—the—the Handi Wipes. And for God's sakes, you can't just leave that shit down there! Take one of those dish towels from the bag and wrap up that club and the knife. Use your head, Collin, what if a cop stopped us?"

His lip quivering, Collin was obedient.

He watched his grandfather wipe the blood off the steering wheel. He had blood on his hands now, too— from handling the nightstick and knife.

"Give those to me," his grandfather said impatiently.

Collin passed the weapons to him, wrapped in the dish towel. His grandfather shoved them under his seat. He thrust the bloodied towelette into his hand. Collin didn't know what to do with it.

"Get the trash bag out and throw it in there. That's why I packed it. And wipe the blood off your hands. Jesus, Collin!"

Collin swallowed hard, nodded, and followed his instructions.

His grandfather pressed the remote, and the garage door opened with a mechanical hum. They backed out to the driveway and stopped. The garage door automatically began its descent. Collin stuffed the black plastic trash bag back into the duffel, and then zipped it up.

His grandfather stretched out his arm and patted the back of his head. "I'm sorry to snap at you, kiddo. It's just that I can't do this alone. I need you to stay sharp here."

"Sure, Grandpa," he murmured.

Collin didn't say anything more. His grandfather's hand was still wet from the towelette. It felt cold and clammy against the back of his neck.

He was so relieved to see there weren't any police cars, ambulances, or news vans around the hotel. During the ferry ride over, he'd had flashbacks to that horrible, chaotic scene in front of the Pelham house ten mornings ago.

As they pulled into the parking lot, Collin gazed at the sprawling three-story motel, one of those institutional tan-brick and glass buildings. All of the rooms had sliding glass doors that led to the tiniest of patios with wrought-iron railings. The first-floor rooms looked like the only ones with glass doors that were actual exits.

His grandfather parked near a side entrance. Collin felt sick to his stomach. He had no idea what to expect. And his grandfather hadn't really explained what he'd planned to do with the duffel bag full of towels and gloves.

"Whatever we find," his grandfather said, shutting off the car engine. "We'll deal with it. Just promise you won't panic or freeze up on me or anything. I need you to be strong, Collin, and do exactly what I tell you."

Biting his lip, he nodded.

They climbed out of the car. Collin carried the bag. His grandfather hit the car's automatic lock device, and then they ducked into the side entrance. The long hallway was dimly lit and had a swirly pattern on the maroon carpet. He heard an ice machine churning. Except for a housekeeper's pushcart outside an open door, the corridor was empty. None of it looked familiar to Collin. He had no idea where room 117 was. So he followed his grandfather, and started looking at the numbers on the doors: *129, 127, 125 . . .*

They skulked past the open door to 123, where the housekeeper was cleaning the room. Collin figured they were coming up to 117 soon. He didn't see yellow police tape across any of the doorways ahead. Was it too much to hope they'd find nothing inside that room?

His grandfather stopped in front of a door with a Do
Not Disturb sign on the knob. Glancing up and down
the hallway, Old Andy pulled out the key card and
slipped it in the slot. Collin held his breath and
watched the green light go on above the slot. His
grandfather opened the door, and they both ducked inside.

Collin balked at the smell.

"Oh, no . . ." his grandfather murmured.

Near the bed, Collin saw the slightly bloated corpse,
facedown on the bloodstained carpet. The head was
turned to one side just enough that Collin saw his gray,
distended face and the washcloth stuffed in his mouth.
The back of Clay Bischoff's shirt was slashed repeatedly and soaked with blood. His hands were tied behind him. One of his loafers had fallen off his foot
during the struggle. Around his ankles was an old cowboy belt that Collin recognized. It was his, and had his
name on it.

He thought he was going to throw up. He tried to
take a few deep breaths, but with every breath he
caught the stench of that body decaying.

"You can't get sick here," his grandfather whispered. But the color had left his face, and he looked a
bit unsteady himself. Collin could tell he was trying to
be strong for both of them. "Do you remember any of
this from last night?" his grandfather asked. "Look
around, is there anything here that's yours?"

"The belt," Collin said, with a hand over his mouth.
He nodded toward the dead man's feet. "That's mine."
His mom had bought it for him about two years ago,
but it had always been too big for him. He would have
tossed it out when he'd moved in with his grandparents. But he hadn't been able to throw out anything that
she'd given him.

"Get the—the—rubber gloves out of the bag," his grandfather whispered.

His hands trembling, Collin unzipped the bag and found a pair of Dee's dishwashing gloves. He handed them to his grandfather, who scowled at him. "I'm not doing it," he hissed. "You tied him up with the belt. You take it off. Maybe it'll help you remember."

Collin stared at him. He started to shake his head.

But his grandfather wasn't looking at him. He grabbed the duffel, took out the other pair of rubber gloves, and put them on. He went to the door, glanced out the peephole, and then fixed the chain lock in place. "Come on, Collin," he said under his breath. "Hurry up." He headed into the bathroom and switched on the light.

Staring down at the dead man, Collin had trouble slipping the rubber gloves over his shaky hands.

His grandfather stepped out of the bathroom and started checking drawers, the nightstands, and the desktop. He frowned at Collin. "For God's sake, we haven't got all day. Get going. . . ."

Collin nodded obediently. He tried not to step in the blood on the beige carpet. He got down on one knee and hovered over the dead man's feet. This close to the corpse the foul odor was even stronger. He tried not to gag as he reached over the body. The man's bloated, swollen ankles pinched against the belt. Wincing, Collin wrestled and tugged at the taut strap. He stared at his name embossed on it.

Suddenly, there was a knock on the door. *"House-keeping!"*

Collin froze.

His grandfather gaped at him—then at the door. "Um, not today, thank you!" he called.

Neither one of them moved. Collin listened to the

squeaky wheels of her pushcart. He heard her knocking on a neighbor's door. *"Housekeeping!"*

"Stupid bitch," his grandfather muttered. "Can't she read the do-not-disturb sign? Good God, Collin, haven't you gotten that damn thing off him yet?"

"Sorry," he muttered. Then he started struggling with the belt again—until he finally pulled it off the dead man's ankles.

His grandfather made him check around the room— even had him poke his nose in the wastebaskets—for anything that might belong to him. Collin didn't find anything. They stashed the belt and the rubber gloves in the plastic bag. Then Collin stuffed the bag back inside the duffel. Once his grandfather checked the peep hole, they quietly slipped out to the hallway. They left the Do Not Disturb sign on the door.

Outside, he gratefully breathed in the fresh air again. Collin couldn't believe they'd made it back to the BMW without anyone seeing them. He threw the bag in the backseat, and buckled his seat belt. Having endured the last nightmarish, revolting fifteen minutes, it was all he could do to keep from breaking down.

His grandfather backed out of the parking spot, found the lot exit, and then pulled into traffic. Neither one of them said anything. If Old Andy had been snapping at him all morning, it was understandable. Collin felt horrible, putting him through this.

He took another look back at the hotel and tried to remember coming here last night. He'd seen Clay Bischoff twice in his life: once from afar at Gail's funeral, and then again, in the lobby of Olivia's office building. Kneeling over that corpse earlier should have triggered something, but it hadn't. And looking at the hotel again, he still came up blank.

He didn't agree with his grandfather's theory that Olivia had given him some kind of post-hypnotic suggestion to kill her estranged husband. Andy didn't know Olivia like he did.

But his grandfather was right when he'd said none of this made sense. Collin couldn't believe that last night—after taking a sleeping pill—he'd gotten up and caught the last ferry out at 12:55 AM. Then after murdering this man, practically a stranger, he'd driven two hours, looping down to Tacoma, over the Narrows Bridge, and back up to Poulsbo. And he had no memory of it at all.

If he hadn't seen the belt around the dead man's ankles, he never would have believed he had anything to do with it.

He thought about that belt and the bloody Handi Wipes in the golf bag. The nightstick and the knife were still under the driver's seat. It didn't seem like much, but he and his grandfather may as well have been carting around that dead, decaying body. Collin knew he'd be carting it around in his mind for the rest of his life. Maybe he didn't remember killing anybody, but he had to take responsibility for what he'd done.

They headed west on Denny Way, past the Space Needle and toward the water. He sighed, breaking the silence between them. "Grandpa, I think we should call the police and let them know what happened."

"What are you, crazy?" his grandfather replied, leaning close to the wheel, intent on his driving. "We tampered with evidence back there. You think they'll go easy on you just because you don't remember tying that man up and stabbing him to death? Right now, more and more, I'm convinced we need to get you on a plane to London—away from all this, away from hypnotists and police inquiries and bad memories. We have to put some distance between you and everything else that's tearing you apart inside right now. Collin, don't you see? If we go abroad, we can start over again. We'll make a clean slate of it in someplace entirely new. You'll be able to forget all about this."

"I really doubt that, Grandpa," he replied. "I know I'm never going to get over it. I don't care how far I run away. I'll still have this hanging over my head. I'll still feel responsible."

"You say that now, but you'll feel differently in a year," his grandfather said, his eyes on the road. "You know, I got into some trouble when I was around your age. I went away and made some resolutions. Being somewhere else is what helped me get over it."

"What kind of trouble were you in?" Collin asked.

"It doesn't matter now." His grandfather got red in the face. "What matters is that I've worked like a dog most of my life and I'll be damned if I spend the rest of it in jail because I cleaned up some murder scene to protect you. I'm in this now—up to my neck. You owe it to me to keep quiet and forget about this. You're all I have left, my only heir, and I don't want you ending up in some insane asylum. You're going to Europe, and you're going to forget all this ever happened. . . ."

At the bottom of Denny, his grandfather took a right. They weren't headed toward the ferry terminal, but in the opposite direction—toward Ballard. "We have to get rid of this knife and the nightstick," his grandfather announced. "Maybe we can dump them someplace over in Magnolia. We still have time before the next ferry."

Collin was half-listening. He thought about how unlike his grandfather he was. He wanted to call Olivia, and then go to the police.

They passed a Chevron station on the left, and he

automatically glanced at the gas gauge on the dash. If he'd driven over a hundred and twenty miles late last night, they were probably low on fuel.

The gauge showed the tank was nearly full.

Collin couldn't imagine himself, covered with blood, stepping out of the car to pump gas. He reached back for his wallet. He'd had about thirteen bucks when he'd last checked yesterday afternoon. He only could have paid for the gas with cash. He didn't have a credit card.

In his wallet, he had a ten and three singles.

"Grandpa, somebody . . ." He trailed off. He was about to say they'd been set up, that he couldn't have made that long drive late last night and filled up the gas tank. But then he remembered Clay's wallet on his bathroom counter at home. He could have used Clay's credit card. Even covered in blood, he could have still gotten out and pumped gas. Who would have noticed him at three or four in the morning?

He still clung to the hope that someone else had done this. But at the same time, he knew the sooner he owned up to it, the better.

"What?" his grandfather said. "You started to say something. . . ."

"Grandpa, I can't take off to Europe like you want me to," he murmured. "I'm sorry. I'm not sure what kind of trouble you were in when you ran away. But I'm sure this is a lot worse. And I can't just shrug it off. . . ."

His grandfather shook his head. "Goddamn it," he whispered.

Suddenly he jerked the wheel, and they turned left—across two lanes of oncoming traffic. The tires screeched as he steered onto a street marked DEAD END. They went over some railroad tracks. The potholed road looped around behind a large deserted warehouse. Grass grew in the pavement cracks. His grandfather stopped the car by a loading dock. To their left was a string of old, rusty, abandoned boxcars. Beyond that, Collin noticed the rail yard with a dozen tracks and several stationary freight trains. A small sign was posted by the tracks: INTERBAY YARD.

He realized they'd pulled alongside the rail yard where Wade Grinnell had been killed.

His grandfather reached under his seat and pulled out the dish towel swaddling the nightstick and knife. "This is as good a place as any for these," he muttered. "They'll think some railroad tramp murdered him." Opening his door, he climbed out of the car. He started to walk away, but then stopped. With his head down, he stood for a moment, clutching the dish towel.

Collin watched from inside the car. He could only see his grandfather from the back, but his shoulders were shaking. Collin realized he was crying. He opened the car door and stepped outside. He took his cell phone from his pocket, and dialed Olivia's number. It rang once.

"What are you doing?" he heard his grandfather say.

Collin looked up. Old Andy started toward him. He dropped the dish towel. The knife and nightstick hit the pavement with a clatter.

Collin turned away—just as Olivia answered on the third ring. "Hello, Collin?"

"Olivia, something happened . . . ," he started to say.

Suddenly, his grandfather knocked the phone out of his hand. He pushed him aside, and frantically stomped on the cell phone as if it were a tarantula. "No one can know!" he barked. He was like a crazy man. "Why won't you just do what I'm asking? Why are you leaving me no choice?"

Collin looked down at the shattered pieces of his phone. Then he gazed at his grandfather. Tears streamed down the old man's face.

"God, why is this happening?" he cried. "When that train ran him down, I thought it was the luckiest thing that ever happened to me. How could he come back?"

Stunned, Collin kept staring at him. He couldn't move.

His grandfather covered his face with hands. "He's dead, goddamn it. Why did he have to come back through you?"

Collin felt as if someone had just sucker-punched him. He didn't want to think it was true. "You—you helped him kill all those people, didn't you?" he heard himself ask. "You were his partner. Fifty years ago . . ."

His grandfather said nothing. Slump shouldered, he dropped his hands to his side. He took a few steps back.

Collin closed his eyes and clutched his stomach. Suddenly, last night and today made sense to him— horrible, clear sense. All morning long, he'd thought someone must have set him up for the murder of Olivia's husband. He didn't want to think the *someone* was his own grandfather. But it was the only explanation. He didn't know when Old Andy had stolen his clothes and the belt from his closet. But he knew his grandfather hadn't attended a city council dinner last night.

"I should have seen it," Collin said, trying to get his breath. "You—you didn't have any problem finding his room this morning—and in a big hotel like that. But you even knew to park by the closest entrance, because you were there last night. You didn't even knock on his door. You used the key card and let yourself in. You already knew no one alive was in there. . . ."

Collin felt as if he were choking with every word he spoke. He couldn't breathe right. He kept thinking last night had been yet another hotel slaying for Wade's partner.

"How could you put me through that?" he asked. "And Gail and her family, you set me up for that, too. Didn't you? How could you? You're my grandfather, for God's sake. . . ."

"I needed your cooperation," he muttered.

Collin numbly shook his head at him. "All these murders now," he said. "My friends and my mom . . ."

"Not your mother," his grandfather whispered. "I didn't have anything to do with that. . . ."

"But you killed the others, didn't you? Or you hired someone to kill them. Why?"

"I had to," he muttered. "You'd introduced them to Wade. They all knew too much. I didn't have a choice. . . ."

His head down, Collin wiped the tears from his eyes.

"You're not giving me a choice now, son," he heard his grandfather say.

When Collin looked at him again, his grandfather was holding the nightstick up in the air.

Before he could do anything, Collin heard the stick crack against his skull. His legs gave out beneath him, and he toppled to the pavement.

As he started to black out, Collin heard his grandfather sobbing.

CHAPTER THIRTY-ONE

Seattle—Thursday, 11:52 p.m.

"*The cellular phone customer you're trying to reach is unavailable now,*" the automatic recording said. "*Please try your call again later.*"

Olivia paced the second-floor hallway outside her brother's bedroom door. This was her second attempt to call Collin back. He'd phoned a few minutes ago. "Olivia, something happened . . ." had been all he'd gotten out before the line had gone dead.

She impatiently clicked off and tried his number once more. The recording came on again. As it played, she peeked in on Ian, asleep in Rex's bed.

This morning, while she and her father had gotten Ian released from the hospital, Hank had run to Ian's apartment for some of his clothes. Ian had been groggy from his medication and was sleeping in the twin single. Rex's vintage illuminated Pabst Blue Ribbon sign was on the wall above the headboard. Baseball and other beer memorabilia filled the small bedroom.

She heard the beep at the end of the automatic greeting on Collin's line. "Hi, Collin," she said, stepping away from the bedroom door. "We got cut off. Are you okay? You didn't sound good. Your grandfather left a message pushing back our session to noon. So I'm hoping to see you in a few minutes. But I'm really worried. Call me as soon as you can, okay?" ·

Clicking off, she checked in on Ian again, and then headed downstairs.

"How soon do you want us out of here?" her father called as she passed by the study.

Olivia stopped and poked her head in the doorway. On their way back from the hospital, they'd stopped by the Essential Baking Company for carry-out. Her dad and Hank were finishing up their lunch in front of ESPN—her dad in his recliner, and Hank on the sofa. They both had TV tables with the sandwiches and wrappers in front of them. They'd promised to move their ESPN fest down to the basement rec room once Collin and his grandfather arrived.

"I wouldn't worry about relocating until they get here, Pop," she sighed. "I have a feeling they'll be late. They might even cancel on me. I'm not sure what's going on."

She retreated to the kitchen, where Sheri Grinnell's Drifters tape was on the reel-to-reel player. Turning down the volume to "Up on the Roof," Olivia checked her phone for the Stamplers' number and dialed it. A woman picked up on the second ring. "Hello?"

"Hi, my name's Olivia Barker. Is this the Stampler residence?"

"Yes, this is Mrs. Stampler."

"Hi, I'm trying to get ahold of Collin, Mrs. Stampler. He has an appointment with me at noon. He called me and we got cut off. I've tried phoning back, but he's not picking up."

"Well, I don't know anything about an appointment

for *Collin*," Mrs. Stampler said. "My husband had an appointment with a neurologist in Seattle this morning, and Collin went with him. I'm expecting them back any minute. What was Collin supposed to see you about?"

Olivia realized Collin and his grandfather were keeping her in the dark about the hypnotherapy sessions. "I'm Gail's aunt, Mrs. Stampler. And actually, they were just going to swing by and say hello while they were in town."

"Oh, yes, I'm sorry, Olivia. You called here the other night. I didn't make the connection. So you're trying to get ahold of Collin?"

"Yes, I think his phone battery must have died or something. Could you give me Mr. Stampler's cell number?"

Five minutes later, she was nervously pacing around the island counter, listening to Andy Stampler's voice mail greeting. The beep sounded. "Hello, Mr. Stampler. This is Olivia, and I'm trying to get ahold of Collin. . . ."

Someone beeped in, and she checked the caller ID. It was Collin's grandfather. She clicked on the incoming call. "Mr. Stampler?"

"Yes, I see you were trying to reach me. . . ."

"That's right. Collin called, and then we were cut off—"

"How long ago was this?"

"About ten or fifteen minutes ago."

"Did he say where he was?"

"No, like I told you, we were cut off. I've tried calling him back—"

"He's run away," Stampler interrupted. "We were on the ferry coming over, and Collin got a call from your husband. It really upset him. He said he had to go to the bathroom, and then he just—*disappeared*. I had half the ferry crew looking for him. They were paging him on the PA system, too. I'm at my wit's end. He must have snuck off as soon as we docked. He left a note on my windshield. 'I'm okay. I need to be alone,' it said. I'm afraid he's going to hurt himself. I'm here driving around the Seattle ferry terminal, searching for him. I have a couple of policemen on it."

"Is there anything I can do?"

"No. I—I'll have Collin call you as soon as we find him. Listen, I need to go. I don't want to tie up the line here."

"Of course," she said. "Good-bye, Mr. Stampler."

Olivia clicked off. She tried Clay's number. It went to the same automatic voice mail as Collin's line. So either his phone was dead or he was out of call range. She didn't leave a message.

If Collin had truly run away, she had a pretty good idea where he'd gone.

On her laptop, she brought up the video of her last session with him. She sent it to her iPhone. Then she threw on her sweater, and grabbed her purse. Heading for the front door, she stopped at the doorway to the study.

Her dad grabbed the remote and muted ESPN. "What's going on?" he asked.

"Can I borrow your car, Pop? I need to go to Ballard."

"Sure. What's in Ballard?"

"I'll let you know when I get there," she said. "Meanwhile, if you hear from Collin or his grandfather, give me a shout, okay?" She turned toward the door.

"All right, well, be careful!" she heard her dad call to her.

* * *

Olivia had left the reel-to-reel player going in the kitchen—with the volume on low. No one in the house heard a break in The Drifters' rendition of "Under the Boardwalk." No one heard a voice come on the tape: *"Testing, one, two, three, testing . . . Hey, Sis. So—ah, here's the thing. By the time you get this, I'll be long gone. And sorry, but I'm probably leaving all sorts of shit for you to clean up. Anyway, I guess I owe you an explanation. . . ."*

Olivia turned out of the driveway and headed down the narrow street. She pulled over for a minivan in the oncoming lane. To her annoyance, the vehicle took its sweet time passing by. She saw DAN DINSMORE CONSTRUCTION on the side of it. Checking her rearview mirror, she watched the minivan turning into her father's driveway.

Olivia shifted into park and turned off the engine. She jumped out of the car and hurried back toward the house to find out what was going on. She heard the minivan's door shut. As she came up the walkway, she saw the man heading toward the front door. He was tall and lean, with black hair and an olive complexion. "Excuse me!" she called to him.

Stopping, he turned and gave her a pleasant smile. His beige jacket had DAN DINSMORE CONSTRUCTION on a label on the left breast. "Hi, how are you?" he said.

"Hi, I live here," she said, a little out of breath. "Is there something I can help you with?"

The front door opened, and her father stepped out on the stoop. "Honey, it's okay. He's here to give us an estimate on the door. I meant to tell you."

The man gave her a little salute.

Olivia smiled back at him. "Hi. Sorry."

"Say, what happened there?" her father asked, pointing to the man's shoulder.

Olivia noticed the brownish-red blotch, too. It was about the size of an epaulet.

The man curled up his nose as he glanced down at it. "Oh, yeah," he chuckled. "My little girl spilled some tomato juice on me." He nodded at the burnt, blister-cracked door. "So this must be it, huh?"

"Excuse me, I'm headed out," Olivia said, backing away. "But could you do me a favor? We have a friend staying with us, and he just got out of the hospital today. He's sleeping upstairs. Could you try not to make too much noise?"

Nodding, the man smiled at her. "I'll make sure to be very quiet, ma'am."

"Thanks," Olivia said. She blew a kiss at her dad, and then hurried back toward the car.

White-knuckled, Andy Stampler clutched the steering wheel and watched the road ahead. Tears streamed down his face. His grandson was lying unconscious in the backseat with a coat covering him. Andy had been barking orders and growling at the poor kid all morning. Maybe finding fault with everything he did made it easier to put his grandson through the wringer like this. The boy hadn't done anything to deserve it.

Andy wondered if it was possible Collin could actually remember back to when he'd been three and a half years old.

Of course, Andy remembered that October day, thirteen years ago, when Wade's sister had tricked him into meeting her. She'd pretended to be a reporter and asked to interview him. His retirement and a slew of awards he'd received in the fall of 1999 had earned him a lot of press. He'd been babysitting three-year-old Collin the day Sheri had wanted to conduct the interview, so he'd suggested they meet at Nelson Park's playground. He'd liked the idea of being portrayed as a proud grandpa—and indeed he had been. Maybe not a proud father, but a proud grandpa.

That sunny autumn day in the park, Andy didn't recognize Sheri at first, not even when they sat down on the bench together. She had shoulder-length white hair and wore too much makeup—which still didn't hide the lines and blotches on her careworn face. The black raincoat she wore looked a bit frayed. She'd brought along a portable tape recorder, which Andy thought was for the interview.

"You don't know who I am, do you?" she said, half-smiling. "But we met each other once—a long time ago. We have someone in common who was close to both of us."

Andy smiled politely and shrugged. He was a bit distracted by Collin, playing on the jungle gym nearby.

"The last time I tried to track you down," she said, "I heard you were in the military, stationed in Europe. . . ."

"That was the mid-seventies," Andy said, his eyes narrowed at her.

"Well, since then I've lived down in Centralia and then in Oregon for a while. I wasn't following the Seattle scene. But then I moved to Tacoma last year, and a few days ago—well, what do you know?—I saw Andy Stampler's name in the newspapers. I read about all your good deeds, and how generous you are. I hope I've caught you in a generous mood now."

She pressed a button on the tape recorder between them.

Andy was still thinking she'd brought the thing for

their interview. Instead, what came out of that little machine was Wade Grinnell's voice—from almost four decades before.

On the jungle gym, little Collin stopped and stared at them.

Stunned, Andy sat there, listening to Wade. His old friend was telling his sister that if the police caught up with him and Andy, he wanted something for the record about exactly how they'd killed those tourist families. There was no regret in his tone. In fact, he was bragging and joking: *"They came to Seattle for the ultimate thrill, and they got it. . . ."*

Collin had abandoned the jungle gym, and he stood in front of them, seemingly fascinated by the tape.

"Go play on the swings," Andy finally told him, a tremor in his voice.

His grandson went to sit on one of the swings, but continued to stare at them—and that box with the voice coming out of it.

Andy remembered when his daughter, Piper, had started getting Collin modeling and commercial roles at age five—just a year and a half later. She'd bragged about how smart he was and how well he remembered his lines. He simply amazed his directors with his memory and imagination.

Had that taped confession planted a malignant seed in the mind of his grandson?

The recording had gone on for fifteen minutes. From the way he'd talked, Wade must not have figured out that his partner in crime had already disavowed him. He'd spoken like they were still a team, a couple of outlaws.

Sheri told him there were copies of the tape, of course. "You know, thirty-seven years ago when I approached your grandfather for money, I was young, stupid, and scared." She let out an abrupt laugh. "I settled for very little—considering how much your family could afford, and how much you stood to lose."

Andy wanted to tell Wade's sister that after thirty-seven years, she was still just as stupid.

But he sheepishly agreed to pay her two hundred and fifty thousand dollars in exchange for the tape and all the copies. Sheri said she would meet him in the park at 2 PM the following day. "And bring your grandson. . . ."

That night, he set her apartment on fire. There was minor damage to the surrounding units in the building. Wade's sister was the only casualty. Before lighting the first match, Andy had thoroughly searched the place for tapes. There had been a bunch of cassettes in her bedroom. He'd figured all of Wade's recordings had gone up in smoke along with Wade's sister.

He didn't think he'd ever have to hear Wade's voice again.

Then ten days ago, he'd checked a video sent to Collin's iPhone. He'd shuddered at the sound of that voice once more—this time, coming from his grandson.

Collin was still unconscious in the backseat.

As much as his grandfather loathed doing it, he was determined to make certain that voice was silenced forever.

"So—is there anyone else at home I need to be quiet for?" the construction man asked, looking down at him with a lopsided smile.

Crouched by the front stoop, Walt held the other end of the measuring tape at the base of the door. He chuckled. "No, there's just our patient upstairs and my new buddy, Hank, glued to the TV there in my study."

"One-oh-seven-point-five inches," the contractor said, holding the tape up to the top of the door. "So this Hank is a *new* friend, huh?"

"Actually, he's kind of a private-detective/bodyguard." Olivia's dad straightened up, then let go of his end of the thin steel tape. It made a hissing sound as it automatically rewound into the receptacle. "It's just a precaution. A friend of my daughter is worried whoever pulled this stunt with the door might come back to try something even more serious."

"Wow, a *bodyguard*?" the contractor said. "Is he carrying a gun or anything like that? I mean, I don't want to say the wrong thing to him and piss him off."

Walt grinned. "Relax. He seems pretty mellow. Say, listen, I'm headed in—if you don't need me for anything else. Would you like a Coke or a glass of water or anything?"

"No, thanks," the man said. He scribbled down something in a notebook. "Just leave the door open a little so I can measure the width."

Walt stepped in and left the door ajar. He poked his head into the study. "Need anything?"

"Nope, I'm doing great," Hank replied, sitting at one end of the sofa. He wore his shoulder holster over his white Izod shirt.

Walt thought he heard murmuring in the kitchen. He headed in there, and saw the reel-to-reel player was still on. But it wasn't playing music or people singing at a party. Instead, someone was talking on the tape: *"Yeah, leave it to Andy. He torched two hotels—the Aurora Vista and the Pioneer Motor Inn. Snap, crackle, pop! I think he ended up frying eight people—nine, if*

you count this bum he set on fire down on the water-
front. That was kind of an accident. That was before we
decided to send a message to those fucking tourists
who came here for this fair. Too bad we couldn't have
killed more of them. Anyway, like I was saying, most
of the time, I held the gun on them and Andy tied them
up. . . ."

A chill raced through Walt. For the last two nights,
Olivia had been playing tape after tape—waiting for
something. Was this what she'd wanted to hear?

Shutting off the tape player, Walt hurried over to the
cordless on the kitchen counter and dialed Olivia's
number. It went to voice mail.

"If you're looking for Walt, I think he's in the
kitchen," Hank said to the contractor.

The man nodded. "Yeah, I know. He's on the phone
right now. I'm just waiting for him to hang up." With
his hand in his jacket pocket, he stepped into the room,
between the detective and the TV. "What are you
watching?"

"*SportsCenter*, and you're a better door than a window." He waved at him to step aside.

"Sorry," he laughed. He backed up until he stood
right beside the Barkers' armed bodyguard. He looked
down at the top of his head—and his receding gray
hair. He slowly pulled his hand from the pocket of the
contractor's jacket. "Hey, I think you got something on
the back of your shirt. . . ."

Hank half turned toward him. "What is it?"

"Here, let me get it," he said. "I think it's a dead leaf
or something. . . ."

Hank leaned forward with his head tilted down.
"You got it?"

The man grabbed him by the scalp and plunged the ice pick into the base of his skull. "Got it," he whispered.

Hank barely uttered a sound.

"Anyway, I think this might be what you were waiting to hear—with all those tapes you've been playing," Walt said on his daughter's voice mail. "It sounds like a confession, only this guy's pretty damn proud of himself. He's bragging about killing tourists at the World's Fair, he and a fellow named Andy. I don't know if it's true or not, but it's pretty disturbing stuff. And now I'm suddenly worried about you. So call me as soon as you get this. Okay, honey? Take care."

He put the cordless back in its cradle, and then turned around to see the contractor standing by the refrigerator. Startled, Walt let out a little laugh. "Well, hey, did you change your mind about a Coke? Or are you finished already?"

"I've barely gotten started yet," the man replied, with a flicker of a smile.

"I get off on Fifty-eighth, a few blocks before Ray's Boathouse. You know—the restaurant? There's a big white stucco house at the top of the Hill . . ."

From the last session with Collin, Olivia had directions to his "safe place." Her iPhone was in the cup holder on the console beside her. It was almost like having a GPS navigation system. But his directions were way ahead of her actual location right now—driving down Market Street in downtown Ballard. She had at least another ten minutes until Ray's Boathouse.

The sky had suddenly turned dark and ominous—as

if a thunderstorm was ready to sneak up on the city. It looked more like dusk than noon. She wished she'd bought a raincoat—and a flashlight for her trek through the forest. A part of her wondered if all this wasn't just a waste of time. But she knew if Collin had run away, he would have retreated to his secret shack in the woods.

At a stoplight, Olivia paused the recording. She noticed someone had called and left a message. She anxiously checked the caller ID. It wasn't Collin or his grandfather. It was home—probably her dad, wanting to know where she was in Ballard.

She saw the light change, and put the phone back in the cup holder. She would check the message and call him back when she got to Fifty-eighth Street.

Olivia pressed on toward Collin's safe place.

"So—what does your daughter do?"

"She's kind of a counselor-therapist. . . ."

Upstairs, in Olivia's brother's bedroom, Ian was awake. For a few moments, he didn't move. He still felt clammy, feverish, and weak. He heard a football game on the TV downstairs, and two people talking in another part of the house. One of them was Olivia's dad. The other voice was familiar, too.

Terribly familiar.

"So where was she headed in such a hurry?"

Olivia's dad's response was a bit muffled by cheers from the football game on TV.

Ian pulled himself out of bed. His T-shirt was soaked with perspiration, and his sweatpants were all twisted around. He staggered over to the bedroom window and glanced down at the minivan in the driveway. The name of the construction company was on it.

Bracing a hand against the wall, he made his way down the hall to the top of the stairs, but he couldn't see anything on the first floor. Still, Ian heard that guy's voice—the same voice he'd heard in the convenience store and in his hospital room last night. He was sure of it now.

Ian's heart was beating wildly. He remembered Mr. Barker mentioning during their lunch on Tuesday that he kept a gun stashed in his bedroom. Ian crept into the master bedroom, convinced with every step he took, they could hear him downstairs. He pulled open the drawer to the nightstand, and almost tipped over the tall lamp on top of it. He steadied the lamp, and caught his breath. He felt light-headed. Bent over the drawer, he sifted through pens, old coins, a rosary, a couple of watches, and several handkerchiefs. But he couldn't find a gun. For a few seconds, it felt as if the room was spinning.

He heard a rustling, flapping noise outside, and headed toward the window. Grasping the window frame to balance himself, Ian stared down at the backyard. It looked like a storm was rolling in. His vision started to right itself again. He noticed a tarp, weighted down with bricks, covering a portion of the garden. But a gust of wind loosened one corner, and it fluttered back—allowing Ian a glimpse of something under the tarp.

It was a dead man, facedown in the mud.

As he bent over in front of the open refrigerator in search for a soda, Walt could feel the contractor hovering behind him. "I know we have a regular Coke in here for you," he told the man. "All my daughter drinks is the diet stuff. . . ."

Walt was starting to wonder about this guy. He

seemed too preoccupied with making small talk, and had spent a total of two minutes assessing the damage to the front of the house. Now the guy wanted a Coke. Talk about a slacker.

The telephone rang. Walt turned around, "Let me get that. It might be my daughter. Here, have a look-see in the fridge. I know we have a regular Coke in there for you."

A resounding cheer came from the fans in a clip of a football game on TV. "Hey, Hank, what game are they showing?" he called.

There was no response.

Walt snatched up the cordless phone. "Hello?" He stepped toward the dining room. In the large mirror above the side buffet, he could see into his study across the hall. Hank was sitting in his chair with his eyes open. The light from the TV flickered on his dull, expressionless face.

"Mr. Barker, don't say anything," he heard Ian whisper on the other end of the line. "Pretend it's someone else calling."

"Hi, um, *George*," Walt said, baffled.

"I'm upstairs on my cell phone," Ian whispered. "That guy you're talking with down there, he's the one who tried to kill me yesterday. . . ."

Walt turned toward the kitchen again. The contractor sat down at the island counter with a Coke. Walt couldn't help thinking Ian might be a bit paranoid. One of the nurses at the hospital had said his medications might make him that way. "Are you—ah, sure what you're talking about?" he asked.

"I know the son of a bitch's voice," Ian whispered. Walt could hear him breathing hard on the other end. "Listen, there's a dead body in your backyard—half-

covered with the tarp over the garden. I—I think he's
the real construction guy. The one you're talking with,
he's a fake. He's here to kill me—and Olivia. Did I hear
you say she isn't home?"

"That's right," he said, wandering toward the big
window. But he couldn't see the garden from there.
He'd put the tarp down himself, so he knew Ian wasn't
totally hallucinating. He caught the man looking at
him. Walt worked up a smile.

"Where's Hank?" Ian asked.

"Uh-huh," Walt said, taking a step into the dining
room. He stared at Hank's reflection in the mirror
again. Some sportscaster on TV was hollering excit-
edly. The detective didn't move a muscle. His open
eyes looked dead. A crimson stain bloomed on the
shoulder of his white sports shirt.

"Mr. Barker?" Ian asked.

Walt swallowed hard, and stepped back into the
kitchen again. The man was watching him carefully.
"Um, George, I—I think the car died. I wouldn't count
on it. You'll—ah, have to think of some other way."

"Oh, Jesus. You—you told me you had a gun up here
in your bedroom—"

"Not anymore, I'm afraid," Walt said, his jaw tens-
ing up. He'd moved the relic of a gun from his bedroom
closet to his desk drawer in the study this morning.
He'd figured it wouldn't do him any good up there if he
was downstairs all day. He nodded at the contractor
and held up his finger to indicate he'd be off the phone
in a minute. "Listen, George," he said. "If you're up for
it, I could certainly use a nice distraction."

"You want me to make some noise up here?"

"Yeah, but I'd wait a minute or two if I were you,"
Walt replied. He wandered over to the sink, and

furtively checked the drying rack. The closest thing to a knife among the few pots and utensils was a potato peeler.

"I'll hang up now and call 9-1-1," Ian told him. "I'll break something in about sixty seconds. Okay?"

"Sounds good," Walt said with a slight tremor in his voice. "And hey, if you see my daughter before I do, give her my love."

Walt clicked off the cordless, and set it on the counter. He smiled at the man. "That was my daughter's friend, George. Sorry, when he starts talking, I can't shut him up." He grabbed a spatula, a ladle, and the potato peeler from the dry rack. Then he moved over to the drawer where he kept the knives and opened it up.

"Hold it right there," the man said. He pulled Hank's gun out of his jacket pocket. "Put that shit down, and close the drawer."

Walt froze and gazed at him. "What is this? What's going on?" He dropped the spatula and ladle. They made a loud clank as they hit the hardwood floor. He stepped back and bumped against the counter, furtively setting down the potato peeler. "Is this some kind of a joke?"

"Your daughter, where is she?"

Walt shrugged helplessly. "She said she was headed to—to Mount Baker someplace. She's supposed to call me when she goes there."

"Get away from that drawer," the man said, eyes narrowed at him.

Walt shut the drawer with his hip and held up his hands for a moment. But he didn't move away. "Why do you keep asking about my daughter?"

"I want you to pick up that phone, and call her," the

man said, casually leaning back in the chair. "Tell her
your friend upstairs has taken a turn for the worse and
you need her to come home right away." A tiny smile
crept over his face. "Oh, and by the way, he will indeed
be taking a turn for the worse, you know."

All at once, a loud crash resounded from the front
hallway.

It even took Walt by surprise. He almost forgot to
swipe the potato peeler off the counter.

Startled, the man leapt up from the bar stool, tipping
it over behind him. He rushed toward Walt and grabbed
him by the front of his shirt. He jabbed the gun against
the side of his head. Walt grimaced in pain as the barrel scraped along the skin. The man started to pull him
toward the front of the house.

He balked at the sound of glass shattering. A thun-
derous boom followed it. As the man hauled him at
gunpoint toward the front hall, Walt couldn't help thinking the last sound had been Ian upstairs collapsing.

*"It sounds like a confession, only this guy's pretty
damn proud of himself . . ."*

Olivia listened to her father's message on her cell
phone. She kept a hand over her other ear to block out
the traffic noise. She stood beside her dad's Mercury
Sable, which she'd parked across the street from the
slightly dilapidated, stately, old white stucco. The lawn
and bushes were neglected. It looked like a haunted
house. Olivia could see the choppy gray water beyond
the trees. A brief flash of lightning illuminated the
darkened sky.

*"He's bragging about killing tourists at the World's
Fair,"* her dad continued, *"he and a fellow named Andy.*

I don't know if it's true or not, but it's pretty disturbing stuff. And now I'm suddenly worried about you. So call me as soon as you get this. . . ."

She knew she'd heard it right: *". . . he and a fellow named Andy."*

She clicked off, and dialed home. She anxiously counted the ringtones, and realized after the fourth, it was going to voice mail. She listened to the familiar greeting and then the beep. "Hi, Pop," she said. "I got your message. Are you there? I wish you'd pick up. Now, suddenly, I'm the one worried about you. Listen, thanks for letting me know about the tape. Whatever you do, don't erase it or anything. The 'Andy' he talked about is Andrew Stampler, Collin's grandfather. I think he's somehow responsible for the fire that killed the Pelhams—and the murder of a teenager named Fernando Ryan. I'm here in Ballard, trying to track down Collin. I think he might have found out about his grandfather and run away. He told me about this place, a tiny shack in the woods near the beach. The trail's beside an old, white stucco—5818 Gilman—off Seaview. I'm about to head down the trail now. I think Collin may be hiding there. I'm probably running out of time here, so call me. Thanks, Pop. I love you."

She clicked off the cell and shoved it in her pocket. With the car lock device, she popped the Sable's trunk open and dug out the tire iron. After closing the trunk, she hurried across the street to the chain-link fence. She found the narrow path alongside it. With all the overgrown vegetation, she couldn't have seen it from the street.

Starting down the crude trail with the tire iron in her fist, Olivia glanced over at the seedy old house again. As she wove through the trees and foliage, deeper into the woods, her sweater collected burrs and bits of dead leaves. Swiping away something that had landed in her hair, she wasn't sure if it was a bug or what. She reached the end of the fence and could smell the beach. The air seemed to get colder and damper. In his directions, Collin had said there was a trail to the right.

Delving farther into the thicket, she wished like hell she had a flashlight. Overhead, tree branches swayed in the wind and leaves scattered. She felt so horribly alone— and lost. She hoped the shack was nearby, and Collin would be there.

Olivia came to a huge, towering pine. She remembered it as a landmark from Collin's directions: *"And just off the path, there's the little shack. It's safe. No one can find us there. . . ."*

She spotted his little hideaway. It looked like a large toolshed. Made up of brick and wood, it had one small window. There was no light coming from inside it.

Olivia tried the door, but it was secured with a padlock. The cracked window on the side had chicken wire in the glass. She peeked inside, but it was too dark. Then she glanced around the gloomy woods. It was pretty obvious she was alone here. She'd come all this way for nothing.

Olivia pulled out her cell phone and tried her dad again. But *No Signal* came up on the screen. She figured all the trees were screwing up the reception. With a sigh, she turned to start back up the path.

But she stopped dead at the sound of twigs snapping and bushes rustling. The noise seemed to come from somewhere up the hill on the other side of the shack. Through the trees, she could see a shadowy figure staggering down the hill.

She wasn't alone here after all.

* * *

The contractor kept him in a choke hold—so fierce he could hardly breathe. Walt twisted and contorted to keep up as the killer dragged him into the front hallway. He felt the blood from the deep scratch the gunbarrel had made. It left a warm, wet trail down the side of his neck. His attacker didn't seem to notice that he'd stashed the potato peeler in his pocket. But Walt wondered what good it would do up against a Glock 38.

Over the TV, the sports announcer on ESPN was shouting his description of a touchdown. Walt caught another glimpse of Hank in the study—slumped back on the sofa, so motionless, the blank stare, and his mouth still open in shock. The light from the TV flickered across his dead face.

In the foyer, Walt almost slipped in a puddle of water on the hardwood floor. He noticed shards of glass, and guessed they were from the tumbler Olivia had left on Ian's nightstand. He also recognized a clunky, heavy baseball bookend from Rex's bedroom.

"Well, look who's here, trying to be a hero again!" the contractor announced. He yanked Walt to one side and crammed the gun barrel into his ear.

Walt let out a sharp cry. Wincing, he looked at Ian on the stairs. About halfway up, his young friend was sprawled across the steps with one of his legs impossibly twisted to one side. Sweating and gasping, he clung to one of the banister posts and glared down at the man. Walt guessed he must have collapsed after hurling the bookend down the stairs.

The telephone rang. Walt felt the man's grip around his neck slacken. The killer froze at the sound of the answering machine clicking on in the kitchen. But the gun barrel was still lodged in Walt's ear, grinding away at the skin.

"Let him go," Ian said weakly. "I'm the one you're after. . . ."

"Shut the fuck up," the man hissed.

Catching his breath, Walt listened with his good ear as Olivia left a message: *". . . I'm here in Ballard, trying to track down Collin. I think he might have found out about his grandfather and run away. He told me about this place, a tiny shack in the woods near the beach. The trail's beside an old, white stucco—5818 Gilman—off Seaview. I'm about to head down the trail now. I think Collin may be hiding there. I'm probably running out of time here, so call me. . . ."*

"Well, now how about that?" the killer chuckled as Olivia finished her message. He tightened his grip around Walt's neck. "Your sweet piece of a daughter just went and told me where I can find her. And she's right, you know. She's running out of time. You too, old man, you've just become expendable. I don't need you for anything anymore."

"Wait!" Ian shouted. "Listen to me for just a second—"

The killer took the gun barrel out of Walt's ear. "You're right," he said, pointing the gun at Ian. "I'll kill you first. Goddamn pain in the—"

The man didn't get another word out—just a gasp as Walt thrust the potato peeler right below his Adam's apple. He plunged it all the way to the handle.

The stunned man fired his gun, hitting a light fixture on the ceiling. Bits of glass rained down on them. Dropping the 38, the man clutched his bleeding throat. He tugged out the peeler, and it fell to the floor. He stumbled back toward the doorway. A scarlet gush came from the hole in his neck, saturating the jacket that wasn't his. He slipped on his own blood and toppled across the threshold. Spasms racked his body, and from his throat came a strange gurgling gasp.

Gaping at him, Walt staggered toward the stairs and clutched the newel post. He turned and looked up at Ian, who looked as if he was ready to pass out. "You okay, my friend?" he asked, out of breath. He nodded at Ian's bent, twisted leg.

Ian clung to the railing. "We better get that address where Olivia went," he said weakly. "Send a cop car over there. . . ."

In the distance, they could hear a police siren.

At the threshold of the charred front door, Andy Stampler's killer-for-hire twitched one final time. Then he was perfectly still.

An ice pick rolled out of his jacket pocket.

Olivia recognized the moaning sound Collin sometimes made as he slipped into a trance.

Hiding behind the thick trunk of the towering pine, she watched as Andy Stampler emerged from the shadowy thicket. He walked backwards along another trail, staggering and stumbling as he dragged his half-conscious grandson closer to the little shack. He kept stopping every few steps to gasp for air and readjust his hold on Collin, who might have been so much dead-weight. Around Andy's wrist was a plastic bag from an AM/PM minimart. It kept swaying back and forth, hitting Collin against his arm.

Clutching the tire iron in her hand, Olivia tried to figure out what Andy Stampler was doing. She thought about him and Wade Grinnell committing those horrible murders together. Somewhere along the line, Andy must have betrayed him. She remembered her first session with Collin. She'd asked his Wade persona how well he knew Collin.

"I've been here with him for a long, long time—years in fact," he'd said. *"I've just been waiting for the right time to come out. This is working out exactly as I wanted. I'm scaring the shit out of him. But I've barely gotten started. I'm really gonna mess with his mind—and then I'll kill him."*

She'd asked him, *"How will you do that without killing yourself?"*

He'd chuckled. *"You don't get it, lady,"* he'd said. *"You don't get it at all."*

But she understood now. Wade didn't care about Collin. All this time, it was Collin's grandfather whose mind he was "messing with."

If Collin—at a young, impressionable age—had heard Wade's voice in a taped confession, then for years and years, he must have buried in his subconscious what he'd heard about his loving grandfather. Wade hadn't come back from the dead. Collin had unwittingly brought him back.

The child actor had no idea about the role he'd taken on.

"We're here, kiddo," his grandfather said, leaning him against the shed. He braced himself against the cabin, and started wheezing and coughing. Asleep on his feet, Collin stirred. He groaned sluggishly. This close, Olivia could see a red welt in the corner of his forehead. He wasn't in a trance. It looked like his grandfather had clubbed him.

Andy Stampler was still panting as he reached into his pocket and took out several keys. He tried a few on the padlock, but he had to keep tipping the half-conscious Collin back against the shed so he didn't fall

on his face. Finally, he found the key to open the padlock. Removing the lock, he pushed open the door. It
squeaked on the hinges.

Collin opened his eyes briefly—as if he recognized
the sound. But he still looked dazed.

His grandfather took him by the arms and led him
inside the shed.

Olivia couldn't figure out what Stampler was doing.
She heard a clatter—like someone had fallen in that little hut. Collin groaned loudly.

She watched his grandfather back out of the shed.
He took the plastic bag off his wrist, reached inside it,
then pulled out a blue and white rectangular tin. The
empty plastic bag caught the wind, and fluttered toward
her, brushing against the pine tree for a moment before
it blew away again.

She heard Stampler sobbing as he aimed the tin at
the door to the shed. Olivia realized he was dousing the
shack with charcoal starter.

She realized what Wade's firebug friend was doing.

"No!" she screamed. Coming from behind the tree,
she charged at him with the tire iron. Olivia thwacked
him on the shoulder, and he howled in pain. He
dropped the can, and a stream of the fluid splashed
him. The can fell to the ground by his feet and made a
hollow clank.

Olivia reeled back to hit him again with the tire iron.
But he grabbed her wrist. "Goddamn it," he hissed. But
Olivia saw the tears in his eyes. She saw that a part of
him didn't want to do this.

"No, you can't!" she cried out, fighting him.

She caught a glimpse of Collin on the floor of the
shed, his back against the wall. He had his head tipped
back, and his eyes were half open. She was about to
yell at him to wake up and get out of there. But then all

at once, she felt a hammer-like blow across her face. It knocked Olivia off her feet, and she let out a frail cry. She hit the ground with a thud. The wind was knocked out of her, but she wouldn't give up. She grabbed the canister and hurled it at Stampler. It hit him on the shoulder and splashed him again.

Olivia saw he had the tire iron now. Desperate, she grabbed a rock and threw it at him. It missed Stampler completely. Gasping and grunting, she heaved another rock at him. It sailed by his face. She let out a frustrated cry.

"Fucking kill her already! She's making too much noise!"

It was Wade's voice coming from inside the shed.

Olivia watched Andy Stampler turn and gape at his grandson.

Sitting up, Collin stared back at him. The cocky, defiant grin on his face belonged to Wade. "Do it, man," he whispered.

Andy Stampler shook his head at him. "Why is this happening?" he cried. "Why are you doing this? God-damn it, you're dead! You got mowed down by a train fifty years ago. And I was happy about it. Understand? I didn't want anything more to do with you. . . ."

Olivia saw the smirk disappear, and a horrified look passed over Collin's face. He covered his mouth with a shaky hand. She'd never told Wade during any of their sessions that he was actually dead.

"What?" Collin whispered. It was his voice, not Wade's. Dazed, he stared up at his grandfather.

Olivia swiped part of a tree branch off the ground. "Collin, run!" she screamed, getting to her feet. She lunged toward Stampler and swung the piece of branch at him. He put up his arm, and the stick broke against it. Pieces of rotten wood flew everywhere.

Grabbing her, Collin's grandfather threw her into the shed. Olivia fell on top of Collin. Momentarily winded, she gaped up at Stampler. Sobbing and shaking, he pulled out a box of matches. Helpless, Olivia watched in horror as he struck the match. The flame sparked.

Then he dropped it.

With all the deadly fires Andy Stampler had started, he'd never once burned his fingers—until now. The lit match fell on his trouser leg, soaked with the charcoal starter. He didn't even realize what had happened. All at once, the flame shot up his pants leg to his waist.

Down near his feet, the fire snaked along the ground—igniting the shed's fluid-soaked door. Flames shot across the doorway, sending a wave of heat and smoke into the little shack.

Past the hissing and cracking, Olivia heard Andy Stampler howl in agony.

Choking on the smoke and fumes, Olivia struggled to her feet. She pulled Collin out of the fiery, blistering hot shed. The two of them clung to each other and gasped for air.

She turned and saw Collin's grandfather swallowed up by flames. He screamed and flailed around helplessly.

Olivia had no idea that fifty years ago, two teenage boys—as a prank—had set an old derelict on fire. His screams and his waggling dance as the fire swept over him had made those boys snicker. The old drunk had burned to death. Andy Stampler might have died the exact same way. But the two people with him wouldn't let that happen.

Shucking off his coat, Collin threw it over his grandfather and tackled him to the ground. He rolled him back and forth in the dirt. Stampler was yelling and twitching in pain the whole time. Olivia helped beat out the flames with her sweater—until it too caught fire. She threw it aside and stomped on it. Collin didn't give up until the flames were snuffed out.

His grandfather lay there, whimpering. His face was blistered and red and his scorched clothes smoldered.

Exhausted and gasping for a breath, Olivia felt a drop of rain on her face—and then another. She heard the gentle patter filling the woods. The rain began to extinguish the blaze that had consumed the shed. Black clouds plumed up to the tree tops and beyond. What remained of the shack was just a charred, cindery shell.

Olivia kneeled down on the ground beside Collin, hovering over his grandfather. She was still trying to catch her breath. "I'll go up the path to the street, where the cell phone reception is better," she said, her hand on his back. "We'll get him some help. You saved his life, you know."

Collin nodded. "And you saved mine."

Patting his shoulder, Olivia straightened up. She glanced over at the blackened remains of the little shack. "Collin, I'm sorry we couldn't rescue your secret hiding place."

"It's okay," he replied, holding his grandfather's hand. The raindrops cascaded down his face. "I—I don't think I'll need it anymore."

Olivia smiled at him. Then she hurried toward the pathway up the hill.

EPILOGUE

Olivia walked her four o'clock patient to the door. Dana Gold-Roberts was a nineteen-year-old UW student who seemed to be conquering her sleep problems. She and Olivia had just discussed how this would be their second-to-last session. For Olivia—and the client, too—the *you're cured, so good-bye* talk was always a happy, yet bittersweet milestone.

Olivia had redecorated her office with new carpeting and a jazzy sofa and chairs set. There was also a Matisse print to replace the framed Monet that had been damaged. She'd decided to forgo another minifountain. The old one had started to get on her nerves anyway.

At home, they had a new red front door. But she wouldn't be using it so much anymore. Next week, she was moving into a one-bedroom apartment on East Capitol Hill, about a mile's walk from work. She'd already started to furnish the place, and even figured out where she'd put the Christmas tree. Clay's family had asked if she wanted any pieces from her old Portland house, but Olivia had politely declined.

Last week, they'd given her an update on Corinne, who was still in the hospital. Apparently, the doctors weren't too optimistic about her chances of walking again—at least, not without a cane or a walker. In addition to malicious mischief and property damage, Corinne had also been charged with manslaughter. She was in no hurry to leave the hospital.

For a while, Olivia was concerned she'd be facing charges, too—for withholding evidence. Before the police and paramedics had found them along the wooded hillside path behind 5818 Gilman Place that Thursday afternoon, she and Collin had agreed on what to tell the authorities about his hypnotherapy sessions. Olivia didn't think anyone needed to know that while under hypnosis, Collin had taken on the persona of a serial killer who had been dead fifty years. No one needed to know the sessions had been recorded either. Collin's grandfather had already destroyed recordings of the sessions on Collin's computer, Fernando's cell phone, and Collin's cell. The story Olivia and Collin had agreed upon was close enough to the truth. In their telling, the first hypnosis session with Gail Pelham had unleashed Collin's subconscious memory of hearing Wade Grinnell's taped confession years before. The sessions with Olivia had drawn out more and more details. All of this was true. The fact that the gifted young actor had actually taken on the part of this killer was something the police and press didn't have to know. As the center of yet another sensational murder case, Collin Cox was under enough scrutiny. If news of this other persona was made public, it would have ruined him.

While rescuers had made their way down the crude forest trail, Olivia had leaned in close to Andy Stampler—so close, she'd smelled his cooked flesh. "If you really care about your grandson," she'd whispered in his ear, "you'll keep your mouth shut about him becoming Wade. This is your chance to make it up to Collin and see he comes out of this okay."

Olivia hadn't been able to tell if the burnt, traumatized man had even heard her. But Andy Stampler didn't say anything to the police. In fact, he didn't utter a single word. The following day, he'd suffered a massive stoke.

Wade Grinnell's taped confession contained several phrases and expressions Collin had used while under hypnosis. Olivia had turned over Sheri Grinnell's tapes to the police. In the middle of four of the reels, Sheri had rerecorded that same confession from her brother. After extorting an initial ten thousand dollars back in the early sixties, Sheri must have hoped to squeeze Andy's family for even more money later on down the line.

In press coverage of the murders, Collin and his grandfather were the reluctant stars while Olivia was relegated to a minor supporting role. That was just fine by her. Still, the exposure brought in a lot of potential new clients. After weeding through the curiosity-seekers and nutcases, Olivia still had twenty-three new names on her appointment list

Dana wasn't a new client. She'd been one of the first people to see Olivia when she'd started up the business in August. After two sessions a week for three months— and many soul-searching conversations—Dana was a bit misty about the prospect of moving on. The pretty blond student had tears in her eyes at the office door.

"You better get out of here before I start bawling, too," Olivia told her—with a tiny laugh. She patted her shoulder. "We still have another session after this. I'll stock up on Kleenex."

"See you in a week, Olivia." Smiling, Dana wiped a tear away and headed through the empty waiting room.

Olivia closed the door. She was about to reach for a tissue when she heard Dana scream.

Flinging open the door, Olivia rushed through the waiting room and out to the corridor. She found an awestruck Dana in the hallway, shaking the hand of a handsome young man. "Collin Cox!" she gushed. "My God, I can't believe I just screamed! You must think I'm such a dork, but I absolutely loved you in the Fragile Bastards video . . ."

Collin wore a wool military coat, a striped sweater, and jeans. In just a few weeks, his slight gawkiness had disappeared. In its place was a relaxed confidence and maturity. A music video he'd shot at the beginning of November had gone viral earlier this week. Fragile Bastards' "Wicked Wasted Life" was a huge hit. Among the young demographic, he was a star again, a new teen sensation—more for the popular quirky, sexy video than for his personal tragedies.

Collin and his grandmother were living in a furnished rental home in Seattle. Though Olivia and he had emailed back and forth, she hadn't actually seen him in over a month. When he'd called asking for some time late this afternoon, she'd quickly cleared her schedule. It was a far cry from their first meeting, when he'd literally begged to see her again.

He had a little brown paper bag tucked under his arm while he autographed the back of a cable bill envelope for Dana. She kept apologizing for making a fuss.

"It's okay, I like it," he assured her. "I haven't gotten jaded yet. This is fun."

A few moments later, he was in Olivia's office, taking off his jacket and glancing around at the new furnishings and the bold colors. "I like this better," he said, setting his jacket and the brown paper bag on her sofa. He seemed a bit nervous.

Olivia sat down in one of two chairs facing each other. "You want to get this over with so we can relax?"

Chuckling, he plopped down in the chair across from her. "You read my mind."

"Okay, *Russ*, I want you to take some deep breaths. . . ."

He laughed. "I have a confession. My real name is Collin Cox."

"Not *the* Collin Cox, star of the Fragile Bastards music video . . ."

"Oh, you ain't heard nothin' yet," he said. "I just signed yesterday for the film version of *Broken Home*, which I keep wanting to call *House Broken*. I'm the teenage son, one of the main characters. They're going after either George Clooney or Russell Crowe to play the father."

"My God, that's incredible," she said—with a stunned laugh. "Can you smuggle me onto the set?"

"I wish I could. They're shooting mostly in Europe. I'm getting a tutor and everything. It's in the contract. It's kind of funny, though. After my grandfather was so bent on whisking me off to Europe, that's where I'll end up for three months—starting in February."

"Well, as long as you brought him up," Olivia said. "How's he doing?"

"The same." He shrugged. "He's still in isolation. The burns are taking their sweet time to heal. The doctors are really worried about infections. Every time Dee goes to see him, she has to wear a smock, gloves, a surgical mask, and this shower-cap thingy on her head. No skin against skin, no saliva, no kissing, no hand-holding. Because of the stroke, he still can't speak. All he does is groan and mutter. The doctors are pretty sure he can see, hear, and understand things. But he can't talk or move."

"Have you gone to see him?" Olivia asked, trying to sound neutral about it.

Collin shook his head. "Not since the last time— over a month ago. Even if I could forgive him for what he did to me, I can't get past him killing my friends— and all those families fifty years ago." He let out a long sigh. "Well, should we get started?"

Nodding, Olivia straightened up in her chair. "Okay, just relax, and think about a place where you feel safe. . . ." She realized he couldn't think of that shack anymore. The memories attached to it couldn't be pleasant or calming. But Collin seemed content; so she didn't say anything. She held her hand in front of his face and slowly moved it back and forth. She watched his eyelids flutter as she guided him into a trance. Once his eyes were closed, she whispered to him, "Collin, can you hear me?"

Slouched back in the chair, he nodded.

"I'm talking to the person inside Collin," she said with uncertainty. She suddenly felt short of breath. "I'm talking to Wade now. Wade, are you there?"

Collin stirred slightly.

"Wade?"

He shook his head. "There's no one else," he murmured in his own voice, "just me."

Olivia smiled. "Okay, Collin, when I say your name and snap my fingers, you'll wake up feeling refreshed and happy. . . ."

Ten minutes later, Olivia was standing by the door, and Collin was putting on his coat. "I'm supposed to meet Ian for dinner after this," he said.

"He's back in town?" Olivia asked. She felt a slight pang in her gut.

After Ian had broken his leg, Olivia had hoped to look after him. But technically she'd still been married to Clay, and there had been a lot to deal with as his new widow. It had cast a pall over whatever seemed to be blooming with her and Ian. She couldn't really object when Ian's family had put him in a wheelchair and on a plane home to Pittsburgh. After a few polite emails back and forth, she'd figured whatever they'd had—or started to have—was gone.

"Yeah, he came back yesterday or the day before," Collin said. "He's got crutches and a walking brace now."

Olivia worked up a smile. "Well, tell him I said hi."

Collin nodded, and then grabbed the small brown paper bag from the sofa. "Before I forget, I thought you might want this." He handed the bag to her.

It was heavy. Olivia reached inside and took out a snow globe with a Disney Pluto figurine inside. She remembered seeing it in Gail's room during one of her and Clay's visits to the Pelhams. "They found it among some of the things stolen from the house that day," she heard Collin explain. "Gail's Aunt Cathy thought I might like it. But I'm pretty sure Gail would've wanted you to have it."

Gail gazed at the snow flurries within the glass ball. "Thanks, Collin," she whispered.

They hugged good-bye in the doorway, and then he headed through the waiting room. He was about to step out to the corridor, when she called to him: "I meant to ask . . ."

Hesitating, he turned around in the other doorway.

"I was wondering where you went in your head

when you were slipping into your trance," Olivia said. "Your 'safe place,' do you have a new one?"

Nodding, Collin smiled. "It's here with you." For a moment, a trace of the gawky young teenager swept over his face. Then it was gone. "See ya, Olivia," he said.

"See you, Collin." She watched him walk out the door.

The two clerks behind the counter at Madison Val-U Mart greeted her as she stepped into the store. Glimmering red and green Christmas bunting and white lights decorated the counter. Over the radio, Harry Belafonte sang "Mary's Boy Child." Glancing at the cigarettes in the display case, Olivia tried to tabulate how many days it had been without a smoke. *Twenty-eight.* She was past the worst of it.

She was on her way home from a Thai dinner with an old UW friend, one of the few who were still single. It was part of her campaign to improve her social life. She'd had a good time.

Swinging by the store, Olivia had hoped against hope she would find his car in the lot. But there had only been a taxi—with a cabbie alone in the front seat. She really didn't need anything there. With a defeated sigh, she headed down the aisle toward the ice cream case, but stopped herself. She pulled her cell from her purse and dialed Ian's number.

Beyond the tall shelves of food, she heard a phone ring in another aisle.

Olivia immediately looked up at the security mirror and saw the man on the crutches three aisles over. He was checking his phone's caller ID screen. He almost toppled over, shoving his fist in the air as if he'd won something.

"Olivia?" he said into the phone. "I was just thinking of you. . . ."

She gazed up at him in the mirror and smiled. "Hi, Ian," she said.

The pain was nonstop. Sometimes, if he stayed very still, he could learn to tolerate it. But one little move under the sterilized bedsheets and he felt as if his body were on fire again. Andy Stampler was convinced the doctors and nurses were purposely skimping on the painkillers—just to torture him. He'd heard them discuss his slow healing process, and knew they had to be undermedicating him or something. He'd stare at them—with their sterilized smocks, the surgical masks and bonnets. One stray hair or a tiny bit of saliva could be fatal for him. At the very least, it could set back his recovery for months. He'd heard it said over and over again.

Except on TV, he hadn't seen one person's face since they'd brought him in here.

Actually, that wasn't entirely true. Last week, a couple of teenagers had snuck past the nursing staff and the guard to steal a peek at him. Security was getting lax now that he wasn't on the news so much anymore. Besides, the police knew he couldn't exactly get up and walk out of there. Andy guessed the two boys who had snuck into his room were about the same age he and Wade had been when they'd killed all those people. These two brats had barely gotten a foot past the doorway. "Oh, shit, gag me," one of them had whispered.

He hadn't seen himself in a mirror since the fire. He'd been curious about the severity of his burns and the swelling, but not after that. Seeing the horrified looks on the faces of those two boys had been enough for Andy. He'd tried to yell, "Get the hell out of here!" But it had just come out as loud garbled gibberish. The two little bastards had laughed and scurried down the hospital corridor.

"You have a visitor," the skinny, young Latino nurse announced, strolling into the room. She wore purple scrubs—along with her mask, bonnet, and gloves. She was one of the few staff-members who didn't glare at him all the time. He wondered if she was pretty.

Andy tried to ask if the visitor was his grandson, but as usual, the words didn't come out right.

"It's your sister-in-law, Grace Freeman," she said, fluffing his pillow a bit.

Dee's older sister hadn't visited in over two weeks. He grumbled an affirmative. The nurse put a straw to his mouth so he could have some water. She fussed with his bedsheets, and then she hurried out of the room.

A few moments later, he heard her going through the drill with Grace: "Please do not touch the patient— even with your gloves. Keep your mask on at all times. If you feel like you have to sneeze or cough, please leave the room. . . ."

"Yes, I know all about it," he heard her reply. But it didn't sound like Grace.

His visitor stepped into the room. Even with the mask and bonnet obscuring her face and hair, Andy could clearly see the thin, older woman wasn't his sister-in-law. "Hello again, Andy," she said.

The nurse disappeared down the hall.

Andy tried to ask "Who are you?" But it came out all muddled.

"I can tell you're in a lot of pain," she said. "I know

you are. I know exactly how you feel." She stepped up to his bedside. From her eyes, he could tell she was older than him. With her gloved hand, she reached down and moved the cord that held the call button. She pulled it over to the far side of the nightstand, where he couldn't reach it. Andy let out a moan of protest.

"You don't know who I am, do you?" she asked. She tugged at her mask and lowered it under her chin.

Andy still didn't recognize her. He tried to shake his head, but it hurt too much. He moaned even louder. He didn't want her breathing on him—what with the risk of infection.

She stared down at him. "I'm Irene Pollack," she said steadily. "And this is for my family, you son of a bitch."

She spit in his face.

Stunned, Andy didn't make a sound. As the spittle slid down his swollen, red-blistered cheeks, he watched her turn away.

He figured she'd waited fifty years to do that.

Mrs. Pollack glanced back at him for a second. She didn't say another word. She just took a deep breath and headed out the door.